A PIRATE'S KISS

Without warning, Jared leaned forward and sensuously sealed Maren's lips. When she did **not** resist him, he continued on, eagerly exploring her mouth. He felt her tremble and press closer to his body. She smelled wonderful, and his senses spun wildly at her nearness. He guided her to the floor and lay half atop her as his mouth conquered hers.

Maren clasped his head, pressed his lips more tightly to hers. It was exciting to be in his arms and to have his full attention. His mouth claimed hers skillfully, tantalizingly, mind-dazingly. A fierce desire for him flamed within her heart.

Jared realized the effect his affections had on her, and his rich voice warned, "Be careful, my radiant siren, or I shall be tempted to take you away with me."

"Surely the flames of fortune burn brightly today, as I can think of no better fate than becoming your willing hostage," she replied.

EXHILARATING ROMANCE
From Zebra Books

GOLDEN PARADISE (2007, $3.95)
by Constance O'Banyon

Desperate for money, the beautiful and innocent Valentina Barrett finds work as a veiled dancer, "Jordanna," at San Francisco's notorious Crystal Palace. There she falls in love with handsome, wealthy Marquis Vincente—a man she knew she could never trust as Valentina — but who Jordanna can't resist making her lover and reveling in love's GOLDEN PARADISE.

MOONLIT SPLENDOR (2008, $3.95)
by Wanda Owen

When the handsome stranger emerged from the shadows and pulled Charmaine Lamoureux into his strong embrace, she knew she should scream, but instead she sighed with pleasure at his seductive caresses. She would be wed against her will on the morrow — but tonight she would succumb to this passionate MOONLIT SPLENDOR.

TEXAS TRIUMPH (2009, $3.95)
by Victoria Thompson

Nothing is more important to the determined Rachel McKinsey than the Circle M — and if it meant marrying her foreman to scare off rustlers, she would do it. Yet the gorgeous rancher feels a secret thrill that the towering Cole Elliot is to be her man — and despite her plan that they be business partners, all she truly desires is a glorious consummation of their vows.

DESERT HEART (2010, $3.95)
by Bobbi Smith

Rancher Rand McAllister was furious when he became the guardian of a scrawny girl from Arizona's mining country. But when he finds that the pig-tailed brat is really a ripe voluptuous beauty, his resentment turns to intense interest! Lorelei knew it would be the biggest mistake in her life to succumb to the virile cowboy — but she can't fight against giving him her body — or her wild DESERT HEART.

JANELLE TAYLOR

FORTUNE'S FLAMES

ZEBRA BOOKS
KENSINGTON PUBLISHING CORP.

ZEBRA BOOKS

are published by

Kensington Publishing Corp.
475 Park Avenue South
New York, NY 10016

First printing: February, 1988

Printed in the United States of America

I dedicate this book to my friend,
Lela Jennies,
for her generous and enlightening research.
She made me fall in love with New Orleans again!

And,
to my talented friends in the music business,
Terri Gibbs and **Mike Dekle,** whose
music relaxes and inspires me.

And,
to my daughter, **Angela Taylor,** a marvelous
secretary and proofer who keeps me on
my toes and on schedule.

And,
to my many friends of **AHS class of '62** who
enjoyed a terrific reunion in Athens in 8/87.

O'er land and sea, the **Flames** of war are raging;
And Fortune's cloaks and faces swiftare changing . . .
What will you do, oh **Destiny's Child,**
When fires of greed and hate run wild?
Searing away barriers and blames,
Baring your soul to **Fortune's Flames** . . .

Chapter One

Maren James stared at the handsome blond man standing before her. She did not want to believe him, but she knew Eric would not lie to her about something this grave. "My parents are dead and everything is lost?" she murmured. When he nodded, she argued, "It cannot be true. Why didn't you tell me sooner? You said everything was fine at home."

"I couldn't tell you this news before we left London because I didn't want to distress our grandparents. They're not strong enough to endure the loss of another son. It's only been three years since my father and mother were killed in that hotel fire and they still agonize over their deaths. Grandfather blames himself for that tragedy because he sent his sons to America to expand his shipping business. With Father gone and this war ruining our trade, I just couldn't place another burden on them. They're old and weak, Maren; they won't live much longer.

9

This news could devastate them." Eric inhaled deeply. "Let them be happy until we're forced to break their hearts again. Surely you understand and agree with my decision to remain silent, don't you, little cousin?"

Maren could not fault Eric's compassion and generosity. Her look and nod said she agreed with his behavior in London.

The green-eyed Eric, now a man of twenty-three, stroked her cheek. "I know this news is hard on you, little cousin, and I wish I didn't have to be the one to tell you. Things have been chaotic at home and abroad since the war started and Uncle Cameron . . . passed away. I tried to get to you sooner, but this damned blockade is nearly impossible to run. I've lost two ships and crews since January, both loaded with expensive cargoes, and we almost got caught several times on our way over here. Blasted British! You'd think they'd be tired of fighting by now. It makes me ashamed of my ties to them. Why can't they be content with Napoleon's defeat? Do they need to crush us too?"

"If it's as bad as I've heard and read, why did you risk a trip to London? You could have been killed or captured."

Eric smiled in response to the concern and affection evident in Maren's whiskey-colored eyes, aware that she was trustful and innocent. "President Madison received a coded message from some British traders and lords who want to help bring about a hasty end to this absurd conflict, secretly of course. It seems that the only ones who want to fight us are the Royal Navy and that mad King. Anyone with intelligence knows Britain can't lick us, at least not easily. You'd think they would have learned their lesson when they tried to conquer us nearly forty years ago. Blast them! It's stupid for either side to refuse to negotiate a treaty. Even if we battle from now until forever, there can be no real winner, and it riles me to watch them destroying everything our parents built. Honestly, Maren, what gets into people to make them behave this way?"

"I don't know, Eric. It seems such a terrible waste of lives and properties. Yet, both sides must feel action is necessary or we wouldn't be at war. What happened at home?" she asked, trying to return the grim conversation to her personal losses, but Eric's mind was elsewhere.

"The President was told to send someone those Englishmen knew and trusted to collect the money. They suggested that my older brother handle the secret dealings because they've done business with the American offices of James Shipping for years and they trust us. But Murray has a broken leg and couldn't make the voyage. Since they know me too, I was asked to take his place. Besides, Murray was born in Britain, so he could be impressed if captured. I'm an American and have 'protection papers' to prove it.

"I agreed to take on this crucial task because I'll do anything to have this war over quickly. I admit I used deceit, false papers, and false flags as a cover in order to fetch you home, but I had no choice. If I hadn't

11

picked you up, my trip to London would have looked suspicious to some people. There are spies everywhere, and traitors on both sides. If you tell anyone about this mission, I could be hunted down and killed. Our President and country are depending upon me, and on this money, to hold our enemy at bay. As I said, little cousin, if I had left you there, I couldn't have told you about Uncle Cameron and Aunt Carlotta. I didn't want you to hear about them from strangers; news like this should come from one of the family."

He hurried on before she could remind him that he had not done the same for their grandparents. "I like peace and prosperity, and I don't want James Shipping wiped out before the war ends. I admit I prefer being rich and important. I guess that makes me selfish and greedy and vain, but I can't help it," he said. Then he chuckled.

Maren did not laugh with him. She did not want to discuss her cousin's problems, flaws, or patriotism. "I need to know about my mother and father, Eric. I was so stunned by your first words that I hardly heard your explanation. It sounds as if I'm returning to nothing and no one."

The playful sparkle left his green eyes and he became serious. "I'm sorry, little cousin; I forgot about your troubles. I've known about this tragedy since last summer, so I've accepted it, as you'll have to. Our parents are gone, Maren, and we can't bring them back. At least yours didn't have to endure the terror and agony mine did during that fire. They would want you to be strong and brave. And don't worry; I'll protect you and take care of you."

As he was speaking, Eric's impenetrable gaze took in the beautiful woman before him. To her Spanish mother, Maren owed her very dark brown hair, which she wore loose most of the time. It was thick and shiny, framing her oval face and ending just below her shoulders, and it waved becomingly. And although her skin was darker than that of most women who caught his eye, it suited Maren's looks and personality. Its olive shade blended perfectly with her dark hair and golden brown eyes. His cousin was slim and shapely, and had a good height for a woman—five and a half feet. With her slightly turned up nose, large eyes, and exquisite mouth, Maren was a beauty who easily captured many hearts and eyes.

She was presently wearing a cream-colored muslin gown, decorated with leafy sprigging, and deep green kid slippers. After sailing, she had removed her green velvet Spencer jacket and had placed an ivory lace shawl around her shoulders to ward off the morning chill. Her day dress had a high waistline, and was banded snugly with a green ribbon directly beneath her breasts, in the current style that immediately drew a man's attention. The short sleeves were puffy, and the round neckline was not too low. The full skirt, gathered into a raised waistline, did not conceal her slim midsection and pleasingly rounded hips. Eric concluded that his cousin would look good in anything, including a man's garments.

Maren wondered why her first cousin was looking at her so oddly yet remaining silent. She decided that he must be seeking the right words to comfort her, or perhaps he was trying to suppress the bitter memory of his own parents' deaths. As she waited for Eric to speak, in an attempt to block out his terrible news, her own mind wandered.

Unbeknownst to Maren, war had been declared before she had sailed to Britain in June of 1812. When she had learned of the conflict, she had assumed it would soon end and her parents would arrive to get her. She hated the war which divided her family; she was an American, but her paternal lineage was English. She was aware of the British and American grievances, and she knew each side was wrong in certain ways, even if both felt they were right.

America wanted impressment halted. Americans wanted to trade wherever and with whomever they pleased. Some even wanted to control Canada and Florida just to prevent enemies or foreign powers from "breathing too closely and hotly on our necks," but most Americans simply wanted peace and prosperity.

Britain wanted to have her way on the high seas. She wanted to control trade, to impress British subjects when her ships needed sailors. And she also wanted to punish America for daring to challenge her, and for aiding Napoleon. To the British it was crucial to protect Canada from American encroachment, to bring America back into the Empire.

Twenty-two months before, Maren had sailed to Britain to marry Daniel Redford, the son of an English lord whose vast estate bordered her grand-parents' land. But her betrothed, having gone to sea when war was declared, had actually left his homeland before her arrival. Within a month after his departure, his ship had been attacked and sunk by an American privateer. Maren had met Daniel during her first trip to visit her grandparents. After that she had spent two months in England every other summer, and she and Daniel had become good friends. She had been very fond of him, but she had not loved him; and it seemed he had been fond of her.

During those early teenage visits, Daniel had taught her to shoot, to fight, to hunt, and to use a rapier. They had enjoyed rides, picnics, swims, and long talks. Between the visits, they had exchanged letters. A few times he had told her about devilish pranks he'd played with other lads or about his amorous conquests of local girls, though she had doubted these tales were true. Daniel had loved to make up wild stories, to see how many people he could fool with them. He had possessed a wonderful imagination and a gift for charming others, and he had been handsome and polished, a marvelous catch for any female. Yet, as far as Maren knew, there had been no romantic magic between them. Oh, they had shared a few kisses and hugs, but there had been no fiery passion.

Their last time together had been during the

summer of 1810 because Daniel had left before she had returned to Britain nearly two years ago. Perhaps it was best they had not wed, for gossip implied that Daniel had changed greatly since she had last seen him four years past. She had heard whispered comments about his wild behavior—his gambling, drinking, fighting, and whoring—and she had wondered what or who had changed him during her absence. One day during an afternoon stroll, a bold female had approached her and had informed her that when Daniel returned from sea she would continue to be his mistress, even after Maren married him! The woman had then told her dreadful things about her betrothed, and Maren had believed her. After Daniel's death was announced, eager suitors had come around to take his place. Always they told her how lucky she was to have eluded the trap Daniel had set for her. They'd said he craved her wealth. Yes, others had been quick to point out Daniel's flaws, but no one would or could tell her what had happened to change him.

No matter now. Her betrothed was long dead and the truth was lost forever. She and Daniel had agreed to marry because their grandparents had wished it, as had Daniel's parents, and because at the age of eighteen, no other had captured either of their hearts. Or so Daniel had claimed in his last letter. It had seemed a good match, socially, emotionally, and economically. Two years ago, she and Daniel had been willing to "do their duty," but it had not been fated that they wed. He had been a good friend and a delightful companion, and despite the nasty rumors about him, Maren had grieved for him for several months. Finally, revelations of the unacceptable changes in Daniel had helped her to get over her loss.

Now, in May of 1814, she was twenty, still single, and without parents and a home. It was as if Fate had turned its back on her. How, Maren wondered, had everything gone awry in only two short years? What would she do when they reached New Orleans?

Maren's golden brown eyes appeared liquid and shiny as she focused them on her cousin. She shook her head of dark brown hair and declared, "It cannot be true, Eric. This must be a mistake or a bad dream. Dead for nearly a year . . . the plantation and business gone . . . Explain to me how such horrible things happened."

Eric pulled her away from the mullioned porthole in the captain's quarters of the *Martha J* and guided her to a chair. This merchant ship could sail from Britain to America in four weeks, if the winds held and they confronted no perils. She had eighteen gunports, but they had been used rarely. Fake logbooks, papers, and flags had seen her safely from port to port. The *Martha J* had been named for their paternal grandmother, whose side they had left that morning. "Are you sure you want to hear it again?" he asked.

"To accept it, I must," Maren answered. She listened as Eric James told of the hurricane that had attacked the lower Louisiana parishes and had caused severe flooding around and in New Orleans.

17

Maren understood this peril of nature. From June to November of every year, that area's inhabitants feared those powerful storms, and many left it to avoid them. But violent weather was not the worst danger; disease bred of displaced waste and refuse was. Bodies of decaying animals could not be cleared away quickly enough. Their carcasses added to the stench and created a health hazard once the hot sun and the intense humidity returned. Mosquitoes and flies rapidly spread infection, and for weeks afterward both water and soil were contaminated. Following most hurricanes, more people and animals died from illnesses than from injuries caused by the storm.

Eric quickly repeated the disturbing tale. "Your father was in town on business, and your mother had accompanied him to go shopping. We had lunch that day, and were to see a play together that night. Except when we were at sea, our lives were little changed by the war. The hurricane struck before anyone realized it was approaching. It was a terrible one, Maren, filth and stench everywhere. I've never seen the insects so bad—big enough and mean enough to eat you alive. Your parents were trapped in New Orleans, but as soon as the roads were passable, Uncle Cameron rushed Aunt Carlotta out of the city. I tried to persuade him to remain where it was safe, but he wanted to get home, he said, to clean water and fresh air. Perhaps it was already too late because the day after they reached the plantation, they lost consciousness. As soon as I could get away, I went to check on them. They were both burning with fever. I summoned a doctor, but nothing could be done. I doubt either knew the other was sick. I had them buried and then placed their belongings in one of my storerooms."

He poured two sherries and handed her one to sip. Draining his glass with one large swallow, he placed it on the table before stuffing his sweaty hands into his pockets. "It took months for workmen to get the town cleaned up and repaired. Your father's losses were heavy. I had to sell the plantation to pay off Uncle Cameron's debts and commitments. With foreign ports blockaded and several ships destroyed or captured, his office had taken a beating. For a time, I feared if I didn't cut it loose, its debts would sink the Baltimore and London offices. But I was determined to save it."

Eric shifted to his other foot and wet his lips before continuing, "I came to New Orleans right after you departed to get things prepared in London. Uncle Cameron had asked me to run this office of the company while he went to your wedding in September; they were planning a long visit to make certain everything went smoothly for you. I'm sorry about Daniel's death, but I know you'll have countless suitors when you get home."

As if he had said something terrible, Eric quickly returned to his previous topic. "After the hurricane, there were workers to be paid, buildings to be repaired, and cargoes to be replaced. I sold everything I could get my hands on, Maren, but it wasn't enough. At that time, I didn't know about Redford's death, so I didn't realize you would need the house, the jewels, and money. If I had known about your bad luck, I would have bankrupted this office and saved whatever I could for you."

He smiled wryly. "Truthfully, I expected to find you happily married and rich enough to make me a loan. I've sunk nearly all I have into the New Orleans office to keep it alive until this war ends. I've worked hard to find men who'll slip a few cargoes through the British blockade; that's how I've managed to stay afloat."

She reasoned, "If you've made it through the blockade several times before, why haven't you fetched me sooner? And why couldn't Papa have gotten at least one message to me? I've been frantic."

"It was too risky, Maren. My schedules were tight, and my voyages were vital to America. We had to stay clear of Britain to avoid capture. I knew you were safe there. My crews and cargoes had to come first. Your parents wrote to you, but the letters didn't get through."

Maren knew her parents had loved her and had tried to contact her, but the war and distance had prevented them from succeeding, just as distance and slow means of communication between New Orleans and Washington had kept news of the outbreak of the war from reaching her before she had sailed so long ago.

Eric was saying, "You can study the books when we reach New Orleans, but you'll see that only my personal investment remains in James Shipping. I would turn it over to you, Maren, but it's all I have. Besides, a man needs work more than a woman. How else can he marry and support a family?"

"But why did you sell the plantation? It was my home. And why didn't its sale bring in enough money to settle father's debts?" Maren inquired.

"The blockade, little cousin. Goods are of little value if you can't export them. By the time your father learned about the war, he had already speculated on several owners' crops. He would have made a fortune if the Royal Navy hadn't prevented him from shipping them to foreign ports. Whole cargoes rotted on the wharf because we couldn't ship them anywhere. We tried to sell as much as we could locally, but everyone was in the same predicament. Running a plantation requires lots of money, and your parents ran out of it for they had little or no income for nearly a year. Things were so bad during that first winter that your father sold whatever he could part with to feed his workers and servants. You can talk with the people in town; they'll tell you how bad it was for him. Maybe death was a blessing, Maren. He was a proud man, and it would have destroyed him to lose everything."

"Even if things were that terrible, Eric, Papa was not a quitter. He would have found some way to survive, to begin anew. A man isn't to blame for a failure he cannot prevent."

"Maren, Maren," he chided softly. "You don't know what it's been like during your absence. Think about it, a blockade of our entire Atlantic coast. War, little cousin. Lives lost in bloody battles. You've been spared the demands of the conflict. I saw Uncle Cam every day. I watched this war take its toll on him. He was helpless. Do you know what that does to a man?''

As she sipped the second sherry Eric had poured for her, her cheeks began to glow and she felt warm and tingly. It seemed that they were discussing strangers and another land. "If things are so bad, why didn't you ask Grandfather for a loan?" she asked.

"The same James pride and stubbornness that our fathers had. I want to survive this mess by my own wits and skills. I want to prove myself to Grandfather and Murray and to our customers and competitors. This is the first big matter I've been allowed to handle; I can't fail. If I told him why I needed the money, I would have to tell him everything. I don't want him and Grandmother to learn about your father's death until it's necessary. If this mission is successful, I should get a reward, and our country will be saved. Captain Hull received a gold medal and fifty thousand dollars from Congress when the *Constitution* defeated the *Guerrière*, and Captain Jones was rewarded with a sword and twenty-five thousand dollars in prize money even though he lost his ship to the British. Surely this vital mission is worth a small reward and a medal. Murray will envy me."

"How is Murray?" Maren had suddenly become curious about her other cousin.

"He's probably fine by now. He wants to keep his

22

accident a secret because he broke his leg at a married woman's house. I think it would be best if you don't mention it to him, or to anybody, if you don't mind."

"I thought he was planning to be married soon."

Eric laughed devilishly. "He is; that's another reason why he wants his recklessness kept quiet."

Maren was annoyed by his brother's conduct because it revived memories of Daniel's alleged deceits. Could no man besides her father be trusted? she wondered. How lucky she had been to have Cameron James as an example, and how fortunate to have such a special mother as Carlotta. Her parents had been strong, intelligent, caring people. And even if they had been ruined financially, they would have found other ways to survive and succeed. "If Murray loves her and plans to marry her, why would he do such a despicable thing?"

"Men take foolish risks when they're about to be imprisoned for life. They become scared and do crazy things. But if I decided to take a wife, I wouldn't cheat on her. I wouldn't want to risk losing her. She would own my heart and soul." He pretended to be embarrassed by his rash confession, thinking that would endear him to her, but recalling Daniel's shortcomings, he quickly changed the subject. "This has been a hard morning for you. Why don't you rest for a while? I'll let you know when it's time to eat."

"Yes, I do need to relax and think," Maren agreed.

After Eric left the cabin, she went over his words several times, and the brunt of them struck her. Alone. It was true; her parents were lost to her forever. She covered her face with quivering hands and wept. Later she would make plans; now she simply needed to release her tension and grief.

Eric stood at the ship's railing with his righthand man. Horben Wolfe's flaming hair whipped about his ruddy face as his pale eyes gazed across the water, eyes which were almost colorless except for a slight tinge of ice blue. The big man's burly frame was propped against the sturdy rail, and his arms were folded over his chest. Horben was at Eric's side most of the time. He was his protector and cohort. No matter what Eric said or did to others, Horben trusted and obeyed him implicitly.

The redheaded man inquired, "Did she believe you?"

Eric laughed and responded, "Why wouldn't she? We've been close friends for years. Maren's smart, but she's too trusting and gullible. Besides, there's little chance she can learn the truth, and if she does, what can she do about it? If she becomes a problem, I know the perfect way to deal with her."

"Are you still planning to get rid of your two brothers?"

"The sooner the better," Eric replied coldly. "I'm tired of Murray's bossiness and interference, and Marc's a weak simpleton. I've done all the work and planning, I've kept the firm afloat; so I deserve to have all of James Shipping, not a third of it."

"What about your grandfather? He still owns part

of the business, and we both know he would hang you if he discovered your secrets."

Eric replied bitterly, "I left a letter telling my beloved grandparents about poor Cameron's death. It should finish them off, or at least keep them out of my hair until it's too late to interfere. I hope that news punishes them for placing Murray in full control of Father's firm. The old beak nose never had any use for me, and the same was true of my dear departed father. In Colin James's eyes, my father had only one son and heir: Murray. God, how I hate them all."

"You still mad at your grandmother because she broke her promise to you?"

"Damn right, Ben! She lied about helping me with Grandfather. If she had kept her word, I would be half-owner with Murray right now, and her youngest son would still be alive . . . well, maybe Uncle Cameron wouldn't be dead yet. I've proven I can handle the New Orleans firm better than anyone. I'd like to see them try to take it away from me," he said, his green gaze cold and angry.

"I can't allow anything or anyone to stand in my way, Ben, not even the American government. But we'll have to be careful and clever. Too many James deaths in a short span will catch someone's attention. Right now, Murray's my main concern. He's getting too inquisitive. After he's gone, Marc won't give me any sass or trouble. Even if Mother hadn't made him into a weakling and a fool, he's too grateful and scared to defy me. Before this year ends, the war should be over and I'll own everything, if there's anything left."

"With what you've got going, it doesn't really matter which country wins this stupid war. You're smart to cover all sides and to keep your identity a secret on this voyage. There shouldn't be any trouble for us with you posing as James Slade and claiming Maren is your wife."

Eric affectionately slapped Horben on the back and replied, "The smartest thing I ever did was to hire you, Ben." They talked a while longer, then went below to eat.

Twenty-six-year-old Peter Thomas stepped from behind a large capstan and several barrels, and was relieved that the deck was not cluttered with men. The sandy-haired seaman wished he had been close enough to eavesdrop, but it had been impossible to get nearer to the two men without being sighted and questioned. Fortunately he had been in Charleston when Captain Canton had hired the crew for this unusual, and suspicious, voyage to Britain. He rubbed his jaw thoughtfully. As soon as possible, he must report to the President to suggest having someone spy on James Slade and Horben Wolfe . . . and perhaps on that beautiful wife James Slade had retrieved from London. . . .

Two weeks passed uneventfully aboard the ship. From recent reports, most of the fighting was being done along the Atlantic coast and around the Great Lakes. To avoid the coastal blockade, Eric's ship had sailed southwest from Britain. They were to pass near the West Indies before entering the Gulf of Mexico and proceeding to New Orleans, after putting in at one of the Caribbean islands.

Maren spent most of her time in Captain Thomas Canton's quarters "to prevent trouble with any beauty-smitten sailor." Only the Captain and first mate knew who she and Eric were, for the crew had been signed on in Charleston and Savannah to insure secrecy for this vital mission.

Once each morning and evening, she was allowed a stroll on deck in the company of the captain or her cousin. Her meals were taken in her borrowed quarters, but she was joined at dinner by Eric, Horben, and Captain Canton. Often they would play games, usually card games or "toss the ring," but sometimes they would talk or read aloud. Confined most of the time, Maren enjoyed these evening meals and visits, except for Horben Wolfe's presence. There was something about the man she did not like or trust. Perhaps it was his piercing stare which made her uneasy.

During one stroll, she and Eric had discussed her problems. It was odd, but her losses seemed unreal to her. She often found herself getting excited and thinking she would soon see her parents and her home. She went over her first conversation with him in detail, but even after she reminded herself that her parents no longer existed, she could not believe it or accept it. She knew she would not until she viewed the evidence. Each day she occupied her hands and thoughts with other things, refusing to torment herself with such an incredible loss.

Nine more days passed slowly, the air warming as they sailed southward. As they approached the tropical islands, laziness began to lap at everyone much like the gentle waves lapped against the ship's hull. During the day, the sky was clear and the sun reflected almost painfully off the seemingly endless stretch of trouble-free water. Sometimes dolphins traveled alongside them, and Maren watched the playful sea creatures from the cabin window. At other times, she studied the men as they tended to their tasks, often forgetting her presence and talking more boldly than they should about certain subjects. She covered her mouth many times to keep from laughing aloud as they discussed women and life. Such eavesdropping was informative and amusing, so she did it frequently.

At night, she heard the canvases popping in the wind, and she listened to the singing of the sailors as they sipped their daily ration of grog and entertained themselves below deck. Often she peered out at the star-filled heavens which inspired a feeling of loneliness and hunger in her, a desperate yearning to be held in protective arms. Sometimes she felt stranded in time, breathlessly waiting for some magical clock to begin ticking once more and to free her from limbo.

On some days and nights, grief plagued her; but most of the time, her losses remained unreal. Since

Eric slept in the same cabin on a cot, she hoped her tossings did not disturb his slumber. At least she had avoided trouble with the sailors, thanks to her alleged marriage to "James Slade," the man who was "considering purchasing this ship and hiring her crew" if she successfully ran the blockade. Yet, Maren found one handsome sailor's gaze on her many times during her strolls. He was a hazel-eyed man named Peter Thomas.

Maren wondered where the British gold was hidden and whether Eric could get it safely to America. It had been a matter of weeks since she had learned of her parents' deaths, and she needed something to occupy her mind, to stimulate her imagination, to fill her dreams. It was exhilarating to know about Eric's patriotic mission and to plan ways to help America win this war before more precious blood was spilt. She was not wholly surprised by Eric's feat, for he had always done things to get attention. She recalled the many letters from Eric's mother, Elizabeth, telling her own mother about Eric's most recent antics. Yet Maren had always found her first cousin to be charming and exciting company, much as Daniel had been.

Many times Maren had felt sorry for Eric as he did not seem able to please his father and older brother. She had been amazed at how different Cameron and John James were. Although she was a girl, her father had spent hours teaching her things, giving her attention and love, whereas her Uncle John had acted as if he'd had only one son: Murray. No wonder Eric had done wild things to get his parents' attention and to punish those who hurt him.

One morning, Eric entered the cabin with a broad smile. "I have a present for you," he told her, then withdrew a gold and ruby necklace from his pocket. "I forgot I had it until I uncovered it in my chest this morning while dressing. I want you to have it. Perhaps it will make up for some of the things you've lost." He fastened it around her neck, and guided her to the mirror to view it.

She was wearing a white batiste dress decorated with tiny red dots and sporting a red band at the high waistline. On the hem and the puff sleeves was red embroidery in a small floral pattern. The day was humid, so she had secured her long hair in a chignon, and the shorter hairs around her face had curled to frame it becomingly. Her gown and her hairstyle accented the expensive necklace she wore.

"It's lovely, Eric, but I couldn't possibly accept it," she remarked as she fingered the exquisite workmanship and pondered its value.

"You must, or I'll be sorely offended," he teased. "It looks perfect around your lovely throat. Within two weeks, we should reach New Orleans, Maren. Think of how the other women will envy you. I'm responsible for you now. Please, let me do this for you," he urged.

"But it's so expensive," she protested.

"It was an investment. If I sell it, I'll take a terrible loss. I would much rather you have it. Think of it as a thank-you gift to Uncle Cam for all he did for me.

During the time I was with him, he treated me more like a son and a man than my father ever did." Eric looked sad for a time, then brightened. "I'll tell you what, wear it for a month or two, then decide whether you want to keep it or not. If you don't want to, you can return it and I won't argue." He caressed her cheek.

It seemed important to her cousin that she accept the gift, so Maren agreed. "If you insist, but I'll guard it carefully until I decide."

Eric grinned and hugged her. "I know you will, little cousin."

When she was alone, she eyed the treasure in the mirror. Something strange is afoot, she decided. If Eric had needed money, this necklace would have sold for a hefty price. Perhaps it was part of the "cargo" he had picked up in London for the President. Eric might be stealing it to make certain he was well rewarded for his dangerous task. She knew her cousin never did anything without a reason, unless her father had changed him. Until she considered the matter further .... Loud yells and the sounds of running on deck seized her attention.

Eric rushed into the cabin. "We're being overtaken by a swift frigate," he hastily explained. "No flag yet, so it could be American or British. Stay in this cabin until I come for you."

Horben entered and went directly to the secret panel which she had seen opened before.

"Be ready to pull out whichever logbook and papers we need, Ben," Eric commanded. "Captain

Canton is prepared to hoist the proper flag." He turned to a wide-eyed Maren and said, "Don't forget, Maren, we're traveling as man and wife, Mr. and Mrs. James Slade. If she's British, we sailed from London and we're heading for Barbados. If she's American or French, we sailed from France and we're heading for Martinique to pick up spices."

"What if they attack and steal the gold?" she asked worriedly.

"They can't know about it, so don't let them bully you into revealing anything. The crew doesn't want to be impressed, so they won't breathe a word. Canton and I can talk us out of trouble if you keep your head."

Eric left her alone with Horben Wolfe who was preparing to place the "correct" papers on the captain's desk and to conceal the others. Maren hurried to the mullioned porthole and gazed at the ship which was rapidly increasing in size. As it bore down on the *Martha J*, it looked as if it were going to sail right into them! Envisioning prison, Maren swallowed hard and her heart drummed in panic.

"Don't be afraid, Miss Maren," Horben said. "We'll protect you. Just keep a clear head on your shoulders and we'll be fine. Eric claims you're smart, so here's your chance to prove he's right."

"Why didn't we run or fight?" she asked. "If Eric's ruse fails, we could be captured or sunk. We can't lose that gold to them."

Horben shook his flaming head. "No way to leave that ship behind. She looks like a privateer; they're about the fastest and deadliest ships on the sea. Don't worry; Eric can outsmart anyone.''

Maren glanced at the brawny man and wished his eyes were not so disconcerting. They made her flesh crawl, and she felt an urge to race out of the cabin into the warm sunlight. From Horben's expression, he realized the effect he was having on her and it troubled him.

Eric returned briefly and informed them, "She's flying a French flag, Ben, and so are we. French, Maren," he stressed.

She nodded. When the two men left, she closed the door, but did not bolt it. Realizing that she was fingering the costly necklace, Maren unfastened it and glanced about for a hiding place. Time was short and the cabin might be searched, so she stuffed the jewels into her bosom. She wondered why Eric had been too nervous to remember the costly item and to hide it. Obviously, she decided, his thoughts were on the hidden gold. She waited apprehensively, wishing she were topside to view this confrontation and to observe her cousin's strategy.

Maren gasped and whirled as the door was roughly thrown open and a powerfully built man entered the cabin. Her golden brown eyes enlarged as they took in his light brown hair streaked by the sun and his eyes, nearly the same color as hers but tawnier. His skin was darkly tanned from years beneath the golden sun and he was handsome. His six-foot frame was clad in snug black breeches and a white linen shirt, and his vivid masculinity took her breath away.

She stared at him as an astonished look came to his tawny eyes. Then his gaze roved over her from head to red-slippered feet, leisurely and appreciatively. She warmed.

"Who might you be, fair lady?" he asked in a rich, mellow tone which teased over her sensitive nerves.

As he approached, Maren leaned against the ship's hull to steady her weakened knees. Her dry lips made it difficult to answer him, and her own gaze drifted down to the expanse of hairy chest revealed by his open shirt. This bronzed man stunned her, and she could not reply.

The privateer halted before her, his gaze slowly raking over her once more. "Relax, fair maiden. Since you aren't British, there's no need to be afraid," he murmured. "Who are you and where are you heading?"

Maren cautioned herself to avoid the slight British accent she had picked up after being in London for so long. "Maren Slade. We're sailing to . . . Martinique to pick up spices and such." She knew she had hesitated while recalling the proper story. It was hard not to do so with him staring into her upturned face. He was so distracting, so intoxicatingly close. She tried to cover her near slip by saying, "You startled me when you burst in. The door wasn't locked."

"Why not?" he asked unexpectedly. "You're a treasure to guard."

Maren flushed slightly and she almost smiled at him, since he was grinning most compellingly at her. "You would only break it down for no reason.

34

We have nothing to hide or fear. Even if you are an enemy ship, most men of the sea do not harm innocent women. Isn't that right?" she inquired apprehensively.

He half turned and ordered, "Check the logbook and papers, Kip, while I search the cabin."

Maren glanced at the other man whom she had not noticed until now. He looked to be in his late twenties, like the man before her. His hair was night black and his eyes were a playful blue. He grinned, then lifted the logbook and read it silently.

Maren observed the intrusive captain as he searched the cabin. When he knelt by her trunks to go through them, she made sure she did not glance in the direction of the hidden panel. She then approached him and began to straighten her possessions and repack each trunk he had rummaged through. "You're ruining my clothing. Why don't you just tell me what you want—or let me help you search?"

His gaze met hers. "Sorry, ma'am, but there are spies and traitors everywhere. I wouldn't put it past those determined Brits to beguile us with a ravishing spy, so I must examine every inch of this cabin for evidence."

"But you're a privateer, no more than a pirate. Why would you be interested in spies and traitors?" she inquired as she refolded and replaced her belongings. She cautioned herself to be alert, but it was hard work with this particular man. Something about his manner and voice told her to be wary of

35

him, but his chuckles and smiles flowed over her like entrancing water, disarming her.

"It was only a jest. I'm looking for jewels and money. You have very little for a woman with such a lovely wardrobe," he remarked as he dangled a bag of money and a pouch of jewels in her face.

Maren instinctively tried to snatch them from his grasp, but as he jerked them out of her reach, she fell against his hard body, sending them both to the deck, where he seized her. "Release me, you pirate," she demanded, aware of how her body trembled in his grasp.

Without moving or looking away, the handsome captain asked his first mate, "Anything of interest there, Kip?"

"Just what the captain told us," Kerry Osgood replied. "The proper French registry, cargo manifests, and bills of landing."

Maren's captor mulled over that information before ordering, "Help the men search the entire ship. I'll join you on deck."

"Aye, Captain Hawk," Kerry responded. Then he left, closing the door.

Maren stared past her captor's strong arm, at the door, and her respiration became noticeably erratic. He had not released her, and his manly smell filled her nostrils, teasing her susceptible senses. Slowly her gaze lifted to meet "Captain Hawk's." He was looking at her oddly, but Maren was certain he did not remember her. After all, it had been five years since she had seen Jared Morgan and had fallen madly in love with him. Nonetheless, that meeting remained vivid in her memory, and he still affected her in that same overwhelming way.

She had first seen him on her fifteenth birthday at the wharf in New Orleans. To accompany her father on his export business, she had dressed as a boy, stuffing her long hair into a skullcap. When her father was busy, she had snooped around. As ill fortune would have it, she had been sighted by some rough sailors who wanted to have fun with an overly inquisitive green lad. While fleeing them, she had bumped headlong into a broad chest, and powerful arms and hands had halted her escape. She had fought like a wild animal until her captor had subdued her with the strength of his body and voice. Finally glancing up at the tall man who was unlike her crude pursuers, Maren had felt her heart leap wildly. When he'd questioned her about her problem, it had taken a while for his words to penetrate her dazed mind.

Suddenly she had realized how terrible she looked, how unfeminine, how ridiculous, how dirty from her explorations. She had wanted to flee the man, yet had also wanted to remain near him. To do so, she had continued to pretend to be a young lad. Jared Morgan had been generous with his time and money that day. He had purchased her lunch and had talked with her; no doubt he had believed her to be a poor wharf rat in need of food and affection.

Jared, twenty-three at that time, had been in port on business for his family in Savannah. Clearly he was an adventurer and a devilish rogue. Maren had been fascinated by him, and by the emotions he had unleashed in her blossoming body and her tender heart. She had fumed each time a woman had flirted with him, and for days afterward, she had sneaked away from her father's warehouse to trail him, to spy on him, and to spend time with him. On the day he had left New Orleans, she had sneaked from her father's office, dressed in her loveliest outfit. Knowing Jared's routine, she had *accidentally* bumped into him. He had not recognized her, and when he had smiled and queried her about any injuries, he had treated her like a child.

Consumed with love for him, Maren had flirted openly and boldly as she had seen other women do, whereupon Jared had grinned knowingly, amused and flattered by her smitten heart. Maren had realized she was being daring, but she could not stop herself. To let her down gently, he had purchased a nosegay from a street vendor, which she had later dried and placed in a small chest. Then Jared had walked out of her life to board his ship. Shamelessly she had observed him until he was out of sight, even waving goodbye twice. How foolish she must have seemed to the grown man who had so kindly returned her farewell gestures.

From a distance, she had seen Jared again during the spring of 1811, when she was seventeen. But he had left town before she could devise a way to get into his path once more. At twenty-five, he had been even more handsome and compelling, and from that day onward, Jared had filled Maren's fantasies and dreams.

Now he was sitting on the floor, inches away from her, talking to her, touching her. As if her body thirsted for his, she greedily drank in the vision of him. He was not yet thirty, but his good looks and desirability had only increased. Still, he was a pirate who was robbing her and this ship. Like Daniel Redford, this man had changed immensely.

Jared was aroused by the way this beautiful woman was looking at him. He had never taken a female captive before, but there was a first time for everything, he thought. A mischievous grin tugged at his lips and an amused glint brightened his whiskey-colored eyes.

Chapter Two

Jared ordered himself to abandon such a foolish idea. His country was at war, and he was raiding a suspicious ship which he doubted was French. Each day he had important work to do, many dangers to confront. His life did not allow him to have a woman at his side. Besides, he wasn't a pirate, only a privateer. Breaking the dreamy aura in the cabin and hoping to catch this ravishing woman off guard, he asked, "Did you see Napoleon during your visit to France?"

"Did I do what?" Maren asked confusedly.

To test this ravishing *intrigante*'s knowledge, he said, "Everyone knows Bonaparte abdicated in early April. Did you get to meet him or visit him? Surely he would receive such a lovely guest in his country."

Maren gazed at him oddly. "Everyone also knows that Bonaparte is in exile on Elba, which every sailor should know is off the coast of Italy, not France.

41

Besides, whyever would Napoleon want to meet me?''

He eyed her appreciatively and grinned. "I would imagine that any man in his right mind would want to meet you. Maren, wasn't it?''

"Yes," she answered, trying to grasp his mood and meaning.

"You sound American. Why are you flying a French flag?''

"Perhaps for the same reason you're flying one, Captain Hawk. I know little of ships and business. I'm only a passenger. Why don't you ask Captain Canton to explain such matters?''

Jared's steady gaze did not reveal his skepticism and curiosity. "But you are American, aren't you?'' he persisted.

"Yes, from New Orleans. If I'm not mistaken, your accent is also Southern, perhaps Georgian," she said, knowing it was not a guess.

"You're very alert and intelligent, Maren. Maren . . . That's an unusual name, yet it sounds vaguely familiar." His keen gaze studied her for a moment. Her hair was a becoming shade of dark brown, and her eyes, the color of aged brandy, were lively. He liked the way her brows arched over those expressive eyes, the way her nose turned ever so slightly upward. Her unmarred complexion appeared to be kissed by the sun; yet, it was obvious the sun had had nothing to do with its hue. She was so warm and responsive, unafraid to reveal her attraction to him, yet she was bold and brave, not wanton or coy or vain. He liked her openness and poise. His eyes settled on her lips. "Familiar, Maren, but I'm certain we've never met. I would definitely remember a woman like you."

"And I would definitely remember a man like you," she replied. Maren was too ensnared by him to realize she was forgetting herself; she was forgetting she *knew* this man, but he did not recall her or realize why she was behaving this way. She was thrilled and titillated by the way he was treating her. Her passions blazed, her body tingled, and her cheeks glowed. She wanted to make him feel the same way she did, wanted him to wish to see more of her.

Jared knew this ravishing creature was getting to him, and he wondered how she could move him so easily and so quickly. This desire he felt was unlike any hunger he had experienced before. It was inexplicable, but it seemed he had known her for years, had waited for her for years. She conjured up visions of lazy days beneath the tropical sun, her in his arms. Why did she make such a curious and powerful impression on him? He had to see her again, and often. He had to possess her fully. "When do you expect to be back in New Orleans?"

"Why?" she asked, as she tried to decide what, if anything, to tell him. Her heart began to drum in panic and wariness. Eric had ordered her to tell their attacker they were heading for Martinique, but she wanted Jared to know where and when to locate her. What if she told Jared she was heading to New Orleans afterward, but had Eric told him something

43

different? After all, Jared was Captain Hawk today, but she did not know what else he had become over the years. If only he weren't so disarming and this encounter weren't so brief . . .

Jared read her hesitation, her alarm, her desire for him. "I would like to see you on my next visit, if you're agreeable. I may be a devil at sea, but I promise I'm an angel ashore," he teased, fingering her lips. "Surely you realize there's a powerful current between us. It should be studied and enjoyed."

Before Maren could respond, Jared opened her last trunk, the one containing her trousseau. She did not want to explain Daniel's death or to expose her sojourn in London. Quickly she pleaded, "Please, Captain Hawk, don't damage them with dirty hands. I swear there is no money or jewels in this one. Let me lift the gowns out and shake each one for you. This was my mother's wedding gown, so it's very special to me."

To eye her ring finger, Jared lifted her left hand and kissed it. He was pleased when he discovered it bare. "I see no need to search this trunk. Relax, Maren," he told her.

"You are most kind. Do you have a name besides Captain Hawk? From what I've heard, pirates rarely use their real names."

He avoided answering by asking her another question, "Why are you aboard this ship, Maren? Wartime makes for dangerous travel."

She tried to reply without using her cousin's false tale that she was married. If Jared had questioned the men above, he knew who James Slade was. Yet, he certainly did not behave as if he had been told she was James's wife. If she was lucky, no one had mentioned it to him. "James is considering the purchase of this ship, so he's aboard to check out her value and the crew's expertise. Until now, we haven't had any trouble. Is this what you do all the time, attack and rob helpless ships?"

Jared smiled and ran his fingers through her silky brown hair. "I haven't killed a single man aboard, Maren, and I don't plan to do so. I only raid enemy ships, so I have to make certain yours is truly French. Are those papers real ones?" he asked, motioning to the desk.

She could not endanger the lives of others or risk playing dumb, so she cleverly alleged, "I have no way of knowing, Captain Hawk, but I assume Captain Canton is an honest man. He's been nothing but kind and polite to me since I came aboard. He insisted I use his cabin, but I cannot say what he does while I am strolling the deck. I was visiting France when the war began and couldn't get home because of the blockade. James picked me up on this voyage. As soon as Captain Canton handles his business and it's safe, he's taking us home to New Orleans. I'm afraid that's all I know." Maren wondered if her deceit was noticeable.

Yes, Jared suspected her of lying, but he did not want to force the matter for he believed she had good reason to fear a pirate or a Britisher in disguise. He assumed Maren Slade was the sister of James Slade, the blond man he had met on deck. She had repeated the same tale Slade had told, yet . . . If he proved she was lying, by choice or by order, and this was an enemy ship, he would be forced to scuttle it and take her captive. Although that was a tempting course of action, he refrained from taking it. The best thing to do would be to sail in the *Martha J*'s shadow for a few days.

Without warning, Jared leaned forward and sensuously sealed Maren's lips. When she did not resist him, his tongue eagerly explored her mouth. He felt her tremble and press closer to his body. She smelled wonderful, and his senses spun wildly at her nearness. He guided her to the floor and lay half atop her as his mouth conquered hers.

Maren clasped his head, pressed his lips more tightly to hers. It was exciting to be in his arms and to have his full attention. His mouth claimed hers skillfully, tantalizingly, mind-dazingly. As a fierce desire for him flamed within her heart, her body yearned to fuse with his. It had been her good fortune to cross his path again today, and she intended to take advantage of her altered fate. Her fingers roved over his sun-streaked brown hair, and they itched to roam over his entire body.

Jared's lips moved to her ear and nibbled on it. He was aware of his effect on her, and of hers on him. No matter who or what she was, he wanted to make love to her at this very moment. How curious, he mused, to feel this way about a total stranger and under these circumstances! His rich voice warned teasingly, "Be careful, my radiant siren, or I shall be tempted to take you away with me."

"Surely the flames of fortune burn brightly today, as I can think of no better fate than becoming your willing captive," she murmured.

Jared leaned back to look into her seductive eyes, and a gleam caught his attention. His molten gaze shifted to her neck, then his eyes cooled and narrowed. One end of the ruby and gold necklace had slipped from her bosom and was snaking over silky flesh as if preparing to strike either or both of them.

Maren remained wide-eyed and rigid as his fingers wriggled into her cleavage and worked the treasure free of its hiding place. "What do we have here, a crown jewel of France?" he asked sarcastically. His probing gaze returned to Maren's alarmed one. He had lost his head to a sly vixen on the floor of an attacked ship! Was he crazy?

Maren paled beneath his chilly glare and his icy mistrust. "Please, take anything you want except the necklace and that one trunk. Because of this damned war, they're all of value I have left. Please." Tears glistened in her eyes, but not for the reason Jared imagined. She was crushed by the reality that the necklace, which she might need to sell to begin a new life, had spoiled things for her. This was probably a cruel joke played by Fate and she would never see him again. Must she lose everyone she loved? "Please, I need that necklace to support myself; it's all I have left. I swear it, Captain Hawk. Surely one measly necklace can't mean so much to you. I beg you, don't take it from me."

Her vulnerability touched Jared, and he made excuses to himself for her deceit. Actually, he concluded, this was the first time she had spoken the truth. He stood, then pulled her to her feet. "I've tarried too long with you, my distracting maiden. Enemy ships could be lurking nearby." He held up the necklace and examined it, wondering how she had come to have it. "It's as exquisite as Maren Slade, but worth far less. If you'll promise to . . . spend time with me when I'm in New Orleans, I won't take anything of yours today."

Maren's astonishment was real and visible, but she misread his meaning. "You want to see me again?" she asked.

Jared was relieved by her excitement. "It is possible?"

Maren could not keep from smiling at him. "It would please me very much, Captain Hawk. Thank you."

Jared was pleased by her response, although he would ponder it later. "You should conceal your jewels and money or the others will wonder why I didn't rob you. We've been alone here too long."

Maren inhaled sharply. "Whatever shall I tell them?"

"That I was reading the logbook and those papers, and searching the cabin," he replied, grinning at her worried look, her innocent look. A sensation of warmth and pleasure flowed over him as he watched her.

Maren hid the two pouches in her trunk and then faced him. Considering what had taken place between them moments ago, she felt awkward. Jared carefully pushed the ruby necklace into her cleavage before trailing his fingertips over the satiny flesh above it. She quivered, and he pulled her into his arms to kiss her soundly, but quickly, before departing.

Maren sank weakly against the bedpost and stared at the closed door. She wanted to run after him, but that was impossible. Would she ever see him again? she wondered sadly. He didn't know her real name or where to find her. She didn't know when, or if, he planned to visit New Orleans. Quickly she went to the mirror and straightened her hair and clothes. She knew Eric would soon be coming to question her about Jared's lengthy presence in this cabin. She tossed the items from one trunk onto the floor and knelt by them to pretend she was cleaning up the mess made by Captain Hawk. Then she glanced toward the large porthole, aware that her love's ship began to move off.

Then the door opened and Eric rushed to her side. "Well, what took so long in here?" he anxiously demanded. "I've been worried sick."

Maren nodded and replied, "That beast dumped my trunks and searched between every item. My clothes are a mess."

"Is that all?" Eric asked strangely.

"No, he seemed most interested in those papers on the desk. He kept shuffling through them and reading them several times." She repeated the tale she was supposed to have told the privateer, the one which Jared had suggested, and, pulling the necklace from its concealed location, she laughed and boasted, "But he didn't get this piece. I hid it before he arrived. I told you I would guard it with my life."

Eric's eyes blazed with relief. Then he laughed joyfully and hugged her. "You're a wonder, Maren James, and I love you."

"Why don't you put it in Captain Canton's hiding place in case something like this happens again?" she suggested.

"That's a splendid idea," he replied, and immediately secreted the necklace.

"What about the gold? Did they find it?" she asked worriedly.

"Nope, but I knew they couldn't," he boasted. "We have one stop to make in a few days; then it's homeward bound, little cousin. Let's drink a toast to our keen wits and to victory."

As he poured two glasses of wine, Maren rose and walked to the porthole to watch the *Sea Mist* sail away. "New Orleans . . . It's been such a long time since I left home," she murmured. "Everything will be so different, but I can't wait to get there." *Please, Jared, visit me soon. Now I know what and who I've been waiting for. . . .*

Two days later Maren was still thinking and dreaming of Jared Morgan. She slipped out of bed, trying not to disturb Eric, and went over to the porthole. She listened to the sounds of wind and water and sail, trying to silence the cries in her heart. She wanted . . .

"Is something wrong, little cousin?" Eric asked from the darkness. Then he joined her by the porthole before she could answer.

"I'm sorry, Eric, but I couldn't sleep. Do you think we'll be attacked again?" she asked without turning, hoping to mislead him.

Eric wrapped his arms around her, drew her against him, and rested his chin lightly on the top of her head. Maren absently curled her fingers over the arms around her chest, rested her cheek against his shoulder, and sighed wearily. Eric followed her gaze across the moonlit ocean. She was one of the few people he truly liked and admired. They had spent much time together and were most compatible. Maren had never judged him or resented him as so many others had. She had joined him in pranks and adventures, and had thanked him for including her in the fun and excitement. Like Daniel Redford, he had let her do as she pleased though she was a girl. He hoped she would not intrude on his plans, for he hated to think of hurting her.

"Don't worry, little cousin. I would never let anyone or anything harm you. We've always been close, and that's important to me. Do you realize you're one of the few people who accepts me as I am? I have to prove myself to others; that's why it's so important that I save your father's company. Uncle

Cam trusted me, so he called me to New Orleans to handle things during his absence. I can't let him down, Maren. Whatever it takes or costs, his office has to survive and succeed, because of me."

"It will, Eric. If anyone can do it, you can. Remember that day at the county fair when your father's horse came up lame and you offered him the one you had trained for months? Your stallion left the others behind during the first lap. He was a winner, like you, Eric. He just needed a lot of care and attention, someone to train him."

Eric recalled that day. His father had laughed and had refused to listen to him. To prove himself, Eric had entered the horse on his own and it had won easily. Despite Eric's victory, his father had been displeased because he had lost a great deal of money betting against his own son. It had always been that way between them. Eric said cleverly, "Your father is the only one who believed in me and helped me. I loved and respected Uncle Cam, and I'm sorry he's gone. I've missed him."

Maren knew her father had been a good influence on many people. Cameron James had been strong, honest, and dependable; but he was also patient, kind, and compassionate. He had possessed traits too many men lacked. "Remember that time when you visited us in New Orleans and Father's dock crew got roaring drunk at a party? You and I were the ones who stayed up all night to help Papa load the cargo. Papa was so pleased that he paid you double wages, and you used half of your windfall to take me to

Marlow's to celebrate. We've shared a lot of good times, Eric. I'm glad you'll be in New Orleans to help me get settled. I'm going to miss my parents terribly; we were so close." Maren shivered apprehensively as she thought of what was before her.

When she began to cry softly, Eric turned her and embraced her. "Let it out, love. Pain hurts too much when you keep it in. No one can defeat us. We'll both make it. You'll see."

"What would I do without you, Eric?" she asked, sobbing in grief.

"You'll never have to know, little cousin. I promise. James Shipping will survive this war, and you will never want for anything."

For anything? Maren's tormented mind echoed. That would be true if she could have Jared Morgan in her life.

Not far behind the *Martha J* was a ship with sails the color of the horizon and a hull painted to blend into the ocean. Indeed, this frigate was so hard to spot she overtook other ships readily. On the deck of the *Sea Mist*, Captain Jared Morgan, known as the Hawk, leaned against the taffrail on the stern section and contemplated the girl aboard the *Martha J*. It was obvious that the other ship was not heading for Martinique or New Orleans, and since Maren's image was haunting him day and night, he prayed he would not be forced to blast that "French" ship out of the water.

His own vessel was one hundred and forty feet long, and her crew of one hundred and thirty-four was totally loyal. Constructed of Southern live oak, the *Sea Mist* was outfitted with forty-two guns: twenty-six long-range twelve-pound cannons on the main deck and sixteen short-range twenty-four-pound carronades on the spar deck. Such imposing firepower combined with her swift speed usually persuaded other ships to give quarter without a battle. And a frigate such as this could carry much cargo, which came in handy when raiding enemy ships or delivering supplies. Furthermore, the *Sea Mist* was swift in pursuit, or in flight if the odds were against her.

Jared pulled from his pocket the note one of the *Martha J*'s sailors had slipped to him. He read it again. "Be wary of Slade and Wolfe. See the President about them." Clearly the sandy-haired man who had sneaked it into his shirt knew who and what he was. But which Slade was he referring to, and what was it that concerned the hazel-eyed man so deeply? Jared wondered. "Damn!" Jared said angrily. He could not destroy the man's cover just to help a female who had captured his eye!

By Friday, he had to deliver the supplies in the hold to the ship which was to meet him in Jamaica. Fortunately it appeared that the vessel ahead of his was heading in the same direction. A British port . . .

Mountainous and fragrant Jamaica loomed before

hem, inspiring Maren to smile. They were heading
or Kingston on the southern side of the island.
Captain Canton had told her of the many valuable
crops grown and sold in Jamaica—sugarcane, coffee,
pices, cacao—and about the exotic birds, tropical
ruits, and rare woods to be found there. After
enduring weeks in the confining cabin, Maren was
eager to go ashore, to experience new sights and
sounds, to explore this exotic place, and to sink her
feet into silty sand.

The *Martha J* sailed into a natural port late in the
afternoon of the second day in June, a beautiful
Thursday in a place far removed from the war that
ravaged her homeland. A British flag waved proudly
from her mast as she dropped anchor, and Maren had
seen the captain place the appropriate papers and
logbook on his desk, in case the ship was searched by
the British authorities.

Now Maren's dark beauty was enhanced by an off-
white promenade dress of Indian muslin with gold
cotton embroidery. Its bosom was finely pleated and
its sleeves were short and puffed. She had donned
matching slippers, but had not dared to wear the
dainty gold necklace which was allegedly stolen. Her
hair was brushed into waves which settled becomingly on her shoulders. Pleased with her appearance,
she smiled at her cousin as he entered the cabin,
trailed by Horben Wolfe and Captain Canton.

The three men removed the false wall to retrieve
several heavy boxes. When she asked what they
contained, not one would say. From their odd

behavior, Maren wondered if they were smuggling illegal goods to this British island. Suddenly she was very curious about what might be in those boxes, and she was confused about why they were being unloaded here. Surely Eric would not turn traitor and hand the gold over to America's foe . . . or try to keep it for himself.

Goods were carried ashore by making numerous trips in the quarterboats. But Maren and the special boxes were taken in the longboat with Captain Canton, Eric James, and Horben Wolfe. It was manned by ten rowers, one of whom was Peter Thomas who furtively watched her.

It was nearly dusk when Eric guided Maren to a small hotel on the edge of town. It was surrounded by tropical trees and plants, and Eric promised he would return to have dinner with her as soon as he carried out his business dealings, probably around nine. Having been told they would sail with the second tide on the morrow, Maren knew her time here was limited, so the moment Eric was gone, she left for a stroll.

As she walked toward the beckoning beach, she admired the beauty of the exotic landscape and listened to its particular sounds. Unfamiliar birds of vivid plumages seemed to serenade her as dreamy shadows slowly cloaked the area, and the air was fresh and invigorating. Breezes danced through her long hair, played through the lush greenery and the profusion of colorful flowers. She closed her golden brown eyes to hear the peaceful sounds of the ocean at low tide. When she opened them, she noticed that everything seemed to be taking on a pearly gray cast. Dusk was near. She had to return to the hotel soon, but not quite yet. She removed her slippers, lifted her hem slightly, and wiggled her toes in the embracing sand. Merry laughter spilled forth then, as pleasure flowed within her.

Maren walked for a time, delighting in the feel of sand against her naked feet, of cool air wafting over her bare arms. She finally halted and leaned against a palm tree with a nature-slanted trunk. She had not felt this calm in a long time, and she wanted to savor the feeling for a while longer. She closed her eyes and inhaled deeply.

"Don't you realize how dangerous it is to be out here alone?" the mellow voice chided. "There are countless wild sailors in port tonight."

Her eyes opened, even though she knew who was there. "I can protect myself. Besides, I was waiting for you," she jested happily.

Jared slipped a leg over the slanted tree and the woman, his body and her semireclining position imprisoning Maren, but she made no attempt to push him aside or to rise. As his eyes locked with hers, he leaned forward and placed his hands on the trunk above her head. "But who will protect you from me, my hypnotic siren?" he teased. Then his mouth gently but hungrily captured hers. As his weight settled lightly against her, Maren's arms slid under his and encircled his body. She flattened her palms against the middle of his broad back and urged him closer.

Jared's arms banded the tree and he used his hold on it to eliminate any space between them. His mouth greedily ravished hers, and when she encouraged him, his lips sensuously wandered over her face and throat.

Maren responded heatedly and uninhibitedly. "How did you find me?" she murmured hoarsely.

Jared tensed briefly, and she noticed his reaction. He ceased his amorous siege to reply, "You found me. I was the one heading for Jamaica; your ship was supposedly sailing for Martinique. Captain Canton does realize this is a British port and we're at war with England?"

"Then what are you doing here, my bold privateer?" she asked, trying to shift her pinioned body so the rough bark did not bite more deeply into her tender flesh and create a discomfort she had not noticed earlier. Her action caused her inflamed body to rub intimately against his, stimulating both of them. "I thought you said the British were your enemies. Is it safe for you to be here?"

Jared moved aside so she could alter her awkward position. He watched her stand and straighten her mussed clothing; then he leaned his firm buttocks and the sole of one boot against the sloping tree which she had vacated. "As long as you have the right papers and flags, you can sail anywhere you wish. Isn't that right, Maren?"

"But you could be in danger if someone recognized you or your ship."

Jared knew she had intentionally avoided his question. "Would that bother you, Maren?" The way she looked at him, she didn't have to answer. "I'll be careful," he promised, "and the same should apply to you."

"We're only exchanging goods. We sail tomorrow afternoon," she said, forgetting he had recently robbed her ship and knew its contents.

"What kind of goods?" he asked. "I may be interested in them."

"I don't know; they were boxed." Too late she realized what she had said.

"Which storehouse are they using?"

"I didn't hear them mention one. You could come to the hotel to speak with James about it. He's to return around nine for dinner." Suddenly Maren noticed how dark it was. "Oh, my," she fretted. "It's late. I must return to my room before I get into trouble."

"Why don't you have dinner with me . . . and we'll have a long talk afterward?" His gaze smoldered, inflaming both of them.

Maren licked her lips. "I wish I could, but I doubt I would be allowed to spend time with the pirate who robbed us a few days ago. In fact, you wouldn't be safe here if you were spotted."

They laughed together. "You're right," he agreed huskily. "Do you think you can sneak out in the morning? Claim you're going shopping or strolling? I'd like to spend more time with you, Maren."

"I'd like to spend more time with you. . . . Do you

59

at least have a first name you can share with me? I hate to call you Captain Hawk."

Moonlight gleamed on the golden streaks in his pale brown hair as he chuckled and pulled her into his embrace. He liked it when she swayed against him and rested her hands on his chest. They gazed at each other for a time; then he remarked, "There's something unique about you, woman, besides your being the most beautiful creature I've ever seen. I guess it's obvious how much I want you, and it impresses the hell out of me that my desire doesn't frighten you."

"I suppose that's because you strike me in the same way. I'd like to get to know you better, starting with at least one name."

They exchanged smiles. "Is Jared enough for now?" he asked.

She did not want to be threatening or overly aggressive. She needed to work on him slowly, carefully, mysteriously. She had to concentrate on now, not the distant future. Her eyes glowed as she replied, "Yes, Jared, it's plenty for now." He had proven that he wanted to trust her by revealing his real name, although he didn't know she knew that.

"Will you meet me in the morning? I'm in room ten of your hotel. With this war raging, I don't know when I can make New Orleans."

Maren knew the risks and consequences of her response, but she was willing to accept them. "I'll come to your room as soon as I can sneak away. Do you have any other plans in the morning?"

"Not anymore. I'll be up by dawn, waiting for you."

Their eyes fused, then their lips. They clung to each other and kissed urgently, caressing pleading flesh, trying to soothe it.

Suddenly Jared drew away. He was breathing heavily. "If we don't halt this, I won't release you on this night."

"I wish you didn't have to," she bravely confessed. "I should get moving or they'll have a search party out for me."

Jared couldn't draw Slade's attention to him right now, so he reluctantly released her. But more importantly, he did not want a swift, primitive mating with her. "I'll follow you back at a safe distance. Get away as soon as you can. Our time together is short."

Maren clasped his face between her hands, drew it down to seal their lips a final time, and kissed him stirringly. "I'll be there, Jared." She then scooped up her slippers and raced toward the lighted area at the edge of town. Sneaking in the rear door of the hotel, she hurried to her room. Eric had not yet returned, so she had time to freshen up and change.

When Kerry Osgood returned to Jared's room, he reported, "I followed them like you ordered, Jared. They took the boxes to a plantation a few miles outside of town. It's my guess they were locked in the cellar. Whatever was inside was a mighty heavy secret. I'd say guns or gold, 'cause it ain't illegal to sell whiskey."

"Did you find out who owns the plantation?"

"Eric James of James Shipping, and it's guarded well. I overheard something else; that ship came straight from London, not France. You were right; they lied to us and those papers were false."

"Did you hear them mention a girl?" Jared asked. Since Kerry was his best friend and first mate, Jared trusted him in all ways. The two men had known each other for years, and had been nearly inseparable for most of that time, so Jared did not have to conceal or deny his feelings.

"Not once," the blue-eyed Kerry answered. Seeing Jared's relief, he then grinned mischievously. "Did you get anywhere with her?"

Jared sent him a playful scowl. "Not like you mean, Kip. I don't know how to explain it, but she's got some crazy grip on me. I'm seeing her in the morning. Maybe I can unravel both mysteries."

"You think she's involved?"

Jared rubbed his jaw and exhaled loudly through his nose. "I surely hope not, Kip. Unless she's got me fooled badly, she isn't."

"But Eric, it's not even morning yet," Maren protested when her cousin roused her and ordered her to get ready to leave immediately.

"Five British warships are arriving today," he lied. "Someone could recognize me or the *Martha J.*

Please hurry, Maren. We've got to get out of here on the early tide or we're trapped."

"Give me twenty minutes, and I'll be ready." Alone, Maren flung on her clothing, then wrote Jared a note. She could finish her grooming aboard ship, but she couldn't vanish without telling Jared she'd had to leave. She crept down the hall and slipped the note beneath his door, returning to her room just before Eric knocked again.

In less than thirty minutes, Maren was watching the island disappear. She threw herself across Canton's big bed and tried to go back to sleep so she wouldn't be tormented by what she was leaving behind.

Jared was up shortly before dawn, eager to see Maren. He hoped she could get away and join him soon. He dressed quickly and carefully, wanting to look his best for her. As he eagerly awaited her arrival, pacing the large room, he noticed a paper on the floor near his door. He frowned as he picked it up, suspecting it was something he did not want to read. "Had to leave. Dangerous here. Hope to see you in New Orleans." Although the note was unsigned, he did not doubt whose message it was.

Jared hoped Maren had not left yet. He went to her room, to find only a cleaning woman. He rushed downstairs, but Maren was not in the lobby. Questioning the man at the desk, he learned that Maren and James Slade had left before dawn, clearly in a hurry to catch the early tide.

Jared sighed heavily, but within moments one of his brows rose. He wondered if she had told James Slade about his presence, had perhaps let it slip accidentally. James Slade was certainly running from something or someone. Jared recalled the words *Dangerous here* and wondered what Maren had meant. At least her message sounded as if her hasty departure was a reluctant one. Yet, something was amiss. Besides probing for his name, she had asked what he was doing in Jamaica and if he had any plans for this day.

If only he could pursue the *Martha J* and check out this curious situation. But he couldn't. His contact here had passed along an order to attack a British flagship heading this way. In addition to rescuing impressed American sailors, Jared was to steal muster rolls and official papers which listed the destination, size, and strength of the British squadron massing near Nassau. Afterward, he was to deliver the information to the President.

Now that Maren was gone, he did not intend to linger. He had asked his contact to learn all he could about Eric James, about his shipping firm, his plantation, and about James Slade. Jared knew that when he reached the President he would discuss James Slade and Eric James with him, for those two men were obviously involved in some secretive endeavor that might be perilous to America.

Chapter Three

On June eighth the *Martha J* reached New Orleans. Maren was apprehensive about going ashore and being confronted by the reality of her parents' deaths and her homelessness. When she had left almost two years ago, she had never expected to return under such sorry circumstances.

Eric guided her to where his brother was awaiting them. Marc was beaming with excitement, his dark blond hair was mussed by the wind, and his green eyes were darting about as if to avoid missing anything. He favored Eric a great deal; even their heights were the same, five feet and eleven inches. Yet, Marc's personality was very different from his brother's. Marc was still green and boyish, and he was much less intelligent than his brother.

He surged forward and hugged Maren, kissed her cheek and asked countless questions, behaving more like a youth of fourteen than a young man of nineteen. Maren smiled and tried to calm him, but Marc was too stimulated to settle down. She related what she could without saying too much in a public place.

Eric clasped his brother's shoulders and lightly shook him. "Let her breathe, Marc. There'll be plenty of time to learn the news."

Marc obeyed his older brother, but he shifted about restlessly. Maren laughed, caught his arm, and cuddled him for a moment as if he were a small child. "You're still the same, cousin Marc," she teased. "Relax, we promise to tell you everything."

The James brothers escorted Maren to the finest hotel in town, and left her there to unpack and rest before they joined her for dinner downstairs. Before closing her door, Maren affectionately embraced both men, but once she was alone she sighed deeply. *What now, Maren James? This isn't London so you can't become Eric's ward. You have to decide what you're going to do with your life.* She must put to use all her parents had taught her, she decided. To get through the difficult days ahead, it would be essential to draw on the courage and strength that had been instilled in her.

As she unpacked, Maren daydreamed of Jared Morgan and of what might have happened between them in Jamaica. She had lost her heart and head to him—she would have proven it that morning if Fate had not intervened—and she was concerned because she had not warned him about the British warships en route to the island. Hopefully he had sailed away as they had . . . but she did not know where Captain Hawk's loyalties lay.

A business problem came up which prevented Eric from dining with Maren and Marc. During their meal Maren related everything she and Eric had agreed to reveal to the immature Marc; then she asked him about things in New Orleans.

In response, Marc told her the tale Eric had ordered him to relate. He didn't know why his brother was lying to their lovely cousin, but he knew better than to cross Eric. When he was obedient, Eric was very good to him; but when he was not, Eric was cruel. Since Murray didn't want him around in Baltimore, Marc had to depend on Eric to take care of him. Besides, he had told only little lies which couldn't harm Maren or anyone. . . .

"Are you planning to sell Lady Luck?" Marc asked.

Maren's head jerked upward, and she stared at the man who was stuffing a rich dessert into his mouth. "I thought Eric had already sold it."

Marc guzzled his drink, then told her, "He tried, but he couldn't. Uncle Cam had a secret partner, so it can't be sold without his signature and agreement. Eric couldn't find out who he is."

"Are you certain about this, Marc? I still own Lady Luck?"

Marc failed to realize that she had not been told of this matter. "Of course I am. Now that you're home, you can tell Eric who the secret partner is and he can sell your half for you." Marc's attention went back to his cake.

Maren was bewildered by this news, distressed by its implication. During the voyage, Eric had not mentioned the fancy gambling house that her father had owned so she had assumed it had been sold. With Lady Luck earning money, how could Eric claim her parents had lacked income for nearly a year? She could not help but wonder if this partnership of her father's was why Eric had come for her. He couldn't sell the gambling house without the consent of the unknown partner. Other questions now troubled her. Had Eric given her the necklace to win her favor so she might agree to sell Lady Luck? And just who was this partner? Why had her father never revealed that he had one? Secrecy was foreign to him, so there had to be a good reason for his resorting to it.

Lady Luck was a beautiful gambling establishment, and a prosperous one. Or it had been before she'd left New Orleans. Perhaps the war had left people with little or no money with which to gamble. If not, Lady Luck could be the answer to all of her problems.

She had to discover why Eric had been silent about this part of her inheritance. Unless Lady Luck was bankrupt, she was not penniless or homeless. She had been to the gambling house many times with her father, during the day when he checked on business and once at night when her father had received an urgent summons from the manager, Dan Myers. On that occasion she had been told to remain in her father's private suite, but curiosity had gotten the best of her. From behind the curtain that concealed the stairway, she had watched people gamble and listen to music. The crowd had been dressed in fine clothes, the ladies had worn jewels, and everyone there had had plenty of money to spend. In later years, Maren had learned every game of chance, and she could probably beat most card players. To the rear of the first floor were the living quarters of Mary Malone, the cook and head housekeeper. Upstairs were two spacious apartments, one for the manager, Dan Myers, and one for the owner's use. She wondered if the other partner had ever stayed there. A place to live, she mused, and a way to earn money. . . .

"Are you worried about something, Maren?" her companion asked as he devoured a second dessert. "You're awfully quiet."

Maren decided not to question Marc further about Lady Luck, and she hoped he would forget he had mentioned it to her. She wanted to find out what Eric would say, what he would do, about the gambling house. And she wanted to find a way to visit it, secretly. There were some things she needed to learn from Dan Myers and Mary Malone, preferably before Eric approached her about selling the place. She was disappointed because she'd thought Eric had really changed for the better. They had been friends, were relatives; and her parents had done a great deal for him. How could he betray her in this selfish way? If

Eric was up to mischief, she wanted him to reveal it. "I was just thinking."

Marc's next words dashed her plans. "About selling Lady Luck?"

Knowing Marc worshipped his brother and wasn't too intelligent, Maren cleverly replied, "Eric must have wanted the news about Lady Luck to remain a secret for a while. I don't think we should mention it to him."

Fearing he had exposed one of his brother's secrets, Marc urged, "Please don't tell him I slipped up. He would be mad at me." To himself Marc added, He might order that Horben Wolfe to beat me up again. Marc James was terrified of the ghostly-eyed man.

"I won't mention that you told me about Lady Luck," she promised.

"Thank you, Maren," he said, his expression and tone almost frantic. Maren noticed how upset he was, and she wondered about that later.

After dinner, Maren returned to her suite. As she paced the floor in deep thought, it struck her that if things were as bad as her cousin claimed, Eric would not have the money to pay for this costly suite. Why had he lied? On the ship, Eric had said he wanted to be rich and important. Had he seized her inheritance to obtain his desires?

Maren hated being suspicious of her cousin, but his explanations did not ring true. If she asked him to clarify the contradictions, he would think she was calling him a liar and a thief, and she knew from past observations that it riled Eric James to be doubted, questioned, or cornered. If she pressed him, he would only become silent or bitter, and she would learn nothing. Her parents had taught her to be persistent and clever, so she decided an investigation was in order. But it must be done gingerly and slowly.

Maren stripped off her clothes and put them away. Having donned a pale green batiste nightgown, she blew out the lamps in her suite, except one. Slowly her eyes adjusted to the changing light as the full moon bathed the room in a soft glow. Only a few muted noises reached her ears, and she became aware of the gentle breeze ruffling the curtains on all windows. She walked to the French doors in the bedroom, and found that they overlooked a lush garden. A waist-high decorative railing acted as a window guard, and she leaned against it.

Glancing skyward, Maren found the heaven filled with twinkling stars. Somewhere beneath them, Jared Morgan was probably sailing the seas as Captain Hawk. She had had time to reflect on her behavior with him, and she wondered what he must think of her. She had thrown herself at him on two occasions, and would have done worse if Eric had not hurried her away from Jamaica. No doubt women did the same everywhere Jared went! Nonetheless, Maren believed that she had handled herself badly, and she fretted over the impression she had made.

Vexed with herself, she recalled that after Jared had attacked and robbed the ship upon which she was traveling, she had practically ravished him on the floor like some rutting wench. And when he had thought he was a stranger to her! That certainly explained why he had been so eager to get her into his room, not the romantic reasons she had invented. If they met again, what could she say and do to correct Jared's dreadful opinion of her? How would she explain Captain Hawk's arrival to Eric? How would she explain her lies to Jared?

From that time years ago when she had met Jared, as a wharf rat, Maren knew he lived in Savannah and had crops to export, unless his family had sold or lost the Morgan plantation. Of course he might have turned to privateering because crops were trapped ashore by the blockade. She wondered what Jared's family was like, wondered if she would ever meet them. She had to be patient!

"A fine mess you've gotten yourself into, Maren James," she chided. "What would Mama do to extricate herself?"

Eric arrived shortly after breakfast with unexpected news. "I thought you might want to visit your parents' graves this morning. I had them buried close by in this parish. I also thought you would want to go through the things left from the plantation. They're in one of my storehouses. I had the servants pack them, and I assume some of that stuff is yours. Are you up to such a task this soon, little cousin?"

"The sooner I get it over with, the better. But do you have time to take me? I'll need the support of a

72

family member in such a difficult moment."

"That's why I'm here, Maren. I wouldn't let you face something like this alone. And we have another matter to discuss later," he hinted.

"What is it?" she asked, surmising it concerned Lady Luck and dreading that conversation.

"One thing at a time, little cousin," he replied evasively.

Due to high ground levels of water and to flooding, few people were buried in New Orleans. Most coffins rested in mausoleums or were encased above ground, one atop another.

Eric pulled Maren away from the white mausoleum which held her parents' bodies. "They're at peace, Maren; let them go."

It had been hard for her to walk down the rows of tombs, realizing that her mother and father were inside one of them, sleeping eternally together. She had wept while reflecting on her life with her parents, and even when she had stood beside the chamber marked *James*, she had found it difficult to accept her loss.

"It seems so unreal, Eric. I keep thinking they're away and will return soon. I can't imagine what it means never to see them again. How long does it take for pain to go away and acceptance to settle in?"

"I don't know. I still think about my parents all the time," he told her, but he did not reveal that his thoughts were dark and cold ones.

"What will happen now, Eric?" Maren murmured sadly.

Misunderstanding her, he replied, "I'll take you back to the hotel so you can rest. Those boxes can wait until another day."

Maren didn't explain her meaning. She shook her head. "I need to be distracted, and I must get that chore behind me."

Eric agreed and took her to the warehouse. He guided her to a back room, which was locked. Once they were inside, he pointed to numerous boxes and trunks and told her all the Jameses' personal belongings were in them. "Do you want me to stay here with you?" he offered.

"If you'll unseal these containers, I can go through them alone. It looks like a big task, doesn't it?"

Calmly, Eric said, "Before you get started with it, I must tell you something. Because of a legal involvement, I couldn't sell Lady Luck to help pay off the firm's debts. Did you know Uncle Cam had a secret partner and the establishment can't be sold without his agreement?"

"What partner?" she inquired, to let Eric think she was unaware of that situation. "I thought Papa owned Lady Luck."

"I couldn't find out who his partner is. All you can do is wait for someone to turn up with the deed in his hand, and keep depositing half of all earnings into an account for him as I've been doing. While you're going through those trunks and boxes, you should look for any papers that might reveal the other owner's name. Even if you don't sell Lady Luck, you'll need to know who your partner is. Your father was giving or sending payments to somebody. I figure the man wasn't a local resident. If he was, he'd have contacted me by now to get his share. Just in case this mystery person shows up one day, I've been placing records of earnings and his share of the profits in a box for him at the bank. I'll give you the key when we get back to your room. You should continue to follow this practice to prevent trouble or a takeover."

"Nobody at Lady Luck knows who this silent partner is?" she questioned.

"If someone does, I haven't been told. Perhaps it's a woman, or someone who needs to keep an interest in a gambling business a secret."

"I can't understand why Papa kept this person's identity to himself. How would I know how to verify this partner, if he or she appeared?"

"Whoever it is would have a legal document signed by your father. But make certain you let a lawyer study it to be sure it's real and binding. Uncle Cam was a smart businessman, but I can't figure his logic in this matter." Eric leaned against a stack of boxes and lit a slender cigar. "Your father drew up legal papers for me to use in handling business for him while he was in London, so I had no trouble using them to sell the plantation and townhouse, especially since I was putting all of the money into the firm. But Lady Luck was in your name, thank goodness, or at least half of it. She seems to be financially stable right now, so you won't have to depend on anyone's charity. I thought if I kept this news to myself until now, it would help you recover from what you had to face this morning. Despite the war, Maren, your income from Lady Luck will be more than sufficient to support you. And if this bloody war ever ends, your business should be even better. You could become a wealthy woman, little cousin. I hope this makes your outlook brighter."

His admission caught her off guard and baffled her. "You're saying I own half of Lady Luck?" she asked, to test him.

"Fate must have made your father put it in your name. If it had been in his, I would have sold it with the other things before I learned you needed it. I know you're a woman and it's a fancy gambling house, but I hope this news pleases you, Maren. You can always find someone to run it for you. Or you can do it yourself," he added, grinning mischievously. "I told you everything would work out fine. Now you can see why I was so confident. I can envision you dressed in a red silk gown, wearing that ruby necklace, and dazzling customers with your beauty and talent. Until you're ready to settle down to a home and family, you'll be an independent woman with a great dowry."

Maren did not want to face any more unpleasant surprises in the future, so she asked, "But what about Papa's debts, Eric? Shouldn't I sell Lady Luck to repay them?"

"I've just about gotten things running smoothly again. I told you, I managed to get two ships through the blockade, plus I made that successful trip with you aboard. Don't you worry about the firm's troubles; I can handle them. Besides, good fortune is smiling on you. You can't legally sell Lady Luck because of your secret partner, and no one can force Maren James to turn over her earnings to pay Cameron James's debts. You run your gambling house, and I'll run my shipping firm. If all goes well, we'll both survive this nasty war and we'll be rich."

"But what about the necklace?" she asked, utterly confused by now. "Don't you need it for an emergency? It's worth a great deal."

"It's yours. Call it payment for some of the things I sold to keep the firm afloat. If I hadn't been here to take care of the business, there wouldn't be one left. I've put my money, wits, and blood into saving James Shipping. It's my child, my wife, Maren. I'm afraid your father's original investment and holdings are gone, but I feel I still owe you something for using your inheritance to clear your father's debts. Uncle Cam trusted me to do the right thing, so I'll make certain you don't lose Lady Luck. I hope you realize I didn't sell everything; Uncle Cam sold a lot of stuff during the hard times to make ends meet. When things improve, I'll try to give you more."

Before thinking this curious statement over, she replied rashly, "Don't worry about it, Eric. You've been wonderful about everything. I'll be busy, and that will be good for me. I have a business to run and a mystery to solve."

"One last thing, little cousin, I have to leave early Saturday morning. I have that gold shipment to deliver and a report to make to the President. After that's done, I'll stop by to see Murray before I return. Do you think you can get along without me for six or eight weeks?"

"Your trip will be dangerous, Eric. What about the blockade?"

"Captain Canton is an expert at eluding the British. We learned a lot from losing several ships to them. We plan to move from cove to cove during the night, too close in for the British to threaten us. Remember, we know our coastline, but they don't. If we're going to win this war, I have to get that gold to the President, but I'll sink my ship before I allow those Brits to take the gold from me and use it to wage war on us. Like your father, the President trusts me."

Maren hugged him tightly and murmured, "As I said earlier, you're wonderful, Eric James. Too bad you're my first cousin."

Eric embraced her and then chuckled. "A damn shame if you ask me. I'll arrange to have some lunch brought to you, and I'll come to take you home at about five."

"That sounds fine." She watched him open the door, chiding herself for her previous suspicions. "Eric," she called out, halting him. "Thank you for everything—especially for being you."

Eric turned and looked at her. He smiled. "Yep, a damn shame, Maren, 'cause you're the best woman around. Don't overdo it today."

"I won't," she promised, and returned his warm smile. Eric had surprised her. Even if he had made mistakes or had been overly greedy, he was trying to make amends, to help her. Could she fault him for concentrating on self-preservation? she asked herself. No, she replied.

Maren began to explore the containers. Many were filled with linens and dishes. In others she found family pictures, an old Bible, clothing, hats, books, letters, embroidery, keepsakes, old dolls, and more. She found no silver, coins, or jewels; Eric must have sold them. She tried not to be annoyed with him, for he had believed she was married to a wealthy man—a man who would be an English lord—and would not be returning home. Each time she came to a trunk or box that contained her own belongings, she pushed it aside to be rummaged through later. First she wanted to look through her parents' things to see if she could find any reference to her father's partner. Later, she would decide what to do with these belongings.

Maren screamed and jerked aside when Horben Wolfe touched her shoulder. Whirling about on the chair, she then glared at him. "Don't do that! You startled me. I didn't hear you come in."

"Sorry, Miss James. I thought you were asleep with your eyes open. I called your name, but you didn't respond. Are you all right?"

Maren swallowed several times before inhaling deeply to slow her racing heart. She did not like this creepy man. "What do you want?"

"Eric told me to bring you this lunch. Can I get you anything else?"

"No, thank you. I was lost in thought about my parents."

"No need to explain. I can see you're hurting real badly today. I wish there was something good I could say to you, but words offer little comfort in times like these."

Maren looked at him, surprised by his insight and by his compassionate tone. "You're right, Mr. Wolfe; this is hard for me."

"Please, call me Horben or Ben. Eric's talked about you so much, it's like I know you. I'm sorry if my looks frighten you, Miss James, but it's like that with most people. Don't worry; I understand and accept it. People can't help themselves. I don't help matters any by getting angry with them. Sometimes nature plays cruel jokes on us."

Shame filled Maren and she flushed brightly. She had a sudden urge to sob, but controlled it. She was feeling very emotional today, but she did not cry easily as many women did, mostly for attention, Maren had decided long ago. It was narrow-minded and insensitive of her to allow this man's looks to influence her attitude toward him. As sweetly as possible, she said, "Thank you for the lunch, Horben."

"Do you need any help?" he offered politely.

"I'm afraid this is something I have to do alone, but thank you," she replied. When he left, she planned to go through the letters to seek information or a clue. Surely her father had recorded something somewhere, and although hers was a lengthy and saddening task, it was a private one.

Horben was pleased with his progress. At last he had her talking to him and smiling at him. With wit, luck, and patience, perhaps he could relieve her revulsion. "Don't worry about your safety; I'll be standing guard out front. I won't let anyone disturb you."

The man's eerie gaze unnerved her, but Maren concealed her reaction, even scolded herself for it. She tried to be friendly. "You're most kind, Horben. I can see why Eric liked you and hired you."

Horben Wolfe nodded and left. When he joined his boss outside, he said, "You know her well, Eric. It worked like a charm. Before we leave Saturday, she'll be drooling over us."

"Relax, Ben, she's out of reach for both of us, unless I change my mind about how to handle my little secret. I just hope I can keep her fooled. Maren is special, and I surely would hate to have to get rid of her."

"If it becomes necessary, can I have her before you do?"

Anyone who defied Eric had to be punished and destroyed, even Maren. He glanced at Horben. "I owe you that much, and more. Hopefully she'll be able to find out who her partner is before we return. I

81

couldn't find a clue in all that junk. Until we know who her partner is, I can't take over Lady Luck."

"It was smart of you to trick her today. She would have gotten suspicious if you hadn't said something about that gambling house. Lordy, it's amazing how clever you are." Horben grinned knowingly. "I can see why you love her and want her—she's a lot like you."

"If I know Maren, she would have remembered Lady Luck and would have done some snooping after we left. This way, she'll believe anything I tell her," Eric vowed smugly. "'Course, I didn't like putting that money in a safety box for some mysterious partner, but it'll be worth doing if it throws Maren off our wake. Besides, the money didn't come out of my pockets." Eric chuckled merrily. "Maren's already been a big help to us. Picking her up in London covered our backs. And she'll keep Josephine's necklace safe for me. If I lost it—"

"Your back would be exposed," Horben finished for him.

"Yours too, my friend," Eric reminded his cohort.

"How do you plan to get it back when we need it?"

"Nothing to fear," Eric boasted. "As easy as a slipknot. When this war's over, we'll recover our treasure from Jamaica and live like kings. As for my dear brother, poor Murray won't be around long enough to catch on to me."

"How do you plan to get rid of him when we reach Baltimore?"

"We'll decide that on the voyage. I've had too much on my mind to give my brother much thought. Do you want to handle it for me?"

"Sure," Horben replied, a wicked sparkle in his eyes.

At midnight on Friday, Maren walked back and forth in her suite. She had never been a pacer until lately, but something was nagging at her. She had finished searching the trunks and boxes that afternoon, without success. Next week she would decide what to do with the belongings. Hers had been delivered to her suite, to be explored leisurely, but only one item had been removed and placed on the lowboy, the dried nosegay Jared Morgan had given her years ago.

She had eaten with Eric Thursday evening and this evening, Horben accompanying them both times. The men were to sail at dawn, and she was glad. Although Eric seemed to say and do everything right, she had perceived that something was wrong. Maybe she had sensed something in her cousin's tone, in his expressions, or in the exchanges and undercurrents between him and Horben.

Yes, she was holding the key to the box that contained money for her secret partner. But was the money already hers? Was there really a secret partner? Was it Eric? If so, why had he given her the key and the records? He could have kept Lady Luck and the money, and she would not have been the wiser. If this

83

was some clever strategy of his, she could not figure it out. However, she felt she was being duped. Possibly the answer to this riddle was Eric's need of her agreement to sell and her ability to discover the identity of her partner.

She had worn the ruby necklace to dinner, and the two men had gazed at it often as if it had some crucial significance. She had been a bit nervous because Horben Wolfe had followed her each time she had left the hotel, as if he were spying on her instead of protecting her. And Marc was acting crazier than ever. He seemed afraid of his brother. Eric . . . he was being too good to be true. Nobody changed that much. Had her cousin forgotten she knew his weaknesses as well as his strengths, his bad side as well as his good? The more she was around Eric, the more she realized she must not trust him, and that saddened her.

Maren halted at her dresser to finger the ruby necklace. There was something odd about it. . . . But what? So many mysteries were plaguing her. When Eric left in the morning, she would begin to solve them.

As Maren approached Lady Luck, she wondered if Mary Malone and Dan Myers knew more than they had told Eric. Perhaps her father had sworn them to secrecy. Just this morning she had realized that Eric had been using her earnings at Lady Luck to pay his expenses, yet he was claiming that the entire shipping business was his. How could that be when only the New Orleans office was Cameron James's share and that had been saved by the sale of Cameron's holdings? Yes, Eric had taken care of the business after her father's death, but it was wrong of him to keep it. He was too smart not to realize he was taking what was rightfully hers. His father had been cruel to him and he had worked hard here, but that did not excuse his greed or his deceit. For weeks her mind had been too cluttered by her tragic losses and her apprehension about returning home to allow her to think clearly. And Jared Morgan's sudden intrusion on her life had flustered her. Now it was time to think, to plan, and to act.

Maren looked at the lovely structure of the gambling establishment, which leaned more to the Federal style than the Georgian. It had two full stories, plus a large wine cellar and several small attic rooms for storage. Built of red brick, it was trimmed with vermilion and white paint. Artistically carved swan pediments graced each window and door, and a large half-moon porch kept patrons dry when they arrived or departed during stormy weather. Maren approached the carved front door and knocked. When no one responded after several raps, she walked around the house and tried to gain access at the back door. While she waited, she turned and glanced at the well-kept stable that served the Lady Luck's clientele.

As she did so the door finally opened, and a woman in her early fifties asked what she wanted. When

Maren turned to her, the woman stared for a moment before smiling in recognition and inviting the young woman before her inside. "Is it really you, Miss Maren?" the cook and head housekeeper asked.

"Yes, Mary," Maren responded, happy to see the cook's warm blue eyes. The older woman's brown hair was slightly streaked with gray now, but only a few lines had etched her genial face. "It's so good to see you. Tell me how you have been," she said quickly, sounding a little like Marc.

"Mister Eric told me you were back. What took you so long to visit me?" Mary Malone teased, pulling out a chair for Maren in the kitchen. "Sit down, child. You're the one with all the news. Speak up."

Maren laughed. She was fond of this woman she had known for so many years. Mary had always made her think of a kindly grandmother, even though the woman had no children and had been widowed since twenty. Maren had often wondered why Mary had not remarried. Mary was pretty and not excessively plump, yet she had been content to prepare light meals and refreshments for Lady Luck's patrons and to keep the gambling establishment clean from top to bottom.

"How have you been, Mary?"

"I've been fine, Miss Maren, staying real busy here. Lord ain't made no occasion which stops eager gamblers from tossing away their money, including war."

"You're saying business is good?" Maren hinted.

"Same as ever, Miss Maren, earning more money

every month."

"Is Dan Myers still the manager?" she asked.

"Certainly is, but he's out on errands. I don't expect him back till four."

"Do you still open at seven?"

"Surely do, Miss Maren. Now that you're the owner, would you like to look around while the place is empty and quiet?"

"I would love to, Mary. Do you have time to join me?"

"Just let me finish these pastries; then I can."

"I'll wait in the other room." Maren responded as she headed toward one of the two large gambling rooms.

In these spacious rooms the moldings were creations of exquisite and painstaking craftsmanship, as were the decorated ceilings of wood and plaster, and because of the southern climate, there were many windows. Numerous chandeliers, candelabra, and sconces provided sufficient light at night, and gilded mirrors were positioned to increase the light by reflecting it, although placed so that patrons would not fear that someone could read their cards. Most of the furniture was expensive: Sheraton, Chippendale, and Adam. Suddenly Maren wondered if Eric had wanted to sell the costly furnishings of this graceful house.

Delicate figurines, flower-filled epergnes, and other expensive objects were strategically placed to enhance the romantic and opulent beauty of the rooms, while heavy red drapes with gold fringe and gold cords afforded privacy. The drapes matched the tablecloths in the eating area. Maren remembered that years ago her father had hired a carpenter to build frames to which loosely woven muslin had been attached to keep pesty insects from coming in through the open windows. The screens had worked so well that other people in the mosquito-infested area had borrowed Cameron's clever idea to keep their own homes and businesses free of annoying insects.

In the foyer between the two gaming rooms, an ornately carved staircase ascended to the second floor. At the first landing, red drapes partitioned off the upper section to allow privacy of those who lived or stayed there. After that turn, the remaining staircase had solid walls on either side. Each room in this building had a marble and stone fireplace for winter use, and imported rugs partially covered the highly polished wood floors. Indeed, the establishment was magnificent, and it was hers.

Maren waited for Mary before going upstairs, as Dan Myers was living up there and she did not know whether he was occupying the same room he'd resided in years ago. From past visits Maren knew that Mary's two rooms were off the kitchen and that there was a private staircase near the pantry and cellar steps. As they mounted the stairs and passed through the drapes, Maren said, "The beauty of this place still makes me breathless."

Mary smiled. "This door goes to Mr. Myers's rooms, and I'm the only one allowed to clean in there."

They walked down the hall and stopped before another door. "Your father stayed here when he was in town alone, and sometimes when he was accompanied by your mother. Nobody's been allowed to use these rooms since he . . . passed away . . . but they're kept cleaned and aired. Over there"—Mary pointed to the other side of the hall—"are the guest rooms."

"Guest rooms? I didn't know we had guests."

"Not the kind who stay overnight. They just rent them for a few hours," Mary explained. "Mr. Myers handles the private rooms."

"You don't mean prostitutes, do you?" Maren asked worriedly.

Mary laughed before responding. "Heavens, no, Miss Maren. Men dally in them with their sweethearts and mistresses for a few hours. None of our girls work these rooms. Your Papa would never have allowed such goings-on." Noticing the younger woman's expression, Mary declared kindly, "You'd lose a lot of business if you closed them up."

Maren decided to ponder that matter later. On the way to the kitchen, as she glanced at the tables where roulette, poker, baccarat, cribbage, piquet, and other games were played, excitement stirred within her, for she knew she was qualified to meet this challenge. She looked at the area where the musicians worked, and could hardly wait to hear them.

As Maren sat down in the kitchen, she turned to Mary and asked, "Did you know Papa had a secret partner in Lady Luck?"

"I didn't until Mister Eric asked about him after

89

Mister Cameron's death. Mr. Myers didn't know either," Mary replied, answering Maren's next question before it was asked.

"Neither did I," Maren confessed uneasily. "It's very strange."

"I know it annoyed Mister Eric because it kept him from selling out."

"That's what he told me Thursday. I went through Papa's things, but I couldn't find any mention of this person. I'll check upstairs," Maren suddenly announced. She had not thought of that while they'd been up there.

"I doubt you'll find anything. Mister Eric searched up there."

"Do you think there will be any problem about my moving into Papa's suite? I don't have anywhere else to go, and I can't live at the hotel."

"Who could stop you, Miss Maren? This place is yours now. I'll be glad to take care of you after you move in."

Maren smiled. "You're very kind, Mary. Right now, I do need help."

"If you like, I can have your rooms ready in an hour or two."

"That sounds wonderful. I'll go pack and have my things delivered."

By three o'clock, Maren was settled into her new home and Mary was busy preparing for a lively Saturday night crowd.

Shortly after four, a knock sounded on Maren's door and she opened it to find Dan Myers standing before her and smiling. Despite his age, forty-eight now, Maren had always called him by his first name. "Dan," she said happily, "it's so good to see you. I hope you don't mind my moving in today."

"Of course not," he replied, "but it surprised me. It's good to have you home again, Miss Maren. I just wish it wasn't due to such terrible circumstances." Dan Myers was a tall and slender man with hazel eyes and salt-and-pepper hair. He had been the manager of Lady Luck since it had opened, and he made no secret of his great love for this place and his job.

Maren assumed that Eric had told Mary and Dan of her troubles, so she didn't repeat her sad tale. "I hope you don't mind teaching me about the business. It's all I have left," she said.

"If I remember correctly, few people could beat you at cards. Will you be keeping me on to manage the place?"

"Do you even need to ask?" Maren replied, laughing. "I want you to carry on as usual. This place couldn't function without you and Mary. I'm glad I have you two. I know this is a complicated business, and I hope I won't be any trouble to you."

"You're a smart girl, Maren James; you'll learn everything quickly. Will you be joining me downstairs tonight?" he asked.

"I've never been present during working hours, so I think I'll just watch from the stairs tonight. Is the schedule still the same?"

"Monday through Thursday it's seven to ten, Friday and Saturday it's seven to twelve, and we're closed on Sunday," he replied.

"Monday should be a slow night, so I'll make my first visit then. That way, I can meet everyone and see how things are done."

"Just like I said, Miss Maren, you're a very bright girl."

Maren was not offended by Dan's calling her a girl since he had known her as one. Soon, he would realize she was a woman, the owner, and his boss. To jump in and take over abruptly might cause problems, perhaps resentment. Maren wanted to keep things running smoothly, so she intended to move slowly and carefully. Men could be strange creatures, especially when it came to having a female boss . . . and one so young. No matter how much she knew about the place and gambling, she decided to pretend that Dan was teaching her everything.

"I'll need lots of help and patience, Dan." She almost told him to call her by her first name, but because of their business involvement, she felt it would be best if he continued to call her Miss Maren.

In case she was sighted by the patrons, Maren put on a pale green dress with tiny black and ivory strips. It was banded beneath her breasts with a wide black velvet sash, and the short sleeves and the neckline were edged with ivory ruche. Having parted her dark hair in the center, Maren had drawn it back with decorative combs, leaving a few short curls over her ears, at her temples, and across her forehead. Since Eric was not here to see the jeweled necklace, Maren secured a gold and jet brooch to a black ribbon, which she tied around her neck. She completed her attire by stepping into matching green slippers.

Maren waited until eight o'clock before sneaking down the first set of stairs to hide behind the heavy red drapes on the landing. Cautiously she drew them back a bit so she could observe the action below, the overly large archways leading to the rooms providing her with excellent views of the gambling rooms. The gambling areas seemed bathed in golden light due to the numerous candles lit, and lovely music reached Maren's alert ears. People were laughing and conversing genially as they enjoyed their games, drinks, and companions. Indeed, Maren was surprised and pleased to discover the genteel atmosphere of Lady Luck. She had expected a gambling house to be noisy and hectic, but this was neither. There was not a ruffian or an unkempt person in sight. Her patrons sported fine clothing and jewels, and good manners. An urge to join them nibbled at her, but she resisted it.

She studied the two men at the door: Ned Jones and Harry Peck, Lady Luck guards for years. With money flowing so freely, it was necessary to have such employees. She made a mental note to ask Dan if Lady Luck had ever been robbed and what security procedures were usually taken.

As if thinking of Dan Myers had summoned him,

she saw him head toward the stairs with a well-dressed couple. As he halted at the foot of the steps and withdrew a key, Maren comprehended what was taking place. Hurriedly she eyed the couple, then quietly rushed to her room. By slightly opening the door and peering through the slit she had created, she watched the pair enter one of those special rooms. She did not have to wonder what they had in mind for entertainment; their intimate expressions and touches revealed all.

Maren closed her door, locked it, and leaned against it. She sighed dreamily as she called Jared Morgan's image to mind. How she wished he were with her. She yearned to see him again, to embrace him and kiss him, to share everything with him, as her mother had done with her father. There were so many problems facing her, and it would be easier to confront them with him at her side. Maren was not a weakling or a coward, but she needed the love and support of someone special.

Her golden brown eyes slowly took in the room. As always, she was impressed by its beauty and tranquillity. It was a lovely sitting room twenty feet long and sixteen feet wide. At the far end was a fireplace, and positioned on each side of it were windows which overlooked the side of the house. On the mantel rested a small wooden box, a painted plate on a stand, and a Seth Thomas clock. Above it were a pair of sconces and an oval looking glass. In all, three mirrors were carefully placed to reflect the natural light from five windows.

She was delighted by the amount of light, natural and man-made, and she was glad that this large and airy room faced a street which was one of the loveliest in town. Maren knew she would enjoy her new home, and she continued to admire it. Before three front windows sat a camel-back sofa. On either end of it were splayed-leg tables, and before it was an oval tea table. Slightly to one side and before the sofa a wing chair and small reading table were placed. The chair and sofa, made of cherry wood that had been polished to a beautiful shine, were upholstered in a material that matched the floral sprays of the Chinese rug which nearly covered the dark wood floor. Curtains in the same design hung over all five windows. On the wall to Maren's left, a masterfully carved secretary was positioned, and she could still envision her father sitting there and writing notes. The pentagonally topped, gateleg table near the door held a hurricane lamp to light the owner's entry, for it was dangerous to keep sconces and candlesticks burning during one's absence. The furnishings were completed by a sideboard, which served as a private bar, and a book case which also held keepsakes and figurines, mostly acquired by her father on his trips abroad.

Maren walked to one of the windows, pulled aside the curtain, and looked into the shadows below. Street lamps glowed at fifty-foot distances, and ornamental iron fences enclosed nearly every yard in sight. The windows had been opened a few inches to allow an air flow, and she could smell the mingled fragrances of flowers wafting on the gentle breeze. Despite the muffled noises from downstairs, she felt alone, trapped in another world, a suddenly lonely world.

To distract herself from her somber mood, she turned and gazed into the alcove near the hall door. It was used for private dining, and she imagined a romantic dinner there with Jared: broccoli, steamed and buttered; baby carrots, gleaming with a honey glaze; roast duckling, baked to a crispy brown; wild rice, gathered from the lowlands and cooked to perfection; finger-licking bread and French pastries, hot and fresh from the oven; and a heady wine to top the meal off. Maren licked her lips and sighed dreamily. After dining, they could snuggle before a cozy fire and relax until they were eager to sneak into the bedroom. . . .

"Behave yourself, Maren James," she chided, then laughed.

She strolled into the alcove. The small area contained a round dining table and two chairs set beneath an exquisite chandelier which held three candles but was made of countless glass prisms. Maren envisioned it sending out glittering light. No doubt it would bathe Jared's handsome face in a mesmerizing glow. She sat down on one of the chairs and looked across the table, imagining her love was sitting with her, eating, drinking, talking, and gazing back at her. Those hungering thoughts made her squirm in her chair, so she jumped up and continued her exploration of this area.

In the back corners were triangular cabinets which held hand-painted dishes and imported crystal. She noticed that the silver was missing and frowned. Eric again, she decided. Silk hangings were suspended from golden cords on either sidewall. On them Chinese birds and flowers had been painstakingly painted by a talented hand whose signature she could not read. And a Chinese tureen, whose surface displayed fragile butterflies and colorful flowers, rested in the middle of the table. As with the other rooms, the walls were off-white and had a Wedgwood blue trim. Abruptly she realized how many of the objects were from the Wedgwood collection, some designed and made by Josiah himself in England.

Maren walked to the doorway of the adjoining bedroom. Here, too, was a fireplace, but this one had bookshelves on both sides of it. A fourteen-inch-high brass guard and a hand-painted fireboard stood before the hearth, whereas in the other room hinged paneled shutters were used to close off the fireplace out of season. In case there was a chilly morning, a basket of wood sat nearby. Two lowboys contained stored clothing and linen. Hurricane lamps were set on them, and a mirror hung above the one against the far wall. This furniture, too, was made of cherry. Maren marveled at the intelligence of the person who had designed this room, this suite, this house.

Maren strolled into the room, stood on carpeting decorated with pink and blue flowers. The drapes and counterpane matched it perfectly. The bed was canopied, and had a crocheted covering which looked lacy and delicate but was probably very sturdy. A night table was placed at one side of it, a writing table at the other. Upon this last was a portable writing desk, and a brass sconce hung over it to provide plenty of light. A wing chair and ottoman stood near the fire, a blanket chest at the foot of the bed. She walked to the large armoire which held her clothes, and fingered its artistic workmanship. Yes, this was a beautiful room, a seductive one. She wondered if her parents had ever made love on the canopied bed, wondered if she would. Tonight would be the first time she slept here, and she was looking forward to the experience.

Maren entered the water closet, which was off the bedroom area. It contained a portable tub with an evacuation line through the wall for easy emptying and a cabinet that held bath linens and grooming items. A looking glass and two sconces were placed above the cabinet. As Maren glanced into the mirror, she noticed two more sconces above the tub and the hand-painted chamberpot to her right.

She removed her combs to brush her hair, then changed her mind about the nightly task. Returning to her bedroom, she put on a nightgown, and after putting away her clothes, she began to look through the books on the fireplace shelves. She found nothing about the secret partner in any of them. For hours she searched every drawer, vase, container, and object in the suite. She checked behind, under, around, and in everything, but found no answer.

"Why did you do this, Papa?" she murmured.

"Surely you would leave some clue for me to follow . . . unless Eric accidentally destroyed it. Maren, Maren, what are you going to do about him?" she fretted.

She wondered why her cousin Marc was keeping his distance. She had expected him to come around her more, to pester her with his boyish antics as he had done in the past and on her first day here. And she could not forget how frightened he had looked when he'd thought he had let something slip about Eric that night at dinner. She recalled the heavy boxes Eric had left in Jamaica, and wondered if some of the British gold had been inside them.

Jamaica . . . A vision of the night on the beach with Jared filled her mind. She remembered how he had held her, touched her, kissed her, entreated her to meet him again. Surely if his only interest in her was physical, he would have taken her then or he would have charmed her into making a nocturnal visit. He had seemed as bewitched by her as she was by him, yet he had not tried to force himself on her. Didn't that mean she had made a good impression on him?

"Oh, Jared, my secret love, if only you knew the truth about me," she murmured. "Heavens above, I need someone to talk to! Beth!" she shrieked in excitement. "I must send a message to her."

Lilibeth Payne was a bundle of energy and mischief, and she had been Maren's best friend. Though she was a year younger than Maren, the two young women had been close for years, out of touch only for the last two. Since her return on Wednesday,

Maren had meant to send word to Beth at Payne's Point, their plantation upriver that belonged to Beth's family. Monday, I will do so, Maren decided.

Suddenly she felt very tired and sleepy. When she saw it was three-thirty in the morning, she laughed. It had been ages since she had stayed up all night. She extinguished the candles and then crawled between the covers. Closing her eyes, she summoned Captain Hawk.

Chapter Four

On Monday evening Maren put on the same attire she had worn to observe business on Saturday night. No one had seen her, so there was no need to select another outfit. Besides, she liked the pale green dress because the material and style were comfortable and flattering. The low-cut bodice was provocative without seeming improper, and the hem was just high enough to reveal her matching slippers but not her slender ankles. Maren deftly knotted the black velvet sash under her left breast.

She brushed her hair and pinned it up in the back, letting curls dangle. Then she set tiny white flowers above the curls, to make a contrast with her dark hair and to match the white stripe in her dress. Finally she secured a black ribbon around her neck and settled the gold and jet brooch it held into place.

Maren locked her door as she left the suite, and she slowly descended to the draped section of the stairway. She halted there briefly to steady her nerves. Music and laughter reached her ears, slightly calming her. She pushed aside the heavy material and gracefully descended the remaining steps.

The two guards, Ned Jones and Harry Peck, ceased their talk to stare at her. They glanced at each other, then grinned and joined her.

"Can this be Cam's little girl?" Ned asked merrily.

"Can't be. She isn't dressed like a boy," Harry jested.

Maren smiled and teased, "Don't you think it's about time I have a clean face and hands, and stop wearing breeches and a cap?"

"I'll bet we'll spend more time protecting you than the house's earnings. Maybe we need to hire another guard just to stick to your side."

"Thank you, Ned, but I can take care of myself."

Harry hinted mirthfully, "Maybe she'll distract our customers so badly that they'll lose more money and we can get a raise."

Ned chuckled and agreed as Dan Myers joined them.

"Help me, Dan," Maren coaxed laughingly. "They're teasing me mercilessly."

The Lady Luck manager said, "Let's leave them to their mischief while I introduce you to our patrons, Miss Maren." Turning to the two men, he added, "You boys stay on your toes; we have a new boss and she cracks a mean whip."

Dan guided Maren from table to table so she would meet employees and patrons. From the way she was received, Maren decided she would not have any trouble taking full control once she set a few flirtatious men and some envious female workers straight. As in most situations, people simply needed to know the rules—her rules. She had to show them she was strong and intelligent and steadfast. Some patrons seemed surprised to discover that the owner of a gambling establishment was "so young" and "so beautiful," and she read doubt of her ability in their eyes.

Nonetheless, Maren accepted condolences for her parents' deaths and wishes for success in her business venture. She listened to advice of all kinds, smiled at compliments and flattery, devoured news of the war as well as local gossip, and received numerous invitations to dine or to attend the theater. At nine, she allowed herself to be persuaded to join a few friendly games to see how much she remembered and how skilled she was. It pleased her and astonished the other players when she learned that she was still hard to beat.

"I tried to warn you boys. She's been playing since the cradle," Dan remarked, provoking nods of concurrence and glances revealing a new respect.

When four men challenged her to a serious game with larger stakes, she smiled as she refused, "I'm afraid I'll need more practice before I take on such first-rate players . . . and it's closing time."

One gambler argued curtly, "You're the boss and owner so you set the hours and stakes. Are you scared, little girl?"

Maren studied the man, without smiling or frowning. She refused to be baited into acting stupidly or rashly. "I am the owner, sir, but not the boss. I employ Dan Myers to set the hours and rules here because I trust him to know what's best for me and my patrons. If I followed my own whims or accepted dares like yours, I could put myself out of business within a few days. I'm not a scared little girl, sir, nor am I irresponsible. If you want more play, return tomorrow night when we're open again. In a week or so, I'll be delighted to accept your invitation for a serious hand of poker or baccarat. I know you nice gentlemen wouldn't want me to break my bank or embarrass myself on my first night, so I'm certain you'll be kind and patient with me."

Dan said, "Gentlemen, you heard the lady, it's closing time. I'll walk you out."

The four men rose and then followed Dan out the front door, which the two guards locked until the manager was ready to reenter. Mary Malone and two workers immediately began to clean up, and the musicians departed. When Dan returned, the dealers, croupiers, bartenders, and serving girls lined up at one table to check in before leaving.

One young woman approached Maren and asked if she could speak with her privately. Maren remembered her. Evelyn Sims was two years older than Maren, but they had been in different social circles. Evelyn's father had worked for Maren's until he had drunk himself to death. Evelyn had corn-flower blue eyes and fair skin with a scattering of freckles. Her curly hair was the color of polished copper, and her indigo blue gown, trimmed with black lace trim, enhanced her coloring. Maren wondered who had selected the colors and styles the female employees wore.

Evelyn smiled and remarked, "I see you like this pretty gown, Miss Maren. Good, because gowns are what I want to talk to you about. I hope you don't mind my giving you a little advice, but there's something you need to know. Is it all right if I speak up? You won't fire me?"

When Evelyn hesitated, Maren said, "Please go on."

"I was watching you move around the room tonight, and I saw how the customers reacted. I think you're dressed a little too prim and proper for a place like this, Miss Maren. Your attire seemed to make our guests uncomfortable. You look too much like a lady, like their wives and daughters and mothers, the women they escape when they come here to have a good time. You're dressed like . . . for church or something. I guess I'm trying to say you look too sweet and innocent, and it was making the men tense. Didn't you notice how many of them left early tonight? Sort of like you reminded them of home and family or made them feel guilty. If you want them to continue coming here, you've got to relax them by dressing like a real woman, like an owner. Do you understand what I'm trying to say?"

"Yes, Evelyn, I understand your meaning. I didn't think about it, but your observation makes sense. I'll check into it tomorrow. Thank you for bringing this to my attention. Good night."

"Good night, Miss Maren, and I'm glad you're so smart and kind."

Evelyn joined the girl who was waiting for her outside. As they walked toward the rooms they rented in an old house a few blocks away, the other girl asked, "Did it work, Ev?"

"Of course, silly. She's eager to fit in and make big money. She'll do as I said. You wait and see. She'll fix up her hair and paint her face and buy some sleazy gowns to prove she's a real woman. I can't wait to see her come down them steps tomorrow night."

"Can she get new clothes by tomorrow?"

Evelyn frowned. Samuel Lewis had told her to make Maren so miserable that she would demand to sell Lady Luck to his boss, Eric James, and Evelyn had decided there was only one way to hurt a woman like Maren James without creating evidence—destroy her reputation. Once Maren realized what owning, running, and living at the Lady Luck was costing her, Eric's cousin would beg to sell the place. "Maybe she can't by tomorrow night, but soon. We'll both work on her until she looks and acts like a whore that no uppity person wants to be around. If she does what I tell her, she'll have men trailing her like a dog in heat, pawing her. We'll prove to her and everybody that she ain't no better than us working girls. Within a week or two, she'll go back where she belongs, or she'll try to when she's treated like a cheap harlot.''

"You're a mean-hearted person, Ev. Maybe I shouldn't do this. Miss Maren seems awfully sweet and nice, and she could fire us.''

"If you don't help me put her down, I'll tell Dan about you stealing money," Evelyn Sims threatened. "That means firing and jailing.''

"You wouldn't, Ev," the girl wailed. "You're my best friend. You know I needed the money for Willy's doctor and medicine, only a few dollars here and there. I can't lose my job.''

"Then obey me, help me. I have to do this; I have to.''

The other dealer pleaded, "You swear we won't get into trouble?''

"How can we? We won't twist her arm. We're only being kind," Evelyn Sims replied sarcastically.

Maren stretched out on her bed and closed her eyes. She tried to envision herself in Evelyn's indigo blue gown or a similar one. If she designed a few gowns carefully, she could look sensational without looking cheap. The redhead was right about choosing clothing that would make her look older, that was more suited to these surroundings. Maren certainly did not want to unsettle her patrons or to discourage their visits. She had looked like a lady tonight. She was a lady, but . . .

Yes, she concluded, she had to alter her appearance

slightly. Mary had been in this business for years, and she could trust Mary's opinions. Tomorrow she would obtain the woman's help in choosing a proper wardrobe.

As Maren slipped into sleep she hoped Beth would respond to her letter soon so they could visit. She could hardly wait to see her best friend . . . and Jared Morgan, who was on her mind most of the time. She wondered if thoughts of her ever troubled him.

Maren would have been delighted to learn she was indeed on Jared Morgan's mind. He was leaning against the rail of his ship, the *Sea Mist*. If the winds held and if he ran the blockade successfully, he would be in Washington by the middle of the next week, and if the President didn't have something pressing for him to do, he would put into New Orleans before heading back to sea. He and his crew needed and deserved a rest, and he wanted to solve a few mysteries. With luck, which he often depended upon as much as skill and knowledge, he could locate Maren Slade and figure out why she, like his shadow, was always present, silent, a part of him and yet separate.

For nearly two weeks Maren had filled his thoughts and dreams. She had enchanted him aboard the *Martha J*, but she had bewitched him in Jamaica. And he had been aching for her since that night on the beach when he had somehow controlled his urgent hunger. She had been warm and willing, but so trusting and open that he had been unable to take advantage of her. He had wanted to share more than sex with her; he had wanted, and still wanted, to make love to her—but when the time and place were perfect. He knew there was a big difference between sating desire and emotional involvement. Maren was pulling at him from all directions at once. She seemed so familiar, yet unlike anyone he had known. He admitted that he wanted her, needed her, and would find a way to have her.

Jared hoped she had reached New Orleans safely. He could not imagine her as someone's captive, other than his. She had lied to him aboard the ship, but her expression and tone had given her away. Didn't that tell him she was unaccustomed to deceit, or that she did not want to dupe him? A bitter war was raging, so it was natural for people to be wary and defensive. He must meet her under better and safer circumstances, so they could trust each other and relax. If she was in New Orleans and if he could go there soon, he would find her and he would determine how strong her hold over him was.

"Maren . . . Maren Slade . . . Maren Morgan . . . Wait a minute, old boy, that's moving a mite fast."

"I've never seen you like this before, Jared," Kerry said.

Jared turned and looked at his first mate. He had been so deep in thought that he had not heard Kerry Osgood approach. "I've never been like this before,

Kip," he confessed readily. "What is it about this woman that has me brainless and weak? Heavens, man, she haunts me. If I don't see her again soon, I'll go crazy."

"Don't you think you should slow down a bit until you check her out? She has some bad connections, friend. She could be trouble, big trouble," the blue-eyed first mate warned.

"What if she isn't trouble, but she's in trouble?" Jared reasoned. "I plan to study her very carefully, so don't worry about me."

"I can't help it, Jared. This isn't like you. She's a stranger."

"Only until I see her again. I can't explain it, Kip. It's crazy, but the line she cast hooked me, and I'm not sure I want to get loose. Would you feel any better if I let you check her out too?"

"Me? Are you kidding? No way. I'm happy she's after you, else I would be chasing her and acting weird like you are," he teased.

"Then you do think the attraction is mutual?" Jared pressed.

"From what I can grasp, she's either really after you or she's the best pretender I know. Just be careful, will you?"

"I promise, Kip. No real woman, no wedding ring."

Kerry stared at his friend and captain, then chuckled. "You're a devil, Jared Morgan. For a minute there you had me going."

"You know what they say, Kip: 'When ye listen tae tha Divil, there be dark days awaitin' ye.' I think I'll put a little light on 'em."

On Friday morning Maren was sitting with Dan Myers while he looked over the papers she had taken from the bank box. She knew something was wrong because the daily receipts for this past week, which she presumed was a normal week, did not dovetail with the amounts listed for her partner. Her suspicions proved accurate.

Dan Myers declared, "This isn't my handwriting, nor are these my figures, Miss Maren. I suppose Eric James wrote them since he was the one collecting the money."

Maren immediately asked, "May I see the books you use for our records?"

Dan glanced at her and replied, "Of course, Miss Maren."

After they went over the real figures, Maren calculated how much was missing. She frowned in dismay. "It's obvious Eric altered the figures on those papers and kept part of the earnings. That's a lot of missing money, Dan. Can you help me replace it without burdening Lady Luck?"

"You're not to blame for this shortage, Miss Maren. Why don't you ask him to replace it, or to explain its absence?" her manager questioned.

Maren sighed. "I can't, Dan. He'll claim he used

the money to save Papa's business and reputation. I can't prove him wrong, so it would only cause trouble. Let's call it part of my education: watch whom you trust, even family."

"We don't know who this partner is or if he'll ever appear. Why not write off the money as stolen and forget about repaying it?"

"I feel responsible, Dan. I don't want to cheat anyone, even a stranger who might never show up to lay claim to his share of the profits. My father trusted someone enough to make him half-owner and to honor his need for secrecy, so I have to do the same. If this person was receiving payments while father was alive and he shows up here one day, he'll know something isn't right and he'll blame me. He could use this situation to take over Lady Luck. The money has to be replaced, and as soon as possible. Perhaps the war and the blockade have prevented this secret partner from questioning the cessation of his payments. But he might come here soon and find part of his payment missing. I can't take that risk, Dan."

"What's wrong with telling him your cousin mishandled the funds?"

"Eric could be jailed. I can't do that to him, not without proof he did it intentionally or maliciously. Besides, Dan, Eric is my first cousin; his guilt might darken my reputation. I'm a woman, a young one, so I have to be extra careful how I handle this place."

"You're talking about thousands of dollars, Miss Maren. How can you earn that in profits any time soon?"

Maren grinned. "I can win it with a couple of lucky hands."

"You're very good, Miss Maren, but that's taking a big risk."

Maren knew what her father would do. She laughed to calm her anxiety. "That's what it's all about, Dan; I'm in the gambling business."

"But you're gambling on losing everything, especially Lady Luck."

Maren smiled as she vowed, "I won't let anything happen to this place. It's my life now."

"Mine too," Dan murmured, then laughed.

When Maren returned to her room, she looked at the gowns which were spread on her counterpane for her inspection. There were five of them. She began her examination with a light rose taffeta; it was the only one which was not décolleté, having been cut to reveal very little of her chest and shoulders. Its waistline banded her halfway between breasts and navel, and dark rose tulle decorated the neckline, bodice, and hem. It was a wise choice. She next studied the green silk with a square-cut neckline, short puffed sleeves, and a slightly flared skirt which fell smoothly from a high waistline. Another wise choice, feminine and stylish.

Her attention was then drawn to an ivory batiste with a gold lace overskirt and flounced sleeves which teased the elbows. The circular bodice was gathered and edged with gold lace ruching. The snug waistline rested in the natural position, and an ivory sash dangled to mid-calf. The skirt, with a hemline that just cleared the floor, was a little fuller than those of the first two gowns.

The last two gowns, both made of deep purplish-blue satin, were beautiful, but slightly provocative. She had ordered two just alike, thinking she would use them to work in most of the time. The necklines dipped to a V shape in the front and back, the material just covering the edges of her shoulders. The sleeves were full and short, snug bands holding them in place, and the waists were cinched just below her bosom. But the skirts seemingly flowed to the floor like tranquil rivers, at the back forming short trains decorated with exquisite silk embroidery a shade darker than the material. That same decoration enhanced the bosom.

Maren could imagine her curls atop her head, tiny wisps dangling down her nape and forehead, and covering her ears. The ultramarine shade suited her coloring perfectly. These matching gowns were her favorites, and she could hardly wait to wear one of them. Mary Malone had taken her to the shop of a talented seamstress, and had helped her select the best materials and styles. Maren knew the bolts of cloth had been bought from the pirates who traded freely in this town. She wondered if Jared ever sold goods here. He was working as a privateer. Jared, everything seemed to remind her of him!

That night Maren wore one of the satin gowns,

and she distracted the men at her table long enough to win two hefty hands of poker. Dan teased her later about using her beauty to obtain victories.

Maren had noticed Evelyn Sims's reaction to her appearance and had been baffled by the dealer's frown, which had been quickly concealed when Maren had caught her eye. Maren looked exceptionally lovely and it pleased her. Others had remarked on the change in her appearance, and many invitations had been extended by eager men.

Maren had politely rejected all overtures, however, claiming it was not proper to see one's patrons socially. Actually she did not want to show favoritism to any customer, and no one had caused her to tingle as Jared had. Single and a gambling house owner, Maren realized she had to be cautious in her behavior in order to prevent wicked speculation and gossip.

Monday was a wonderful day; Lilibeth Payne came to call after lunch. When she was shown to Maren's door, the happy friends greeted each other affectionately, both bubbling with questions. After Beth entered, they seated themselves on the sofa to talk.

"It's been so long, Maren, and you look marvelous. Please, tell me everything you've done since you left home."

Maren laughed gaily. Beth's fair complexion was flushed with excitement and anticipation. "First, I must hear all of your news," Maren said.

Beth lowered her tone conspiratorially and urged,

"We have to keep this visit a secret from Papa; he would kill me if he learned I had been to Lady Luck. I'm supposed to be shopping while he handles business. After I received your letter, I could hardly wait to see you. It's been so long," she said once more.

"In nine days, it will have been two years. So much has changed for me, Beth. What about you?" she asked her nineteen-year-old friend.

"I was supposed to get married at Christmas time, but Bart was off fighting the British somewhere. This war has ruined everything for me. Papa can't get crops to market on time, so half of them spoil. And if it weren't for the pirates in those bayous, we would be without imports. Their goods are in such demand that those men walk the streets like regular people. Some of them are wicked looking, and I'm certain they would snatch up a proper lady and sell her into slavery if she were not careful," Beth asserted, jumping from topic to topic.

To settle down her friend, Maren asked, "Which Bart?"

"Barton Hughes of course," Beth replied, sighing dreamily.

"However did you snare him?" Maren asked in amazement. Barton Hughes was, or had been, the richest bachelor in the area. He was also well educated, highly polished, and very handsome.

"It was at a picnic. He was racing with some other men and nearly ran right over me. I was knocked into a mudhole and my new dress was stained forever. Naturally I pretended that my ankle was twisted to hold his attention for a while." Maren and Beth laughed merrily. "He carried me all the way to the hotel and sent for a doctor to check on me. By the time he got me there, we were both a mess, but talking and laughing like we had known each other forever. He then began to call on me, and asked Papa for my hand within three months."

"And?" Maren inquired eagerly.

"We set the wedding date, but the war intruded. I begged him not to leave, or to at least marry me first, but he said we should wait until he returned. I know he's fine because he sends messages every few weeks. Mercy, Maren, he makes me quiver down to my toes."

"You're still living at Payne's Point?"

"I'm afraid so. Papa wants Bart to return and marry me just so he can squeeze a loan from his new son-in-law. Things have been bad for most of the plantation owners."

"Eric told me about the sorry conditions here since the war began. You remember my cousin. Have you gotten better acquainted with him during my absence?"

"You know I never liked Eric James. He was always talking you into those silly pranks and games. It's a miracle you didn't get into more mischief and trouble than you did because of him. Would you believe he's actually tried to court me since Bart left? Such nerve!"

"You can't blame him, Beth; you are very beautiful." Maren did not want to say that during wartime lovers often did not return. She had known

117

that Beth had not cared for Eric James, and obviously her friend had not changed her mind about him.

"If you don't hurry and tell me about Daniel Redford, I shall die of curiosity. You didn't sign his name to your letter. I would have known who Maren Redford was. Why did he allow you to leave England during a vicious war? And won't he be angry with you for coming here?"

Maren realized that her friend did not know about Daniel's death, so she slowly related the tragic tale. She watched Beth's green eyes enlarge with disbelief, then narrow as the girl grimaced in empathy. When Maren bravely told of the allegations against her intended, her long-time friend frowned in vexation.

"How dare he treat you like that! I'm glad you discovered the truth before your marriage. Served him right to be slain. Don't you worry; you can have your choice of men here—except for my Bart," she teased. "How did you get home? What about the blockade?"

Maren explained that Eric had run the blockade to get to London and rescue her, then had skirted it on their return. Since the President was involved in her cousin's secret mission, Maren kept quiet about that part.

The perky blonde eyed her brunette friend, and said playfully, "All right, Maren. Something happened on that voyage. Tell me about it."

Maren had the perfect solution to her friend's curiosity. "I met a man, a simply divine one." She grinned slyly.

"Who? Where?" Beth asked, her eyes glowing.

"The privateer who raided our ship," Maren replied calmly.

"The what?" Beth asked. "Surely I did not hear you correctly."

"Do you remember the handsome sailor I met on the wharf when I was fifteen? The one I followed around for days?"

"You mean the one you fell madly in love with, and pursued dressed as a boy?" she teased.

Maren laughed and nodded her head. "That's him. He's a privateer now. He attacked our ship, without a battle of course, and he flirted outrageously with me, as I did with him."

"Maren James! Do you know how dangerous that was? Pirates are known to take women as captives, to use them or to sell them as slaves. Did he remember you?"

"Heavens, no! And I didn't tell him we had met before. But when he comes here to see me again, I'll reveal all."

Lilibeth Payne stared at her friend. "Whatever has come over you in the last two years, Maren James? Are you living here because he robbed you? Why doesn't Eric support you? He's one of the few men in shipping who can conquer this damnable blockade. But he charges a fortune, so Papa and a lot of others can't afford him." For the moment, Beth decided not to reveal the price at which Eric had agreed to help her father. Maren had enough problems without adding another one.

"You can't blame him, Beth. It's dangerous and costly to challenge the British line. He's already lost two ships since January."

Beth replied skeptically, "Really? I've heard he's always victorious. I just wish he could have learned his skills earlier; your parents were desperate to get a message to you. The ship you were on did make it back here, so at least they knew you had reached London safely. They wrote to you every week, but I doubt the letters ever got shipped."

"They must have been terribly worried, but there was no way for me to reach them. It was terrible being out of contact for so long."

"Well, they did know you were safe with your grandparents. What are you going to do now, Maren, run your father's businesses?"

Maren did not mention that she had been in Jamaica because it was an enemy port and that stopover had to do with Eric's mission. "Eric owns the shipping firm and he sold everything else. This is the only place I have." Maren related some of her episodes at Lady Luck. "Actually, Beth, it's wonderful. This place is mine," she concluded.

Beth argued with her. "But you're a lady, Maren. You shouldn't be living here, working here. Why don't you sell this place? Surely you realize that people will gossip about you. It isn't proper for a woman to be managing a gambling establishment, especially one of your age. To tell the truth, I've already heard wild stories about you," Beth confessed uneasily.

"What stories? I've done nothing wrong."

"You're beautiful and single, Maren, and only twenty. You're a James, a lady from one of the most prestigious families in this area, but it is said you've been playing cards downstairs—you, Maren James, my best friend, gambling and drinking, in public! It is also said that you've been cavorting with your . . . customers."

"I do play a few games downstairs, I'm good at cards, and I need the money I win. Besides, it's merely good business to join in with your patrons once in a while. I don't know who started the other tales, but it isn't like that here. A glass or two of wine in an evening can't be considered heavy drinking, and being friendly can't be called cavorting. Beth, I'm very careful about how I dress and behave. I even refuse all social invitations so people won't get the wrong idea. You know people will talk whether they speak the truth or not. They simply need something besides a nasty war to discuss. Let the novelty of my position wear off and they'll move on to another topic."

"I'm not sure about that, Maren. You've attracted a lot of men, and many women are miffed at you."

"They're only jealous because I'm doing something exciting."

"That's partly true, but there's more to it. I've been told that you dress in low-cut, flaming red gowns that are so snug you can hardly move, that you wear red plumes in your hair and use them to tickle guests."

Maren could not believe what she was hearing. "Those are lies, Beth. Come with me," she commanded, then rushed into her bedroom. Jerking open her armoire, she yanked out her gowns and showed each one to her friend. "Not an immodest or sexy one amongst them."

As Maren was replacing them, Beth asked softly, "Does it really matter if the rumors are true or false? Some people are spreading them and others are believing them. Sell this place, Maren, and start over."

"I can't, Beth. I have a partner, and I would need his agreement to sell. I don't even know who he is."

"I don't understand."

Maren explained her curious and frustrating situation. "That's why Eric couldn't sell the Lady Luck to cover Papa's debts."

"What debts?" Beth inquired. "Your father was one of the few who was surviving. Papa said it was because he had so many local contracts that weren't affected by the blockade." When Maren looked bewildered, Beth explained, "You know, supplying restaurants and stores with food and goods. And this place was always busy."

"But Eric said Papa was broke, that he owed lots of people. He said he sold nearly everything to pay Papa's debts and to keep the firm going."

Lilibeth Payne was as baffled as her friend. She reflected a few minutes, then asked pointedly, "Have you ever considered that dear Eric is pulling another of his pranks, or simply lying through his teeth?"

Maren's expression revealed her suspicions, and

she admitted, "Lately I have. Too many strange facts have been surfacing since I returned. If he were in New Orleans, I would ask for some explanations, but he sailed on the eleventh and won't return for six to eight weeks. Papa trusted Eric enough to give him full authority over James Shipping, so I regret doubting him."

"But your father was such a good man, Maren. He believed the best of everyone. I've often wished he were my father. But your cousin is clever. Eric could have fooled him or betrayed him."

Maren asked unexpectedly, "Was Payne's Point damaged during the hurricane that killed my parents last year?"

"What hurricane? Your parents died of some kind of swamp fever."

Maren stared at her friend. "But Eric said . . ."

"Eric said what?" the girl pressed, her gaze filled with suspicion.

As Maren revealed what he had told her on the ship, Beth's astonishment increased with each sentence. "There was no hurricane, was there?" Maren finally asked, her heart thudding painfully.

Beth responded sadly, "No, Maren, there wasn't."

Maren paced her room and did not go downstairs that night. She had discovered many distressing things. She had not been invited to the homes of "friends," not because her parents were dead and she had been away for so long, but because people were gossiping about her. Eric had altered her partner's records and had stolen money from him. Worse, Eric had lied about her parents' deaths. What is going on? she wondered. Suddenly she felt alone, and alarmed.

Far away in Washington, Jared Morgan had reported to President Madison, Secretary of War Monroe, and Secretary of Navy Crowinshield. Peter Thomas, the spy from the *Martha J*, had been present. The five had discussed Jared's recent missions and victories, and what they needed him to do next. They had speculated on James Slade's voyage to London, on his motives and on what had been in the boxes he had delivered to Eric James's plantation in Jamaica. They had talked of the grim rumor that the pirates who frequented New Orleans, and the Indian tribes around it, were joining with the British. Then they had discussed the possibility of a slave revolt. Peter Thomas had even said he wondered if Maren Slade, James Slade's *wife*, was involved in whatever was going on!

After pacing his hotel room for an hour, Jared halted near a window and stared outside. His keen mind was racing. If Maren was married to James Slade, why had she dallied so wantonly with him? What was it she had said aboard the ship? Yes, he remembered: "I can think of no better fate than becoming your willing captive." Had she been enticing him to take her with him so she could spy on him, use him, entrap him? She had claimed to be almost destitute and had pretended to be vulnerable, but she wasn't. And what of her behavior when he had confronted her in Jamaica when she was supposed to have been in Martinique? She had led him on, then had warned her husband to flee. She had bewitched him and duped him. By damn, she owed him!

After leaving Jamaica, Peter Thomas had overheard James Slade tell Horben Wolfe that Maren had a big part to play in their scheme, and that she'd already proven herself clever and trustworthy by fooling that privateer. That report had stung Jared.

Unfortunately, during the three days when Eric had been in port, Peter Thomas had been too weakened by dysentery to go into New Orleans and spy on "James and Maren Slade." But by the time the ship had docked in Baltimore, Peter had been well enough to purchase another crewman's shoreleave so he could ride the thirty-seven miles into Washington and meet with the President. Afterward, he had hurried back to Baltimore to continue his observation of "James Slade."

Chapter Five

After lunch on Friday, Maren went to visit Eric's younger brother at the office of James Shipping. She had waited long enough to see if her cousin was evading her. She needed to learn what, if anything, Marc knew about Eric's schemes.

She greeted the young man exuberantly. "Marc. You've been very naughty to avoid me."

Marc James whirled about, knocking over several things. "M-Maren, what are y-you doing here?" he asked.

Maren realized that her cousin was unsettled by this surprise visit. Good, she decided. He might let something slip. "I've been home for more than two weeks, yet I've only seen you twice, and both times on my first day in New Orleans." As she eyed him furtively, she remarked, "This is the first time I've visited Papa's business since I returned. His office has changed."

"It's Eric's office now. But you can't see him today; he's gone to Baltimore," Marc told her nervously.

"I know. Why haven't you been to Lady Luck to visit me? You don't seem glad to have me back. Are you angry with me? Did I get you into trouble with Eric? I didn't tell him about your slip."

"I've been busy since Eric left."

"With the blockade, how much work is there to do?" she teased. "Are you in charge while he's away?"

"Not really," Marc confessed, lowering his gaze. "I just watch the office and send customers to Mr. Andrews at the wharf."

"Why doesn't Eric train you to handle things while he's away? With a little help and patience, you could learn to run the business for him."

"Eric says I'm not smart enough. He says I would mess things up. He's right," Marc added quickly. "I ruined a whole order trying to show him I could help out. He was real mad."

Maren thought it sad that Marc believed he was so incompetent, and she found it cruel of Eric to keep him that way. However, her younger cousin was so frightened that he kept revealing things without meaning to do so. "You work all day, but surely you're off at night. Why not join me for dinner?"

"Eric told me to stay out of Lady Luck so I wouldn't cause problems for him and for you. I don't know how to play cards. He said I would make your customers nervous by watching them, that people don't like to be observed when they're betting. And he says I'm clumsy. I might knock things over and make people real mad."

"I didn't know about that, Marc. I suppose Eric could be right, but I'll bet I could teach you to play cards. At least we could visit sometimes. Wouldn't you like that?" she asked as if she were speaking to a child.

"I suppose," he replied sullenly. "But let's wait for Eric to return; then we'll ask him if it's all right."

"Do you do everything Eric says?" Maren asked.

"Course I do," he quickly replied, fear dancing in his eyes.

"Why, Marc? You're smart enough to think for yourself."

"I'm not," he argued. "Ask Eric; he'll tell you I'm not smart."

A well-dressed gentleman called in from the doorway just then. "Could you please tell me where to find a Mr. Andrews?" he asked.

"He's in the warehouse at the wharf," Marc responded.

"Where is that, young man? I'm from upriver."

"I'll show you," Marc said obediently. He turned to Maren and told her he had to leave.

"I'll wait here for you," she declared. "I'm not finished with our visit."

Marc seemed reluctant to leave her in Eric's office. "You should come back later. Mr. Andrews might have some work for me to do."

"If you're not back within thirty minutes, I'll lock the door and leave. Since I have nothing else to do this afternoon, I can wait."

When her cousin lingered, Maren said sternly, "Show the gentleman where to find Mr. Andrews. You're wasting his valuable time. Go on."

"Yes, ma'am," Marc responded.

Maren watched the two men until they rounded a corner. Then she locked the office door. She hoped Eric had not changed the safe's combination. Since the numbers matched the month and day of her mother's birthday, she could hardly forget them. She twirled the dial as quickly as her quivering fingers would allow, then yanked on the heavy door. Nothing. She frowned.

She coaxed, "Try again, Maren, maybe you missed a notch."

This time the safe opened, and she smiled. She searched the ledgers and papers, but found nothing suspicious or incriminating. No doubt Eric kept his important papers elsewhere. Suddenly she wondered where Eric lived. She hadn't been told, nor had she asked. As she lifted the last stack of papers, she noticed a ribbon-bound set of letters beneath them. Lifting the packet, she saw that the letters were addressed to Miss Maren James. They had been written by her parents during her absence. . . .

Maren was in a quandary. If she took them, Eric might notice and realize she had been in the safe. If she didn't, she would never know what they said. They belonged to her, but she didn't want to alert him to her knowledge of the safe's combination. Suddenly she grinned. She could read the letters and replace them before Eric's return. She stuffed them into her reticule, locked the safe, and left the office.

Maren settled herself on the sofa in her suite at Lady Luck. She lifted the first letter and opened it slowly, praying she was ready for this task. She read only ten letters before she was forced to halt for a time. Glancing here and there at the last few days gone by, remembering her parents. She recalled books they had discussed, plays they had seen, events they had shared.

Maren recalled the day her mother had questioned her feelings for Daniel. As in their many talks before that one, they had discussed love, sex, duty to one's self and to one's heritage, and other people's behavior. Maren had told her mother that she wanted to marry Daniel, and it had been true at the time because it had seemed like the best thing to do at that point in her life. Her mother had advised her to marry for love, not wealth or position or responsibility, not even to please her grandparents in London. Guilt now overwhelmed Maren, for she had agreed to marry for those very reasons. Until Jared had opened her eyes to love, she had not imagined truly winning her heart's desire.

Maren was mystified as to why Eric had kept the letters from her, especially since they spoke so highly of him. Had he withheld them to "surprise" her as he had with the news of Lady Luck? Or did he think they would serve him better on another day? Since the envelopes had never been sealed, she could not tell whether Eric had read these missives, but she assumed that he had. But why did he keep them, unless he intended to give them to her? If not, he would have burned them long ago.

"Papa was very smart, so how did Eric fool him?" Maren murmured pensively. Then she chided herself, "You'll drive yourself mad trying to figure out Eric's behavior."

So far, all of the letters had praised Eric's hard work and the growth of his character. Her parents had referred to the many happy times they had shared with their daughter, but they had also mentioned that Eric had moved into the townhouse with them and that he often spent time at the plantation, trying to learn how it was run.

Her father had written, "Eric is becoming like a son to me. I don't know what I would do without him. Much as I hate to fault my own brother, John never gave this boy a chance. I've watched Eric mature since he's been here, and I'm very proud of him, Maren. You will be too. I can see love and gratitude in his eyes because of what we're doing for him, and I'm pleased. He can't seem to do enough for us. He even embarrasses me by working harder than I do."

Another letter said, "When this war is over, I won't have the slightest qualm about leaving the firm in Eric's hands while we visit you and Daniel. He's kept my business from sinking on more than one occasion. I've tried to reward him, but he refuses to accept payment. I honestly believe the only thing he wants is to prove himself. Too bad John and Elizabeth aren't here to see the man he's become."

The following missive had more to say about her cousin. "Every day Eric tries to persuade me to run the blockade, but I think it's too risky. Others have tried and failed miserably. He's purchased a raggedy ship, and hired a crew with his own money to prove to me that he can break through the British line. I won't be like John was about that horse race. I told Eric if he succeeded, we would send out one of my ships."

And the next one revealed even more. "He made it, Maren! He sailed to the islands and back—safely. He exchanged goods with foreign ships and made more than enough to cover his expenses. It looks as if James Shipping might make it through this war after all, thanks to Eric. Mercy, he's stubborn and persistent, just like me. He ordered us to keep writing and promised to get these letters to you one day. Knowing Eric, he'll find a way. I wish we dared to visit London, but the islands are as far as we should risk sailing right now."

Then Maren came upon a page written by her mother. "I slipped up on Eric crying the other day. It broke my heart to hear him scolding God for giving him John as a father instead of Cameron. He's been hurt badly, Maren, and I think it's good for him to live as we do for a change. He gets kinder and more thoughtful every day. More and more I can see your father rubbing off on him. They enjoy each other's company, and I must say it's been delightful having him with us, Maren. He's done your father so much good. They spend nearly all day together. It warms me to witness the love and respect they have for each other. Eric is a very special young man. He's had a hard time, but he opens up to us a little more each week. Cameron is strong, but it's been wonderful for him to have Eric to lean on in hard times."

The letters went on in much the same vein, which caused Maren to wonder if she was being fair to Eric. She deliberated the . . . *evidence*. He had saved the firm, had worked hard for it, so wasn't it natural for him to feel as if it were his? He hadn't stolen Lady Luck from her, nor had he destroyed these letters. He had given her an expensive necklace to cover some of her losses. He had turned over the money in the bank, even though it was short by several thousand, and he had risked his life and ship to rescue her and to help America's war effort. They had been separated for years and they both had changed. Perhaps she shouldn't put so much weight on Marc's words and behavior. Perhaps Lilibeth Payne's opinions were biased; Beth had never liked Eric. Perhaps she herself was blaming him too much for her losses. After all, his decisions had caused them. Perhaps some of her suspicions were petty or groundless. Eric might have a good explanation for each of her charges against him.

"Oh, Eric, if only I could trust you . . . Either you cleverly duped my parents, or I'm fooling myself badly. Lordy, which is it?" she fretted.

Maren lit most of the candles in both rooms to chase away the rapidly increasing shadows. She would finish the letters tomorrow, then replace them. It would be interesting to see whether Eric passed them along to her. She concealed the two stacks, one read and the other unread, in her bedroom.

It was late, as Maren bathed and dressed quickly. Needing her mood lifted, she wore the rose-colored gown and secured her dark hair in a chignon. Perhaps she should have a red dress made to match the ruby necklace, as Eric had suggested on the ship. No, she decided, recalling the gossip about her wearing "flaming red gowns." She recalled that Evelyn Sims had talked with her about new gowns, and wondered if there was any connection with the gossip circulating about her wardrobe. It might be a good idea to give that woman a sweetly laced warning, she thought.

That evening Maren ached for some distraction from the problems which plagued her. She played poker at several tables before joining the same four men who'd challenged her to play on her first evening at Lady Luck. She did not realize she was unconsciously accepting the previous challenge of one of them to prove herself, but tonight she did need to do that, to herself and to others.

After winning two hands, the man who'd challenged her scoffed, "I told you, girl, I've never seen the day when a twit like you could beat me. Why don't you go back to the kitchen where you belong? I'll bet you can handle pots better than you handle cards. Want me to prove it again?"

The other three men scolded him and apologized to Maren for his rude behavior. But she smiled genially and replied, "Give it a try, sir."

This time, Maren intended to concentrate on the game. She desperately wanted to beat the arrogant snake across from her. As the antes were paid and play began, the card game drew attention. After a series of passes, raises, calls, and draws, it was time for a showdown.

"Well?" Maren's obnoxious challenger said with a sneer, as he looked at the large pile of money on the table. He had insisted they play with cash instead of chips.

Only three players remained in the game. As their hands were revealed, one man had a full house; the offensive gambler laid down four of a kind, grinning triumphantly; and Maren gracefully and nonchalantly spread out a straight flush. Only a royal flush could have bettered it.

Her competitor's face became redder than the hearts on Maren's cards. He quickly downed his drink, then said loudly, "You baited me, girl. I think you cheated. One of you men check those cards."

Dan Myers came to stand at Maren's side, but she clasped his hand to signal that she would handle this repulsive man. "I did not bait you, sir, and I never cheat. I think you've had enough liquor for a whole week and enough cards for tonight. If you desire to come here again, leave your crude behavior at home. And," Maren added, "I'm not a girl."

"You can't tell me how much to drink or order me to leave. I've been playing cards and socializing here for years. If you persist in this, none of my friends will ever come here again, and you need us."

"Dan, will you kindly show this . . . man to the door. Tell Ned and Harry that he isn't allowed in here again."

"Afraid I'll whip your pretty ass next time?" the irate loser shouted.

The house fell silent, and Maren stared at the man, wondering if he was as drunk as he appeared. Frankly, she didn't think so. In fact, she believed he was intentionally creating a scene. "Look around, sir. You're making a spectacle of yourself. Walk out like a man, or I'll have my guards toss you out."

The offensive man snatched up his companion's drink and gulped it down. "I'm more of a man than those slugs you've been bedding upstairs."

Belatedly Maren realized where this scene was heading. This man was out to harm her. Others were trying to reason with him, but his dark eyes gleamed with a light which told her they were wasting their time and breath. She collected the cards and handed them to the man at her right. "To assure this man that he's been beaten fairly, please check each card in this deck."

Maren prayed that the troublemaker had not tampered with the cards during the game. Fortunately, he hadn't thought of doing so, and his companions could find nothing wrong with them. "Your own friends vow that the deck is clean, sir. Are you ready to leave politely?"

When Maren revealed that she was not going to back down or burst into tears, the man glared at her. "I'll get revenge tomorrow night."

"No, sir, you will not. You are no longer welcome in Lady Luck."

"Don't be a fool, girl. I can cost you plenty of business."

"If that business is like yours, sir, I will gladly lose it. Lady Luck is known for her refined atmosphere; your drunken outbursts are out of place. I cannot allow you or anyone else to subject my patrons to such vulgarity and discourtesy. Leave, sir, and tell your boss the ploy didn't work," she remarked meaningfully.

A look of surprise briefly crossed the obnoxious man's ruddy face before he stalked from the room. Maren glanced around, noted that the focus was still on her. She smiled. "Please, everyone, return to your games and conversations. I'm terribly sorry for the interruption. Dan, serve everyone a glass of wine on the house."

When Dan joined her near the steps, he said, "That was a generous thing to do, Miss Maren, but a costly one. Our wine stores are almost depleted."

"I know, Dan; I checked the wine cellar with Mary this morning. But I had to do something to relax our patrons after that nasty scene. Has that man always been such a bastard?"

138

"He's always been a tough player and heavy drinker, but I've never seen him drunk or crude before. I don't know what's gotten into him."

"I think someone paid him to harass me tonight." Maren related the gossip circulating about her and Lady Luck. "I think somebody wants me to fail, to give up."

"Who?" Dan asked. "For what reason?"

"I don't know, Dan. Just make certain that man stays out of here."

In her room, Maren vowed to herself that she would never again play cards for such a large stake when distracted. Unable to sleep, she retrieved the letters and read more of them.

"Damn you, Eric James! From these letters, you're getting better and better all the time. My parents were good judges of character, so they couldn't be so wrong about you. That means I can't be right about you. Damn. If you aren't my enemy, then who is?"

The following Sunday, at lunchtime, Dan Myers informed Maren that he was moving into a house down the street from Lady Luck. She looked at him in surprise. "Why, Dan? Have I done something wrong? You aren't quitting, are you?" she asked worriedly.

"Certainly not, Miss Maren," he responded pleasantly. "I think it would be best for you if you didn't have a man living here."

"We aren't alone, Dan; Mary lives here too."

"She lives downstairs, but we live upstairs. Gossip can be ferocious, Miss Maren. I don't want it to devour you."

"What do I care if people talk about me?" she scoffed angrily.

"You care, or you wouldn't be so careful about your behavior. I was a friend of your father's, so I have to do what's best for you."

"That would leave Mary and me alone here, Dan. Is that wise?"

"I'll make certain everything is locked up tightly every night. Maybe you're right about somebody harassing you. You're a young woman, a single one, and a very beautiful one. I'm not old, I'm single, and presentable. That makes us a perfect target for rumors. If I remain here, my presence can be used against you. I don't want that, Miss Maren."

"But free living quarters are part of your pay. If you move out, I insist on giving you a raise to cover your rent."

"You can't afford to do that. Don't worry about me."

"If necessary, I'll use the money in the bank to pay you and to buy more wine. My partner may be dead or nonexistent. I'll worry about him and his money later."

"Your father would be very proud of you, Miss Maren."

On Thursday evening Maren donned the ivory and

gold dress. Since she needed to feel relaxed, she let her long dark hair hang loose and wavy. She did not mind going below because there had been no more trouble downstairs since last Friday night.

And this week she had learned something. On Tuesday, she had visited Marc at the office again, and she had managed to find out that Eric was "renting" her family's townhouse from the "investor" who had purchased it following her parents' deaths and Eric's takeover. Reluctantly Dan had helped her lure Marc from the office long enough for her to replace most of the letters; she had read all of them except the last few. Those she had kept, for she had hoped that Eric did not know how many there were. Of course Dan had merely thought she had wanted to look around the office. She had not told him she knew the safe's combination.

Later, Dan reported that he had made contact with a pirate who had promised to deliver fifty crates of wine on the following afternoon and fifty every two weeks thereafter. Maren knew the wine was stolen from ships taken at sea. But if she did not purchase it, someone else would, and she needed wine to stay in business.

Maren circulated in the gaming rooms, chatting with her patrons before agreeing to join three men for baccarat, a game which depended upon the luck of the draw as much as a player's skill. One of the three was the banker, who dealt each player two cards face-down. If a third card was desired to achieve a total of nine or nineteen, and to win, the third card was dealt face-up, creating suspense. Tens and face cards did not count, and all bets had to be equal to or less than the banker's.

The game proceeded genially, Maren sipping a glass of wine, the men inbibing stronger drinks; but Cameron James's daughter did not allow the conversation to dull her wits. She had set a limit on what she could afford to lose and had vowed not to exceed it. She hoped to earn more money tonight, to help replace the amount stolen by Eric.

As Jared Morgan entered the gambling house, he nodded a greeting to the guards, then paused in the large entry hall to scan his surroundings. He wanted to take his mind off his frustrating search for James and Maren Slade, who seemed unknown here. After docking at dawn, he had managed to locate James Shipping, but according to the lad in the office, Eric James and the *Martha J* had been gone for weeks. To make matters worse, Jared had been told of Cameron James's death and of Eric's takeover of the firm. He wondered who was in control of Lady Luck and whether he would face problems here. Fortunately he had put in at Savannah to check on his family, so he was now prepared to handle his other business.

When familiar laughter reached Jared's alert ears, his head jerked toward the room to his right and his tawny gaze focused on a brunette who had her back to him. His tall body stiffened and his heart pounded. He almost dreaded checking the looking glass beyond her, but he had to view the woman's face. His eyes narrowed. How was it possible that no one he'd questioned had known of the beautiful woman who was calmly playing cards with three men!

Quickly Jared's gaze searched both rooms for Maren's husband, James Slade. Surprised and pleased to find the man was not about, he made his way through the large room to stand behind her.

Maren sensed a male presence, but she was caught off guard when she received a kiss on the cheek. Simultaneously his manly fragrance assailed her nostrils, then her head turned and their gazes fused. She inhaled sharply and her eyes widened. His smile beat upon her like the blazing sun.

"Maren. It's been a long time."

"Jared," she murmured, suddenly short of breath and very warm. Her hands trembled so that she nearly dropped her cards.

"You're very hard to locate, I must say. I've spent all day looking for you. I see you're a woman of many surprises," he teased.

With great difficulty, Maren pulled her eyes from his handsome face and glanced at the men at her table. Their curious gazes were locked on her. "Let me finish this game, Jared, then we'll talk," she told him, but she dared not look at him again.

"I'll wait right here. I can't allow you to slip through my fingers," he replied in a strange, but mellow, tone.

Maren tried to concentrate on the game, but Jared's close proximity prevented it. Aware of his hands on her chair, she vainly tried to suppress the quiver this slight contact inspired. And when his strong fingers slipped beneath her hair and began to caress the back of her neck, she shifted in her seat. She could not ask him to halt his bold behavior without calling more attention to it, but she gradually became annoyed with him for displaying such familiarity in a public place, her place. After Jared's unexpected arrival, Maren lost every hand except one, and she rapidly reached her loss limit for the night. Having done so, she smiled, thanked the players, and excused herself. Jared then pulled out her chair and extended his hand to help her rise. After Maren led him to the foot of the stairs, she turned to face him. "Don't ever embarrass me in public like that again," she scolded. "I have enough trouble keeping a clean reputation without you strolling in and discoloring it."

Jared did not apologize. Why should he worry about sparing a reputation she was so loose with at times! The *Martha J*'s cabin had been private, but the beach in Jamaica was certainly a public place where they could have been discovered in an almost intimate situation. He knew he had been unnerving her; he had done it intentionally. He leaned against the sturdy stair post. "You've led me on quite a merry chase, woman. I didn't find your note until you were long gone, and now I have wasted all day trying to track you down. Let's go where we can talk."

Maren erroneously assumed that Jared had discovered her identity. "I can't take you to my room," she whispered. "People would gossip." She observed him as he grinned mischievously. He was dressed in a fawn waistcoat. Its narrow shoulders and tight-fitting sleeves revealed his masculine torso. His fawn-colored breeches halted below the knee, and silk stockings then covered his legs until they disappeared into soft leather shoes with rounded tongues and silver buckles. Underneath his vest, he wore a soft linen shirt. A neatly tied cravat completed his attire. His hair was combed back, and parted on the right side. His garments were clean and fresh, as was he. He smelled delightful, and he looked magnificent, refined.

Jared was eying Maren as she looked him over. He liked the ivory gown she wore. The fitted waist revealed her slender midriff, and modestly accentuated her nice bosom. He wanted to stroke the satiny flesh her low neckline revealed. Indeed, his passionate nature was responding to her undeniable sensuality; his snug britches made him aware of this. Touching the gold necklace at her throat, he remarked, "I'm glad I didn't take this that day; it's at home around this lovely neck."

Maren actually blushed, something she did infrequently. "I, too, am glad," she replied, unable to come up with a wittier response.

"However, you don't look as desperate or as helpless as you did that day on the ship. In fact, I don't recall this gown," he said.

Maren looked surprised. "Do you remember everything you see?"

"I try to. Sometimes even a tiny piece of information could save my life. In any case, you seem to have made out well since your return."

"I've had my share of good luck. What about you, Captain Hawk?"

Jared quickly glanced around to make certain no one had overheard her. "If you don't mind, would you keep that name to yourself?" he asked. Jared didn't need to be secretive about it because he was a patriotic privateer who worked under the president's aegis, but he thought it might charm this exquisite woman if she believed she shared a secret with him.

"Then what shall I call you, Jared?"

"Morgan," he answered calmly.

"Well, Morgan, what are you doing in New Orleans?"

He chuckled. "Jared Morgan is my name. You do recall your promise to spend time with me if I didn't rob you? And your note in Jamaica?"

Maren smiled when Jared shared his real name with her. Now, she wouldn't have to worry about making a slip before she confessed that they had met years ago. "Surely you didn't spend so much time and money just to pay a social call on me," she teased merrily.

"To be honest, I'm here on business, and for pleasure. Can we take a walk so we can talk privately? It's beautiful outside."

"That would be nice, Jared," she replied, but as they approached the door, Maren smiled and told the two guards, "I'll return later."

Ned Jones and Harry Peck nodded, and Ned said, "Don't worry. We'll keep an eye on things, Miss

Maren. We won't allow any trouble tonight."

Maren thanked them, then left with Jared, who had assumed the guard was referring to trouble with James Slade.

As soon as they were a short distance from Lady Luck, Jared teased, "You really like to live dangerously, don't you, Maren?"

She halted and looked at him. "What do you mean? I don't usually lose very many hands, but you did distract me with your sudden arrival."

"How about playing a game with me?"

"And let you win the shirt off my back because you addle my brain?"

"That sounds most enticing, but I had a much different game in mind, my enchanting siren. Let's go to my hotel room and play a game without any rules," he suggested bluntly.

Maren's cheeks colored slightly. "I can't do that, Jared. Someone might see us. Besides, I think you have the wrong impression of me. Actually we should go back inside, but perhaps we can have lunch tomorrow."

"You weren't concerned about getting caught with me on the ship or on the beach," he reminded her. "You were warm and willing then. Why so cold tonight? I've come a long way to collect on your promises."

Maren was dismayed by his words. "That just happened, Jared. I was foolish."

"Then be foolish again tonight," he coaxed huskily. "You owe me, woman. You led me on twice, then ran out on me in Jamaica."

"I left you a note. I told you it was dangerous there and we had to leave. We had been told British ships would arrive that day."

"Why didn't you warn me about them?" he asked.

"I was aroused before dawn and rushed out, half-asleep. I barely had time to write you that note. I'm sorry. But you should be used to looking out for your own safety. Are they your enemies too?"

"Of course. I'm an American. Thank goodness someone warned me to sail quickly. We barely cleared the island before they arrived."

"I said I was sorry. I couldn't risk getting caught waking you. If you'll recall, Captain Hawk, you had robbed us a few days earlier, and I only had twenty minutes to get ready. But I did say goodbye. You don't have to be so hateful, Jared. I don't owe you anything."

"Are you spurning me after luring me into coming so far to have you?"

Maren was shocked. "I did no such thing! I've never behaved like that before. You just . . . charmed me into misbehaving."

"Oh, little Maren can't help misbehaving," he teased huskily.

"You're wrong about me, Jared. Let me explain what—"

"Where is your beloved husband tonight?" he asked abruptly.

"Husband?" she echoed, momentarily confused.

"You do recall that you have one, don't you, Mrs.

James Slade?"

Maren was astonished by his insinuation. "You knew?"

"It seems you forgot to reveal that piece of information to me. If a man needs to watch out for an irate husband, he should be warned. Then he can decide whether the woman in question is worth the risk. You are."

Maren stared at him as his words sank in. "If you thought I was married, why did you carry on like that with me? Do you always accost married women when you attack ships?"

"I didn't know the truth about you that day. I found out later."

"But you pursued me again in Jamaica," she accused.

"I pursued you?" he taunted mirthfully. "You were more than eager both times. You didn't mind betraying your husband before, so why act the innocent tonight? You know you want me as much as I want you."

"Damn you, you lecherous bastard! Get away from me."

Maren started to head back to Lady Luck, but Jared seized her arm. Thoughts of her had tormented him for weeks. "Not so fast, my lovely tart. Nobody makes a fool of me or refuses to pay a debt."

"You made a fool of yourself, Captain Hawk. I'm not Maren Slade; I'm not married to anyone. In fact, James Slade doesn't exist. That was a ruse to protect me from the sailors aboard Eric's ship."

149

"Eric's ship?" he repeated evocatively.

"My first cousin, Eric James, owns James Shipping. I was trapped in London by the war. Eric ran the blockade and rescued me. I own Lady Luck and I live there. I don't need any man to take care of me or to tell me what to do, especially not one who fools around with married women. Don't you ever come near me again."

Jared's mind was working swiftly and keenly. "That would make you Maren James, Cameron James's daughter."

"That's right, Captain Hawk. But my father's dead."

"I heard that today," he replied, his tone noticeably different. "I thought you said you had nothing but that necklace and those clothes."

Maren wasn't about to explain her situation to this man. He had dallied with her while thinking her a married woman, and there was no telling what other bad traits he possessed. She concluded sadly that Jared Morgan was not the man she had thought him to be. "I did not lead you on, you foul beast, but you cannot say the same. Leave me alone before I call my guards."

"You say you own Lady Luck?" he probed. "But you're a woman."

"I am, but I can run it better than any man."

"I imagine you can," he murmured with a grin.

"What's that supposed to mean?" she demanded.

"I've witnessed your talents at work in many areas, Maren. I think you can do anything you wish. You tricked me easily enough."

"If you're referring to how I misled you on the ship, surely you didn't expect me to be honest with a pirate."

"I'm not a pirate; I'm a privateer."

"I doubt there's little difference."

"That depends on whose side you are on. I'm an American so I'm helping to show the Brits that we can defend our waters."

"I suppose that gives you an excuse to raid ships whenever you wish."

"You're a hard woman, Maren James," he teased.

"I don't like being duped, Mr. Morgan."

"Nor do I, Miss James," he retorted. "I thought you were married."

"I know you did," she replied frostily, her accusation clear.

The quick-witted Jared said, "But not until you left me. I was being honest with you those two times. You've bewitched me, woman."

Maren watched Jared closely. She doubted him.

"Are you going to break your promises to me?" he asked softly.

"I made those promises to someone else, not a wife stealer."

"I told you, I heard that false tale later."

"I don't believe you. You were aware of it when you found me tonight, yet you continued your lewd pursuit. How long did you plan to keep your false impression a secret? Until I kept my . . . promise?"

"Maybe," he responded honestly. "I believed you

had lied to me and led me on. You hooked me good, and I wanted you."

"As you can see, I owe you nothing."

"You're mistaken," he murmured mysteriously, then smiled.

Something else was gnawing at Jared's mind: Eric James and his voyage to London. Had the man actually gone there to rescue his cousin? Why risk trying to get her through a blockade when she was safe in England? And since her parents were dead, why had Maren hurried home during a war? He knew from stolen official papers that the British had their eyes on New Orleans which offered a base for an inland invasion via the Mississippi River. Was Eric James a traitor? A spy for the British? What about that stop in Jamaica and those concealed boxes? His hasty flight when the American agent, Captain Hawk, arrived? Was Maren Eric's helper or his cover? Lady Luck was the perfect place for contacts. Maren owned it, and she had returned at a curious time. She had tricked him easily and expertly, just as Peter Thomas had heard Eric say. Kip had warned him that this girl could mean trouble, that she must be watched.

Maren observed how pensive Jared was, and she wondered what was going through his mind. His next question stunned her.

"What is Eric James up to, Maren? Why did he really go to London? And why did he make a stop in a British port?"

Maren asked herself why Jared had asked about

such things and why he was suspicious of her cousin. If Jared also worked for the Americans, then he would know about Eric and the London mission. She recalled what Eric had said about being sought out and slain if his mission was exposed. Jared had been in a British port, Jamaica, and he had acted strangely during the attack on their ship. Perhaps he was a spy. . . .

Chapter Six

"I could ask you those same questions, *Captain Hawk*, but I doubt you would answer them, at least honestly. Just stay away from me." Maren tried to free herself, but Jared refused to release her. "I will scream for help," she threatened.

"And reveal our quarrel to your friends?"

"You wouldn't dare expose yourself," she murmured.

"Why not? Everyone knows I'm Captain Hawk," he responded.

"You're a devil." She corrected him tersely.

"Some say I am, but others call me an angel, an avenging angel."

"Oh, yes, I remember, 'an angel ashore,' wasn't it?"

Jared chuckled. "You know me so well, Maren."

"I know you better than I want to, Mr. Morgan."

"I think not, Miss James, at least you didn't act

that way earlier."

"Only because I had you confused with someone else!"

"Who might that be?" he inquired, lifting one brow.

Maren bridled her loose tongue. "Someone I met a long time ago. But you're nothing like him. Let go of me, you bastard."

"Is there a problem here, Miss James?" a voice asked politely.

Maren glanced at the other man and smiled. "Nothing I can't handle, Dan. I'll walk back with you. Good night, Mr. Morgan."

"We aren't finished, Maren," Jared said firmly.

"Yes, we are. Don't come near me again. Dan, make certain Ned and Harry are ordered to keep this man out of Lady Luck."

Jared chuckled at her last statement. "You can't escape me this easily, Maren, but we'll let it go for tonight. Think about what I said, and I'll see you tomorrow. 'Nite, Dan."

Maren missed Dan's reply for she was watching Jared Morgan stroll away, whistling a merry tune. "Of all the nerve," she murmured angrily.

"Anything wrong, Miss Maren?" Dan asked.

"Just a very persistent suitor, Dan. I tried to convince him I wasn't interested in him, but he's too arrogant to pay attention."

Dan Myers realized these two had met before and were close, despite their squabble. He replied evocatively, "Jared Morgan usually isn't like that.

Maybe he was upset about something."

"You know him?" Maren asked, eagerness brightening her eyes and enlivening her voice.

The manager nodded. "He's been to Lady Luck many times during his visits to New Orleans on business. He's a well-liked man. You sure you want to exclude him? He was a friend of your father's."

That revelation startled her. "Jared Morgan knew my father? I've only known him a short time, but why didn't he tell me that when we met?"

"I suppose Jared thought you knew. Actually, Jared's father, Benjamin Morgan, was a good friend of Cameron's. That's how Jared met your father. Ben died a few years back; he was a good man, too. I'm surprised you've never met him or his son."

"So am I, Dan. But I guess Papa had many friends I didn't know. He was a popular man and did business with a lot of people."

It was after midnight and Maren was still sitting on the sofa and thinking about Jared Morgan. She recalled his curious reaction to her identity. Now it made sense to her. But, having known her father and having been his friend, why had he kept taunting her? And why had he not revealed that relationship? Another mystery to solve, she decided.

Her father might have introduced her to Jared Morgan years ago! If only she could have told him her real name that first day on the ship . . . Would Jared have behaved differently to the daughter of an old friend? There was something unusual about Jared Morgan, and she intended to discover what it was.

Jared was having a similar debate with himself. Cameron James's daughter . . . his partner in Lady Luck . . . He chuckled as he wondered how Maren would take that shocking news. Keep him out of the gambling house of which he was half-owner? "No way, my little siren," he said aloud.

Jared had not imagined an entanglement like this. He wished he hadn't mentioned her alleged marriage before learning it had only been a pretense. Could it be she was telling the truth about everything? Was she a pawn in Eric's schemes? Of course, she could be a willing participant. After all, her grandparents were English, and she had been in England for years. Maybe she had been talked into aiding the other side. Eric might have duped her, or she might be indebted to him in some way.

"I wonder just where you stand in all of this mess, my little siren. I must uncover the truth before I let you get too close to me. And by damn, I want you real close."

Jared jingled the keys to Lady Luck and grinned. "Soon, my lovely one, but not tonight."

He stretched out on his bed, and called Maren's image to mind. She certainly had a sparkle in her eyes when she was mad. He wanted to run his fingers through her silky hair and over her satiny flesh, wanted to see her smile again, hear her laugh, feel her in his arms. And he wanted to kiss her until she breathlessly surrendered to him. He said aloud, "I want you, Maren James, and I'm going to have you."

The wine was delivered as promised the next afternoon and Maren paid the man who delivered it with money from the bank box. She recorded the transaction and then left the receipt with the remainder of the money. She was tempted to remove the cash, but decided to wait until the war was over, if there was any left. If no one showed up to make a claim on Lady Luck by then, she would consider the cash hers.

That night, Maren slipped into one of the matching purplish blue gowns and styled her hair in cascading curls. She had revoked her order for Dan to keep Jared out of the place, for she knew if she was going to learn more about him, she had to see him again. Now her pulse raced wildly as his smiling face loomed before her mind's eye. His golden brown eyes had danced with mischief last night, and she loved the way his hair had waved playfully, settling into sun-tipped locks. She longed to trail her fingers over his hard, tanned body, to kiss him, embrace him. If only . . .

"Stop it, Maren. You have work to do, a devil to unmask," she said suddenly.

Jared did not appear until eleven o'clock, an hour before closing time. He saw Maren speaking with people in one room, so he entered the other and found a game to join.

As Maren strolled through that room to see how things were going, she noticed Jared Morgan. She halted and watched him until he looked up and smiled at her. It was hard not to return the smile, but she merely nodded in response. She talked with a few people and tried to keep her mind off the enticing man who kept glancing at her.

When Jared's table cleared of the other players, she boldly went to sit across from him. "Dan told me you knew my father."

Jared counted his winnings and pushed them aside before meeting her probing gaze. "For many years. Too bad he didn't think me worthy of an introduction to his beautiful daughter."

"If you were anything like you are now, Mr. Morgan, I can easily understand why he didn't."

"Then that is why, because the only thing that's changed about me is my age. I suppose your being Cameron's daughter made you seem vaguely familiar to me that day on the ship. You favor your mother, but you have traces of Cam in you."

"You knew my mother, too?" she inquired, more intrigued.

"I had the honor and pleasure of meeting her on several occasions. As best I can recall, you were usually visiting your grandparents in London when I was around. Too bad. We could have started our private war years ago. I'll bet if your father had known how daring you are, he wouldn't have allowed you to go away alone so many times."

"I'm only daring when I'm around devils like you, Captain Hawk. Besides, my parents trusted me, and with good reason."

Jared's twinkling eyes drifted over her. He liked the way she looked with her curls cascading—older, romantic, sensual, but also very feminine and spirited. "Thank goodness there aren't many of us infamous devils around to lure nice little girls like you into trouble."

"I'm not a little girl; I'm twenty years old."

"And still single. That amazes me, Miss James. Can't you find a man to suit you? Or is it that you've been waiting for me all these years?"

Maren reacted guiltily to his last jest, but her reply was delivered in a decisive tone. "I'm single because my betrothed was killed when this bloody war began. I went to London to be married. That was my wedding gown you saw on the ship."

"You were going to wed a Brit? And in that exquisite gown! Shame on you, Maren. You certainly have a bad habit of lying artfully."

"Well, I'm certainly glad you don't have any bad habits that need correcting," she taunted.

"Oh, I have plenty of them, but you're just the woman to change them. Want to give it a try?"

"Perhaps," she replied with a compelling smile. "Frankly, you are a man of contradictions, and they intrigue me."

"What contradictions?" he asked, propping his elbows on the table and leaning forward.

"I think I prefer to keep them a secret for now. I wouldn't want you changing on me before I can figure you out."

"Don't you keep enough secrets from me without adding a new one?"

"Me, keep secrets from you, Captain Hawk? You appear to be a man who knows everything, a man who gathers every 'tiny piece of information' that can save your life."

"Is my life in danger here, Maren, or only my freedom?"

Maren watched his eyes glow with desire, and she warmed to the flames that burned in his tawny gaze. Her eyes drifted appreciatively over as much of him as she could see. "There's freedom, Jared, and then there's . . . *freedom.*"

"I believe you once told me you would like to become my willing captive. Is that offer still open?"

"It was a silly jest made by a terrified woman during a pirate attack."

"But I'm not a pirate and you weren't under attack."

"Wasn't I?" she playfully retorted, enjoying their word game.

"I would never attack you, Maren, but I would love to . . . get to know you better," he said, his eyes darkening as his hunger increased.

It was as if they had suddenly forgotten they were in a room full of people. Jared came around the table and sat down beside her, their gazes remaining locked as he did so. As he covered her hands with his and bent forward to dispel most of the remaining distance between them, Maren did nothing to discourage him. For some moments they watched each other, his thumbs absently stroking her hands.

"Will you, Maren?" He finally broke the seductive silence between them when he posed the question. He wanted to yank her into his arms, to whisk her away to his room. As always, something in her eyes called out to him. To revealed her yearning for him, bound her to him whether she realized it or not.

"Will I what, Jared?" she responded, lost in his gaze.

"Will you let me get to know you better?"

"Should I?" She was asking the wrong person, the right person. He was so overwhelming that he made her feel weak with need for him. He caused her body to sing with joy, to tense with anticipation, to blossom.

Jared felt comfortable with Maren, even when they quarreled or misunderstood each other. A bond was growing between them, one he could not resist. Jared knew so much about raiding ships and stealing supplies, but did he know how to steal a heart, this woman's heart? "If you refuse, Maren, we'll miss something special. Can't you feel the pull between us? Can you resist it?"

Maren trembled. He had a powerful effect on her, but his behavior on the preceding night kept flashing into her mind like destructive lightning. Hoarsely, she said, "I have to resist it, Jared. I don't know you anymore, and I'm afraid to trust you."

"You weren't afraid on the ship or in Jamaica. Don't fear me now."

"That was different. You were different," she told him, then hurriedly left him. She was unprepared for this romantic siege, and she had to put distance between them to think clearly.

Jared watched her leave in a panic, and wanted to pursue her. But he couldn't. He would not compromise her. Later, he promised himself. Noting that Dan Myers was observing him, Jared decided that he had to win Maren's confidence, but without jeopardizing his investigation of Eric James. He sighed heavily and left.

Dan Myers glanced at the front door, then at the stairs. He knew something was going on between those two, and he wondered how it would affect him. . . .

Jared went to Lady Luck on Saturday to invite Maren to lunch, but she wasn't in, or so he was told. When he asked to speak with Dan Myers, he learned that the manager no longer lived there. The housekeeper, Mary Malone, would tell him nothing more.

That night at ten-thirty, Jared showed up again to play cards. He joined Maren and three men at a table. They played poker for over an hour, with Maren or Jared winning nearly every hand. The talk centered on the war and Jared shared what news he could. The main topics they discussed were Andrew Jackson's battle at Horseshoe Bend in Mississippi and the abdication of Napoleon Bonaparte, which would allow the British to concentrate on the war with America. Jared told the men that the blockade had been extended up the eastern coastline to Maine and that there was a great deal of fighting along the Canadian border.

Maren nearly choked on her wine when one of the men asked, "Is it really as bad as they say at sea, Captain Hawk?"

Jared grinned at Maren before replying, "Worse, sir. The Royal Navy had the advantage by over a thousand ships when this war began, and I'm afraid things haven't improved much. Our nine frigates and three sloops can hardly battle four hundred of theirs, and that doesn't include their nearly two hundred warships. About a hundred to one odds, gentlemen, but we do our best to destroy as many British ships as possible."

"You're mighty brave to go against such odds, Captain Hawk."

Jared played his hand, then replied, "Brave, or reckless, I don't know which. We need money and supplies to fend off our determined foe. New England has plenty of both, but she's stingy with them. Talk is those Easterners are whispering about secession, about rejoining the British Empire. Too bad we can't toss them out like rancid meat. Many of their businesses still deal with the British, shipping them goods that help defeat their own country. Worst of all, the New Englanders make the rest of America pay heavily for supplies. Until the Brits bottled them up last May, they controlled most of the commerce and manufacturing. Somebody needs to break their control."

"Damn traitors, if you ask me," one man declared angrily.

"Yep, this country is full of them," Jared said. "Most describe themselves as loyal Americans while they sell us out to the Brits."

"It's up to you, Miss James," one of the players said.

Maren pulled her gaze from Jared's handsome face, glanced at the hand spread before him—a royal flush—and frowned. Only five of a kind could beat him and they were not playing any wild cards. "I'm afraid Captain Hawk is the winner tonight, gentlemen."

Jared smiled and stood. "It's closing time, so I'll collect later. I can trust you to hold the money for me, can't I, Miss James?"

"She runs an honest house, Captain Hawk, the best one."

"You should take your winnings with you, sir. You can't ever tell when you'll be called to sea to battle our enemy." The moment Maren had said that, she winced inwardly, for she knew he would leave some day soon.

"Better it be in your lovely hands than those of the British if I'm captured," he replied, provoking laughter from the men who were rising to leave.

"What if I collect it tomorrow when I take you to lunch?"

"I'm sorry, sir, but I do not see my patrons socially."

"But I'm an old friend of your father's and a sailor soon off to war."

"So you are, Captain Hawk, but that doesn't prevent gossip."

Maren sighed heavily as she turned onto her left side. Then she screamed as her sleepy eyes touched on the man leaning neligently against her bedpost. The night candle revealed his face as he sat down beside her. "What are you doing here? How did you get in?" she asked quickly.

Jared smiled. "I'm a soldier at war; we have our ways of getting into the enemy's camp. I came to collect my winnings."

There was a loud knock at the door of Maren's suite, and Mary Malone called out, "Miss Maren, are you all right? Miss Maren?"

Maren flung the bedcovers aside and rushed to the door. Opening it, she said, "I'm sorry for disturbing you, Mary. It was only a bad dream. I'm fine now, but thanks for checking on me."

When Maren returned, Jared was stretched out on the warm spot she had so swiftly vacated. "I need to work on your bad habit of lying," he stated coolly.

"You devilish rake, what did you expect me to tell

her?" Maren whispered as she stood beside her bed in a thin nightgown, her tousled hair tumbling about her shoulders. "How did you get in here? If you can enter at will, so can thieves. Tell me so I can correct it."

"I'd like to think I have talents they don't, Miss James. Relax, you're in no danger from thieves or from me. I only wanted to talk privately with you. I tried at lunch, but I was told you were out."

"I went to visit my cousin Marc, Eric's brother."

"Did you have a nice time?" he inquired casually.

"No, I couldn't find him."

"Is he that blond lad I met on my first day here?"

"At James Shipping?" she asked.

"Yes."

"Then it must have been Marc. He isn't too bright, and I worry about him. I can't imagine where he is."

"What about at home on a Saturday?"

"I tried there, but no one answered the door. He lives with Eric in the townhouse we used to own."

"Used to own?"

"Yes, Eric had to . . . You're mighty nosy, Jared Morgan."

"I know; it's one of those bad habits you'll have to break."

"I'm going to break your neck if you don't get out of here, after you tell me how you got in. What if someone saw you?"

"No one did, Maren. I can move like the mist."

"In case you don't know it, Captain Hawk, mist isn't invisible."

"Heavens, woman, haven't you heard my legend? Captain Hawk and the *Sea Mist* can't be seen or heard until they're down your throat."

"Very amusing, Jared. Are you going to answer me?"

"And give away my best secret?"

"You're impossible!"

"No, my fetching siren, I'm not, at least where you're concerned."

"What do you want, Jared? It's late and I'm tired."

"Tomorrow's Sunday; you can sleep all day."

"No, I can't. I have books to do. I work, remember?"

"Why don't you hire someone to do them for you so you can relax?"

"I can't afford any more employees," she said, then quickly added, "There is a war going on and business is not at its peak."

"It doesn't look to me as if it could get much better. People around here are carrying on as usual. The war is some distant nightmare to them, and I hope it stays that way," Jared murmured. He wondered why Maren was handling the books instead of letting Dan do them? Had she changed that procedure?

"You must leave, Jared. I can't afford idle gossip. It's hard enough to be a woman in business without having more trouble."

"More trouble?"

"Must you pounce on every word I utter?" she asked, exasperated.

"You said it, so it must be important."

"Why must it be important, especially to you?"

"Because everything you say or do or think means something to me," he replied tenderly, sitting up and pulling her down beside him.

"Don't do this, Jared," she softly pleaded as she clutched his hand.

He was glad she had not fully realized the facts: he had broken into her room, she was attired in a nightgown, and in the middle of the night they were sitting on her bed, talking. "Do what, Maren?"

"Confuse me. You aren't behaving the way you did years ago."

Jared considered her words for a minute before asking, "What do you mean, years ago?"

Maren jumped up and turned her back on him. But he rose and pulled her around to face him. In the candlelight they could see each other's faces. When Maren's gaze lowered, Jared lifted her chin, and she bravely met his eyes.

"What did you mean?" he persisted.

"All right," she yielded. "We met years ago, when I was fifteen, actually on my fifteenth birthday. I was smitten with you. That's why I acted so . . . foolish on the ship and in Jamaica. I remembered you."

"Cameron never introduced us," he argued. "I would have recalled."

"He didn't," she confessed, then revealed the entire story to him. Withdrawing from his arms, she retrieved the dried nosegay from her lowboy. "I found it when I was going through my things after I returned. It sounds so silly now, and I acted so . . . stupid on the ship and in Jamaica. You see, Jared, I remembered you, but you could not have remembered me. No wonder you thought me so wicked."

When Jared chuckled, she punched him in the stomach and chided, "It isn't funny. I was a very impressionable young girl. I thought I had forgotten about you until you sailed into my life again."

"Maren, my bewitching siren, it makes perfect sense, wonderful sense. The only silly thing about it is the misunderstanding. That's why you seemed familiar. Honestly, I remember you as a young girl and a wharf lad. You touched me as both. Let your dreams of me come alive." He drew her against him and hugged her tightly, and his lips wandered over her brown hair and her cheek before they found her lips. As their mouths fused and explored, Maren clung to him and responded to his demanding siege on her senses. Her body was pressed snugly to his.

"I want you, Maren James," Jared murmured against her ear.

"And I want you, Jared Morgan," she responded ardently.

Jared leaned away from her and asked, "Are you sure? I don't want you to be sorry about this later."

"I'm twenty, Jared. I know what I want and need— you."

"I'm not a girlish fantasy anymore. I'm real, Maren, and this night will be real. But I'll have to leave soon. Can you accept having only this part of me until the war is over?"

Maren allowed her gaze to roam over his face. She had time to make her decision; he was not rushing her. She caressed his strong jawline and fingered his lips. She did not want to talk about the future; this moment counted most, these feelings. She must not intimidate him with a demand for a commitment. She must be honest to a point, then remain mysterious. She had to entice him to come back to her, and to keep coming back because he could not survive without her. She had to feed him little by little from love's frightening dish, until he was addicted to her ambrosia and had to feast on it each day for survival. She must not pose a threat to his freedom, until he was willing to discard it. She had to begin this relationship on the bottom step, then mount the stairs with him one at a time. If they were to become friends, more than lovers, they had to climb together, slowly, deliberately, carefully. Starting at a romantic peak left no place to go but down if things did not work out. Yes, this romantic ladder had to be climbed one rung at a time, beginning tonight. . . .

"Yes, Jared, it's enough for now."

"Swear you won't make any more dangerous voyages. Swear you'll remain here in New Orleans where you'll be safe."

"I can't make such promises, Jared. My grandparents are old; their time is limited. If this war is prolonged, I'll find a way to visit them again."

"But we're at war with Britain. How can you go back there? How can you socialize with our enemies?"

"They aren't my enemies, Jared. I'm not at war with my family and my friends."

"During a war, Maren, you have to take a side, a stand."

"Not against my grandparents or my friends."

"Then why did you leave London during the war to return to no one? You were safe with your grandparents."

"When I left London with Eric, I didn't know my parents were dead. We had been out of contact since June of 1812. Eric told me they'd died after we were underway." Maren brushed over the explanation of her parents' deaths and of what she had believed when she'd met Jared on the *Martha J.* "I didn't know I still had Lady Luck; that's why I needed to keep the necklace. I intended to sell it so I could make a fresh start. I think Eric was right to withhold the tragic news of my parents from our grandparents. How could they endure the death of their last son?"

"That still doesn't explain why Eric came after you at such an inopportune time. Why did he sail into the arms of the enemy and risk losing his ship and crew? Why didn't he leave you there until the end of the war? He took you away from your grandparents when their years are short, deprived you of their support and of good surroundings to drop you into a gambling house. It doesn't make sense, Maren. Why did he visit London?"

"I can't tell you, Jared. Please don't ask again. Besides," she said softly, "this isn't the time to discuss war or business."

Maren's first words had implied there was something she could not reveal, something important. Being a presidential spy was an arduous task, one that demanded a great deal of Jared, and he must keep his mission secret, even from his newfound love. Much as he craved Maren, he had to press her on this urgent matter before things went any further between them.

He said firmly, "You must tell me the truth this time, Maren. Why did your ship stop in Jamaica and why did you sail so hurriedly after my arrival? Where is Eric now? What is he doing?"

"I've told you all I can, Jared. Please let this subject go, especially tonight."

"I can't, Maren," he responded. "We have to settle this matter before we get any closer."

"You seem overly interested in my cousin," she said accusingly. "In fact, you seem more interested in Eric than in me. Why is that, Jared?"

"That isn't true, Maren, but I have to know everything about him. He had a reason for being in London, and it wasn't to rescue you. All that stuff about sailing from France and carrying French papers, it wasn't true. Why did an American on an American ship put into a British port? Will it help you to decide to answer my questions if I tell you I'm working for President Madison? I am, and this information could be vital to America, to our victory."

Maren took offense at Jared's tone, look, and implication. She wondered if this mysterious privateer had learned about the gold shipment and had been trailing them to steal it. When he had been unable to locate it during his attack, perhaps he had followed them to Jamaica, then to New Orleans. Was he manipulating her, using her love for him so he might learn where the gold was hidden? She spoke to the man who was with her, to this stranger Jared had become. "If you thought we were French, Captain Hawk, why did you rob us? If you didn't believe it, why did you let us sail away? And have you forgotten that you also entered that enemy port? We had export business there, but you didn't. You were trailing us, weren't you? Perhaps you should tell me the truth for a change."

"I told you, Maren, I'm working for the President, for America. I use Captain Hawk and the *Sea Mist* to carry out my secret missions. I think Eric James is a traitor and a British spy. Convince me he isn't."

Maren was stunned by this accusation. She knew what happened to traitors and spies—they were executed—but she could not believe Eric was guilty of either crime. Nor could she betray her own kin, not even to Jared, unless she had undeniable proof. Fragments from her parents' letters came to her mind. Perhaps she was wrong about Eric. She had no proof that he was misleading her; she had only suspicions which might have logical explanations. After reading those letters, she could believe a lot of things about Eric James, but that he might be committing treason and spying were too much for her to accept. Maybe Jared was the one she shouldn't trust, at least not so blindly and quickly. If he was working for the President as he claimed, wouldn't he know about Eric's mission? And she could not forget how Jared had treated her upon his arrival in New Orleans. Was he only after the gold?

"Well?" he prompted. "Can you?"

"Even if you didn't already have your mind set against him, why should I try? If you knew Eric James at all, you wouldn't say such things."

"If that's an invitation to hang around until he returns, I accept. Since you're so protective of him, I'll just study him on my own. I hope you learn to trust me, Maren. If what I think about your cousin is true, he could get you into real trouble if you stick with him."

"If that's supposed to scare me into betraying Eric, it won't work."

"I was voicing a concern, Maren, not threatening you. But I hope you're more willing to betray Eric than to betray yourself and America." He ran his fingers through his light brown hair, then sighed wearily. "I think it's best if I leave. I'm sorry for spoiling things between us tonight. But before we get together, Maren, we have to like and trust each other. Once I allow you to get under my skin, I'll be forced to help you whether you're right or wrong. I won't put either of us in that awkward position, so until I decide that you're as important to me as my country is, I have to resist you."

Jared walked toward the door, but he halted and said, "In case you need help or change your mind, I'll be around for a while."

Maren's heart was pounding furiously, but she did not know how to respond. Her mother had told her many things about men. She knew they played games with women, and she had to decide whether Jared was playing with her emotions before she reacted. Why was he hesitating in the doorway? What should she do or say?

"I promise I won't tell Eric about your suspicions," she finally responded. "If what you think is true, then convince me of it. That's as far as I can bend tonight. Can you accept only that part of me until this matter is settled?"

Jared half turned to look at Maren. With her back to the candlestick, her face was in shadows. He tried to see it clearly, but could not. He wanted to trust her, but it was so hard for him to open up to a woman. Willa Barns Morgan had done such terrible things at home that he had trouble trusting any woman, especially with his life and freedom. To ease his tension, he jested, "I hope it's settled quickly, my fetching siren, before you drown me in this flood of desire."

Jared left before Maren could react. She then slowly went to the door, and locked it. She again wondered how he had gotten into the gambling house and into her room. Could someone else do the same? Dan Myers was no longer here to protect her and Mary, and many people probably knew he had moved. Perhaps she should get a pistol. Yes, she must do that. The next time, it might not be Jared Morgan who was sneaking into her room.

Maren returned to bed and snuggled into Jared's indentation. His manly smell lingered and inflamed her anew. Three times he could have taken her, three times she would have surrendered, and three times he had resisted her. Was she being foolish? Too willing and eager?

Maren flung the cover aside once more and lit another candle. She retrieved the haunting letters from a drawer and read them once more. Two in particular troubled her. Those were the ones that had caused her to defend Eric, even at the expense of spoiling her time with her love.

Cameron James had written, "It amazes me, Maren, but Eric continues to improve in all areas. He's been able to get several ships in and out of the Gulf, but only as far as the islands. He worked out a deal with a privateer in Martinique. The man picks up our cargoes there and takes them to European ports for us. Naturally we don't earn much, having to go through another shipper who takes the main risks, but that approach is keeping us in business while others are failing. . . . Eric takes little reward for himself, always putting nearly everything earned back into the firm, except for what he insists that your mother and I use for ourselves and the plantation. I promised to repay him for his hard work by making him my partner after the war. You should have seen his face when I told him that news. He was so choked up he could barely speak for over an hour. He's a hard worker, Maren, and a good man. He is cunning, yet he can be totally unselfish. . . .

"Eric has a real patriotic streak which I greatly admire, but he is reserved about it because he doesn't like people to make much of him. This is so unlike the old Eric who did anything for attention. But secrecy is necessary to protect Eric and to aid his missions, as we call them. If the British captured him or one of their spies (yes, spies here in our land, Maren) unmasked him, our beloved Eric could be slain. When I try to give him credit publicly for saving me during this mess, he pretends everything is my doing and he scolds me later for making him seem too important."

Another letter, written shortly before her father's death, followed a similar vein. "Despite his previous loudness, Eric is really quite shy and sensitive. It's taken me nearly a year to force some confidence into him; John made him feel so useless and inferior. I'm ashamed of my brother for almost destroying his own son. . . . Eric's very proud of what he's done for me and for himself, but what seems to matter most to him is that I recognize and appreciate his growth. I often wish he were my son instead of John's or that he could become my son-in-law. Of course that is not possible since you are first cousins. Nonetheless, he misses you terribly and wishes you had married someone closer to us (we assume you went ahead with the wedding when war was declared). He's told me about some of the pranks you two played. It's clear you're Cameron James's daughter. Eric really loves you, Maren, and talks about you often. All of us wonder how you're doing, and we hope you're happy with Daniel. Naturally your mother worries about your having a child without her there at your side, and every morning and night we pray for this war to end so we can visit you. We love you, Maren, more each day."

That was as much as she could read before anguish overtook her. Her father and mother had admired Eric James. In fact, it seemed that he had gotten better and better, which was certainly possible under her father's influence and guidance. Several times the letters had stated that Eric was helping the American cause in secret ways, but that more could not be revealed in a letter. And twice he had mentioned that Eric had financed certain missions out of a "special fund which you will understand later." Maren hated to think Eric had used the missing money from the bank box, the money she had accused him of stealing.

If she had not finished reading the letters this afternoon, she would have answered Jared's questions, she admitted. But having read them, how could she betray the man her parents had loved so dearly? Eric had almost become a son to Cameron and Carlotta James and, through their letters, a brother to her. All of the good times and feelings she had shared with her first cousin in the first eighteen years of her life had resurfaced, and she had been unable to reveal anything about him to Jared Morgan. Even if Eric was guilty of some crime or foul deed, it would have to be someone else who betrayed him.

* * *

When Maren got out of bed at eleven the next morning, she knew Mary Malone was attending church and would then have lunch with friends. She washed her face and brushed her hair, but did not dress before going downstairs to prepare her wake-up tea. She smiled as she realized that Mary had left a fire in the stove for heating water and for warming the fresh pastries which were on the table. She set the kettle in place and turned to the pastries. Suddenly she screamed, and Jared chuckled.

"Damn you, stop sneaking up on me! Did you stay here last night?" she asked, trying to sound vexed, but it was difficult because he looked so appealing in a billowy white shirt, snug ebony breeches, and shiny black boots.

"No. I slept in my room at the hotel."

"How do you get in?" When he merely grinned, she shouted, "Blast you, Jared Morgan, tell me! This could be dangerous for me and Mary."

"Not anymore, I moved into Dan Myers's old room. I'll be here to protect you and Mrs. Malone. That tea about ready?"

Maren gaped in disbelief. When she found her voice, she shrieked, "You can't move in here! Who do you think you are?"

"Your partner. So I have every right to live here, just as you do, Miss James. After we have tea and pastries, I'll show you the papers your father signed years ago making me half-owner of Lady Luck. By the way, I haven't received any earnings since the war began. After breakfast, we must figure out how much you owe me. Your father was to hold my earnings until I came to collect them, and I do hope you haven't spent them. Somehow I doubt that you want to be indebted to me. Oh, you also owe me for my winning streak last night. But since I was a patron, I do hope you don't pay me with my own money. As to how I get in and out," he added, dangling keys in the air, "I have my own keys. Cameron gave them to me on my last visit."

Chapter Seven

After a lengthy silence, Maren demanded, "What are you trying to pull, Jared Morgan? You can't be my father's partner."

"I'm not, Miss James—I'm yours."

Maren did not like the way Jared grinned. "Give me those keys. You can't come in and out of here like you—"

"Own half of this place." He teasingly completed her statement.

Maren observed him intently. His teeth looked exceedingly white in contrast with his tanned skin, and his brownish gold eyes appeared to be balls of warm honey. He had not shaved yet, and his stubble was very dark for a light-haired man. Though his hair was combed, it still settled into windblown waves with sun-laced tips. She eyed his features. They were strong, manly and appealing, as was his lean and muscular physique. Like his stubble, the hair on his chest, visible because of his half-open shirt, was very dark. She had trouble accepting what he'd said. Jared Morgan, the man whom she had dreamed of since the age of fifteen—Captain Hawk, the roguish privateer who had romantically besieged her three times—was her mystery partner. The man was sharing her home and . . .

"You can't live here, Jared. People will gossip. You might not care about your reputation, but I must protect mine. Vicious rumors can ruin me and my business. After you sail away, I'll be living here. What are you really after?"

"Why, my rightful earnings, among other things. Perhaps I'll use the money to make an investment while I'm waiting for Eric's return. I'm not one to let money sit in a bank." When Maren shifted apprehensively, Jared asked, "You do have my money, don't you?"

Maren knew she had to think of a way to delay him until she could replace his stolen earnings. If she told Jared that Eric had taken them, it would make her cousin vulnerable to this clever deceiver. Obviously Jared had come here about Lady Luck and Eric, not to locate her. Maybe he had known who she was all along! Perhaps he had been playing mischievous games with her! No, she decided, not unless he had been pretending on that first night. But, her warring mind argued, what if he had discovered the truth after his arrival but before he saw her that night?

"You're not answering me, Maren. Your father said he was keeping my share in a special fund.

Surely you were told that you have a partner?"

"Special fund." Maren thought of her father's letter. Things looked worse now than before; there were not two years' earnings and records in the bank box! "I spent some of it. The rest is in a box at the bank, and it's closed on Sunday."

"Why would you spend what isn't yours?" Jared inquired. He walked to the stove and removed the hissing kettle. After calmly preparing two cups of tea and placing them on the table, he took a seat.

Maren remained standing so she would not feel more trapped in the chair than she felt on her feet. "I used some of it to buy wine and liquor from pirates, privateers as you call yourselves. We can't run this place without a supply, and they charge heavily because of the blockade. I recorded my expenses. I had to pay my hotel bill and buy some new clothes. They don't come cheap during these times either. After my father's death, I had nothing left except this place, and you know how much money I had with me when I left London. It was all in that little pouch you so generously didn't steal," she said sarcastically. "And since you recall my wardrobe, you know I couldn't wear those prim gowns in a gambling house. It made my customers nervous to see me dressed like a proper lady. I reminded them of their wives and daughters or of a church social. Don't worry, Mr. Morgan, you'll get every dollar coming to you. But there is one problem."

"What is that, Miss James?" he asked, barely controlling his mirth.

"I have no record of your earnings before my father's death. I didn't even know he had a partner until my return on June eighth. Whatever your arrangement with him was, I know nothing about it. Eric was the one who started putting my mysterious partner's share in a bank box, and he told me to continue to do so every week to prevent trouble or a takeover in case the half-owner of Lady Luck ever appeared. I've followed his advice. It's all there except for the expenditures, which are noted in your records. Now I would like to see the paper which confirms your claim to the partnership. And I advise you not to settle in here until I have a lawyer study your partnership agreement."

"I can give you the same advice, Miss James. I only have your word you're Cameron's daughter and heir," he teased merrily.

Maren frowned at him as he chuckled. "How do I know you didn't steal that deed from the rightful owner during one of your raids?"

"Because it has my signature on it, as well as your father's. You see, my lovely siren, we had the papers drawn up again after my father's death to make certain there was no misunderstanding. I'm sure you'll recognize your father's handwriting. You're fortunate I believe you're Cameron's daughter. Still, during the last two years he could have willed his share of the place to someone else to cover a debt. I have proof Lady Luck is half mine. Do you? And I wonder what the law would have to say about you . . . borrowing my earnings without permission.

It sounds a wee bit like fraud and theft, don't you think?''

Anger and alarm surged through Maren, and her golden brown eyes revealed it. ''How could I obtain your permission when I didn't even know who you were? And if I had known, what if you had been killed or captured at sea? What if you had never showed up to make your claim? Did you expect me to allow Lady Luck to go bankrupt or fall into disrepair while that money stayed nestled in the bank like a fragile egg?''

''How can I be sure you spent my money as you say? You might have lost it playing cards? And why should I trust you to run this place for us? You're a woman, Maren James, a very young one, inexperienced and a temptation to our patrons.''

''I'm a damned good card player, one of the best. Ask the patrons; I've lost very few games, only small ones. Not that it matters to you, Jared Morgan, but I'm using my winnings to repay you. Check the books since I took over. You'll see that I'm more than qualified to run Lady Luck. If you don't trust me or believe me, check with Dan Myers.''

''How do I know he wouldn't cover for you? He did move out to protect your name, and he came to your rescue on the street.''

''I'm not going to answer any more of your questions until you prove you have a right to ask them. Why did you keep your partnership a secret?''

''Cameron James and Benjamin Morgan were the original partners; we inherited their shares when they died. My father bought into this place to give me an inheritance. He knew my older brother would get Shady Rest, the family's plantation in Savannah, so he wanted to give me a business to fall back on when I had to quit the sea. I didn't know about this for a while; he wanted to make certain Lady Luck was successful before he told me about it. My ship, the *Sea Mist*, was purchased with earnings from this place, but over the years, things changed. My father remarried—he's dead now—and my brother Jeremy was hanged by the British after he was impressed. He refused to bend to the Royal Navy, so he was killed. A lawful execution, I think they called it."

Jared sipped the hot tea to wash down his bitterness. Maren remained silent and watchful. "My father didn't want anyone to know about his interest in Lady Luck, not until the business was prosperous and it was time to hand it over to me. He might have wanted to make sure I had settled down enough and had the brains to keep it going. Since you met me years ago, I don't need to tell you I was a wild and reckless youth. Nonetheless, my father willed his partnership to me and asked me to keep it as long as I could. So far, I've had enough money to live on without selling my share, and I've had no reason to disclose my partnership. Besides, as long as people here thought your father owned this place, it made him appear more prosperous, more of a man to trust with their business. And if anything happened to me, no one could approach your father about my debts."

A playful tone laced Jared's voice when he added,

"There was another reason to keep the partnership a secret: your protection. If you didn't know who to contact and couldn't sell without my signature, you would always have a source of income. That would prevent a greedy husband, or cousin, from selling this place and leaving you penniless and homeless. Admit it, Maren, if it were not for this secret, you wouldn't have Lady Luck today. I've heard that Eric sold Cameron James's holdings and took over the shipping firm. Why haven't you tried to recover your fortune?"

"Who told you such things? Are you spying on me?"

"Why, Miss James, it's common knowledge he's cheated you out of a fortune. Or I should say, cleverly beguiled you into giving up one."

"Then you must also know how and why he sold everything. It was done legally, and out of necessity. My father loved and trusted Eric; he gave my cousin the authority to manage his holdings. Eric wouldn't have sold anything of mine if he had known I was . . . That's all you need to know. I'll turn over your money and records tomorrow."

"And then we can discuss how you plan to repay your debt to me."

"Stop worrying about the blasted money. You'll get it back."

"I assume it's a great deal or you wouldn't be so upset about it. Have you asked Eric about that money and the earlier records?"

"How could I? I didn't know they were missing

189

until you told me. Besides, I only have your word that you haven't been paid since the war began. What did Papa say he would do with your earnings?''

''He said he would keep them in a safe place, in a special fund.''

Maren couldn't reveal that she knew anything about a "special fund" without letting Jared read her parents' letters, and she could not do that. When Eric returned, she would straighten out these dismaying matters with him, then deal with Jared. "I left here in June of 1812 and had no contact with my parents during my absence. When I returned, I went through their belongings, which were stored in Eric's warehouse, but I found no money or records among them. That's all I can tell you, Jared.''

Jared noticed how softly she had spoken his name, although she had done it unconsciously. He could tell something was troubling her, something she could not or would not share with him. "We can question your father's lawyer when you have him go over my deed. He might know something about this matter.''

''Papa's lawyer! Why didn't I think about that? It's just that things have been so hectic since my return. It was harder to visit their graves and go through their things than I had imagined. And trying to get settled in this place . . . Why am I telling you all of this? You can't live here, Jared. Please, it could hurt me and our business.''

''With Dan Myers gone, you and Mrs. Malone need a man here to protect you. People won't talk after we announce our partnership."

"You're going to tell everyone?"

"Why not? There's no need for secrecy anymore."

"But people will think you're running the place because you're a man. They'll give you all the credit for our success. I was doing fine before you showed up; I don't need such an intrusion. Go back to sea and leave me alone. You've been nothing but trouble since we met."

"Is that a fact, my tempting siren?"

"Don't start that again, Jared Morgan. I know why you came to New Orleans, and it wasn't to look up Maren Slade!"

"I swear you are one of my main reasons for being here, Maren."

Maren declared curtly, "Because you think you can trick me into turning Lady Luck over to you, that you can charm me into betraying Eric?"

"Why is it that Eric James always seems to be coming between us? I think he owes you about as much as you owe me. Why don't you sell me your half of Lady Luck and settle down?"

"Never!" she shouted at him. "It was a gift from my father, and it's all I have left. I don't want any man taking care of me as if I were one of his possessions. I like being on my own."

"How much do you owe me, Maren? Enough to permit me to legally take over Lady Luck, like Eric took over your firm and your plantation?"

"You're trying to scare me or to trap me into helping you, aren't you?"

"I'm only trying to force you to see the truth, Maren. You owe me a sizable amount."

"If you take Lady Luck, I won't have anything, Jared. Why are you doing this to me? You were my father's friend, his partner."

Jared recalled that she had admitted dreaming of him for years and he thought of how she had behaved since finding him again. He wished it hadn't been so long since he had seen Cameron because so much had changed. And he wished he had met Eric so he would have an idea of what the man was like. For that matter, he felt if he and Maren had met long ago matters wouldn't be so difficult to settle. He deliberated on how he wanted to use the edge he had over her because of the debt. Maren had lost her fiancé and her parents, and most of her inheritance. She was afraid, by her own admission, to trust him. He had confused and angered her. To win her, he had to be sly and firm, to play the devilish rake. He had not meant to handle things this way, but doing so could be helpful to both of them. Yes, there was only one course to sail. . . .

"You can have the ruby necklace, the one I hid from you on the ship," Maren offered. "I'll sign a paper stating how much more I owe you, and if I can't repay you within a year, I'll sell you my half of this place. Is it a deal?"

"No," Jared replied. He watched her become pale.

"No?" she echoed hoarsely. "Then, what do you want from me?"

"It isn't what I want from you, Maren. What I want

is you."

A sharp inhalation left her dry lips. "You can't be serious. I know I behaved wickedly on the ship and the beach, but I'm not a harlot. It may sound stupid, but I had reality and fantasy all mixed up. If any other raider had attacked our ship, I would never have acted that way. Believe what you will, but that's the truth."

Jared realized that she had misunderstood him. She thought his only interest in her was physical; that was not true. Oh, he wanted her badly, but he had to make certain she wanted to belong to him in all ways before he possessed her. His father had told him over and over that sex did not prove love, only desire. She was embarrassed by her past behavior, and he didn't want her to be uncomfortable about their special attraction. He had to make her aware of how much, and of how seriously, he craved her. "I believe you, Maren, and I'm glad those girlhood dreams caused you to respond to me. Otherwise, I wouldn't have chased you. I'll give you six months to repay me. If not, I get you. Everything about you, Miss James, including all you are and know."

Maren began breathlessly, "If you think I'll become your mistress to repay a de—"

Jared interrupted. "My wife, Maren. You repay me or you marry me. That's the only deal I'll accept. While I'm at sea, you had best keep that wedding dress locked in a trunk. If you wear it to wed someone else, I'll see that you're put in jail for theft. Shall we say you'll repay your debt to me one way or another on January first?"

Maren was stunned. He had vowed she could not escape him. Was this just a clever way to entrap her? And why marriage? Was his offer real or a disarming trick? "This is madness, Jared."

"Not to me. It would settle all of my problems."

"What about my problems?" she asked, utterly confused.

"It should settle them, too. You'll be getting all you need and want. Blame yourself, Maren; you're the one who enticed me with promises of becoming my willing captive, and you rashly indebted yourself to me. January first, Maren, one way or another," he said, grinning. "That is, unless one of us dies. In that case, Lady Luck goes to the survivor. If you're lucky, I might not return from this war."

Maren wondered what was going on with Jared Morgan. Her mother had told her about men's desires, urges, and unsated frustrations, and she had mentioned the games men played with members of the opposite sex, men's fears of losing their freedom. Maren had been advised to chase her heart's desire until he surrendered, believing he had ensnared her. But things were topsy-turvy with Jared Morgan. She, the cunning woman, was supposed to subtly pursue him, the elusive and intimidated man; she was supposed to flirt, entice, and beguile—to fight to attain her heart's desire. But Jared was doing the pursuing and capturing! Maren wasn't sure how to deal with this upside-down situation. If he wanted to marry her, why didn't he just ask her? Why did he play this elaborate game? Was it only a ruse to beguile her?

"What about your suspicions of Eric? If you really work for the President, why are you trusting me with such a dangerous secret? How do you know I won't expose you to Eric or someone else?"

Jared knew he had made her think his pursuit of Eric was more important to him than she was. He had given her reason to be wary and suspicious. "It's the only way I can earn your trust and help. You said you weren't at war with your English family and friends, but America is—I am. You said you couldn't take a stand against them. What if you have to do that someday, Maren? If someone asked you to aid the Brits, would you? If someone asked you to defend America against them, would you? Don't answer now, just think over those questions. Maybe you haven't been forced to make such a difficult decision yet. But what if Eric has? And what if he's involved you without your knowledge? How would that appear to American authorities? After all, you have English roots, your fiancé was an Englishman slain by Americans, and your parental ties to America are gone. If you are my wife, I can protect you."

Maren mulled over the points he'd made. What if Eric was a British spy and Jared was an American agent? Did Jared distrust her? She really did not want to discuss such crucial matters at that time, so she asked, "What about the ruby necklace as payment?"

"Keep it for an emergency, or as a stake if you decide to elude me. Believe me, Maren, there are worse fates than marrying me."

"Such as?"

"Marrying a Brit like the one who hung my brother Jeremy," he replied unwittingly. "What happened to your Englishman? Who was he?"

Maren caught Jared's bitterness over his brother's grim fate. Yet her grandparents and her father were British; she was partly British. Did he bear resentment toward her? "Are you sure you want to hear about my colorful past?"

He hated being jealous of a dead man, but he was. "Eventually you'll have to tell me about it."

"If you insist . . . His name was Daniel Redford, Lord Redford's son and heir. We were to be married in September of 1812, but he went to sea before my arrival. You men seem to think war is so much fun that you embrace it eagerly. Soon after the fighting began, his ship, the *Merry Maiden,* was attacked by an American privateer and everyone aboard was killed. Is that sufficient for now, sir?"

"Did you love Daniel Redford?"

Maren wondered if the truth had been noticeable in her eyes and her voice, but she did not want to vow or disavow love for her deceased fiancé. "Does it matter to you now? He's dead, his body is lost somewhere in the sea."

"Do you still love him?" Jared altered his question slightly, for he was the privateer who had sunk the *Merry Maiden*.

Reflecting on and talking about Daniel had changed Maren's mood. She was now thinking of death, of the deviousness of men, of her many losses, of lies and broken dreams, of silly mistakes. "I think I'll get dressed now. Make yourself at home, but since Mary is out for the day, you'll have to eat elsewhere or prepare your own meals. I have a previous engagement." She headed for the kitchen door.

"What about our deal, Maren?"

She halted and looked at him. "Will you put our deal in writing, just in case some British privateer prevents you from returning to collect? I wouldn't want you willing your share to another conquest."

"We'll handle everything tomorrow."

"Tomorrow is July fourth. Some people make a holiday of it. What about Tuesday?"

"That's fine. I'll see you tonight. Oh, how about having dinner with me at the hotel? We have to eat, so why not dine together?"

"I have other plans for today and tonight, but thank you."

Jared spent the afternoon searching Maren's rooms for clues. He found the letters from her parents, and after reading them, he could understand why Maren was protecting Eric James: their past friendship, their kinship, her parents' feelings about Eric, and her cousin's alleged patriotism. She undoubtedly felt he was risking death for treason or espionage. The letters had mentioned Cameron James's intention to make Eric a partner in James Shipping. They had spoken of Eric's secret work for

America, and they had mentioned a "special fund," which meant Maren had already known of it. He hated to realize how easily and frequently she had deceived him. He had to teach her to trust him.

Jared knew something which Maren did not; there was a hidden compartment behind the bookcase by her bedroom fireplace. He went over the papers hidden there, and learned some grim facts. Cameron had given Eric legal authority to handle his business, but he had been about to revoke it. There was a letter there for Jared, a shocking one. It began, "If you find this letter, please take care of my daughter Maren for me. Protect her from her cousin Eric James. How could I have been so wrong about him? He's evil, Jared, evil and sly. I'll tell you what he's done and what he's planning to do. . . ."

He left the papers with the "special fund" he had found in the secret compartment. After reading about Eric's deception and hearing about how he had begun to act shortly before the Jameses' deaths, he suspected that Eric had had something to do with their sudden demises. Of course, he couldn't reveal such dark suspicions to Maren; they would put her in danger and would break her heart. Aware of how dangerous Eric could be, especially to Maren, Jared must wait for the proper moment to use this grim evidence. Maren was vulnerable, and he wanted to protect her. He decided to see Dan Myers to gather more facts. He realized that he must let Maren discover this terrible truth on her own; if he forced it on

her, she would resist him. But he would guide her to
it, and he would defend, comfort, and love her.

Maren walked around in the sitting room of the
old James townhouse, the one Eric now "rented."
She had arrived there just as Marc was returning
home, so he could not avoid her. She informed her
younger cousin that she had discovered who her
partner was and that the man had moved into Lady
Luck. She knew if Eric kept to his schedule he should
return to New Orleans around the end of the
month or the beginning of the next one, and the
impending confrontation between Jared and Eric
worried her. It would reveal the truth.

Jared had told her that he would resist her until he
decided whether she was as important to him as his
country, yet he was yielding to her. Did that mean he
had decided she was vital to his happiness, or was he
tricking her because he had realized she was not
important to him? Jared had confided so many
things to her, secrets she found hard to believe: tales
of treachery and treason. She had to think.

"Do you mind if I stay here today, Marc? Mary isn't
home and I don't want to be alone with that man."

"I guess it's all right."

"I'm sure Eric wouldn't mind. I loved this place,"
she murmured, glancing around the room. "Eric's
kept it much the same. I'm glad he was able to rent it.
He lived here while working for my father, didn't

he?" she asked casually.

"Yes. Why didn't you move in here with us?"

Maren replied deviously, "I wanted to live at Lady Luck and take care of myself. How long have you been living with Eric?"

"He brought me here after your parents died. Murray didn't want me around, so Eric takes care of me."

That told Maren why Marc was obedient to his brother, gratitude and the fact that Marc was afraid of Eric James. "That's nice of him. Do you have any plans for tomorrow? Would you like to visit me?"

"That man, your partner, is he the one who came to the office and asked me all those questions?"

Maren decided to learn whether Eric had recognized Jared as Captain Hawk during the raid on the *Martha J* and had mentioned it to Marc. "Worse, Marc, he's the awful pirate who attacked us at sea. Eric will be furious when he gets home and finds that beast living at Lady Luck. I tried to persuade Mr. Morgan to sell his half to me, but he refused. Imagine, me in business with the notorious Captain Hawk!"

"I don't like him. Eric won't like him either. I'd better stay away from him or Eric will be mad. He doesn't like people nosing around here."

Maren did not want to argue the point with the sulky youth. She had other things on her mind. In fact, she intended to spend the night here and avoid Jared until her head cleared. It might do that cocky rogue good to suspect she was with another man.

"You relax, Marc, while I prepare us a nice dinner. We'll talk and play cards afterward."

By midnight, Jared was worried about Maren. There were many lowlifes abroad in New Orleans, and he had upset Maren. She might not be thinking clearly. He tried to imagine where she had been all day. Mary Malone had returned after four, and he had had a long talk with her. He liked Mary, and she appeared to like him. She had cooked him a delicious meal, and they had eaten together. However, when he had questioned her about Maren's absence, the woman had known nothing and had been just as worried as he was.

A knock drew his attention, and going to the door of his suite, he found Mary standing before it. "She isn't home yet, Mr. Morgan. She must be in trouble."

"Can you think of any place where she would go to be away from me?"

"To be away from you? Whatever for?" the woman inquired.

"I gave her a good start today. I may as well confess that I've been pursuing her for a long time and I've asked her to marry me. I think she wants to say yes, but this mystery partner stuff has her annoyed and baffled. She's probably off somewhere pouting."

Mary was pleased by that news because she had been impressed by Jared Morgan. She replied honestly, "I hope she says yes, but she is a headstrong, independent girl. What about her cousin's place? She could be there. He lives in Mr. Cameron's old townhouse."

Jared recalled the address, and hurried over there. When he peeked through the sitting room window, he saw Maren and Marc at a game table. He knocked on the door until Marc responded, looking frightened. "Tell Maren I'm here to take her home."

Maren suddenly appeared behind her cousin and asked, "What are you doing here, Mr. Morgan? How dare you follow me about and give me orders! I'm staying here tonight."

"No, you are not. Remember that precious reputation you have to guard? When people see you returning home in the morning, how are they to know you stayed the night with your cousin? Your behavior is rash and childish. Mary is worried sick about you."

Maren conceded on this point. "I should have left her a note. We were having such fun that I lost track of time. When I saw how late it was, I decided to stay the night. How did you find me?"

"Mary suggested I check here before scouring the city for you. Fetch your things and let's return before she becomes more frantic."

Maren didn't argue further. She retrieved her shawl and reticule, and joined the tawny-eyed man at the door. "Good night, Marc. I'm sorry to leave in the midst of our game. I'll see you on another day."

Marc did not respond; he just kept staring at Jared Morgan.

When Jared mounted his borrowed horse and

reached for Maren, she tried to back away, but he seized her arms and lifted her up before him. She protested, and he ordered, "Be quiet, woman. You've caused me enough discomfort tonight. It's late, so no one will notice us."

To prevent the clattering of hooves, Jared walked the animal back toward Lady Luck. "Next time you pull something like this, you'd best let us know where you'll be. And don't try to provoke me. These bayous are filled with pirates and smugglers who would love to get their hands on a treasure like you. I won't tolerate such recklessness. You'll do as you're told or our deal is off."

"Just what am I being told not to do, Mr. Morgan?"

"Since you've agreed to my terms, you're promised to me if you fail to repay your debt. That means you may not see other men or try to irritate me at every turn."

"I wasn't seeing another man. Marc is my first cousin."

"But you wanted me to think otherwise, didn't you?"

"Why would I do that?" Maren asked, lowering her lashes.

Jared reined in the horse. Grasping her chin, he raised it, and his gaze bored into hers. "Either to make me jealous or to punish me."

"Don't be silly," she chided, trying to free her chin.

"Do not toy with me, Maren," he warned, then his mouth closed over hers. The kiss was swift, to the point, staggering.

"Toy with you, Jared?" she scoffed, though dazed by the kiss. She wanted nothing more than to rush home and get into bed with him, but she could not. Even if he were being honest, he had to be taught how to treat her properly and fairly. She must not allow him to take her for granted, to think only of his wishes. Her mother had told her that a man had to learn how to treat a woman, that he must not be allowed to get away with even a minor offense. Yet, this training had to be done carefully and gently and slyly. "Why did you wait four days to reveal our partnership? And why are you making these crazy demands?"

He ran his tongue over his lips for another taste of her. "I wanted to look things over, to see how you were handling the place, and yourself."

"And?" she prompted. "Were you satisfied or disappointed?"

"Both."

"Would you mind explaining that answer?"

"You're doing great with the place, and business is wonderful."

"And?" she said impatiently. "You only covered satisfied."

"Well, on the other hand, I seem to be out of a lot of earnings. We both know you can't possibly repay so much money, no matter how you scrimp or how many games you win. If I take over to cover what's due me, Cameron James's daughter will be out in the cold. I can't do that to the offspring of my old friend and partner, so I will lose the money but I will gain a wife."

"Leave my father out of this. And don't feel sorry for me. I can take care of myself. I may surprise you by coming up with the money. If I can't, I'll marry you before I'll give up Lady Luck."

"That sounds like the perfect compromise. Think about it, Maren. You're twenty and single. I'm twenty-nine and single. Most people are married at our ages. You love Lady Luck, and I need someone to manage my half while I'm at sea. We both need a home, money, and respectability. And it doesn't hurt that we're attracted to each other, just in case we might want children some day."

Maren stared into his eyes and murmured sultrily, "When you add up the facts, Mr. Morgan, it does sound like a perfect arrangement. But I wonder . . . perhaps I could find a better one with someone else."

As they covered the remaining distance, he ordered, "Just make certain you don't seek one out until your debt to me is settled."

After Jared eased her feet to the ground, Maren inquired saucily, "Does that stipulation also apply to you when you are in ports, Captain Hawk?"

Jared dismounted and grinned. Before heading for the stable, he reasoned in a playful tone, "Why should it? I'm not the one in trouble."

"Until January first, I'm not either," Maren informed him; then she went inside while he tended to the horse. After making a quick explanation to Mary, she hurried to her room.

On Monday morning Maren asked Mary Malone to send Dan Myers to her room. She told Mary she would talk with her later over tea, but first there were some matters she had to settle with her manager.

Maren hated to put Dan on the spot by asking him whether Jared Morgan had talked privately with him since his arrival, so she did not. She hoped Dan would be loyal enough to tell her anything so crucial. After explaining that Jared Morgan was her previously silent partner, but that he was planning to make public his half-ownership this week, she told Dan about the missing money that Jared had claimed was due him even before the war had begun.

"I told him I wasn't responsible for his understanding with Papa, but I have to find a way to pay him everything he's got coming since Papa died. If he discovers Eric's theft, there's no telling what he'll try to pull."

"Jared Morgan isn't a devious or cruel man, Miss Maren."

"That's what you think, Dan. He's asked me to marry him. Or, I should say he demanded it. He ordered me to repay him by January first or to marry him. I'm not sure which prospect is worse."

Dan looked shocked and dismayed. "Why would Jared Morgan try to force you to marry him?"

"He says it's because we're partners, we're too old

to be single, and we both need homes and respectability. He made it sound like a business deal instead of a marriage. He's so arrogant and bossy! I have to repay him, Dan, so I won't be indebted to him."

Myers remarked, "From what I observed the other night, you two were attracted to each other."

"I don't have to marry a man just because I'm attracted to him. You don't marry every woman who catches your eye. But this isn't a simple matter. To be honest, Dan, I don't really know what I want to do. Can I ask you a question?"

"Certainly."

"Did you know about Jared's claim on Lady Luck before he arrived last Thursday?"

"If I had known who your partner was, I would have told you."

"Have you talked to him privately since he came here?"

Dan answered her truthfully. "Yesterday. If you want to fire me, you can, but I told him the truth about the missing money."

"Why, Dan?" she asked sadly. "He hates Eric."

Dan thought it wise to say, "Because I didn't want him blaming you for taking it. Plenty of people suspect that Eric James stole you blind, and Jared claims he only wants to help you."

Yes, Maren scoffed silently, *help me right into his bed!* "You might trust him, Dan, but I don't. There are some things I must learn about the infamous Captain Hawk. For one, what did he say when you told him about Eric taking his share of the money? For another, is he going to send him to jail?"

"He promised not to do anything about your cousin or the missing money until you agree to proceed based on the evidence."

"It is more likely he won't make any move until he gets Eric trapped like I am. What kind of man blackmails a woman into marrying him?"

"You can always repay him or reject his proposal and marry someone else," Dan suggested, observing Cameron's daughter closely.

"You call those choices, Dan?" she murmured dejectedly. "If only he weren't so damned cocky and secretive! I don't even know if this so-called deal is a genuine offer."

Outside the door, Jared suppressed a chuckle. But when he heard someone heading for the stairs, he hurried to his room.

Maren looked at Dan and said, "You're right about one thing; I do want to marry Jared Morgan. I have wanted to since I was fifteen. But if you tell him, I swear I'll break your neck before I fire you and vanish!"

The manager hated to imagine how such a marriage would alter his life, yet he could not speak against it and remain here. He wondered how Eric James was going to take this news. Dan was wary of Jared Morgan because of his sudden arrival during wartime, his pursuit of Maren James, his revelation of half-ownership in Lady Luck, and his interest in Eric James. Dan knew he needed to think over these matters, and he had to think carefully.

Chapter Eight

Maren did not know where Jared had vanished to that morning, but she had not seen him. She had just decided that he might have gone to his ship, when a note from Lilibeth Payne was delivered.

Maren was already wearing a lovely promenade gown of sky-blue muslin, so she put on a straw bonnet trimmed with ribbons and flowers, took her parasol and string bag, and left Lady Luck. All she told Mary Malone was that she would return before nightfall.

July fourth celebrators were in a festive mood, and Maren James quickly cast her worries aside. As she went to meet her best friend for lunch, the poised, young brunette smiled and nodded at everyone she met.

When she was seated at the restaurant, Maren said, "I'm so glad you're here, Beth. How are your parents, and how is everyone at Payne's Point?"

Her blond friend laughed merrily. "Everyone is fine. Papa came to town to amuse himself, and I persuaded him to let me come along to visit with friends and have a little fun. But you know Mama; she despises the heat and the insects so she remained at home."

Beth's Southern accent became more pronounced as she asserted, "I do declare, Maren, life will leave Mama behind for she only sits around sewing and reading. I've heard Papa tell her she's as boring as a faded strap on a cotton bale. It's true, Maren; she's like an old sow. If I were Papa, I would stick a cocklebur in her drawers and liven her up. If Mama isn't careful, Papa's going to become too entangled with one of those fancy little piglets he sneaks off to see. Can you imagine the proper Mr. Payne having several tarts?" Beth giggled, but Maren tried to keep a straight face.

"There's so little to do at home," Beth wailed. "I wish we lived in New Orleans, or Baton Rouge. There's always so much going on here, so much to do and see; and I sorely need distractions while Bart's away. I'm going mad at home, but I plan to have lots of fun today. I hope you'll join me," she coaxed. "It seems to me that these celebrations get larger each year, especially since this nasty war began."

"It's probably a show of defiance," Maren suggested. Then, in order to let Beth ramble on while she collected her thoughts, she asked, "Have you heard from Bart since we talked?"

Beth's green eyes glowed with love before they were

210

dulled by worry. "No, and he couldn't be much farther away; he's in Maine. He told me not to fret, but he said there's heavy fighting there. Men," she scoffed in annoyance. "They act like little boys playing a game. But war isn't a game, Maren; it's lethal. I do wish he would return soon so I can see for myself that he's all right. Sometimes I think about going after him and dragging him home by the ears," she whispered.

Maren smiled at the petite girl with the fair skin. "I don't blame you, but it would be very reckless. You might be captured and used against him. I'm afraid that women always get left behind."

"I know, but it isn't fair. I'd bet you and I could fight as well as most of the men on the front lines. And I would be with Bart. I do miss him so, Maren. I shall wither and die if anything happens to him."

"He'll be careful, Beth. He has you waiting for him."

"But I am dampening our festive mood," she scolded herself. "I promise to be cheerful the rest of the day."

As they dined, they talked about old friends, past occasions, and their plans for the day. Slowly they consumed a crisp salad, steaming shrimp creole, hot bread, and a dry white wine. Later as they sipped dark coffee with a heady aroma and savored rich slices of cake, their conversation shifted to the future.

"Now that you're back, will you stand with me at my wedding?" Beth asked eagerly.

"You know I will," Maren replied quickly. "It will

be wonderful. I'm so glad you snared Bart. I know you'll be happy."

"Have you met anyone to spend time with, someone special?"

Maren had been waiting for this moment. "Do you remember when we talked about my secret partner?" she asked, and Beth nodded, fully anticipating Maren's next words. "He appeared last Thursday and made his claim. Yesterday, he moved into Lady Luck without even telling me first. He took over Dan's old suite. Oh, I didn't tell you; Dan moved out last Sunday. He feared there'd be gossip about us living there together, and that would hurt me and the business."

"Well? Are you going to keep me in suspense? Tell me who he is."

Maren did not laugh with the bright-eyed Beth. "Would you believe it's Jared Morgan, alias Captain Hawk?"

Beth's mouth flew open, and she gaped at Maren. "You're jesting!"

When Maren shook her dark head, Beth clamped a hand over her mouth and tried to suppress her giggles.

"What's so amusing, Lilibeth Payne?"

"For years you've wondered where he is and if you'd ever see him again. Now he's suddenly thrust into your life. First he attacks your ship and then he strolled into your home and moves in with you. It's perfect, Maren. You have him right where you want him, right where you can work on him. How romantic and tantalizing. Whatever did you say when he appeared? And what did he say when he realized his partner was a victim of his last raid?"

"This might be funny to you, Beth, but it's very serious to me," Maren declared. She told her friend about the money she owed Jared and described his proposition.

"You mean he actually said you must marry him or go to jail?"

"That's his proposition. I must repay him by the first of the year. Heavens, Beth, that's less than six months away, and I owe him a lot of money. I thought he was just joking at first, trying to get . . ."

"To get you into bed with him?" Beth teased after her friend fell silent. "What's wrong with that, Maren? You've craved him for years."

"Lilibeth Payne," Maren whispered sternly, "that's wicked."

"How so? You love him, and he's asked you to marry him. I've made love to Bart several times," the blond young woman confessed shamelessly. "It's the most natural and wonderful thing in the world to share yourself with the one you love. Don't be a coward; that isn't like Maren James."

"Your situation is very different from mine. You and Bart know all about each other; you've spent so much time together. I'm just learning about Jared Morgan. But sometimes I forget he's practically a stranger to me. When we're together, it seems we've always known each other, and I end up acting foolish and bold, like a flirt or a tart."

"Obviously he doesn't mind; he's determined to win you. Why not let him? At least give him a chance to woo you properly. Mercy, girl, you've got him snared, so why cut him free?"

"But how will it look with us living in the same house?"

"You can't spend your life worrying about what other people think. Mercy, Maren, are you going to risk losing him when you've just found him? Don't reject him without ever giving this romance a chance to bloom."

"That's good advice, Beth, but following it can be dangerous."

"What do you mean, dangerous?"

Maren worried over how much she should confide to her best friend. After all, they had been separated for two years, even if neither of them seemed to have changed much. "He's a privateer, almost a pirate, Beth, and I don't know what else. How would you feel about being blackmailed into marrying an arrogant, domineering rogue?"

Beth sighed. "You're right, Maren. He could be dangerous, and he could be after more than your hand in wedlock."

"Yes, like my share of Lady Luck. He's already tried to purchase it, but I refused to sell. And he was here for days before he dropped the stunning news that he is my partner. He claimed he was checking things out before enlightening me. There's something about Jared Morgan that I can't put my finger on. He questions me all the time, as if I were a criminal. He seems very suspicious of my British roots and of my sudden return home. Like you, he hates Eric and wants to know everything about him. He's admitted that he's hanging around to study my cousin. And would you believe, he and his father were friendly with Papa? He claims that's why he wants to marry me, to take care of Cameron James's daughter."

"Criminal . . . a spy, a traitor, a thief, or what?"

"All of them. He's ordered me to prove that I'm innocent of any wrongdoing or to become his slave. What shall I do, Beth?"

"First of all," she said seriously, "don't tell anyone what you've just told me, particularly Eric James. Second, I would prove myself to Jared Morgan. You must admit, Maren, your recent adventures would sound a mite curious, especially to a certain Captain Hawk. I think the best course to pursue is the one you've already decided on, to learn more about him. Get close to him. Let him get close to you. It's surprising how much you can learn from a man when his head's next to yours on a pillow."

"What if I discover he's all wrong for me, even dangerous?"

"Do you honestly believe either of those possibilities could be true?"

"I guess not, but I'm so afraid I'll fall prey to temptation."

"From where I'm sitting, Miss Maren James, that's already happened," Beth declared. "Jared has dropped his apple at your feet; you've picked it up and studied it. Now, decide on whether you want to bite it or not."

"Wanting to bite it isn't the problem. What happens afterward is."

Following their lengthy lunch, Maren and Beth strolled about, observing the holiday activities and enjoying the beauty of New Orleans. They halted here and there to peer into shop windows; and they chatted as they walked. After a while they stopped to have tea and cookies at a sidewalk café which was surrounded by numerous flower boxes. Refreshed, they then strolled on. New Orleans was a city which enlivened the senses with its unique blend of sights, sounds, smells, and people; and both women were delighted to be part of it.

It was after five o'clock, and they stood watching dancers in the street, when Beth reminded Maren that she had to be back at the hotel by six, "Papa said things could get wild on the streets tonight, so I promised I would have dinner at the hotel with the Bleakers and would stay in tonight. I wish I could sneak into Lady Luck with you, but Papa might be there or someone might tell on me. Until I get away from home, I have to obey him, at least as far as he knows."

"Good evening, ladies." The skin-tingling voice came from behind them.

Both women turned and gazed at a handsome face, tawny eyes, and a stirring smile. Jared's unexpected nearness made Maren quiver, and her smoldering heart melted.

"I thought you might enjoy a fresh one, Maren," he remarked, holding out a lovely nosegay as he had done years ago in this same city. "If you like, we can escort your friend to her hotel; then I can walk you home. It's getting a bit rowdy on the streets for ladies to be alone."

Beth smiled. "I take it you're Captain Jared Morgan. I'm Lilibeth Payne, Maren's best friend."

A broad grin captured Jared's lips and eyes. Executing a half bow, he told her, "It's a pleasure to meet you, Miss Payne."

"Beth, please," she corrected genially.

"Only if you call me Jared," he replied, impressed with the blond Lilibeth.

She, too, was impressed, and she understood why Maren was so smitten by this attractive man. No. He was more than a man; he was a male animal and it showed in his gaze and stance. Hoping to help her friend discover more about Jared through observation, she remarked, "Maren tells me you're her partner in Lady Luck. Is it too presumptuous to ask whether you plan to remain here to help her run the business or you intend to go back to sea?"

"I intend to do both, depending on Maren's needs," he replied rather boldly. "My crew is taking a much-needed rest while my ship is being repaired and resupplied. While I'm here, perhaps you would join Maren and me for dinner one night." He glanced at Maren.

She immediately said, "That sounds wonderful to me. Would it be possible for you on this trip, Beth?"

217

Lilibeth's disappointment was evident. "I'm afraid Papa insisted we return home the first thing in the morning. But I'll be coming back in two weeks to stay for several days. I'll send word ahead so we can make plans. I'll be getting some things I'll need for my wedding when Bart returns."

Maren turned to Jared. "When the war began, Beth's fiancé was attacked by a severe case of patriotism, and to soothe his ailment, he sailed away to fight the British. As with so many eager patriots, he left before their wedding, so when he returns he and Beth plan to be married. Perhaps you've met him, Barton Hughes?"

"I'm pleased to say I have met Bart. I've done business with him. I don't know who is luckier, Beth, or Bart. This appears to be a very good match. I'm certain you both will be very happy."

Maren added, "Bart is fighting near Maine, but he manages to get messages to Beth every so often. You know how it is, Jared, some people will do anything to earn money during a war."

Jared chuckled. "Including buying a wife," he jested. "Did Maren tell you I proposed to her yesterday?"

"Proposed? Is that what you call it?" Maren protested.

Jared winked at Beth. "I know she wants to say yes, but she's stubborn and proud. I think she's more afraid of giving up her freedom than I am. Maybe you can talk some sense into her."

"Me? Surely you jest, Cap— Jared. I've never been

able to control this wild seed, especially where that blasted Er— Whoops!"

Maren frowned at Beth, who shrugged her shoulders and made a wry face. "I think you'll be late for dinner if we don't hurry, Miss Payne," she said in a frosty tone.

"You're right, dear friend. I'll take one strong arm and you take the other," Beth suggested, then slipped an arm through Jared's.

Jared smiled at the petite woman to his right and then cocked an elbow toward Maren. She sighed resignedly as she laced her arm through his. Then the three of them walked jauntily down the street, Jared and Beth chattering away like old friends.

At the hotel, Maren asked Jared to wait outside while she went in with Beth to speak with the Bleakers. Assuming Maren wanted to have a few private words with her friend, he did as she asked. He hoped Lilibeth liked him and spoke in his favor, and he wondered if he could sneak back later to ask Beth why she detested Eric James.

Inside, Maren was scolding Beth, "You shouldn't have mentioned Eric to him. Jared hates him. He blames Eric for all of our problems."

"Then perhaps you should listen to your fiancé."

"Jared isn't my fiancé."

"Oh, but he is, dear friend. Why not be happy about it? He's the best thing I've seen besides Bart. Go after him, Maren," she coaxed.

"Are you sure to have to leave in the morning? Couldn't you persuade your father to let you stay

219

with me for a few days? I desperately need a friendly ear."

"Papa let me stay at Lady Luck?" Beth laughed.

"Perhaps in two million years," Maren added, and they both laughed.

"Papa's probably afraid I'd see him there with one of his sugar-teats. Maybe I should tell him I know all about his fooling around so he'll stop pretending with me and dashing my plans to protect his secrets. When I come back in two weeks, I'll find some way to sneak a night or two with you. I won't show my face downstairs, but I'd love to get a glimpse of the action. It must be exciting."

After Maren told her she could observe from behind a drapery, Beth asked in a whisper, "Do men really take women to private rooms upstairs to play around for a few hours?"

"We don't allow any prostitutes there, but a man sometimes brings his sweetheart or mistress for a rendezvous. As to what goes on while they have the room rented, we can only guess."

"I'll bet Papa used to rent one of those rooms regularly. But, he might be leery of playing around at Lady Luck since you took over. Do you know any of the men who use the rooms?"

"Even if I did, Miss Nosy, I couldn't tell you or anyone."

"Just imagine, hours alone with your true love . . . If Bart were home, I'd let him rent one all night. Maybe for two nights straight."

"Lilibeth Payne, whatever am I going to do with you?"

"Let me stand with you when you marry Jared Morgan on January first. Darn it, Maren, if this war continues, you'll have married your second fiancé before my first one returns. If I could get a letter to Bart, I'd warn him to get home before I find me another man—such as Jared Morgan if you foolishly reject him."

When Maren returned to Jared's side, she was grinning playfully. He questioned her behavior, but she refused to explain it. "I'm starving, partner. Let's hurry back so we can eat before we open. From the look of things, it's going to be hectic tonight. I hope so; I owe a big debt to some persistent rogue."

"Agree to marry me and you won't have to worry about repaying it."

Maren glanced at him and smiled provocatively. "It's certainly a mighty tempting offer, Mr. Morgan. I will promise you one thing; I'll give you an answer before you sail. That way, if I say yes, you won't be searching for a wife in every port you visit."

"You're tempting me to sail at this very moment just to get your answer."

"Please don't. I need a little more time to decide. And if I were to say yes, would you remember you have a fiancée waiting for you no matter where you sailed or how long you're gone?" she probed coquettishly.

"Would it make you happy to know I haven't been

out with another woman since I met you?"

"You're a clever rake, Captain Hawk, but I won't fall for that ruse. How could you see another woman at sea? Do you normally carry women aboard your ship?"

Jared halted their progress and faced her. "Let me put it another way, my fetching siren; I haven't wanted to see another woman since I met you, nor have I thought about one."

"You flatter me, sir," she murmured in a heavy Southern drawl.

Grinning, he replied, "No flattery intended, ma'am. I'm afraid I've met an all-consuming vixen who doesn't know when she's licked."

Maren suggestively licked her lips; then she fluttered her lashes mischievously. "Oh, sir, but I do. And I must confess that I find it most intriguing . . . and stimulating."

"Maren James, have you been drinking in the middle of the day?"

Again she affected a heavy Southern accent. "Little ol' me, Captain Hawk? Why shame on you for thinking such wicked thoughts about me." When Jared eyed her humorously, she grinned and explained, "I just feel particularly good today. I needed to spend time with a friend, and Beth is my best friend. I guess I've been a little lonely since I returned, sort of feeling sorry for myself. But if you dare tell that to Mary and Dan, I'll deny every word I've said."

"It's only natural for you to feel low, Maren,

considering all you've faced since your return," he said tenderly.

Maren's gaze lingered on his, and she responded to his gentleness. "You constantly amaze me, Jared Morgan. Thank you."

Jared was not embarrassed in the least by his show of emotion, and realizing that, he knew how deeply Maren had affected him. Since he could be this open and relaxed with her, his feelings for her were special. That discovery pleased him. He smiled. "I should be the one to thank you, Maren, for entering my life at the perfect moment."

They seemed totally absorbed in each other until a carriage clattered by and startled them. They laughed and then continued their walk homeward. Fragrant flowers bloomed all around them as the hot sun lowered, allowing the heat of the day to cool. The sky was changing from intense blue to tranquil gray, and not a cloud was to be seen. As dusk approached, the trees became a darker green and the shadows became longer and longer. Despite the festive occasion, most people were dining at this hour, so the streets were quiet. It was a pleasant time of day, calm and relaxing.

"I liked Beth."

Jared's words broke into Maren's dreamy state. "We've been best friends since childhood. She's a very special person. We can tell each other anything, everything. I just hope Bart makes it through this damnable war alive. It would crush her to lose him."

"Like it crushed you to lose Daniel Redford?" he

asked, before he could stop himself. "I'm sorry; I shouldn't have said that."

Maren looked directly at him. "Before me, have you ever loved anyone? Not desired, but truly loved her?"

Jared feared the point she was about to make, but he answered honestly, "No, Maren, I haven't."

"Neither have I, Jared," she confessed, then left him standing on the front steps of Lady Luck.

It was thirty minutes before closing time when the trouble struck. Maren and Jared had eaten a quick meal in the kitchen with Mary, then they'd gone their separate ways to bathe and dress for the evening. After mingling with the patrons, Jared had joined one table of card players and Maren had joined another. A party mood filled the rooms that night, and the pirated wine and champagne flowed steadily. When Mary Malone carried some refreshments to the stablemen, a scowling man sneaked through the back door. Suddenly a jeering voice came from behind Maren. "You cheating anybody tonight, my fancy tart? You boys watch her good 'cause she's got quick and sneaky hands. She uses that pretty face and lovely mouth to distract you while she cheats you," he accused, trailing his sweaty fingers over Maren's cheek and lips.

Maren rose and faced the troublemaker, staring at him coldly. "You were forbidden to come here again, sir. Get out."

The room had fallen silent the moment the supposedly drunken man had spoken his first insulting words. But his speech wasn't slurred, and he was steady-handed. When the instantaneous silence alerted Jared to a problem, he quickly excused himself and hurried to Maren's side.

By this time, the offensive man was saying, "We didn't have any cheating or trouble when Dan Myers was running this place. Why don't you take your fancy gowns and cheap ways and leave us men in peace? This ain't no place for the likes of you. Cheating gets people killed."

Maren grasped Jared's hand and squeezed it to signal him to remain silent. "You are mistaken, sir," she declared. "We didn't have any trouble until you showed up, and we only have it when you do show up. If you cannot accept my ownership, then I suggest you find another gambling establishment to frequent. I, for one, do not like your manner or your presence. Everyone was having a wonderful time until you spoiled the fun. It's awfully strange that you're the only sore loser I've played against. Ned, Harry, show this . . . gentleman out."

"You little bitch, you'll be sorry for cheating me and embarrassing me. Come on, everybody," he shouted, "let's get out of here. Let this bitch go under. She can't cheat us and prosper."

Jared seized the man by the front of his vest and yanked him close to his rage-flushed face. Between gritted teeth, he warned, "Unless you have proof of your accusation, don't speak it aloud. And if you ever insult Miss Maren again, I'll stuff your words down your miserable throat. Now, get out of here, you sorry bastard, and don't ever step foot in here."

The man was frightened, but he jerked himself free of Jared's loosened grip. "You can't talk to me like that. This doesn't concern you, Morgan."

"Oh, yes, it does. I'm half-owner of this place, and it's an honest one. If you have a problem with Miss James, then you also have one with me. She's never cheated anyone; she doesn't need to. She's one of the best players I've seen." Jared glanced around the room as he said, "Most of you knew Cameron James; surely you realize his daughter is just like him: honest to a fault. Like Maren said, anybody who dislikes gambling in a place run by a female should go elsewhere. I've given her full authority to handle Lady Luck as she sees best."

The repulsive man scoffed, "You're just defending her because she lives upstairs with you an—"

Jared's blazing eyes burned away the remainder of the man's crude words. "You'd best leave before I'm riled," he threatened coldly. "I've killed men for lesser offenses than you've committed tonight."

The man began to back away. "I'm leaving, but you ain't heard the last of me. I'm going to the law about this place. Ain't nobody going to cheat Howard Heath and get away with it."

Jared challenged, "Prove you've been cheated and I'll pay you three times your loss. The same goes for any patron here. Miss James is one of the most honest people I know, just like her father Cameron. That's why I went into business with him, and with her."

Dan joined them and, grasping Heath's arm, escorted him outside. When he returned, he said, "I think this war has been too hard on Mister Heath. He's about lost everything he owns, and his wife ran off with another man. Of course that doesn't excuse his bad behavior, but it does explain it. I'll keep him out of here for you."

After everyone had gone and Mary had turned in, Jared poured himself and Maren a glass of wine, and they sat down at one of the red-clothed tables. Nearly all of the lamps and candles had been extinguished, and those still lit made only a soft glow. It was quiet inside and outside the gambling house, and the room where they sat suddenly seemed very large.

Jared watched Maren stare into her wine, and he wondered what she was thinking. He murmured, "I'm sorry about the trouble tonight." Then he touched his glass to hers and said, "To peace and independence."

Maren met his mellow gaze and replied, "No, to Jared Morgan." She brought her glass to his. "I appreciate what you said and did tonight. I'm sure you realized I've had trouble with that man before. Mary told me how he probably got in." She repeated the housekeeper's explanation, then added, "Actually, this interruption was a good thing. It showed us that a determined person can sneak inside. We must take better precautions. One night, it could be a thief."

"Something is up, Maren. He wasn't drunk or

stupid or suffering."

"I know, Jared, and he wasn't the other time either. He's out to cause trouble, and I don't know why or for whom. Yet . . ."

When she shrugged and halted, Jared stated, "I hope you realize he isn't doing it for me, Maren."

"If there's one thing I know about you, Jared Morgan, it's that you're not a man to hire another to settle your problems." She smiled. "Well, at least your ownership and the fact that you're living here are in the open. Now we have to learn if it makes a difference to anyone."

"Besides Eric," he declared rashly, then added, "I'm sorry. It slipped out. You make me lose control of my tongue and my wits."

She stood and said teasingly, "Little ol' me make you lose self-control? Don't exaggerate or I might try to do it more often." Her mood waxed serious as she added, "Thanks again, Jared. Good night. About ten in the morning?"

"For what?" he asked confusedly.

"To meet with Papa's lawyer to go over our papers and terms. Then, we can go to the bank so you can take possession of your money."

"You sure you want to handle all that tomorrow?"

"I think we both need to know where we stand, don't you?"

Jared rose and looked down into her upturned face. His fingers lightly drifted over her parted lips. "I suppose you're right," he concurred. Taking her hand, he guided her to the steps. "You go on and I'll douse the remaining candles."

Maren hesitated indecisively. She wanted to embrace him, to kiss him, but she feared what that would lead to. Was she ready to follow Beth's advice? Mary's advice? Her own desires?

Jared gently pulled her into his arms and murmured, "No matter how much we want each other, Maren, tonight's not the right time. But I would like to hold you for a moment and kiss you good night."

"I would like that very much," she bravely told him.

Jared gently cupped her face between his hands and gazed into it for what seemed like a long time. Slowly he leaned forward and kissed each of her eyes closed. His lips brushed her forehead, the tip of her nose, and her cheek. Then they attempted to cover every inch of her face before drifting over her neck and ears. Abruptly and tightly he embraced her.

Maren felt his rigid body tremble, and she could hear his ragged respiration. He had pressed her head to his chest and was holding it there with one hand. The other, at her waist, kept her locked against him. Her eyes shut, Maren listened to his thundering heartbeat, thrilled by her effect on him. She was very aware of the sturdiness of his body, his compelling shape and size, his manly smell, his sensitivity. His hands had the strength to crush her, but they gently caressed her, inflaming her. Many impressions and images flooded her enraptured mind, and she warmed to each of them. She savored this heady contact with him, and nestled closer.

Slowly, appreciatively, uncontrollably, his hands wandered up and down her back, stroking her tenderly while his body experienced enticing sensations. He smiled and relaxed as he heard her sigh peacefully, dreamily. It felt so good to simply hold her in his arms. He rested his chin against her dark hair and inhaled its floral scent. She fit perfectly in his embrace, and he wanted her to remain there. But first, he had some business to handle, dangerous business. After Thursday, he could concentrate on winning and possessing Maren, but not tonight. Once he took her to his bed or hers, it would be to stay, so he would not do it without explaining his impending absence, which he could not do.

He lifted her chin and sealed their lips, but the kiss was brief. It had to be. He dared not lose mastery over his wits and body, or he would whisk her upstairs and make her his. He looked deeply, longingly, into her golden brown eyes, and promised huskily, "Soon, Maren, this powerful bond between us will be shared. It must be shared."

Maren's right hand rose to caress his strong jawline. Her voice was husky with emotion as she replied, "I think I sensed that the first time I met you, when I was only fifteen. But I was certain of it on the ship and the beach. No matter what happens between us later or what you think about me for being so wanton, I will surrender to your irresistible siege when you finally decide to make your attack."

Maren pulled his head downward as she eased onto tiptoe and their lips met in a breathtaking and intoxicating kiss. Moments later, she gazed into his tawny eyes and smiled. "Good night, Jared Morgan."

He inhaled deeply and erratically to slow his racing heart, but flames of desire leapt from his brownish gold eyes as he declared, "Thursday night, Miss Maren James; be ready to yield or be gone from here, for I shall not take no that night."

"Nor will I, my skittish rogue," she climbed the stairs gracefully, as Jared observed her swaying hips and mopped perspiration from his brow.

With her stableman's unknowing assistance the next morning, Maren returned her parents' letters to Eric's safe. At her request, Marc left the office to help load two of the trunks containing her belongings onto a supply wagon, and while he was away, Maren quickly unlocked the safe and replaced the letters, unaware that Eric had had them in a certain order. When the men returned, she was sitting calmly in a chair and fanning herself. She rose, leisurely bid her cousin goodbye, and left.

At the lawyer's office, Jared came forward and helped her down from the wagon. She waved to the stableman as she watched him depart.

"What's wrong, Maren?" Jared asked, glancing from the man's retreating back to Maren's pensive expression.

"He was just helping me get some of my trunks from Eric's warehouse to Lady Luck," she replied, feeling deceitful. "Well, partner, let's get this matter settled."

"Was there trouble at the warehouse?"

"Of course not. Why should there be?"

"You're in a strange mood this morning."

"Oh?" she responded noncommittally. "Ready for business?"

When Jared eyed her intently, she turned away. "Ready," he answered when he realized she was not going to reveal anything to him.

The meeting began with Jared presenting his deed for Samuel Lewis to study. When the lawyer passed it to Maren, he asked, "Is that your father's signature?"

Maren eyed it closely and nodded. After reading over a second paper, the wiry man passed it to his alert client. "Are those Cameron James's notes and promises?"

Maren read this paper twice. It stated that her father would hold Jared's money in a "special fund" until the war ended or until it was safe for Jared to claim it. It also gave Jared the right to go over the books at any time he wished, and the authority to decide how Lady Luck should and would be run, a stipulation which troubled Maren. When she glanced over at the handsome man beside her, he knew which section she was concerned about and he smiled encouragingly.

Maren returned to the page, certain it contained

"clues" her father had planted to let her know this paper and partner were valid: the date she had broken her left wrist in a fall, the date he had given her an exquisite doll and vase from China, the Wedgwood pieces in his private collection, and the book which was their favorite reading. Revelations only her father would know.

"Did my father leave this special fund with you?" she inquired, and the man shook his head. "Did he tell you where it would be kept?" Again, he shook his head. "What happens if I can't locate it and turn it over to Mr. Morgan?"

The man could not lie with Jared Morgan sitting before him. "The contract and deed are binding, Miss James. As your father's heir, you're responsible for resolving the matter."

"But if I don't have the records and money, how can I?"

"Then Mr. Morgan can do one of two things. He can legally take over Lady Luck to cover his losses, or he can allow you to repay him." Samuel Lewis hoped Jared would choose to do the latter. Finally the secret partner's identity was known, but it could become a big problem. Eric would be infuriated by this turn of events, and Jared Morgan's fame and wealth would make him a formidable foe.

Maren broke her pensive silence by inquiring, "How do I know he hasn't already claimed this special fund?"

"His word on the matter. He is well-known and respected."

"Is his word more binding than mine?"

"That wasn't my meaning, Miss James."

"What if I swear he's collected the money?" Maren asked, not once looking toward the silent Jared.

The lawyer had to reply, "How can you, Miss James? You've been gone for the past two years. Did you receive any messages from your father during this time?"

"No," she replied honestly.

"Do you have any reason to doubt Mr. Morgan's word?"

"No," she replied again. "But I do have most of his earnings from the last year; they're in the bank. I'm handing them over this morning."

"Mr. Morgan, is it your intention to allow Miss James to repay you, or do you want to press for total ownership?"

The lawyer was shocked when Jared stated, "I'm giving her until the first of the year to repay me. If she can't, then she's to sign over her share to me or marry me. I want this deal put into writing today."

Samuel looked from one impenetrable face to the other. Eric James would definitely be enraged upon hearing this news! Eric had wanted to discover the identity of her partner and then get rid of him so he could take over Lady Luck. But he had not anticipated an obstacle like Captain Hawk. "I . . . I'm not sure that would be legal, sir. It reeks of blackmail."

Jared responded confidently, "Since Miss James is agreeable to those terms, I see no problem, and I do not want them to be revealed to anyone else. We also want it recorded that in case either partner dies, the other inherits all. That would include my ship and my personal possessions, as well as hers."

Lewis was surprised. "It's most unusual to make a stranger your heir. Miss James, do you go along with such terms?"

"Yes sir, I do. This is the only way I can keep from losing all I own."

Jared wished she had not added the last line. "I assure you, sir, Miss James will be taken care of before and after this matter is settled. Cameron was a friend of mine, and I would never harm his daughter."

Samuel Lewis decided this cloud had a silver lining: when Jared Morgan died, all he possessed would go to Maren, Eric's cousin. "If you two are sure of this arrangement, I'll write up the contract for you."

"There's another matter I want you to handle, sir," Jared put in. "I want you to check out the legality of her cousin's takeover of James Shipping and his selling of her property without her knowledge or approval. At the least, Eric James owes Maren James monetary compensation and half-ownership of James Shipping."

The lawyer appeared to become nervous at this point. "I handled those transactions myself, Mr. Morgan. Rest assured, they were legal. Eric—Mr. James—had a letter of authority from Cameron which gave him the power to take whatever measures he deemed necessary.''

Jared had evidence to prove those sales were illegal, but he dared not reveal it at this time. "How do we know that power was not revoked?" he asked casually as he witnessed the lawyer's alarm increase.

"I would know, Mr. Morgan; it was in my possession. Cameron never canceled it. After his death, Eric James settled Cameron's debts by selling off the property. No one expected Miss James to return and contest his decisions.''

"I haven't contested them, sir," Maren injected. Staring oddly at Jared, she told her love, "This is not your affair, Mr. Morgan. It's family business, personal business which I'll settle with my cousin.''

"You're wrong, Maren. If I'm going to back up my deal with all I own, then you need something of value to back up yours. Even if most of your inheritance was sold off, surely your cousin owes you for your losses and his gains. I would imagine that you still have a claim to all or part of James Shipping, since it was your father's money which saved it, in fact yours which saved it. What can be done about it, sir?''

Lewis squirmed in his seat and tried to think rapidly. Jared Morgan was asking him to recover property he had helped Eric James steal from this woman. He became frightened. He could not allow Morgan to press this matter before Eric returned. "I . . . I'm not sure anything can be done. I would have to study the matter closely. I would need to go over the firm's books. I can't do that with Mr. James out of town. It wouldn't be ethical. Besides, Miss

James would need strong legal grounds on which to challenge her cousin. Do you suspect him of cheating you, Miss James?"

"Certainly not," she replied too hastily. "But I suppose it would be best if you went over the books and records just to appease Mr. Morgan. It was a lot of money to lose, and I can't see why Eric would mind. Would you handle it for me when he returns?"

The lawyer who followed. At least Eric's lovely cousin was resisting Morgan on this. "I see no reason why not. You and Mr. James can meet with me after his return and we can settle this matter quickly and quietly. You don't want it to appear that you're accusing him of a crime. I'm sure you realize a public scandal such as that could ruin the firm."

"Our discussions will not go farther than this office, sir."

"Do you want me to approach him on the matter, or will you?"

"I think I should," Maren responded. "I'll contact you when Eric and I are ready to meet with you."

"After you speak with him, you might not need my services. I've always found Mr. James to be open and honest in his dealings, both business and personal."

"What about her father's townhouse? We would like to repurchase it so Maren won't have to live at the gambling house. It was her home and it's close to her business. Is that a problem?"

"No problem with the owner, but it could be with the tenant. Mr. James has lived there since moving to New Orleans. He loves it, and I doubt he would want to move. If he will relocate, I'll gladly sell it to Miss James for a fair price."

"You own it?" Maren asked, intrigued.

"Yes, I bought it as an investment when Mr. Eric James was selling off your father's holdings. He rents it from me."

"But you're willing to sell it back to me if Eric is agreeable?"

"For what I paid for it, plus its increase in value since then."

"You're very kind, sir. I would love to have it back and it would be nicer to live there. Some people think it's improper for me to live at Lady Luck, so it would halt a lot of nasty gossip."

"I'll draw up the papers for your arrangement with Mr. Morgan, and you can sign them on Friday morning. When Mr. James returns, we'll handle the other two matters. Is that all for today?"

"One last question," Jared said. "If anything happened to Eric James, who would inherit all of his holdings?"

"Why do you ask that, Mr. Morgan?"

"Running the blockade is dangerous, and can be lethal. If Maren's cousin met with . . . an early demise, would she recover any of her losses from Eric's estate? After all, her inheritance built it."

"Mr. James doesn't have a will that I know of, and I'm not sure what the legal ruling would be. I take it you're aware he has two brothers who would precede a cousin as higher heirs. I can check on both matters when he returns. Is that all?" he asked once more, his eagerness to have them gone apparent to both Maren and Jared. But Lewis was glad they had come to him, not gone to another lawyer!

On the way to the bank, Maren was silent and thoughtful. Once they'd arrived, she turned the key over to Jared and they checked the money and records. Maren had not corrected or replaced the falsified pages, and now she watched Jared look them over, then glance at her.

"This isn't your handwriting, or Dan's. Eric's?" Jared said sharply.

"I told you he was running the business until I returned. He put the money and records here."

"Yes, I can see Eric's greedy little hand at work."

"What do you mean?" Maren asked anxiously.

Jared's gaze fused with hers and he said, "You know what I mean. I'm certain Dan told you that he and I have already discussed this irritating matter. You forget about it; I'll handle it because I don't want you to annoy me with your continual defense of Eric." He promptly dropped the matter. "Keep the key in case you need money while I'm gone. We do have expensive wine to pay for. Perhaps the next time I raid a ship it will be loaded with it."

Maren didn't follow his lead. "You didn't believe half of what that lawyer told us, did you?"

Jared eyed her squarely and asserted, "You didn't either. I think your family's townhouse was his payoff for helping Eric fleece you. When Eric returns, that nervous snake of a lawyer will tell him every detail of our meeting. Eric will know I'm suspicious, and such a man is dangerous when he is nervous. I would advise you to claim you had nothing to do with my performance in there this morning. I was trying to ask questions that would open your eyes about Eric James, but obviously you prefer to keep them closed. I don't know about you, woman, but I despise letting him or anyone get away with deceiving and betraying your father—and you."

Chapter Nine

Trying to clear their heads and calm their agitated nerves, Maren and Jared returned to Lady Luck without discussing Eric James. After Maren went upstairs, Jared asked Mary to prepare a nice meal for them to be served at five, and to chill a bottle of champagne. He requested the early dining hour so they would have time to eat in a leisurely fashion before their employees arrived at about six. Jared grinned at the genial housekeeper as he left her.

But Maren was surprised when Mary came to her room and revealed Jared's plans for that evening. Noting her reaction, Mary told her, "He's something real special, Miss Maren; I hope you realize how much he likes you."

Maren didn't respond, but after Mary had departed she scoffed, "Or how much he wants from me. Damn you, Jared Morgan, what are you up to?"

Suspicions flooded her mind. Suppose she did

241

recover her losses from Eric, when she had "willed" everything to Jared, couldn't something happen to her? The man she loved and desired might be the greedy conniver, not her cousin. But what if Jared was right about Eric? And if she surrendered to Jared, did he really care for her?

Flustered, Maren muttered, "Life is all about taking risks, isn't it, Maren ol' girl? If only there wasn't so much at stake . . ."

When Maren descended the steps at five o'clock, she was dressed in a light rose taffeta gown. A darker shade of tulle edged the hem, the neckline, and the puffy sleeves. And the gown had a raised waistline, but it was not banded tightly just beneath her breasts, nor was the bodice cut very low. Maren had removed several tiny roses from the nosegay Jared had given her the day before, and had secured them amidst the curls atop her dark brown head. She wore no jewelry, so nothing drew attention from her silky shoulders and her slender neck, which was made more noticeable by her unswept hairstyle. She trod softly in the dark rose slippers, but Jared's keen ears heard her approach.

He met her at the base of the stairs, and, entranced, he let his gaze roam over her appreciatively. "You look beautiful, Maren. I'm glad you agreed to join me for dinner, even if I did irritate you today."

"One has to eat, doesn't one?" she replied politely, still somewhat miffed because of their earlier dispute. "Thank you for the compliment, Mr. Morgan. You look quite dashing yourself."

Jared's slim hips and hard-muscled thighs were clad in close-fitting breeches with button fastenings below the knees. His matching dove gray coat was cut square across the front to the waist, and had wide lapels and revers. His white ruffled shirt had a high collar, and a neatly tied dark gray cravat set it off. His coat sleeves were slashed at the wrists, and his exposed shirt cuffs were also ruffled. A green- and wine-striped vest, gray silk stockings, and leather shoes completed his immaculate attire.

Maren noticed that his sun-tipped locks had been brushed away from his tanned face, and that some curled over his collar at the nape of his neck. His tawny eyes glowed as he looked her over from head to toe, and she was glad he was so tall. His height made him seem so masterful and so self-assured. She even liked the way his jawline curved, and the shape of his nose. Even his brows enhanced his looks. Indeed, Jared was a man who seemed to have everything: looks, wealth, confidence, breeding, intelligence, and prowess.

Jared was deeply affected by her admiring scrutiny. "Do I pass inspection, partner?" he teased, to gain time and regain mastery of himself.

Suddenly aware of her devouring gaze and predacious mood, Maren silently chided herself for such a display. She meant to think her next words, but she spoke them aloud. "You look perfect, Jared, too damned perfect."

"Why should my gentlemanly facade annoy you, Miss James? Don't you want me to keep our female patrons as happy as you keep our male ones?" he inquired, grinning at her dismay and her slip.

"How do I deal with someone who knows and has everything? With a man who has no faults— according to him."

"I don't recall ever claiming to be anywhere near perfect. What's wrong, my lovely feline? Something has your back up tonight."

"Sorry," she murmured, vexed with herself for acting so foolish. "I guess I'm still upset over our quarrel this morning."

"Can we forget about business for tonight?" he entreated. "I was hoping we could have a nice dinner to celebrate our agreement."

"Forget business or celebrate your victory, which is it?"

A look of disappointment came to his eyes. "It seems as if my idea was a bad one."

"No, Jared," she protested quickly. "It's a wonderful idea and a kind gesture. I'm the bad one. It's just that . . ."

"That what, Maren?" he inquired tenderly. He captured her hand in his and, carrying it to his mouth, let his lips lightly brush her fingertips. "What's wrong, love?" he asked, kissing her palm.

Maren shuddered with an overwhelming need for him. She withdrew her hand from his. "You stroll into my life and instantly try to change it. You don't even ask what I think or how I feel or what I want. You make demands, make decisions, and you make threats. You want everything to go your way. I am supposed to fall in with your plans as if I have none of my own, as if I have nothing to lose. For your information, Jared Morgan, I have a lot at stake, financially and personally. If you expect me to take great risks with you, then allow me to have some say-so, and if I feel it is necessary, I will change. I'm not a child or a dunderhead."

"I know you aren't, Maren. If you were, I wouldn't be interested in you. I suppose I have been too bossy and overbearing. I'm a man, and such behavior comes naturally to me. And I'm new at partnerships, especially one with a woman. I'm used to being in charge of everything and everyone around me, to doing things a certain way, but suddenly I don't know where I stand or what I'm doing. That makes me a little edgy and defensive, perhaps too demanding. I apologize for my behavior."

"If this partnership is going to work, we both must make some changes and some compromises. Just because I'm a woman, it is no easier for me to accept the situation. You seem used to women who obey your every command, but let me tell you, women have feelings and goals, too."

"You're right, Maren. I'll do my best to remember your warning."

Maren closed her eyes for a moment. "It wasn't a warning, Jared. Why do you see everything as a power play?"

"Calm down, Maren. It really bothers you to think

I have power over you, doesn't it?" he asked seriously.

"Wouldn't it bother you if our positions were reversed? You make me feel helpless and vulnerable, insecure and utterly confused. My father taught me many things, but not how to deal with the emotions I'm feeling or the predicament I am in. He taught me to be strong and independent, to attack problems head-on. But you strolled in and decided to take control of me and my life. Why did Papa give you so much authority?"

"Please don't take offense at my answer, but he did it because I'm a man, and because I'm older and I know more about business. I think Cameron would have changed the terms of my agreement with him if he had lived until you were older and knew the business better. I'm sure he only intended to protect you while you were young, or from . . ."

"From what? Go ahead, say it. From Eric."

"From anyone who might take advantage of you during my absence."

"Darn it, Jared! I'm not stupid! Don't you think I realize things are strange when . . ." She frowned and, turning from him, leaned against the staircase, intending to get some self-control.

Jared remained silent and alert. He could tell how troubled she was. He had been pushing her a mite hard since his arrival. After all, she didn't know of Eric's evil deeds, so he shouldn't expect her to react in the same way he did. He had to relax and pull back or he was going to spoil everything. "I seem to be saying

246

this a lot, but I'm sorry."

Finally Maren faced him again. "All right, Jared, the truth. Yes, I'm suspicious of Eric; I have been since I left London. But this is something I have to handle myself, and without intrusion. You've already alerted that lawyer to my doubts about him. He'll tell Eric about our visit; then Eric will close up tighter than a clam. I was planning to work on him when he returned, but now he'll be on guard. I've known him all my life, and we've been very close. We're kin. I can't just turn my back on him, believe the worst of him, until I gather proof. And I must do it, Jared, not you or anyone else. Maybe Eric's in trouble; maybe he's been greedy, made mistakes or intentionally erred. If so, I can help him. Please, let me stand on my own two feet for a while so I can resolve this situation."

"That's dangerous, Maren; he's dangerous," Jared warned.

"That's only your opinion," she declared. "You could be wrong, and I hope you are. No matter what I just said, you aren't perfect."

"But I'm not wrong this time, Maren, nor is the President. He ordered me to look into Eric James's dealings with the British. There was an American spy on the *Martha J;* he passed me a note when we boarded her. He's the one who asked me to sail in your shadow and to watch your cousin closely. And he asked President Madison to send me here to unmask a traitor."

Maren quickly reflected on that voyage. "It was Peter Thomas, wasn't it? The sailor with sandy hair."

"How do you know about Peter?" he asked worriedly.

"It would have to be him; he was always watching me."

"Did Eric notice him too?"

"How should I know? Why?"

"He's still sailing with your cousin; his life could be in danger if Eric suspects him."

"I don't think so. Maybe he was just admiring me," she jested.

"That's more likely," Jared agreed. "Peter overheard Eric tell Wolfe you had fooled me completely, and when Peter told me you were James Slade's wife, I thought that was what Eric had meant. Later, I realized he was referring to the ruse you used to keep the necklace. Eric also said you had a big part to play in his scheme, that you were clever and trustworthy. I believe he was referring to you having provided a cover for his trip to London. Can you see why I was angry and doubtful?"

"Do you still mistrust me, Jared?"

"Certainly not," he vowed. "Peter left us in Washington to return to Baltimore and rejoin your cousin. One way or another, the truth about Eric James will be exposed in the next few months."

"So, you did come here for a reason other than finding me."

"I have several missions in this area, but I

volunteered for them so I could be with you while carrying them out," he admitted. "Take a chance on me, my talented gambler; I'm worth the risk."

"Perhaps you are, Captain Hawk, perhaps you are. Let's eat."

"I guess that means our conversation is over?"

"You're right, Jared, at least for now. No more talk of wars and business tonight. Please."

They dined on a juicy duckling which had been baked and browned to perfection, along with low-country wild rice, succulent carrots, hot croissants, and creamy butter; all delectably washed down with champagne. Mary served them in the front room, at a table near an open window through which a gentle breeze carried a floral odor.

When they were alone, Maren teased Jared as she sipped her second glass of champagne. "Isn't it a bit early in the day to be getting me intoxicated, Captain Hawk? I could go wild and attack you."

Jared laughed. "You're limited to two glasses, so that's your last one. Your reputation would definitely be endangered if our patrons arrived to find you chasing me around the house. I can't allow that."

"Why would I have to chase you? I thought you were going to pursue me."

"This isn't Thursday night; my siege begins then."

Maren put her glass aside and asked, "Are you truly making an appointment to seduce me, as you would arrange a business meeting?"

Jared did not chuckle when he said, "Never, my enchanting siren. It's a promise, an enticing threat you might call it. I don't want to start us boiling like wild rice when we don't have time to cook properly. That would only create a sticky mess. I'm giving you plenty of time to decide what you want in a man, because once you're mine, I don't want you to think I pressed you unfairly. At midnight on Thursday, I'm going to knock on your door. Don't open it if you have any doubts about me or about us. If you do open it, I'll consider that an acceptance of my proposal and we will marry on January first or when the war ends, whichever comes first."

"The war could end any day, Jared, even tomorrow."

He grinned devilishly. "I know."

Maren shook her head very slowly. "You are the most exasperating and bewildering man I've ever met. I never know when you're joking."

"Yes, you do, Maren; you're just afraid to admit it to yourself." He pulled a box from his pocket and passed it to her. "For you."

Maren's heart began to thud heavily, and she wondered if he could hear it. "What is it?" she asked, clutching the small gift tightly.

"There's only one way to find out."

Maren lowered her gaze to the box and with shaky fingers, she opened it. She withdrew an oval locket on a gold chain. "Where did you get this?" she asked. "When?"

Jared came around the table and bent forward to

explain. "I stole your parents' picture from your rooms upstairs and I already had the one of me on my ship. I had an artist do miniatures of both. When I left this morning, I went to pick up this present. I ordered it yesterday, before I met you and Beth. It may be presumptuous and vain of me, but do you like it?"

"It's beautiful. Thank you, Jared."

He looked into her misty eyes and said, "If you reject me, you can always remove my picture and replace it."

Maren focused her dewy gaze on his painted image and smiled. "If you don't mind, I think I'll leave it here for a while. Will you put the locket on for me? I'm so excited and pleased that my hands are shaking."

Jared stepped behind her and fastened the clasp, allowing the locket to settle near her heart. After Maren caressed it fondly and thanked him again, he strewed kisses from her left ear to her shoulder. When she lifted her head to look at him, their eyes locked, and for a long time they gazed at each other. Then their hands joined, and their lips drew nearer.

"Jared, I hate to disturb you, but I need to speak with you on an urgent matter." It was a man's voice, loud and intrusive. It came from the kitchen doorway.

Jared straightened and turned in that direction. "What is it, Kip?"

Kerry Osgood hesitated a moment before claiming falsely, "There's a problem at the ship. I think you should come handle it."

Maren had turned in her chair to study the raven-haired Kerry. She remembered him from the raid on the *Martha J,* and she noted that he was dressed very casually, in a white linen shirt and dark trousers. She decided he was close to Jared in height, size, and age.

"I'd like you two to meet before we leave," Jared said.

Osgood came forward, and Jared said, "Miss Maren James, my partner and ladylove, this is Kerry Osgood, known as Kip to those who put up with him. He is my first mate and my best friend. If you do not spurn me, he will stand with us when we marry."

Kip bowed gallantly and clasped her hand. "It is a pleasure and an honor to be formally introduced to you, Miss James. Our first meeting was rather unexpected and tense, so please forgive my behavior."

"I'm delighted to meet you, sir, and as for our first encounter, it was an exciting moment in my life. However, that wasn't the first time I'd met Jared, though he didn't recall me until I later nudged his memory. He'll have to tell you that amusing story one day. Are you enjoying your visit here?"

Jared broke in. "If you two will excuse me for a minute, I need to change before we leave. This isn't exactly shipboard attire."

As he hurried upstairs, Kip picked up the conversation. "This is a beautiful city, and you are a beautiful woman. I'm amazed that you captured him, but I wish you both happiness."

"Frankly, I didn't ensnare him; he captured me."

"And I can see why. He's a lucky man, always has been."

"How long have you known Jared?"

"Seems like forever, but it's more like years. He's a good captain, and friend. Do you plan to stay here or will you move to Savannah?"

"We haven't discussed it. I had forgotten we have homes in different states. Is Jared close to his family?"

A closed look spread over Kip's face. "I heard about the loss of your parents. I'm sorry; that must have been rough on you."

Maren realized the man had evaded answering and she wondered why. But Jared returned then, almost breathless from rushing and dressed like his friend.

"I hope we have time later to get better acquainted," Kip said. "There are some things you should be told about your intended," he jested. "But right now, we have to hurry."

Jared quickly apologized. "I'm sorry to leave like this, Maren, but duty calls. I don't know when I'll return."

"Do you trust me and Dan to take care of the business?"

"Of course. Just be alert for more trouble."

"I shall. It was very nice meeting you, Kip."

"A pleasure, Maren."

The two men left by the back door after speaking with Mary Malone, and when they had gone, Maren went to thank the housekeeper for the lovely meal.

She offered to help her clear up, but the older woman insisted that she avoid ruining her gown and suggested she go upstairs to rest before opening time. Maren hugged Mary and obeyed, for she needed time to think.

It was obvious that Kerry Osgood had not been surprised by Jared's announcement that they might marry, which told her how close the two men were. She suspected that Kip's summons had nothing to do with trouble on Jared's ship. Jared probably never had trouble on his ship. If she had been dressed differently, Maren would have trailed them! Yes, she was going to take a risk with Jared Morgan, but it would be nice to make certain beforehand that her decision was a wise one.

Jared had claimed that he had several missions to accomplish in this area. She wondered what they were, whether they were dangerous, and how long they would take to complete. If he would let her tag along, he might convince her of his honesty, and she could prove to him that she was patriotic, intelligent, trustworthy, and brave.

She then became preoccupied by another mystery: Jared's family, or what was left of it. She wondered if Kip had refused to talk about them by choice or at Jared's behest. If Jared's father and brother were dead, who was left in Savannah?

Everything went fine that night at Lady Luck, but Jared didn't return. Maren was worried about him, though she knew he could take care of himself. A man in his position, a privateer during wartime, had to be skilled at self-defense. She fingered the locket he had given her at dinner, opened it to study the images inside, pictures of the three people most important to her. She was touched by his gift, mostly because of its meaning. Suddenly Maren wanted to speak with Jared, to hug him and kiss him. She waited for him until three in the morning, then lay down on her bed and fell asleep.

Arising at noon, Maren hurried to the kitchen to see if Jared had been down for breakfast yet, but she learned that he had not returned. When she expressed concern, Mary advised her not to worry and she revealed that Jared had told her not to expect him back until later that day. Maren stared at Mary when she was informed that Jared had asked the older woman to watch over Maren for him.

"If he knew he wasn't coming back until tonight, why didn't he tell me that so I wouldn't worry about him? Unless he wanted me to worry! Darn him, Mary, he acts like he trusts everyone but me!"

"That isn't so, Miss Maren. He just didn't want you to worry. He probably figured you would go to bed thinking he would be home soon."

"Well, I didn't. I waited up until nearly dawn. How do we know something hasn't happened to him?"

"Mister Jared can take care of himself. He has a whole crew of men to help him. Why don't I prepare you a nice breakfast?"

"Thanks, but not yet, Mary. I'm not fully awake. I think I'll bathe and dress, then take a refreshing walk."

"That sounds fine. Let me know when you're

ready to eat."

Maren hurriedly washed herself. Then she put on a thin muslin day dress, a pale yellow one. Having secured a matching fichu around her shoulders, she arranged her hair in a chignon and then covered it with a bonnet which had a shallow crown and a deep brim. She gathered a silk parasol and a dainty reticule, and left while Mary was hanging out the wash and couldn't argue with her bold behavior.

It was easy to find a carriage that would transport her to the wharf at which Jared Morgan's ship was docked. Surely she would be safe there at midday, she thought, recalling that New Orleans had grown immensely since her harrowing experience years ago, when she had been hurled into Jared's arms. In any case, she had to make certain his ship was still in port and he was safe. Perhaps he would invite her aboard. Then she could learn more about him. Seeing his ship and his crew should teach her a few things. And she wanted to see him in command, see him in his chosen surroundings. Presently, she didn't care if he became annoyed with her. She had to take that risk.

Maren's gaze slowly scanned the ships which were trapped by the blockade. Some had been kept in fine shape, while others were in dire need of repair. Cargoes stood in the dock area, some old and rotting, others new and hopeful, and men bustled about. But they were not too rushed to halt and stare at her. She ignored them and continued to stroll on, searching for Jared.

As she proceeded, her heart began to beat fran-

FREE

BOOK CERTIFICATE

ZEBRA HOME SUBSCRIPTION SERVICE, INC.

YES! Please start my subscription to Zebra Historical Romances and send me my free Zebra Novel along with my first month's Romances. I understand that I may preview these four new Zebra Historical Romances Free for 10 days. If I'm not satisfied with them I may return the four books within 10 days and owe nothing. Otherwise I will pay just $3.50 each; a total of $14.00 (a $15.80 value—I save $1.80). Then each month I will receive the 4 newest titles as soon as they come off the press for the same 10 day Free preview and low price. I may return any shipment and I may cancel this arrangement at any time. There is no minimum number of books to buy and there are no shipping, handling or postage charges. Regardless of what I do, the FREE book is mine to keep.

Name _____

_____
(Please Print)

Address _____ Apt. # _____

City _____ State _____ Zip _____

Telephone ( ) _____

Signature _____

_____
(if under 18, parent or guardian must sign)

Terms and offer subject to change without notice.

MAIL IN THE COUPON BELOW TODAY

GET FREE GIFT

To get your Free Zebra **HISTORICAL ROMANCE** fill out the coupon below and send it in today. As soon as we receive the coupon, we'll send your first month's books to preview Free for 10 days along with your **FREE NOVEL.**

ACCEPT YOUR FREE GIFT
AND EXPERIENCE MORE OF
THE PASSION AND ADVENTURE
YOU LIKE IN A
HISTORICAL ROMANCE

❦

Zebra Romances are the finest novels of their kind and are written with the adult woman in mind. All of our books are written by authors who really know how to weave tales of romantic adventure in the historical settings you love.

Because our readers tell us these books sell out very fast in the stores, Zebra has made arrangements for you to receive at home the four newest titles published each month. You'll never miss a title and home delivery is so convenient. With your first shipment we'll even send you a FREE Zebra Historical Romance as our gift just for trying our home subscription service. No obligation.

BIG SAVINGS
AND **FREE** HOME DELIVERY

Each month, the Zebra Home Subscription Service will send you the four newest titles as soon as they are published. (We ship these books to our subscribers even before we send them to the stores.) You may preview them *Free* for 10 days. If you like them as much as we think you will, you'll pay just $3.50 each and save $1.80 each month off the cover price. *AND you'll also get FREE HOME DELIVERY.* There is never a charge for shipping, handling or postage and there is no minimum you must buy. If you decide not to keep any shipment, simply return it within 10 days, no questions asked, and owe nothing.

tically. The *Sea Mist* was nowhere in sight. She had to get some answers! She questioned several dockmen, but each said he hadn't seen the *Sea Mist* or Captain Hawk in port recently. When she asked if he could be anchored in the Gulf, she was told that was too far out for someone staying in town. Maren insisted that Jared Morgan had been in New Orleans until last night, but the men remained firm in their ignorance.

How could these men know nothing about such a legendary ship and captain? Maren fretted. They couldn't all be sworn to silence, or be unaware of their surroundings. If Jared had sailed into port . . .

If not, how had he gotten here? And where had he gone? When was he returning?

Kip had said there was trouble. Surely his crew had not become mutinous and stolen the ship. And she was certain he hadn't gone to sea without telling her. This riddle made no sense.

A group of sailors halted to ask if she needed help or was lost, and she was delighted to learn that there were nice men among them. "I was looking for Captain Jared Morgan of the *Sea Mist.*"

"Lots of women are," one man teased, but the others hushed him.

After receiving the same responses the dockmen had given her, she argued politely, "But he's been here for a week. We're in business together at Lady Luck. He was called away last night on an emergency. When he didn't return, I became worried about him, but I can't seem to locate anyone who's seen him or his ship. How can that be?"

"I can't rightly answer that, miss," one man responded. "Some of these privateers know secret coves to hide in just like them pirates. Barataria and Grand Isle ain't far. Maybe they're letting Captain Hawk anchor there."

"Captain Morgan associate with pirates? Certainly not."

The men laughed and nudged each other. Then another sailor informed her, "Most pirates ain't bad men. Some of 'em just got turned around. Some of 'em ain't got no homes or families, no place to go. Some of 'em escaped from prisons in other countries or from slave ships. Most of 'em only attack enemy ships. The people here love 'em 'cause they keep the town well supplied with goods."

Maren didn't want to debate with them, so she smiled and said, "Perhaps you're right. If you hear anything about Captain Morgan or the *Sea Mist* and you bring the news to me at Lady Luck, I'll pay you."

After Maren left, one man turned to another. "Ain't that the woman who buys the wine from us?"

"Yep, she is. She's a real lady, just like the Water Snake said. 'Course, our cap'n only saw her at a distance. He don't want her to recognize him as René Blanc when she passes him on the street."

"We'd best head back to the *Sea Serpent*. Cap'n says we're sailing with the night tide. Maybe we'll capture more wine for that purty lady."

"Why didn't you tell her where Captain Hawk is?"

"If he wants her to know, he'll tell her. Ain't our place."

The first pirate turned and watched the retreating Maren. "Yep, I can see why René is burning over her. Think he'll go after her?"

"Not if Cap'n Hawk has a claim on her. Nobody challenges him."

Maren spent hours strolling around just to see if she could get a glimpse of Jared. The July sun was hot, and the day was humid. Maren realized her clothes were becoming soaked from her exertions. She hadn't eaten all day. She was exhausted, hungry, and miserable.

"I knew you couldn't handle that place alone. I see you found you a big man to help you. Where is the cocky Captain Hawk today?"

Maren walked on past the shop door in which the gambler who'd made trouble was standing. But the man dogged her, making crude remarks and asking vulgar questions. Finally she halted and glared at him, "Who's paying you to harass me and besmirch my name? I'm not a fool, nor is Jared Morgan. He plans to have you followed day and night to discover the truth about your little pretense, and once we learn who's hired you and why, Jared plans to deal with you personally."

Maren saw real fear creep into the man's eyes. She enjoyed verbally wounding this hateful man, and she could not resist adding, "We know you haven't been drunk during your silly tirades at Lady Luck. We know you're being paid to drive me out of business. It won't work. Before Jared sails, he'll expose you and you'll be punished. What I can't understand is why you would humiliate yourself over and over. People are laughing at you behind your back. They think you've gone daft. But we know better, don't we, sir?"

When the man glanced around as if making certain they weren't being overheard, Maren went on. "In fact, I suspect I have you to thank for all the gossip about me. Jared is furious about those lies, and he's checking them out, one by one. If I were you . . . Never mind, I'm certain a smart man like you doesn't need advice from a mere woman, and an alleged cardsharp at that."

Suddenly the man's eyes narrowed and chilled. "Give me any trouble over this and you'll be sorry, dead sorry," he vowed. "And call off your lover before he gets hurt real bad or finds himself floating face down in that ocean he loves." He stepped closer to Maren and warned, "If you provoke me again, I'll pay a few pirates to take care of you. Take my advice"—he sneered—"Lady Luck means nothing but trouble for you. Get out while you can, and take Morgan with you. When I see my boss tonight, I'll tell him you're dumber than we thought."

Maren glared at the man. She hoped that her terror was not evident as she scoffed brazenly, "You miserable little bastard, you must be simple-minded. If you think you're scaring me, you're wrong. I don't need Jared Morgan or any man to fight my battles for me. I can fence and shoot better than most men, and I will gladly duel with you on any day, if you have the guts to show up and fight a mere woman. Cameron

James did not birth or rear a fool or a weakling. Don't come near me or my place again, or I will personally toss you out. Report that to your boss, and maybe he'll hire a *real* man to take your place."

"You arrogant bitch, you'll be sorry you ever returned home. By the time he finishes with you, you won't even have a chamber pot to use."

Maren quickly and cleverly retorted, "Eric wouldn't go that far!"

"Don't be so sure of it, Prisspot."

A runaway carriage thundered down the street just then, and the man assumed she had missed his slip when she failed to react to it. While Maren stared at the swiftly moving menace, he walked away, thinking she was distracted.

Maren glanced toward his retreating back, then walked over to a carriage. She paid the driver to take her back to Lady Luck. It was six-thirty. Her head was pounding due to the heat, lack of food and liquid, and her emotional dilemma.

Mary met her at the door. "Where have you been?" she asked.

Maren was too fatigued to lie to the anxious woman. She related her adventures and explained her sorry physical condition. Mary said she would prepare a soothing bath and a meal, and she recommended that Maren lie down and remain in her room that night. A weary and grateful young woman agreed.

After her stomach was filled and her skin was refreshed, Maren felt pleasingly relaxed. She donned a cornflower blue nightgown and brushed her hair. Music and laughter and muffled voices came from beneath her, but she knew Dan Myers could handle everything for one night. She had already asked Mary if there had been any news from Jared, and there had not.

When the housekeeper returned for Maren's tray, she said, "I found a letter under the edge of your bed while I was cleaning today, an old one from your parents. I put it on the desk near your bed."

"Thank you, Mary. You're so generous and thoughtful. I don't know what I would do without you."

"You're kind to say that, Miss Maren. I love working here, even more so since you moved in. Get some sleep. I'll see you in the morning."

"Mary, if Jared returns, will you wake me and let me know?"

"Of course, child," the housekeeper responded soothingly. "I'm sure he's fine."

Maren locked her door and walked to her bed. As she sat down to remove her slippers, her aimless gaze touched on the letter. It was in a blue envelope. Her brow knit in puzzlement for she did not recall any of the letters being in colored envelopes. She reached for it. It was not sealed, but she knew she had not read it. And since Mary had told her this suite was cleaned regularly, it must have fallen from the packet she had taken from the safe. She decided to read it and then replace it without delay. Eric had been gone for only four weeks, but he might cut his trip short and return before the six to eight weeks he'd planned to be away.

Maren withdrew the pages and read the baffling letter. Propped up by her pillows, she studied part of it: "I know you won't mind my using this lovely stationery for you know how I love blue. Soon you will have been away for a year, and we miss you terribly. We have no one else to love besides you, yet you are so far away. Things have been going badly of late, and I am glad you are not here to witness them."

Maren sighed. "What do you mean, Papa, no one else to love? What about Eric? What was happening last year?"

She read more. "I'm worried about our family. We've never been devious before, but much has changed lately. It's a tough battle, Maren, a bitter one. If you get back here one day, don't forget to take your China doll back with you. And my favorite Wedgwood piece. Between them, you should be very happy. You've always been such a clever girl, so I am certain you remember that poem we loved: 'Blue is me. Red is you. Cut them in half; And you still have two.'"

"Whatever are you talking about, Papa? Did you write this letter in clues because you were afraid Eric would find it?"

Maren jumped up and went to the bookcase by the bedroom fireplace. Her father had placed the doll there. She took it in her hands and checked it over to see if a message was hidden upon it; she found none. She hated to do it, but she took the treasure apart to make certain nothing crucial was concealed inside;

she found nothing.

Then she reached for the Wedgwood box with the familiar design and color, but there was nothing unusual inside it and no message scratched on it. As Maren replaced the box, she noted that the doll would have to be repaired. She returned to her bed and again looked over the strange letter.

"I wish I had stopped you from going to London to marry Daniel," it said. "After your mother told me why you had consented, each morning I prayed you haven't gone through with the wedding. One should marry for love, Maren, for no other reason. If I had been as smart as you believe I am, I would have introduced you to the perfect man for you, the son of a friend of mine. You'll meet him one day, and I just hope it won't be too late for him to turn your head like your mother turned mine. He is a man you could trust with your life, this Jared Morgan. I've been very wrong about some men, but not about him. Lastly I bid you not to be afraid to take risks, Maren; you are Lady Luck."

Maren went to bed, her curiosity aroused. Something vital was concealed at Lady Luck. But what and where? She couldn't tear the place apart to find whatever it was her father wanted her to know or to have, and Lady Luck was so big it could take years to find his hiding place. That night she was too tired to decipher the clues. The secret had waited for this long, and it could remain hidden one more day.

A smile teased over her face as she thought of her father's description of Jared. Cameron would be pleased if he knew they had gotten together. Well, she mused, almost together, soon to be together.

She sat up in bed and frowned. How convenient it was that this missing letter vilified Eric and championed Jared. . . .

Jared had gone upstairs last night to change his clothing before he left. He had gotten into her room before, so he might have placed the letter where it could be found during his absence. What, she wondered, could his motivation be? And how had he gotten the letter? No, she had to be wrong. She was just thinking wildly because she was tired.

She went to her father's liquor cabinet and poured herself a whiskey, then drank it, coughing and wheezing after each swallow. Having done this, she returned to bed and was asleep within twenty minutes.

Evelyn Sims asked, "What are we going to do about that James tart? She isn't failing over there or getting scared like Lewis wants."

Howard Heath looked her in the eye and said, "Kill her, of course."

Evelyn argued, "That isn't what we're supposed to do, Howard. Besides, I thought you wanted a taste of her. You said you were going to kidnap her and rough her up good. That's the best way to send Miss James fleeing."

He smiled wickedly. "I plan to take the bitch before I cut her throat. I'll do that just as soon as

Morgan's out of my way. We'll have to charge Lewis double for getting rid of Captain Hawk."

"Kill Jared Morgan?" she asked fearfully.

Hatred was evident in the man's eyes and voice. "After the way those two treated me in public Monday, I'll enjoy every minute of their pain."

"Check this plan out with Mr. Lewis first," she cautioned.

"Hell no!" Heath snorted. "I don't want that snooty lawyer interfering with my plans. He said to scare her out, and you can't get any farther out than being dead. I might even do the Morgan job for free."

Chapter Ten

Thursday night Maren walked from one room to another in her suite, unable to relax. Jared had been gone since early Tuesday evening. She had received no messages from him, and she was alarmed by his lengthy absence. Due to the strong whiskey she had drunk the preceding night, she had slept until noon. She had gone downstairs that evening, but had not stayed long. Unable to concentrate on business and not feeling like smiling and talking with the patrons, Maren had decided a long bath would refresh and calm her. But as time passed, she became more annoyed with Jared for worrying her so.

If something terrible happened to him, how would she learn of it? How could she aid him?

Clad for bed in a thin nightgown, she doused nearly all of the candles and lamps in her suite. The contents of the letter that Mary had found yesterday kept flashing across her mind. Surely her father had been beseeching her to trust Jared Morgan and to doubt Eric James.

"It's all about trust, isn't it, Maren?" she asked herself.

"Yes, it is." Jared's voice came from behind her.

Maren whirled and suppressed a cry of panic. She had not heard him enter. "You must stop doing that, Jared," she chided.

He came forward with a purposeful stride, one which revealed his agility and confidence. "Do you trust me, Maren?"

"Can I, Jared? Should I? Where have you been?"

Jared's gaze took in her concern and vexation. "I trust you, Maren; that's why I'll answer. I've been meeting with some troublemakers in this area. The British are hoping to stir up three factions against us: the pirates, the slaves, and the Indians. I've been trying to see what I could find out about this plot. Do you realize how vulnerable we would be to a British attack if we are busy battling other enemies? I must uncover the details of this plan and try to thwart it."

"You mean the British would incite brutal conflicts just to weaken us?"

"This is war, Maren; our enemy will stop at nothing to defeat us. I'm sorry you've been so frantic; I couldn't get word to you. I thought I would be back yesterday morning."

"Is it really that bad, Jared?"

"Not yet, but it can be if I don't halt them."

"Is there anything I can do to help you?"

He smiled as he reached forward to caress her cheek. "If I think of something and it's not dangerous to do, I'll let you know. I don't want you killed. You're special to me, woman."

"I looked for you yesterday," she confessed.

"I know. Perhaps I should have told you my ship is anchored in Lake Borgne. If the Royal Navy heads up the river to attack New Orleans, I would be able to escape from that anchorage and nip their rears."

The war had remained almost unreal to Maren until this moment. Now Jared's words and his peril brought it to life. "How can you stop this madness they're plotting?"

"By warning the plantation owners to be on the alert against agitators and by making the local authorities aware of a possible Indian uprising. If the right people know how and where trouble will be stirred up, they can prevent it or squash it quickly. I also need to persuade the pirates to join us instead of the British."

"You want pirates to join us?"

"A soldier is a soldier, Maren. The Royal Navy is powerful and large. We need every man, gun, and brave heart we can find. Those men have as much at stake as any of us. Some of them have suffered under the British, have been impressed. We need their help, Maren; they have guns, ammunition, supplies. And they have ships with which to attack the British warships."

"Can you trust them?" she inquired skeptically.

"It's amazing what some men will do when you

show them respect and trust, and when they are truly needed."

Maren sensed that Jared was referring to more than the dangers at hand. His words sounded almost accusatory. She traced his lips with her fingers as she said, "If anyone can obtain their aid, it's you, Captain Hawk. I've learned you can be most persuasive."

The candlelight danced lovingly over Jared's face, exposing the warm glow in his eyes, and a fiery flush suddenly consumed Maren's receptive body. His light brown hair with the tawny tips was mussed, but that only enhanced his appeal. His skin, what she could see of it, was tanned and unmarred. His billowy shirt—cloud white like his teeth when he smiled—was open to a few inches below his heart, where she longed to nuzzle her cheek. Drawn to him, she was helpless to resist the pull. Like leaves in a brisk wind, her senses were suddenly scattered, wild and free. Jared was mesmeric and persuasive, and Maren felt a curious tension mounting between them, around them, within her. This tension was heavily laced with anticipation, not restrictiveness or fear. She did not move or speak as her gaze communicated with his.

Jared was alert and perceptive. He sensed that she was ready to explore the bond stretched tight between them like a hawser, the emotional rope that urged him to tow her into his arms and moor her there forever. As he looked deeply into her limpid eyes, he had to battle the golden brown currents there to keep from losing his wits and being set adrift, rudderless. The aura around her spoke of *paradise,* and he desperately wanted to visit it. He wanted to bask in the radiant glow of her eyes, to spend exotic days in her sultry arms. Her hair flowed in dark waves around her head and shoulders, and she drew him to her as powerfully as a whirlpool, yet as gently as a small eddy.

A talented artist might have placed her features on the figurehead decorating the bow of a ship. Her lips were parted as if in invitation, and even though her skin was darker than most women's, he could tell it was unblemished and creamy soft. His heart was thudding heavily and his breathing was quickening. She was unintentionally causing him to lose some of his self-assurance and to neglect his seductive skills. He feared doing or saying the wrong thing. He wanted this night to be perfect for her. He wanted her heart as much as he wanted her body. He had waited a long time to possess her, and he did not intend to rush this precious moment.

Unable to keep from touching her, his quivering fingers slipped into her shiny hair and pleasured themselves in its fullness. He watched her shut her eyes dreamily and then lean her head into his palm, nuzzling it like an affectionate kitten being stroked by an adoring owner. He brushed his lips over her forehead, then trailed them ever so slowly and enticingly over her brows, temples, nose, and cheeks. He kissed her closed eyes and finally, tentatively, claimed her mouth, at first softly and then hungrily.

He groaned, expressing his rising need for her, and banded her tightly against his trembling body.

Their tongues touched, savored, and teased; snailishly at first, then swiftly and demandingly. Spontaneously, their hands joined in the sensuous and tantalizing quest. Tonight they would delve into the magic which enchanted and united them, and they would solve its mysteries. They would challenge this heady sea together and travel each knot side by side, through calm or turbulence. Tonight there would be no captain or first mate, only loving partners. They would examine their feelings, their attraction; would test its strength and uniqueness. Undeniably paradise beckoned.

Maren's head steadily drifted backward as Jared's seeking mouth wandered down the silky column of her neck. His teeth gently nibbled at her collarbone, and his tongue played in the hollow of her throat before his provocative journey was halted by her garment.

"It's Thursday night," he murmured into her ear before playfully nipping its enticing lobe, causing her to quiver and squirm.

She laughed softly. "You didn't knock first," she reminded him, her voice constricted by desire. She felt as if she were aflame and nothing could douse the fire.

It was the same for Jared. He had difficulty breathing and speaking, thinking, moving, holding still. His body felt heavy, yet light. He was tense, yet free. He was experiencing a strange and unfamiliar range of emotions and sensations. He looked into her seductive eyes and asked, "Do I need to?"

Maren returned his gaze as she shamelessly responded, "The only no you'll receive tonight is to that question."

"Are you sure you're ready for this?" he asked, suddenly feeling as if his vast experience and skills were insufficient. He didn't want to hurt her, and he knew there was pain involved during a woman's first union with a man. He wanted her to find pleasure and satisfaction with him, yet he wondered if he could restrain himself long enough to give them to her.

"Yes, Jared, I'm ready; I have been for years." Color slightly tinged her cheeks, but it was due more to blazing passion than modesty. "I don't know what to do, so you'll have to guide me through this adventure."

"Just relax, Maren, and allow your instincts to take command. Anything that doesn't come to you naturally, I'll teach you."

"Teach me everything, Jared. I want to experience all with you."

Jared unbuttoned her gown, but did not remove it. He must cover this new territory carefully and leisurely, allowing her time to deal with her modesty and apprehensions. No matter how brave and hungry she was at this moment, haste could spoil her willing surrender.

Jared's lips captured hers as he slipped a hand into the opening of her gown and gently covered a breast.

His tongue invaded her mouth, savoring its sweetness, while he caressed the fleshy mound and tenderly thumbed the taut bud on it. He was amazed by the contrast between the rigidity of the peak and the satiny texture of her breast. With great care, his mouth trailed down her throat and closed over the nipple. As he lavished moist and hot attention there, he felt her shudder, heard her moan. His tongue circled and flicked the joyous bud while he eased her gown off her shoulders. It quickly snaked to the floor, to lie around her bare feet.

Maren instinctively disentangled them and kicked the garment aside. His strong hands were caressing her bare arms and back, and she gave herself to the blissful sensations dazing her. Lost to the sounds coming from below them, she was aware only of their rising passion.

Jared tensed briefly as her quivering hands impatiently drew his billowy shirt over his head and her fingers roamed his bare torso. Her long hair gently caressed his body as she pressed kisses to his chest. Then she buried her fingers in his hair and drew his lips to her aching, pleading breasts. Because of his height, Jared was in an uncomfortable position, but he hated to move just yet, even to the enticing bed not far away. His mouth returned to hers and greedily feasted there, and though his body craved swift union with hers, he labored lovingly to arouse her to an even higher plane of urgency. His hand touched the incredibly silky curls which guarded her womanhood, parted her downlike maidenhair, and located the satiny folds which were fiery yet damp.

The peak they hid was hot and hard. It begged to be pleasured. Very cautiously, because he knew an aroused bud was sensitive at this point of love-making, he massaged it until it craved to burst into bloom, skillfully tormenting her to a frenzy of yearning.

Maren's legs were shaky and she knew they would not support her weight much longer. "Jared, you're making me weak with longing. I can hardly stand. If we don't lie down, I shall melt to the floor."

Jared scooped her into his arms and placed her on the bed. In the pale candlelight his adoring gaze traveled her full length, and his desire intensified. "You're a treasure, my beautiful and bewitching siren," he murmured in a low, thick voice.

Maren opened her arms. "Then lay claim to me, my roguish pirate, because I can endure no more plundering."

Jared chuckled happily, the sound mellow and soothing to her ears. "Let me eye you a moment longer, for your beauty steals my breath and plays havoc with my self-control."

"You can study your prize later, my love. Now please come and enjoy it. Do you want this carefully ignited fire to cool before it can consume us?" she teased, feeling marvelously free spirited and bold.

"My fire needs to cool a mite, my blazing booty, else I might ravish you the moment our bodies touch."

"And waste all that wonderful kindling?"

"Nothing is wasted on you, Maren, nothing."

Their gazes locked and they smiled, each realizing how aroused the other was.

Even more than the scent of the sea, her fragrance called out to him, intoxicating his senses. As he removed his boots and unbuckled his belt, he suddenly wished the room were dark for he feared the sight of his tumid manhood might frighten her.

But Maren's mother had discussed this aspect of sex with her daughter. She had told Maren not to panic over a man's size and eagerness, had explained what would take place on her first night with a man and later. Naturally Maren was nervous because of her inexperience, but she knew that Jared would be gentle and patient with her. She witnessed her love's hestiation and was touched by it. To relax him, she teased, "Don't tell me you're shyer than I am, my lusty privateer."

"This is new for you, Maren, and I don't want to frighten you. Actually it's new for me too love, so bear with me." He removed his pants and tossed them onto the floor. Strange, he had never felt more naked and vulnerable in his life! He prayed she was too aroused to be frightened by the sight of his prominent manhood.

But before he could join Maren, she said, "Please wait a moment, Jared. Let me see you as you've seen me."

He halted and gazed at her, and her eyes slowly roamed over his lean, hard body. His golden brown shoulders were broad and powerful, his midriff flat, his hips narrow. She noticed the ripples of his rib cage and the way his muscles rose and fell, reminding her of gently rolling hills covered by supple grass. His flesh looked smooth and snug, and his tan halted at his waist. She eyed the curling fuzz on his chest, followed it down his sleek abdomen.

Jared was thrilled by her courage and admiration Inflamed by her pervasive study of his naked frame, he joined her on the bed. Lying half atop her, he longingly gazed into her flushed face and entreating eyes, relieved that she had not been discouraged or intimidated by him. His lips and hands again caressed her, rapidly arousing flames of raging desire.

She loved everything he did to her, each caress, each kiss, each unspoken promise of what was to come. Her hands roved his body, and she nibbled on his shoulders and neck. Then, waxing between tension and relaxation, she responded wildly as his fingers and lips brought delightful sensations to her nipples. The bud of her womanhood tingled and pulsed with pleasure, and she encouraged him to continue. Blood raced madly throughout her head and body, heating her to a feverish level and burning away all inhibition. Every inch he touched was sensitive, responsive, alive. She thought if he didn't move on to the next stage of this drama she would burst into flame and be totally consumed. When Jared's finger eased within her, her feminine recess eagerly accepted it and reacted to its wondrous movements, becoming more moist and beginning to ache with need of him.

Jared had tantalized her and had restrained himself for as long as he could endure the blissful torment surging through him. As gently as possible he entered her to avoid prolonging her discomfort with clumsy probings and pokings.

Maren tensed, inhaled, and involuntarily arched upward as if seeking his protection and comfort. Her urge to withdraw and protest vanished like quicksilver, along with the sharp and brief pain. But, an odd feeling lingered within her. She was on alert, her senses temporarily cleared. She felt him tremble and heard him breathe erratically. He was rigid, as if fearing to move. Then, his lips claimed hers and stole her wits once more. He withdrew and entered her several times, very slowly and gingerly, then halted again. His chest hair teased against her breasts, stimulating them. His gentle hands sensuously fondled her flesh and made her aware of every part of her body. Then he began to move rhythmically, his movements giving her great pleasure, but arousing an intense hunger.

A strange tension kept building in her until she wanted to claw at him and demand that he do something to end the ache deep within her core. She began to lift her buttocks toward his probing flesh each time he retreated. Mutely she pleaded that he satisfy the urgent hunger gnawing at her. She clung to him and kissed him feverishly.

"Jared, Jared, you're driving me mad," she murmured. "What must I do?"

"Ride the waves with me, my sweet siren. Wrap your legs around me, and hold me tightly. Come to me, Maren, come to me," he coaxed huskily. "Be mine tonight and forever."

Her arms and legs encircled him, and soon the core of her womanhood began to spasm wildly. "Oh, oh," she moaned into his mouth, surprised and stirred by the sensations assailing her. Clinging to him, she matched his pace as rapture's waves crashed over them and around them. She had expected their lovemaking to be wonderful, but not this blissful and staggering.

Jared knew she had obtained her release, and he was glad because his was spilling forth rapidly, joyously, uncontrollably. Within moments they lay limp in each other's embrace. He held her snugly and possessively as they nestled together, sharing tender kisses, their bodies content.

Despite the war between America and Britain, which could tear them apart at any time, they were at peace for the moment. All was quiet below them and through the windows came fresh air. Occasionally an animal broke the serene silence, and the scents of flowers and of lovemaking wafted on the gentle breeze which cooled their flesh. The bedside candle was guttering, but the moon was almost full.

The last full moon had occurred when she'd come home, and Maren was amazed by how much had changed for her since then. She thought of her parents making love in this bed where she had found pleasure with Jared. *Trust*, she mused. Yes, she trusted the man she loved, the man in her arms and bed. She closed her eyes and went to sleep, knowing Jared was safe and he was hers at last.

Jared lifted his head and glanced over at Maren. She was breathing evenly, so he knew she was asleep. He longed for this war to end so he could remain at her side, and he dreaded the day when he would be compelled to leave her and go to sea. Yet, he must. The Royal Navy was powerful and his country needed his aid, despite the risk to his ship and his life. If only they weren't so pitifully outnumbered and outgunned . . . Every day at sea could be his last, and life was suddenly too precious to lose. But no matter what he and Maren wanted and needed, he could remain with her only as long as his missions justified his presence. Anger and panic raced through him. Before he left her alone, he decided, he had to deal with Eric James.

Thoughts of separation from his love tormented him. He had to be assured that she was safe before he departed. He imagined her alarm at the news that he must leave. She would probably fear losing him as she had lost Daniel Redford. No, he silently argued, it was different with him. By her own admission she had not loved Daniel . . . but she had not declared her love for him. He gazed at her until he was consumed by a need to claim her once more, to fuse their bodies and hopefully to fuse their hearts. Perhaps it was selfish to awaken her, but he could not banish such feelings. . . .

*   *   *

Maren stretched and yawned lazily as she awakened. Smiling at the first images which came to mind on this new and glorious day, she rolled onto her side and her smile faded. Jared was not lying beside her. She flung the covers aside and looked for him; he was gone. Disappointment nibbled at her until she realized he must have sneaked out of her suite before dawn to avoid gossip and to allow her additional sleep. Once they were married . . . That thought brought a broader and happier smile to her face. He had made love to her twice last night, the second time with an urgency which had astonished and baffled her. Yet, he had been extremely gentle and passionate both times, and she warmed as she recalled those stirring unions. Eager to see him, she bathed and dressed quickly, then rushed downstairs.

Mary was busy with her chores when the blissfully happy Maren reached the kitchen. "Where's Jared?" she inquired, trying to sound casual.

Mary glanced at her and replied, "He left early this morning."

"Where did he go? What time did he say he'd return?"

"He didn't tell me, Miss Maren, but I did notice a cloth bag in his hand, the kind sailors pack their clothes in."

She shrieked, "You mean he's *gone?* Without telling me?"

Barely suppressing a merry chuckle, Jared answered from the doorway, "Certainly not. Next time I have business to handle, I'll leave you a note so you won't worry about me."

As their eyes met, the housekeeper's presence was briefly forgotten. They lovingly scrutinized each other, as if looking for changes since their last meeting, which Mary did not know had occurred last night. But the older woman did sense the tender aura surrounding them, and she smiled secretly.

"I'm starving," Jared announced huskily, never taking his twinkling eyes from Maren's. "It seems like ages since I've tasted anything delicious. How about you?" A half-grin teased at his lips, which she wanted to kiss.

"Ravenous, Mr. Morgan," she replied. "Shall I prepare us a tempting meal?"

"Lunch is ready, unless you prefer breakfast," Mary told them.

Their double entendres lost to Mary, Maren and Jared laughed as they sat down and continued to have eyes only for each other. When the housekeeper began to place food on the table, Maren jumped up and said, "You're busy, Mary; I'll get this."

"It's no trouble, Miss Maren. I enjoy doing things for you two. Just sit and talk while I fetch things."

Complying, Maren said to Jared, "Tell me about your family and your home."

A curious expression crossed Jared's face before he smiled and said, "Later, partner, we have a busy day ahead."

"What have you planned?" she asked excitedly.

"We have an appointment with our lawyer about some papers, remember? Unless you've changed your mind about signing them."

"Never," she murmured.

"Good. Now eat and get ready to leave or we'll be late."

The lawyer was very formal as he explained the contents of the papers to be signed. He then promised to look into the other matters they had mentioned on their last visit, after Eric James returned, and he advised them to keep the papers in a safe place, as they were also wills. As quickly as possible, he completed the business and dismissed them.

After Maren and Jared had strolled a short way, he asked, "Did you notice how eager he was to be rid of us? No doubt he's in a panic, wanting your cousin to return so he can report our doings to him. What will Eric have to say?"

"I imagine he won't like any of it."

"You're still going to press the matter, aren't you?"

"I suppose," she answered absently, wanting to avoid the subject.

"You suppose?" Jared probed, stopping to look at her.

Maren halted too, but hesitated before turning to meet his gaze. "Let's handle it after he's back," she coaxed. "We can't solve anything until I speak with him, so why keep going over and over it?"

"You can't back away from this problem, Maren. It's important to both of us."

"Both of us?" she echoed in bewilderment.

"We are partners now, in every way possible. I want you to get back what is rightfully and legally yours. It angers me to think he duped you and your father. I want it settled before I leave."

"Leave? When?" she asked.

"When my business here is finished, I have to return to sea. My ship and I are needed."

"How soon?" she probed sadly.

"A few weeks, more or less. Don't worry, I'll be back as soon as possible. I have some important investments here."

"I hate to think of you being in danger."

"I'll be careful, especially now. But if anything does hap—"

She clamped a hand over his mouth. "Don't say it."

He gently grasped her hand and moved it so he could speak. "I have to say it, Maren. If anything should happen to me, you're taken care of."

"I don't care about the money. I care about you, Jared."

"Then trust me to stay alive and return."

"I trust you; I just don't trust the Royal Navy. You said they would do anything to defeat us. What trophies would the British want more than Captain Hawk and the *Sea Mist*?"

"You flatter me, woman," he jested to calm her.

"Flattery, ha! You know it's true."

"Don't ask me not to go, Maren. Please."

"I want to, but I can't. I know you have to defend

our country, but swear you won't take any unnecessary risks."

"Everything in war is a risk, love, but I won't take any foolish ones."

His words of endearment warmed her. She wanted to fling herself into his arms, but they were on the street. She hoped he would ask her to marry him before he sailed. She would say yes. She decided to let him know that she was willing to wed him at any time.

"Where did you go this morning? I missed you when I awoke."

"I had to see a man who is to do a job for me. The less you know about my work at this point, the better. As soon as this is done, I'll explain everything."

"You're afraid I'll drop hints in the wrong ears?"

"It happens sometimes by accident, Maren. People drink too much, they get ill and delirious, or they don't notice an eavesdropping spy like Peter Thomas," he explained. "I have to be extra careful now that people associate me with you. If the wrong person got wind of my assignments, you could be captured and tortured for information."

"You're right; I can't let drop what I don't know."

"You're serious? Just like that, you accept my terms?"

"Just like that," she replied, smiling at his astonishment.

"I don't believe my luck. I've found the perfect woman."

"Didn't you know, Jared? I am Lady Luck."

Jared was so relaxed that he almost reminded her that her father had called her that in his letter. Soon he would show her the hidden cabinet behind the fireplace; he would reveal all he knew to her. Right now he wanted to get closer to her.

Maren noticed Jared's curious reaction. Though she felt he had been about to say something, she let it pass.

They stopped at the bank and placed their papers in the box they kept there. Jared told Maren to hold on to the key in case she had need of his will or of the deed to Lady Luck.

"When this war's over, Lady Luck will be very prosperous. We could become rich, Maren. And if we can take back James Shipping, we can have the best of two lives: one on land and one at sea."

"It sounds wonderful. I would have Jared Morgan at home and Captain Hawk at sea—two adventurous men to sate my every desire."

"If you take a nap this afternoon, I'll begin my task late tonight and I'll work at it for hours."

"Agreed, Mr. Morgan."

"That sounds as if I had better take my nap with you."

"That would be wise, partner. I have lots of learning to do."

Maren put on the green silk gown with the squared neck and raised waistline. It had short sleeves and a slightly flared skirt. She then eased her feet into matching slippers, and fastened the locket Jared had given her about her neck. She drew her hair up on the sides and secured it with decorative combs, allowing it to cascade down her back. She was eager to see Jared, to be with him again tonight. She couldn't seem to have enough of him, and she hoped it would always be like this.

She waited until seven-thirty before heading downstairs. Praying that her expression would not give away their intimacy when she looked at Jared, she halted at the landing and inhaled deeply to slow her racing heart. She was as nervous as a kitten beneath a hawk's shadow. You're being silly, Maren James, she chided herself. He belongs to you now.

As she made her final descent, her left foot was caught by something, and she tumbled down the stairs. When she grabbed at the railing to check her downward plunge, her body twisted and her head slammed into the bottom post. She heard herself scream before blackness claimed her.

When she roused, Jared and Mary were leaning over her and she was in her bed. "Are you all right?" they asked in unison.

"What . . . happened?" she asked confusedly as she tried to sit up.

Even if she hadn't swayed, Jared would have pressed her back onto the bed. "Lie still. The doctor is on his way. You took a bad fall, woman. One of the steps became loose and threw you off balance."

Maren's head ached, but it was clearing. "Where

was everyone? Did anyone see me fall?"

"I'm afraid not. The guards were out front and everyone else was busy. We heard you scream and fall, but when we reached you, you were out cold. Dan's having the step repaired right now. You'll have to be more careful, woman; that accident could have killed you."

Accident? The word echoed in Maren's mind. It hadn't been an accident. The step hadn't been loose. She had felt a hand seize her ankle. . . .

Chapter Eleven

After the doctor checked Maren over and assured Jared and Mary that she was fine, the housekeeper returned to her tasks to allow Jared to talk privately with Maren. Maren wanted to get up, but the doctor had advised her to remain abed until morning and Jared had insisted she obey him.

She was quiet for a long time, too quiet. Jared was worried. "Are you sure you're all right, Maren?"

She met his concerned gaze and smiled. She loved him and trusted him. "It wasn't an accident, Jared."

Sitting beside her, he stroked her head and teased, "Don't worry, I don't think you're clumsy. Just be more careful in the future."

"That isn't what I meant. Someone was standing under the stairs. Whoever it was tripped me. I felt a hand on my ankle. Obviously the board was loosened to make it appear an accident. Who was around when I fell?"

289

Jared realized she was serious. "It happened so quickly, Maren, that I doubt anyone saw anything suspicious. We were all busy and the hall was empty when you came down. After we heard your scream and a thud, you were surrounded by people. If anyone was under the steps, he melted into the crowd."

"Not *if*, Jared," she corrected him, alarmed by this attempt on her life.

"Relax, love, don't jump on an innocently spoken word," he softly scolded. "I believe you. Whoever did it is smart; it was timed to occur when no one was around. I don't recall seeing that gambler who's been giving us trouble, but I'll ask the others about him. And I'll go check under the steps right now."

"Jared, there's something I forgot to tell you," she began, then revealed her confrontation with Howard Heath during his absence.

"Damn it, Maren!" he declared angrily. "That man is dangerous, maybe crazy. How could you let something like this slip your mind?"

Maren caught his hand and kissed it. "We've been kind of busy since your return, Mr. Morgan. My mind was somewhere else."

"When we talked about Eric this afternoon, you should have recalled that incident. Please don't keep on protecting him," he urged.

"I'm not protecting him or defending him, Jared. Honestly, it slipped my mind until now. Besides, he had said he was seeing his boss that night, and Eric is far away."

"His boss must be working for Eric. Blast it, woman, you heard the slip he made. How much evidence do you need against Eric?"

"What if the threat doesn't come from Eric? What if someone wants to trick us into thinking he's to blame?"

"Maren, Maren," he chided, "you know that isn't true."

Unshed tears glistened in her eyes as she admitted, "I know, Jared, but it's hard to believe him so wicked. I've been close to him for years. I can't believe he would harm me, or have me harmed."

"After you told that troublemaker we were on to him and he reported it to Eric's cohort, their plans may have been changed. We've already added that sneaky lawyer to the list of men working for your cousin. They both know we're suspicious of Eric and plan to work against him. They probably think Eric will go along with any actions they're taking."

"I know what you say is true, but someone else could want Lady Luck. The place is valuable, and will be worth even more after the war."

"You aren't referring to me, are you?"

She nipped his hand before saying, "Don't be ridiculous. If I didn't trust you, would I be telling you all of this?"

"Then prove it," he challenged, his gaze imprisoning hers.

"How so?"

"Marry me tomorrow, but in secret."

Her eyes widened and she stared at him. "Marry

you? Secretly?"

"We both know what we want, Maren, each other. So there's no reason to wait for months to marry." He stroked her hair as he explained, "But we'll have to do it secretly to protect you from our enemies. If Eric learns he can't get Lady Luck by scaring you out, he might have no use for you. It's my guess he brought you home so he could take it from you." Jared came to some other grim conclusions. "And don't forget, I'm a threat to many men, traitors and spies who wouldn't hesitate to use my wife to get at me. Until all of this is worked out, no one can be told, Maren, not even Beth. You know her tongue moves faster than her wits when she's excited."

"Who would perform a secret ceremony?"

"I know the perfect man. He's right outside of town. Are you willing?"

"If you're serious, the answer is yes."

"I'll make arrangements tomorrow, and we can have it done Sunday afternoon. I mean it, Maren, don't reveal this to anyone. Promise?"

"I promise."

"Get some rest now. I'll see you in the morning."

"In the morning?" she repeated, frowning disappointedly.

He playfully tugged on a long curl. "You'll have me all to yourself very soon, Miss James. Take it easy tonight. That's a nasty bump on your head, and you're supposed to remain quiet."

"If you insist, Mr. Morgan. At least kiss me good night."

Jared leaned forward, and as their lips met, Maren's arms encircled his neck. They held each other tenderly, both of them trembling with desire.

As he spread kisses over her face, he murmured, "What am I going to do with you, woman? You steal my wits and self-control."

Maren laughed happily. "Evidently not as much as you steal mine, my selfish pirate. You're the one rejecting me tonight."

"That isn't fair," he teased, kissing her again. He stood up and said, "That's all for tonight, woman. When you're my wife, I'll give you more, lots more."

Wife, she mused. "Maren Morgan, it has a nice sound, doesn't it?"

"Yes, my love, it does. Now get some sleep."

Jared went downstairs and entered the curtained-off area beneath the steps where supplies were kept. He found several extra chairs there. Standing on one would have enabled someone to reach the step on which Maren had tripped. The board had been repaired immediately so he could not examine how much space had been created by moving it, but surely it had been large enough for a hand to slide through to seize Maren's foot. In the commotion after her fall, anyone hiding under the stairs could have slipped unnoticed into the crowd gathered around her. He decided to investigate this matter without alerting the guilty person to his suspicion.

"Looking for something, Jared?" Dan Myers asked.

"We have a problem, Dan," Jared replied. "Maren's fall wasn't an accident. Someone hid under here and tripped her. Did you notice anyone acting strange?"

Dan looked surprised. "I'm afraid not. Who do you think was responsible?"

Jared shrugged. "I don't know, but we'd better keep an eye on her. Don't tell anyone about this until we know more."

"I'll watch over her when you're not here," the manager promised. He wondered what was going on.

"I'd appreciate that," Jared said. Then he asked about the troublesome gambler, but Dan told him the man hadn't returned since he'd been kicked out earlier in the week. "I think Eric James is behind this danger, but I don't know who's doing his dirty work for him. Keep an eye on his friends," Jared told his manager.

"Does Miss Maren agree?" Dan asked.

"She's beginning to accept the truth about her cousin, but it's hard on her. We have to find a way to unmask Eric before I'm forced to leave."

"When will that be?"

"I hope I can stay another couple of weeks. He should be back by then. I'm sure you realize he cheated Cameron's daughter out of most of her inheritance, and now he wants Lady Luck. Once I obtain evidence against him, I'll let the law handle him, if I don't kill him first. But I want to unmask his cohorts so they are no threat to Maren after I leave New Orleans."

"Who could be working for a snake like Eric James? Setting up an accident like that . . . Maren could have been killed. He's a smart one, Jared. Be careful."

"I plan to be, Dan."

"How will you get evidence against Eric and his hirelings? And how do you intend to stop him from taking over Lady Luck after you're gone?"

"He can't get it so long as I'm her partner."

"I know that, but so will he when he returns," Dan said pointedly. "He was real anxious to learn who her secret partner was. That could be why he brought her back, to unmask you."

"But Maren had the accident," Jared reasoned.

"Yes, but you also live upstairs. You could have tripped as easily as she did and broken your neck. Then Maren would be sole owner. Or Eric might want both of you out of the way. Who else stands to inherit Maren's holdings but her nearest kin?"

"You have a point, Dan. With me dead, he wouldn't have to worry about the no-sale stipulation." According to the papers he and Maren had signed, their estates were interlocked. Yes, a smart lawyer could find a way for Eric to take over everything. Maybe the accident had been meant for him.

Jared started toward the door. "I think I'll go nose around that lawyer's house. And do you know where that other bastard lives?''

''Next door to Lewis,'' Dan replied, causing Jared's brows to rise.

At Jared's insistence, Maren remained inside the house on Saturday, and the doors were kept locked. As a further precaution, Jared had had the downstairs windows nailed shut at the bottom and opened at the top to allow air to flow through the rooms. Since the windows were tall and high off the ground it would be difficult for anyone to get inside, at least quietly. Jared left around noon to meet with Kerry Osgood and to make the arrangements for his marriage on the following day, July tenth.

Around two o'clock, Marc James came to visit Maren. She was surprised to see her cousin, who claimed he had come to check on her after hearing about her recent fall.

''As you can see, Marc, I'm fine, just some bruises and a knot on my head. How did you hear about my accident?''

''Mr. Heath told me. I saw him at the dock this morning?''

Howard Heath, that obnoxious man . . . ''How did he know about it?'' she asked. ''He isn't allowed in here.''

''His friends told him. He doesn't like you, Maren. He laughed about your fall, said it was too bad you didn't break your . . . neck.''

When Marc hesitated and flushed, she knew the

revolting Heath had used more vulgar language. She casually related the trouble she had had with Howard Heath, just to see how Marc would react.

"That sorry no-good brute! Why didn't you have someone beat him up for you, Maren? He can't treat my cousin that way. I'll tell Eric when he gets home. He'll be fighting mad."

"Don't worry about me, Marc; Jared is taking care of Heath. How are things going at the office?"

"Mr. Andrews got two ships in and one out. Eric will be happy." Marc grinned as if the credit for this success was his own.

Maren smiled. "I'm glad business is so good. Eric will be proud of you for taking such good care of things."

"You think so?" he asked, eagerness shining in his green eyes.

Maren's gaze swept over Marc's dark blond hair and boyish features. In another year or two he would look even more like Eric. "I'm certain of it. Would you like some refreshments? It's hot out today."

"No, thanks. I have to get home. A cleaning woman comes on Saturday afternoons and Eric doesn't like anyone in the house alone."

"Why not?" she asked in a teasing tone.

"He's afraid something might be stolen. And he gets real mad when anybody disturbs his stuff. I have to watch her the whole time. I'm not supposed to let anyone in while he's away, but that don't mean you."

About an hour after Marc left, Evelyn Sims came to call, ostensibly to check on Maren's injuries. Her copper-colored hair shone as she fastened her blue eyes on her employer. "I was so worried about you, Miss Maren. Are you hurt?"

"I'm fine, Evelyn. I'm lucky that board wasn't totally broken. I do hope someone didn't loosen it on purpose. I know I can be a demanding boss at times and make people mad," she jested slyly, hoping to evoke a reaction.

"Do you think someone made you fall?" the fair-skinned woman asked, her eyes fixed on Maren's face.

Maren replied calmly, "Why would anyone do that? I was teasing."

"Everyone was worried about you. I couldn't wait until tonight to make sure you weren't hurt badly. You should be more careful."

"I will. Did you happen to notice anyone hanging around last night?" As she asked this, Maren noticed that Evelyn Sims paled slightly and fidgeted.

"You mean someone pushed you down the stairs?" Evelyn asked, wishing she hadn't allowed Howard to entice her to do such a crazy thing. But he had promised to marry her, if she did as he asked. Still, should Samuel Lewis learn it wasn't an accident . . .

Maren realized Evelyn Sims was reacting oddly to her questions, so she changed her tack. "No. I'm just telling everyone to be alert for trouble. If strangers come around looking things over, I want to be told. We take in a lot of money, and I don't want to risk a robbery. Nor do I want any more incidents like those Howard Heath caused. He's a vicious man."

*   *   *

At six, Ned Jones and Harry Peck, the two guards, arrived. As with Marc and Evelyn, Maren questioned them slyly, but learning nothing new, she returned to her room.

When Jared knocked at her door twenty minutes later, she let him in, hugged him, and spread kisses over his face. "I'm so glad you're home. I've missed you terribly," she declared.

Jared scooped her up into his arms and, walking to the sofa, sat down with her on his lap. He nuzzled her neck and caused her to giggle. Then his mouth sought hers and they kissed hungrily. When they broke apart, his head dropped against the sofa back and he inhaled deeply. "That's what I call a proper greeting. How was your day?" he asked, his fingers pushing straying locks from her lovely face.

Maren excitedly related her news, telling him about her visitors. At one point in her tale Jared's jaw tensed and his brownish gold eyes narrowed. He grasped her forearms gently and stared into her eyes. "What's wrong?" she asked.

He sighed annoyedly. "You've certainly had a busy day. I leave you home where I think you're safe, yet you still manage to endanger yourself."

"I didn't reveal anything to them. I was careful. Besides, if any attacker knows I'm on to him, maybe he won't try to harm me again."

Jared set her aside and faced her. "Or maybe he'll be more clever and try harder next time. You've alerted him to our suspicions, Maren. He'll be more careful now, harder to trap."

"Well I can't just sit here doing nothing. My life is

in danger."

"And I'm responsible for it," he told her angrily.

"So am I," she retorted, matching his tone.

He exhaled loudly in frustration. "I know you want to help, love, but please don't intrude again. This isn't a game, Maren. I'm experienced in such matters. Let me handle them."

"I'm not trained as you are, Jared, but I'm not stupid. We need answers, and we can't get them without asking questions."

"There are ways to get information without exposing ourselves. I want you to remain upstairs tonight. It would give us away if I was guarding you."

"I can't become a prisoner in my room," she protested.

"Damn it, Maren! Please do as I ask until you're safe. I can't concentrate when I know you're dangling yourself before a crazed man."

Maren noted his genuine concern. "All right, we'll do it your way," she conceded. "Just visit me as much as possible."

"My willing captive, that's what you once promised to be and I'm holding you to your vow. You know the rules; a wife obeys."

"Oh? Perhaps I should give this marriage further consideration," she teased as she ran her forefinger over his lips.

"Oh, no, you won't. You're marrying me tomorrow. It's all set."

"When? Where?" she asked, anticipation flooding

through her.

"We'll go over the plan later. Right now, I've got to get downstairs and keep my eyes open. I want to memorize every face in case there's another attempt."

"You really think he'll try again, don't you?"

Jared did not want to worry her by revealing that they both were in danger. "Not if I can catch him. If anything happened to you . . ."

He pulled her roughly and pulled her against him, pressed his mouth urgently to hers. His kiss was forceful, nearly desperate, and a little frightening. His tight grip was bruising Maren's arms and his lips were ravaging hers, but she yielded eagerly to this show of intense emotion.

She was breathless when his mouth left hers and he clutched her to him. She could hear his heart beating, swiftly and heavily. He is afraid for me, she concluded and smiled.

"Please don't let any harm come to you, Maren," he urged hoarsely. "I need you and I want you. I can't lose you, too."

Maren leaned away from him and met his troubled gaze. She started to ask for an explanation of his last statement, but decided it was best to wait until he offered one. The look in his eyes touched her, ensnared her. "I feel the same way, Jared," she said.

He smiled and hugged her again, this time tenderly. Then he rested his head against the sofa and closed his eyes, and Maren realized how weary he seemed. He had many burdens: his missions, her safety, and something painful from his past. She cuddled against him to offer him comfort.

When he didn't move or speak for some time, she finally asked, "Do you want to lie down for a while? You seem tired and depressed."

"I only want to relax for a minute. It's nice to have you beside me and in my life. But it feels strange to be open and vulnerable again; it'll take some getting used to. I haven't needed anyone or leaned on anyone since my father and brother died and . . . Be patient with me, Maren. Don't lose faith in me. There are some things I must settle in Savannah before we announce our marriage. If you don't mind, I'd rather not discuss them just yet."

Jared had told her that he had never loved before, so Maren assumed his problems did not involve another woman. Still, she wondered if he had ever been married . . . if he had children at home? She would have married without love; suppose Jared had done the same. She hadn't seen him in years, and his life could have changed more drastically than she had imagined. The thought of another woman being that close to him sent ripples of jealousy through her. His words and his tone haunted her, but she replied, "You can tell me everything when you're ready."

He cupped her face and tilted her head so their gazes locked. "You do trust me completely, don't you, Maren?"

"More than I trust myself, Jared. I need you and I want you."

"You are my Lady Luck, Maren. You're going to fill all the empty spots in me and in my life. I'm not forcing you to marry me tomorrow, but I need to know you're mine before I'm called away."

"And I need to know you're mine, Jared, all mine."

They moved toward each other and kissed, again and again. They began to caress each other, to share their great need, but when fiery passion seized them, Jared reluctantly drew away from her.

"The next time I make love to you, I want my ring on your finger. I want it to be perfect. I want us to give our all to each other. Is that all right with you?"

Maren smiled radiantly. "Hard, but I agree."

"Let's make it easier on ourselves. I'll leave."

Maren locked the door after he departed, and leaned against it. She sighed happily, then suddenly danced around the room, nearly bumping into a table. Halting her dizzying twirl, she laughed softly. His wife, she was becoming Jared Morgan's wife— tomorrow! He was no longer alive only in her dreams and fantasies. He was hers.

Maren spent the time trying to distract herself with reading, but every so often she halted and lowered the book. Her father's letters kept coming to mind, as did the mystery he had created in them. Unable to concentrate on the book, she went into her bedroom and approached the bookcase. She looked at the doll, which Mary had repaired, and at her father's favorite Wedgwood piece. The doll was mostly in red and the piece was in blue. They were on opposite ends of the same shelf. She called the letter to mind: "Cut them in half. . . ."

She searched the shelf for another clue, but could

find nothing. Perhaps the objects had been moved since her father had died. "And you still have two." Two more what? she wondered. "Shelves!" she concluded aloud. Quickly she searched the second shelf above the doll. Nothing. She knelt and searched the second one below it. Her fingers encountered a catch on the underside of the shelf. As she worked with it, the bookcase moved slightly and squeaked.

Maren shoved it open and stared inside. The space revealed was large enough to conceal a person standing up! She noticed more shelves to the rear. Fetching more light, she stepped into the secret enclosure. She could not believe what she had found: letters, papers, and money.

Maren checked the records and the money first, and realized she had found the missing "special fund." This was Jared's money, his share of the profits before Eric took control. The deeds to Lady Luck, the townhouse, and the plantation were inside, as were the ownership papers of the shipping firm. Instantly Maren wondered how Eric had sold everything—anything—without these deeds. Then she knew. That devious lawyer had forged copies. The sales were not legal and she still owned everything! But how could she recover her inheritance? Some of the properties might be out of Eric's hands?

She read the letters, all in blue envelopes. They were addressed to her. In them her father spoke of his worries and fears about the changes in Eric, or rather the dropping of Eric's lengthy pretense, and he revealed his disappointment in his brother's son. Her

father sounded deeply concerned about Eric's behavior toward their clients and about the way her
cousin was running the business. He charged Eric
with trading with the British, and said he was going
to revoke Eric's authority and send him home!

There was another letter on the shelf, addressed to
Jared, unsealed. She read it and was dismayed to
sense the anguish her father must have endured. He
begged Jared to help him get Eric out of his life and
firm, and to correct Eric's wrongs if anything
happened to him. Maren's heart lurched, but she
closed her mind to such an idea.

As she read on, her father told Jared all about her
and encouraged him to consider her for a wife! Maren
reread that line. The next few surprised her even
more: "Maren is a strong and stubborn girl, but she'll
bend to the right man, a man like you, Jared. I can't
believe she'll go through with her marriage to Daniel
Redford. She doesn't love him." Maren's eyes
widened as Cameron exposed her reasons for agreeing to the union, the ones she had confided to her
mother, but the next lines were heartrending. "If
anything happens to me, I beg you to find Maren and
help her. Eric isn't to be trusted at all, Jared. Don't let
him disarm you and fool you as he did me."

Maren lay the letters aside, then leaned weakly
against the wall. Jared was right; Eric was dangerous
and greedy. Maren's emotions were a maelstrom of
fury, sadness, anguish, bitterness, and alarm. She had
to outwit and punish her cousin. With Jared's help,
she would do it very soon.

But they had to be careful. Eric had many men working for him, and perhaps Evelyn Sims. Maren didn't want to endanger her love, and she knew Eric would retaliate. Since her cousin could return at any time, she dreaded the confrontation that was imminent. She had to show this compartment and its contents to Jared. The letter . . .

She straightened. Jared often came in and out of her room. He had been in business with her father for years. The letter she'd found on the floor had been blue, like those in this secret place. Did Jared know about this compartment? Had he already checked it out?

Maren snatched up the letter to her love and finished reading it. She clenched her teeth as she read the last line: "When you check here for your money and find this letter . . ."

"Damn you, Jared Morgan! You asked me to trust you, and I did. But you deceived me. You knew about this place—this evidence. Why did you make a fuss about the missing money? Why did you intend to force me to marry you? Why didn't you confide in me?"

Anger and torment gnawed at her, and when Mary came up to bring her refreshments, she asked the woman to send Jared to her. While the housekeeper left, Maren paced the room anxiously. She was not going to marry Jared just so he could take care of Cameron's daughter. She was going to confront him with everything!

If this was a misunderstanding, it would be

resolved promptly. Her mother had warned her about such tricky matters. "Don't simmer until you burst, Maren," she'd said. "If something troubles you, take care of it quickly before it causes problems." Maybe Jared had a good reason for keeping his secret, and maybe he didn't.

The housekeeper returned with the message that Jared would come up later, that it wouldn't look proper if someone saw him going into her room at this time of night.

Maren thanked Mary and dismissed her. She then replaced everything in the compartment and closed it. She was tempted to dress, go downstairs, and drag him up to her room to make an explanation. But she dared not do that in her agitated state. She sipped some wine to relax her tension, and she cried about the implications of her discoveries. Soon, physically and emotionally exhausted, she fell asleep.

Jared entered her room shortly after twelve. He watched her slumber for a time, then decided not to awaken her. Tomorrow they would be married and would be together all night.

At ten, Jared knocked on her door and called out, "Up, woman, we have a busy day. Don't keep a nervous groom waiting."

Maren knew Mary was always gone on Sunday morning, so she unlocked the door and walked away from it, halting with her back to him.

Jared's sunny smile faded when he detected the

chill in the room and saw that she was not dressed to leave. "Don't tell me you're miffed with me for not answering your summons last night," he teased anxiously. "You were asleep by the time I finished and came upstairs. I didn't want you to be grumpy and tired today from lack of rest."

Maren whirled to face him. "You demand that I trust you, Jared; then you refuse to trust me. Don't you think it's time to be honest?"

Jared tensed and stared, trying to figure out the change in her since last night. She was distant and cool, nearly hostile. She could be referring to many things, so he asked, "Be honest about what, Maren? I'm utterly confused."

"About everything," she retorted, her tone curt.

"You want to hear my life story before we get married? Heavens, woman, you're marrying the man I am today, not my past."

In response she declared gravely, "If you don't tell me the truth, we won't be getting married, today or any day."

Jared stepped forward and reached for her, but Maren avoided his embrace. "Don't touch me until you explain everything," she said.

"Explain what, Maren? How can I answer you when I don't know what you want to know?"

"Me, I'm the question. Tell me everything about your connection to me." When his brow wrinkled in bewilderment, she added, "You can begin with the secret panel in Papa's bedroom and what's in there."

"You found it? When? How?"

"Does it matter? You lied to me, Jared."

"No, love, I didn't. I just kept silent. I didn't want you to see what was in there just yet. I wanted you to accept the truth about Eric before you saw Cameron's allegations. That's all they are, Maren, your father's fears and charges. And we still have to prove those deeds are the real ones. Eric is a big man now, with powerful friends. If we reveal those papers too soon we could be accused of fraud. Your cousin is clever, Maren. He knows the real deeds are hidden somewhere. He probably hoped you could lead him to them after your return."

"Is that why you asked me to marry you, as a favor to my father?"

"Never, Maren. I didn't even go through that stuff until Monday, and you were already under my skin before that."

"Under your skin so deeply that while I was out with Beth you were snooping through my room? Why didn't you tell me later? Certainly after we spent the night together! Did it slip your mind?"

"No, Maren, it didn't. I wasn't ready for you to learn such things."

"It isn't your place to decide what I should and shouldn't know!"

"Blast it, woman! Don't you realize what those letters imply?"

Pain knifed through her. "Yes. . . ."

"After I read them, I was afraid of how that information would affect you. I didn't think you were ready to hear those things so soon. Heavens, you've only known about your parents' deaths for a few months. How could I hit you with the possibility they were . . . killed by Eric? Don't you see, love? Eric wants more than Lady Luck from you. He needs that evidence."

"That's what you believe, isn't it?"

"Don't you, Maren? Deep inside, don't you?" he asked softly.

"Yes," she admitted through trembling lips. "But your missing money is there, so why did you threaten me with the necessity to repay it?"

"I needed to be able to make you turn to me. I was going to show you everything this week and explain my secrecy. I just wanted time to get closer to you before I sprang this on you. I wanted you to trust me enough to let me comfort you and help you."

"You don't have to marry me to lend me support. I'm not a little girl, Jared."

"I admit I dropped that letter so you would find it while I was gone. I was hoping it would make you doubt Eric. I was trying to move slowly and carefully on this, Maren. I knew how much it would hurt you. I read what your father said about me, and I hoped it would entice you to trust me. You were closer to your father, so I thought you might obey his last wishes. I'm marrying you because I love you, Maren, because I need you. I was hoping you would learn to feel the same way about me."

The admission was all she needed. "How could I learn to feel something I already felt?" she responded. "Haven't you guessed the truth by now, Jared? I yielded to you because I love you. I've loved you since I was fifteen. You read father's letter so you know my foolish reasons for agreeing to wed Daniel. Even if he hadn't been killed, I wouldn't have gone through with it. Don't you see, Jared, you're my destiny? I've been waiting years for you to come after me."

Jared lifted her in his arms and spun her around, laughing joyfully. "Say it again, Maren, so I'll know I heard you right."

"I love you, Jared Morgan," she declared as he set her down. Their eyes met and she repeated, "I love you."

"Maren, Maren, my dream come true. I love you, woman."

They kissed and hugged and laughed.

"Does this mean you'll marry me today?"

"Yes, but we need to talk over breakfast."

Hurriedly, they prepared the meal and then sat down to eat. As they breakfasted, Maren told Jared everything Eric had told her during the voyage from England and after her arrival in New Orleans. She also told him of the letters she'd found in her father's office safe, and she related the facts she had gathered from Marc. Finally, she explained how she had found the compartment.

"You and your father are clever; I didn't realize those were clues which would help you find that hidden cabinet. I merely thought he was rambling because of his emotional state."

"The truth is still hard to accept, Jared. Eric's always been difficult, but that he would do such evil things . . ."

He captured her hand and squeezed it. "I know, love. The only thing worse than death is to be deceived by someone in your own family."

Maren perceived the anguish in his voice and she knew that statement also referred to his own experiences. Soon, she decided, he would explain them.

"You can bet that gold Eric transported isn't to be used to aid America. It's my bet he left it at his plantation in Jamaica." Jared then revealed what he had learned on the island.

"That's where my money went!" Maren declared angrily. "To buy that plantation. We have to get everything back, Jared. Help me."

"I will, love. He won't get away with such crimes. You found the deeds, so you know those sales were illegal. It's my guess deeds were forged, with that lawyer's help. Now you understand why I was baiting him, don't you? To catch a greedy shark. Before our meeting with Lewis, I didn't tell you what I'd planned to say because I wanted you to appear genuinely surprised and annoyed."

Maren complimented him. "Your clever strategy worked."

"Good, because I don't want them to be suspicious of you. Eric could be in Jamaica right now, collecting that gold."

"Jared, what if there never was any gold aboard that ship? What if Eric just told me that story to win my trust?"

"When I leave here, I'm sailing to Jamaica to see for myself. Our country can use that gold for its defense. And wouldn't it be amusing to have the British supply the gold that helps to defeat them."

They laughed as they cleared the table and went upstairs to get ready for their wedding. Jared changed quickly and went to hire a carriage for "a Sunday ride in the country."

Maren wished she could wear her mother's wedding dress, but that was impossible. Though white was becoming the accepted color for a wedding gown, and her Spanish mother had worn a beautiful gown of cloudlike lace years ago, its style was outdated. She donned a gown with a snugly fitted waist and a gathered bodice. The sleeves were short, and had lace flounces, and the hem was decorated with lace. This fine muslin was soft blue with a darker blue sprigging splashed over it, and Maren's slippers were also dark blue, as was the trim on her light blue hat.

Because of the July heat and humidity, she pulled her hair up and arranged it atop her head. The only piece of jewelry she wore was the locket Jared had given her. She lifted her lacy parasol and joined Jared at the back door. "Ready," she said.

His eyes roamed over her and he smiled. "You look ravishing."

Maren eyed his buff-colored breeches, matching waistcoat, and white shirt. "So do you, my love."

"Let's go before I whisk you upstairs and forget our plans."

"I wouldn't protest," she teased.

He pulled her into his arms and kissed her soundly. "Soon, you'll be mine forever, Maren. My luck has never been better."

"Nor mine," she replied, caressing his handsome face.

Halfway to the preacher's home, Jared halted and turned to her. "Do you know how to handle a carriage?"

"Only since I was eight," she told him with a grin. "I can probably beat you at riding anything. Papa taught me well." Sadness suddenly came to her eyes. "I wish my parents could be here today."

"So do I, love. They were special people."

Jared climbed down after telling her to drive a ways up the road while he checked to make certain that no one was following them. She did as he asked, and was relieved when he joined her, dusting himself off with his hands.

He met her gaze and grinned. "I don't like shadows," he teased.

"Did you take good care of him?" she asked.

"Let's say he's tied up for a while."

"Did you recognize him?"

"Just a common wharf rat. He claimed he wasn't following us and refused to tell me anything. If I wasn't in such a big hurry to have you all to myself, I would have convinced him to confess."

"He'll probably give up his job when he gets loose."

"If he gets loose. I tie a wicked knot, woman."

"Should we untie him on our return trip—hand him over to the law?"

"No. We can't prove anything. The longer he stays bound, the more time he has to think over the hazards of his job."

When they arrived at the preacher's house, Jared said, "I know you would prefer a priest, Maren, but I don't know any around here."

"A religious man is all we need, Jared," Maren declared, and before she could say anything else, Kerry Osgood rode up and joined them. He was grinning.

"I see you caught him," Jared's dark-haired friend remarked. "I didn't notice anyone else sailing in your wake," he added.

"You are a most cautious man, Jared Morgan." Maren turned to Osgood. "Good morning, Kip."

"Good morning, Maren. I'm seeing this, but I don't believe it. You must be some woman to capture the likes of Captain Hawk."

"It's the reverse, Kip; he's some man to entrap me. But I'm in shock; that's why I couldn't refuse him."

"All right, you two, stop taunting me about my weakness. It's all your fault, Kip. You were the one who sighted that ship and advised me to attack. And as you can see, I kept the best treasure for myself." Jared embraced Maren, proudly and possessively.

Then they went inside, and found the preacher and his wife awaiting them. From the greetings exchanged, Maren knew the couple was well acquainted with Jared. The preacher then said he hated to rush them, but that he had visitors on Sunday afternoons. Showing them where to stand, he opened the Bible. He accomplished the marriage ceremony as quickly and reverently as possible, and after the marriage certificate was signed, witnessed, and bound with a ribbon, the newlyweds and Kip left.

When they were outside, Kip congratulated them. Then he mounted his horse and said, "I'll meet you Wednesday at the dock."

On the way back to Lady Luck, Maren sat on her side of the carriage, in case they encountered anyone on the road. She wanted to be in her new husband's arms, and she kept envisioning the night before them. Their "shadow" was still tightly bound to a tree when they trotted past him. The man struggled against his bonds and gag, but Jared ignored him.

As they walked into the kitchen of Lady Luck, Mary was just leaving a note for them. The housekeeper smiled and blushed as she said, "Your food is in the oven. I'm having dinner with Dan at the hotel. Do you mind?"

"Of course not, Mary. Sunday is your day off. Have fun."

The housekeeper left when Dan arrived in a carriage, and Maren recalled that the manager was three years younger than Mary. But she decided that didn't matter. After she and Jared watched the pair drive off, he locked the door.

"It seems we're not the only ones around here who have a claim on romance," he said.

"I should hope not, Jared," Maren replied.

"Are you hungry?" he asked, his ravenous eyes feasting on her.

"Only for you," she murmured as she went into his embrace and drew his mouth down to hers.

Evelyn Sims snuggled into Howard Heath's arms and begged him to stop scolding her. "I thought it was Jared Morgan coming downstairs," she lied, not wanting Howard to get his hands on Maren James because she feared the beauty's effect on him. "Don't worry, Howard, she doesn't suspect a thing. She told me so herself."

But Howard persisted. "I need Morgan out of our way, Ev. How else can we get to that bitch? I don't care about the money anymore; I just want them punished for humiliating me."

"Has Mr. Lewis said anything about her fall? Does he suspect us?"

"He's upriver for a week or so. This is the perfect time to get rid of them. What can he do after they're dead? Nothing!"

"But we agreed to work for him, so that means we're actually working for Eric James. I'm scared, Howard. What if they turn against us or Morgan learns about us?"

"He won't, if you keep your head. As for Samuel Lewis and Eric James, I ain't afraid of either of them."

"When can we get married? Your wife's been gone nearly a year."

"Good riddance too!" he declared coldly, but Evelyn missed this clue. "We'll get married when those two are dead."

"But how? When? They're wary now."

"You said they didn't suspect anything, but no matter. I have a few ideas," he murmured satanically.

Chapter Twelve

Maren and Jared gazed into each other's eyes as they undressed. They had put away the food so Mary wouldn't realize they hadn't eaten, and they both hoped she would stay out late with Dan Myers. They could wait no longer to have each other.

Their intertwined garments lying across a chair, they embraced, pressing their unclad bodies together. Sighing in unison, they clasped each other. The contact of their flesh enflaming their passions, their fingertips trailed over naked skin, noting contrasts and textures. He nibbled at her neck and shoulder while she brushed her lips over his chest. They were eager to unite their bodies and to share their desires, but they proceeded to make love leisurely.

Maren caressed his chest with her cheek, delighting in the feel of its ticklish hair, and Jared's hands wandered down her back, stroking her spine and caressing each inch they encountered. Then her

319

hands roved up his back and savored the feel of his powerful muscles, while his fingers drifted to her arms and teased up and down them as if he wanted to touch every part of her. As her lips and tongue played in the hollows near his throat and danced over his collarbone, Jared felt her breasts, hot and firm with desire, against his chest. He had to touch them, to taste them, to arouse them even more.

He broke their contact to bend forward, to run his arms around her knees and waist, and lift her. He was strong and she was light, so the feat was easy for him. He carried her to the bed and placed her upon it; then lay on his side beside her as he did not want to obstruct his view of her. His fingertips trailed over her chin, through the valley between her breasts, over her stomach, across the furry mound of her womanhood, and down her legs for as far as he could reach. This beautiful territory was all his to explore, to cultivate, to enjoy. Pride and love surged through him.

His hand slowly, provocatively, made the return journey to her face and moved lightly, caressingly, over each feature. She was exquisite, and she was his. When his hand halted at her lips, she kissed each fingertip, and he looked into her eyes, content to lose himself there for a time. He saw no apprehension or doubt in those golden brown depths. Like a mythical siren, she had lured him at their first meeting. Now, entranced by her, he did not want to seek freedom, did not want to resist her magical song. He welcomed this bewitchment and willingly entered her world.

His head came down to kiss her, and his hand began its heady exploration.

Maren gazed at the crocheted canopy positioned above them like a lacy sky, then she closed her eyes because she wanted to block out any distractions so she might fully enjoy each sensation he aroused. Her senses heightened by the self-imposed darkness, she inhaled deeply to let his manly smell tease her nostrils. He was wearing a cologne which she did not recognize, and its masculine scent suited him perfectly. His lips tasted of the Irish whiskey he had drunk while they cleared the kitchen, perhaps to calm his tension, and his hands were bold, but gentle and skilled. As his tongue played with the taut buds on her breasts, pleasure seemed to begin in her belly and then flash through her body like lightning before a violent storm. His left leg had slipped over hers and now rested between her thighs, and his manly shaft was hot and stiff against her hip, its intimate contact arousing her. She felt tense, yet totally relaxed.

Jared's tongue circled her breasts and assailed their peaks over and over. His lips then explored her sensitive neck and chest as he stroked her from her firm mounds to the downy triangle between her legs. Finally he buried his fingers there, enticed by the warmth and softness of her. He gently nudged her thighs apart and thrust one finger into her welcoming crevice to roam its silky valley and taut peak. Lightly teething her nipples, he continued his expedition into her moist cave.

Maren moaned softly as she surrendered to his demands. She didn't even realize her hands were playing in his hair and caressing his neck and shoulders. Every inch of her seemed responsive to his touch, alive and craving him. Although she received enormous pleasure and satisfaction from his skillful caresses, they created a fierce hunger in her.

Jared was thrilled by his wife's responses. She writhed and moaned as her hunger for him increased. He enjoyed giving her pleasure, but he was also savoring his conquest of her. How smart he had been to lay claim to this virginal land. Its peaks, valleys, plains, and caves cried out for his possession— demanded it. Her passion was like a crop he would harvest. He had planted it, had helped it grow, and its fruition delighted him. Tonight and always he would sensuously till her flesh, tend it carefully, cherish it and nourish it, and watch his cultivation bring forth a harvest of love.

Maren's need for him became so great that she pulled him atop her and insisted he enter her. "Take me now or I shall perish from need," she murmured against his lips.

Jared urged his probing manhood into her dark recess to examine that inviting chasm and then rapidly enter and reenter it. Abundant moisture allowed him to penetrate her easily and rapturously. Jared was burning with such intense desire that he wondered if he could hold out much longer before his fiery torch exploded like one of the volcanoes he had seen during his travels.

Maren arched to meet his every thrust, and provoked him to a swifter pace with her words and movements. He hoped he was reading her signals correctly or she would be left behind when he seized his victory, for there could be no retreat now. Maren almost cried aloud when her rapture was achieved, but he sealed her lips with his.

Despite the perspiration which glistened on their faces and trickled from their bodies, they clung tightly to each other, and quivering fingers trailed over damp flesh, fondling, caressing, adoring.

She didn't mind the salty taste of him as she spread kisses over his face, neck, and chest. She didn't mind the enormous heat they had created and endured while making passionate love, nor did she mind the musky scent of lovemaking which filled her room. She giggled as sweat dripped from his body onto hers and rolled down her sides.

Jared lifted his head and asked, "What's funny, my sated siren?"

As she flattened her hands against his ribs and stroked upward to his shoulders, she teased, "We sort of heated things up a bit, my love."

Jared laughed. "You've only yourself to blame, my fiery fortune. You set me ablaze every time you touch me, Mrs. Morgan."

Maren cupped his handsome face between her hands and smiled into his tender gaze. As she scanned his face, her heart pounded ecstatically. "That name sounds wonderful, Mr. Morgan, like a dream. Please tell me I'll never awaken."

323

He propped his folded arms on either side of her head, and loosening the damp curls stuck to her serene face, he pushed them back into place. After brushing his lips over her moist brow, Jared murmured, "It isn't a dream, Maren. This is real; I'm real. You're mine now, my greedy wench, and I'll never let anyone or anything take you from me. I've waited for this moment since I attacked your ship—and practically attacked you on its deck," he added, chuckling.

Maren fluttered her lashes playfully. "I was terribly wanton that day, wasn't I? But I couldn't help myself. The moment you walked through that cabin door, my wits and poise deserted me. I'm afraid I couldn't restrain myself or remember I was supposed to be a lady. All I could think about was how I had wanted you for years, and suddenly you were there within my reach. I was utterly enchanted, a captive of your many charms, my rakish pirate."

"You will be pleased to learn I didn't think of you as wanton or forward. I only saw a woman who found me as irresistible as I found her. Frankly I thought you were damned brave and honest to show your feelings. But I must confess I wanted to strangle you when Peter Thomas told me in Washington that you were Mrs. James Slade. When I came here, I was ready to punish you for enticing me into wanting someone out of reach, someone I wanted desperately. Do you realize how happy I was to learn you were not married?"

When Maren grinned and hugged him, Jared

nibbled at her lips as he murmured, "If you had been Maren Slade, I think I would have taken my first slave away with me. I would have kept you imprisoned in my cabin, in my bed, and in my arms. You see, Mrs. Morgan, I can be a determined man when I want something, and a dangerous one to cross."

"Dangerous only to your enemies, my love, never to me." A tranquil glow entered her eyes as she said, "I can't believe this, married to the man who stole my heart at fifteen, and less than two months after he took notice of me. I was right to throw myself into your arms."

"I'm neither blind nor a fool, Maren Morgan. I recognize a rare treasure when I see one and I wasn't about to risk losing it even when dangers abounded. I guess it's my pirate blood."

They made love again before falling asleep in each other's arms.

They were awakened by persistent pounding on Maren's door. A whale-oil lamp was burning low near the bed as Maren and Jared quickly sat up and glanced at each other.

"What are we going to do?" Maren asked in a whisper.

"See who it is," he replied softly, getting out of bed.

Maren went to the door. "Who is it?" she asked.

Mary responded in a nervous tone. "Me, Miss

Maren. Mister Jared isn't here and I think someone is trying to break in downstairs. I keep hearing strange noises."

Maren looked to Jared for help in handling this unexpected situation, and he whispered in her ear. "The windows are nailed at the bottom and the doors are locked. It's probably nothing. Slowly make your way downstairs with Mary while I get dressed. To be safe, don't carry a light, then you two can't be seen."

"Let me grab a robe, Mary, and I'll join you," Maren called out. She then rushed into her bedroom, and covering her nakedness, she left as Jared was pulling on his trousers.

The two women sneaked down the steps, careful to make certain none were loose. On the first floor, they halted and listened.

Maren detected noises in two directions, but she didn't think these sounds indicated intruders. Still, she moved quietly toward the room to the left and paused near its large archway. Mary came up beside her, cautioning her to be careful. Everything was silent there now, but sounds in the other room caught her attention. She slipped across the entry hall, halted in the other archway, and tried to pierce the darkness. The muffled noise was coming from behind the musician's platform. She heard glass break in the other room and knew the sound came from the bar. Two odd disturbances. She froze. Then Jared was with them.

He drew the two women to him and whispered, "Wait on the landing. I've checked upstairs and it's safe. Don't come down until I call you."

The women obeyed as quietly as shaky legs and creaky steps would allow, but Maren's heart pounded in fear for Jared. She clutched Mary's hand tightly for comfort as she waited tensely, straining for any sound.

Noises she did not recognize came to her ears, and she heard Jared scurrying about in the shadows and bumping into things. When a chair fell over, she suppressed a scream of panic. Then candlelight brightened the room he was in, and masculine laughter reached her ears. Quizzically, she glanced at Mary.

"Come on down, ladies. It's safe," he called out to them as he traversed the hall and illuminated the other room.

Maren ran down the steps and hurried to his side. She stared at the terrified creature hunkered down on the roulette table and seeking a way to escape. It suddenly bolted off and raced around the room in confusion and fear. "A squirrel got inside?"

"Two of them, one's in the other room. They must have sneaked in over the top sashes. I'll have to figure out how to entice them outside."

Mary, who had joined them, sighed with relief. "That's never happened before. They nearly scared me to death, sneaky little varmints."

"Why don't we open the front doors and urge them out?" Maren suggested. "If we work together to guide them in that direction, they'll smell the fresh air and go to it. That's what we used to do at the plantation

327

when they got loose inside."

"Clever idea, Mrs. . . . Maren." In his eagerness to praise her, Jared had made a slip. "Let's work on this frightened fellow first," he added quickly, nodding toward the squirrel eying them anxiously.

After Mary opened the door, they chased the furry creatures around the two rooms. At one point, the larger rodent took refuge atop the drapes and refused to be coaxed or intimidated from his lofty perch. Shaking his tail and chattering loudly, he warned them to keep their distance from his sharp teeth, but Mary's skill with a broom finally encouraged him to flee into the entry hall where he found the exit. Then they went to work on the second gray invader, which darted under, around, and atop nearly every item in both rooms. Twice the squirrel knocked over vases and broke them, and once he toppled a burning candle which Maren quickly extinguished. Jared tried to entrap the creature in a tablecloth, but the fuzzy little beast evaded him and raced here and there, seeking a place to hide. Evidently this squirrel was smart because no one could sneak up on it while the others held its attention. It required an hour of trying and lots of energy to flush this second intruder back into the open.

As they leaned against the double doors laughing, Maren suddenly straightened and asked, "How did they get inside? There are muslin screens over the windows to keep out insects."

Jared wished she wasn't so clever because he had already thought of that, but he replied casually,

"One of the screens must be torn, or the squirrels might have pulled it loose to get inside and search for food. I'll tell Dan to get it repaired tomorrow."

"I'm sure he checked the screens when he sealed the lower sashes. It sounds odd to me." Maren noted his expression and frowned. "It does to you too, Jared Morgan. This was done on purpose, to scare us."

"I think you're right, Maren. I'll look around," he told her.

Mary and Maren exchanged glances as Jared went from window to window. After a moment, he called them over to one near the front porch and pointed to where the loosely woven screening had been ripped from its frame.

"It must have been done tonight. Otherwise Dan would have noticed that tear and he'd have mentioned it to me," Mary remarked.

"I know. I think it was cut and the squirrels were shoved inside. Someone could have stood on the railing to do that. I'll close and lock this window; then I'll make certain no others are within our trickster's reach."

"New strategy to frighten us, Jared?" Maren inquired angrily.

"More like a taunting or a warning, love," he replied absently as he went from window to window. "But the doors and lower sashes are sealed, so no one can get inside to harm us. All our nemesis can do is pull pranks like this one."

As Mary watched Jared and Maren, she realized where Jared had been when she could not locate him earlier. She did not know whether to be delighted or disappointed, but she knew she could not judge them. If Dan desired her, she would yield to him in a moment. Life was too short to be miserable, and Dan had recently shown her just how empty her life had been. She hadn't realized how much she missed a man's company, his touch, his affection. She had been friendly with Dan for years; now she wanted more from him. "Now that the excitement's over, I'll turn in again. Good night," she said.

"Good night, Mary," Jared and Maren replied in unison.

Jared put out the lamps and then escorted Maren upstairs. "I should go to my room, love, even though she's probably guessed our little secret."

"Only part of it, my beloved husband," Maren teased.

"Don't get modest on me and reveal our real secret to her."

"I won't," Maren replied. Then she hugged him and kissed him before returning to her room and to her mussed bed.

Monday passed peacefully at Lady Luck. Jared and Dan checked every window and door, and secured those that were accessible. That evening, Maren spent only a short time downstairs with the patrons, and later Jared sneaked into her room and they made passionate love for hours before he returned to his own suite.

On Tuesday, with Dan's help, Maren and Jared slipped into Eric's townhouse to search it. Dan remained hidden outside with a pistol, ready to fire a warning shot if Marc returned unexpectedly from the shipping firm. Maren didn't know of any hiding places in that residence, and finding nothing suspicious, they were both disappointed.

Dan was nervous when they joined him outside. He asked, "Did you find anything incriminating?"

"Nothing," Jared replied thoughtfully, "but I didn't expect to. Eric is too clever to be trapped so easily. What we need is probably locked up in the bank and there's no way we can get to it."

"What now?" Despite his question, Dan seemed more relaxed.

"We'll have to keep an eye on Heath and Samuel Lewis, and on Evelyn Sims."

"Evelyn Sims?" Dan echoed quizzically. "Why?"

"I think she's in on this scheme too. Hopefully she'll break soon."

Dan considered that disclosure, and said, "I'll watch her closely."

"Thanks," Jared replied. "We need your help to catch this lot."

That night, Maren and Jared lay curled up in her bed after making love. They had discussed their problems, and Maren wished her husband would talk about himself, about his family in Savannah, but she did not press him.

As he was rising to leave, he murmured tenderly, "One day we won't have to sneak around to be together. Just be patient, love."

Early on Wednesday Kerry Osgood appeared and asked to speak privately with Jared. While Kip waited in the kitchen with Mary, Jared then told Maren that he had to leave for a few days.

"A friend of mine sent news of a supply shipment we must seize," he added. "I'll have to take my ship out, but I'll be back before Sunday."

"A raid? On a British ship? One this close to us?"

"Yes, love. But don't worry. We'll be careful."

"Do you have to be the one to go, Jared?"

"The *Sea Mist* is the best ship for such an attack. Another ship and captain will be helping me, and between the two of us, we can take this vessel easily. I have to do this, Maren. This ship is carrying ammunition and guns to be distributed to Indians and renegade slaves. I can't allow those weapons to fall into such hands. Think of how many innocent people could be slain."

Maren knew his mission was unavoidable. She hugged him tightly and pleaded, "Be careful, Jared."

"I'll talk with Dan, tell him to have Ned and Harry hang around here while I'm gone. And Dan can sleep in my room so you and Mary won't be alone at night. I'm sure Mary and Dan will enjoy being together."

Maren half smiled at his mischievous remark, but Jared added a warning, "If Eric returns, don't go near him and don't be alone with him. Stay with people we trust. Don't leave the house. Understand?"

"Yes, Captain Hawk," she replied merrily to relax him. She had known this moment would come, but she hadn't expected it to come so soon. She dreaded being parted from him and she feared for his life. She gazed longingly into his eyes.

Jared seized her and embraced her. "I can't stand the thought of leaving you at a time like this, but it would be more dangerous to take you with me. Damn it, Maren, it's hell to be torn in two. Be careful and alert, woman, or I'll tan your hide."

"Return by Sunday or I'll hire a ship and come looking for you."

"I'll bet you would, you brazen wench."

They kissed and then Jared went to meet with Dan. After he told Dan of his sudden departure, the two men made plans for Maren's safety before Jared left with his first mate.

After lunch, as Jared had instructed, Dan went to find Ned Jones and Harry Peck to hire them to guard Lady Luck during the day. In case there might be trouble during his absence, he left a pistol on the kitchen table within the women's reach, for he wanted no problems while he was responsible for Maren's safety.

A well-mannered sailor delivered a note to Maren only fifteen minutes after Dan rode away. He waited patiently while Maren read it aloud to Mary: "'Didn't sail yet. Need to see you. Come with John to the dock. He'll protect you. Hurry.'"

"You think something's wrong?" Mary asked.

"I don't know. I'll be back as soon as I can." Maren

went to get her parasol and bonnet.

While she was upstairs, Mary asked the young man, "Is there a problem at the dock?"

He smiled charmingly and shrugged. "I don't know, ma'am. I was just ordered to escort Miss Maren to him and to protect her."

Maren returned and left with the neatly clad young sailor. They rode in a carriage to Eric's warehouse, where the sailor helped her down and told her Captain Hawk awaited her inside. When Maren hurried into the wooden structure and called his name, she heard a muffled reply from the room in which her parents' belongings had been stored. She rushed into it, and the door was slammed behind her. Whirling about, she found herself trapped by two men. There was no lock on the inside of the door, but one wasn't needed. The men stood between her and escape.

"John will guard the front door until one of us finishes and relieves him," the burly man said. He grinned lewdly as he leaned against the door. "Scream if you like, me beauty; no one will hear you in here. Fact 'tis, I like me a fighting woman."

Maren backed away as both men stepped toward her, but she was finally halted by a stack of crates. The men laughed wickedly when she screamed for help several times.

"This is one job I'm gonna enjoy," the second man said as his lecherous gaze assaulted Maren.

"I knew that, Davy, that's why I included you and John. We've been paid to take as much of her as we can hold, but I would have accepted this job for free. Ol' Cap'n Hawk won't even recognize her after we're finished. He'll be wanting a new partner to chase."

"You're a devil, George. You're too rough with your wenches."

"I'm a hungry devil, Davy. Let's stop jawing and git to eating."

Maren knew she couldn't flee past the men and get away, and she silently scolded herself for falling for this treacherous ruse. Perspiration broke out over her body and her heart beat rapidly. Her eyes widened in alarm and her breathing became constricted. If there had been only one man, she could probably have fought him off, but two burly sailors with bulging muscles and stout bodies . . . Terror seized her.

"Someone will be searching for me soon," she warned. "Let me go."

"No one knows where to find you. Anyway you'll be used up before they do."

"Jared Morgan will hunt you down and kill you if you harm me."

The two men glanced at each other. Then they chuckled as if she had told an amusing joke.

Maren was petrified. Was there no way she could save herself? She glanced about for something to use as a weapon, resolved to fight to the end, but before she could spy anything, two pairs of rough hands grabbed her. Maren screamed again, provoking more chuckles from her attackers who made no attempt to cover her mouth or to silence her. Their behavior told her that screaming was futile, only a waste of energy.

She struggled with them as one held her hands and the other fumbled with the buttons on the back of her dress. Twisting about and berating them, she tried to pull free from one and to prevent the other from undressing her. Suddenly her head darted forward and she savagely bit George's hand.

He yelped and shoved her backward. The wind was knocked from her lungs as she struck the wall, and he immediately jerked her toward him. Grabbing her by the hair, he slapped her hard across the face, dazing her. "We're wasting time being gentle and nice. Let's rip it off, Davy. It's more fun to tussle with a naked woman."

Hands pulled at Maren's garments, and as she heard the material of her day dress give way, horror flooded through her. It was torn from neck to waist in front and back, but she fought anew with an energy born of desperation and fear. Then the one called Davy locked her arms behind her back, and he nibbled her bared shoulders before tracing a slobbery path up her neck and over her ears.

Meanwhile the man called George gripped her chemise and parted it easily, baring her silken flesh to his wild eyes. He tugged the shredded garment off her torso and pulled its remnants down her imprisoned arms, exposing her body from the waist up. "Look at these beauties, Davy. They're just begging to be sucked." As George's hands closed over Maren's breasts and kneaded them not too gently, his face became flushed and, as his lust increased, his breathing became erratic. He shifted from foot to foot, his tight breeches strained now. Then he bent forward and his mouth engulfed one peak.

The noises he made as he ravenously feasted on her nipple made Maren nauseous. As humiliation consumed her, and anger and hatred, she raged against her lack of strength to battle these brutes, berated fate for allowing this evil to befall her. Her abduction had been perfectly timed. Someone had known she would be defenseless and receptive. How had he known about Jared's sudden departure? How had he learned that Dan would be away? She suddenly realized the timing was a little too perfect. . . . She threatened her tormentors, but when they paid no heed, she decided she must somehow endure their abuse.

"It was real smart of you to send that baby-faced John to fetch her," Davy said. "Ever'body trusts his innocent look and his charming ways. Wonder why our new boss didn't want the first piece of her?"

"He said he don't like virgins. He wants us to train her good for him. We're supposed to take her to him after dark. When he's done with her, he'll dump her body in a well someplace or in the ocean."

As he had been instructed to do to fool Maren, Davy said, "I thought you said he was going to burn her up in here and lay the blame on Eric James—git rid of both of them at one time."

"He changed his mind. Said it would look too suspicious to point the finger at James while he's gone. Mr. High-Farting James will get his later. All we got to do is have fun with her before delivery time."

Maren listened to their grim and vulgar words even as she desperately tried to think of a way to escape them. But nothing came to mind, and she felt helpless, trapped, and stupid. She should have suspected this was a trick. Howard Heath had threatened to pay pirates to "have fun" with her, but she had not taken the threat seriously. If she survived such brutal ravishment, how would Jared feel toward her afterward?

Jared . . . she had revealed Heath's threat to her love! Her problems had all begun after his unexpected arrival, and he had plenty to gain from her death, especially since Eric's takeovers were illegal and her property could be recovered. . . . No one else could have known about his abrupt departure in time to plan this sly attack. And the broken step and the squirrel incident were pranks pulled by someone inside Lady Luck.

No, Maren's heart protested, her foe could not be Jared. It was someone insidiously clever and evil, someone who'd been watching them, someone who was prepared to act on a moment's notice. But who? And what if this enemy had lured Jared away? What if her beloved husband was in grave peril too? Maren's panic increased.

When George raised her skirt and petticoat and slid a filthy hand between her thighs, she clamped them together tightly. But he put painful pressure on her sensitive flesh and tortured her muscles until he was able to wedge his leg between hers to prevent her from closing her thighs again. He then ran his dirty fingers back and forth over her most feminine region. "Lordy, it feels real hot in there, Davy. She's probably gonna set this thing afire when I stick it in 'er." He stroked himself through his breeches and mumbled crude remarks as he fondled Maren's most private area.

"Git on with it, man. Mine's a-burnin' too," Davy pleaded.

George took his hands from Maren in order to yank off his shirt, but as he was removing his pants, the door opened and everything went crazy. Dan shot George as he tried to pull up his pants. Then he pointed his pistol at Davy. It was a Ducksfoot pistol, a favorite with sailors for it had several barrels which could be fired separately or collectively. One shot had taken down George, so several bullets remained.

"Release her, you bastard," Dan ordered coldly. His hazel eyes gleamed with fury. He had no doubt that this assault, and the step and squirrel incidents, could be credited to Howard Heath and Evelyn Sims. As soon as Samuel Lewis returned from Baton Rouge, he would warn the lawyer to control those fools! Obviously his little talk with Howard on Monday night hadn't deterred the man. Still, he couldn't figure out how those two idiots had thought up such a cunning plot, unless they had help from . . . Surely not!

Davy threw his left arm around Maren's throat. He

had drawn his knife with his right hand. He was nearly choking Maren, and she tried to loosen his hold so she could breathe. Feeling her struggle, Davy slightly let up on his pressure. As she gasped for air, Maren attempted to cover her bare breasts with her torn garments.

"If I don't git out of here alive, she don't either," Davy warned, placing the knife point at her throat. Then the two men silently studied each other.

Dan realized the sailors had not completed their assault on Maren and he was greatly relieved. Since her return home, she had not tried to push him out of Lady Luck, and she was Cam's daughter. He was all mixed up. He had not expected his job for Eric James to be this difficult, or lethal. He had assumed Maren would give up the gambling house easily and quickly, or be frightened into doing so. Who could have suspected she would not fall for her cousin's lies and his charm? But it was too late to back away; he was in this mess too deeply. More was at stake now than a partnership in his beloved Lady Luck. When Eric had approached him on this matter before making the trip to London to fetch Maren, the proposition had sounded simple and profitable. As payment for his help in getting Eric Maren's half of Lady Luck, Eric was to give him her partner's share. But who could have imagined that Maren's partner was the famed Captain Hawk! Dan had not wanted to tangle with Jared Morgan, a man he had known and liked for years, but he had been determined to protect himself and his prize. To throw off suspicion, he had pretended to be against Eric. To make this ruse believable, he had to keep Maren safe while she was in his care, and he had to prevent his cohorts from implicating him. Besides, he liked Maren James. He hoped she would accept Eric's generous offer and give up her fight for Lady Luck before she was badly hurt.

Dan finally broke the lengthy silence. "You harm her any more than you have, and I'll carve you into little pieces with your own blade. Relax, Miss Maren, you'll be free and safe soon."

As Maren gazed at Dan Myers she wondered how he had found her so quickly. She had never seen Lady Luck's manager so furious. His gaze revealed determination, a willingness to kill, and awesome anger and hatred; but Maren understood Dan's unspoken warning: do nothing to provoke the nervous Davy. She wanted to jab her elbow into her captor's gut, to slam her head into his nose or pound her balled fist into his sensitive groin; but she restrained herself. If her move was too slow or too weak, Davy would cut her up badly, perhaps even fatally, before Dan could save her. She bade herself to exercise patience and self-control.

"Where's John?" Davy asked, keeping Maren pinned against him.

"If you mean the guard outside, he's dead. You're next."

"Not unless you want me to slice her up good before you get me. Then you can explain to Cap'n Hawk how you got her killed."

Dan instantly recognized the sly opening the man had provided for casting suspicion from himself. He asked, "What does Jared have to do with this?" When the man remained silent, Dan told him, "Jared's gone, so I'm responsible for her safety. Now who's behind this plot against Miss Maren and how was it carried off so perfectly?"

"I ain't telling you nothing, gambling man!"

"Name your price for giving us information," Dan offered rashly.

The sailor eyed Dan mistrustfully, then shook his head. "You ain't tricking me. I'm getting out of here and she's my shield. Try to stop me and this blade will kiss her liver."

"Listen to me, man; let her go and you can walk out safely. I swear it. Miss Maren's life is my only concern."

"I'm taking her with me to make sure I get away clean."

Dan refused to buckle. "I can't allow you to take her out of here so you can harm her and dump her somewhere. Lock us in and then leave. Somebody will find us and free us. That's the deal I offer you, you bastard. But if you injure her, you'll never get past me alive."

Davy considered Dan's words, and realizing he was trapped, he agreed. He edged toward the door and paused, watching Dan carefully. Then he shoved Maren forward to block any attack from Dan and quickly slammed the door, bolting it from the outside. Dan broke Maren's fall by rushing forward and catching her. They heard the clattering of her attacker's shoes as he fled, then a shot. Maren jumped in surprise.

As Dan removed his waistcoat and placed it around her naked shoulders, he explained, "Ned and Harry are outside. They got him."

Harry unbolted the door, but Dan ordered him to leave it closed. "We got him, Mr. Myers. We'll be waiting outside."

Maren had never been one to faint or to weep, but she felt she was about to do both. Her forehead rested against Dan's shoulder as she struggled for control. "Thank you, Dan," she murmured hoarsely.

He embraced her comfortingly. "It's all over, Miss Maren. I knew something was wrong. Jared wouldn't have sent for you like this; he would have sent a message to me to bring you to him. Mary heard that sailor tell the carriage driver to bring you here, and we came as fast as we could. We took care of the guard; then I sneaked in. I told Ned and Harry to set a trap outside in case there was trouble."

"I was stupid to fall for such a ruse," Maren said, trembling.

"It was an honest and natural mistake. Even Mary was fooled," Dan remarked. "I'll get you home where you'll be safe. We'll figure all this out later."

"What about Jared? Do you think he was lured away so someone could get at both of us? He could be in terrible danger."

"Jared can defend himself, Miss Maren. Besides, we don't know how to reach him." He added, "What

I can't figure out is how this was timed so perfectly. Who could have known Jared would leave so suddenly this morning? Something's funny here."

"I know, Dan, and it worries me." She revealed her assailants words to her father's old friend.

To mislead her, Dan responded skeptically. "You aren't saying you believe that malarky about Eric's innocence?"

"No, I'm sure it was meant to deceive me, yet I can't help but wonder if Eric's men are not harassing me on their own."

Dan pretended to think over her words before seeming to concur. "I have to admit it seems rash for your cousin to institute schemes which point toward him as the guilty party. And I think you're right about him being too smart to be responsible for your current troubles. I believe we should begin a serious search for the real culprit, but right now let's get you home."

"Not like this, Dan. We could be seen in the carriage or someone might come to work early. I don't want anyone to know about this incident. My mother's trunks are still here. I'll find something in them to put on."

After dragging George's body out of the room, Dan joined Ned and Harry while Maren searched for a gown to wear. Having found one she could get into alone, she hurriedly donned it. Then she tried to rearrange her hair and put on her bonnet, aware it didn't match the yellow muslin dress which Carlotta James had owned. She rolled the torn gown and chemise into a ball and took them with her. She would destroy them at Lady Luck.

Before leaving, she looked around the storage room, grateful that she had no more than bruises and scuffs to show for her time there. Once outside, she thanked the men for their timely rescue.

Maren was escorted back to Lady Luck by three protective men. Then Mary prepared a hot bath and she soaked in it until the water was cold. As she dried herself, a dismayed Maren saw bruises forming on her arms and legs, especially on the inner surfaces of her thighs. And she had scratches on her chest made by ragged fingernails. Tears filled her eyes as she recalled how those vicious men had abused her.

And this time she could not prevent herself from crying. She needed the cleansing effect of the tears. She wished Jared were there to hold her. "Jared, my love, my husband, please beware of those around you," she whispered.

Mary checked on her several times that evening, and when Maren told her what had happened at the warehouse, the older woman blamed herself for not preventing her charge from leaving with the sailor. "I'm so sorry, Miss Maren. I would die if any harm came to you. We promised Mr. Morgan we'd look after you day and night. We'll have to be more careful. Those ruffians are dangerous beasts, unfit to live on God's earth."

On Thursday Maren kept to her room and again

went over the papers in the hidden compartment. She couldn't forget what her attackers had said about Eric, and she wondered if his cohort was betraying him. If so, how could she and Jared make use of that situation? She kept halting during her chore to worry about her husband. She knew Jared was smart and alert, but would he be careful enough on his own ship?

In Howard Heath's home, Dan Myers roughly shoved Heath against the wall as he berated him. "You bloody fool! I've warned you to settle down or you'll put all of us in jail or in the cemetery. Those stunts with the stairs and the squirrels and that foul business you pulled yesterday will have the finger pointing right at me!"

"Why would they suspect you, Myers?" Heath argued.

"Because the timing indicates someone inside planned it. Jared and Maren are already on to Evelyn Sims. When Jared puts the grips on her, she'll talk plenty, and then we're all done for. Evelyn's so stupid she visited Maren after her fall and let information slip. When Jared gets home and hears about this attack on Maren, he'll be all over her, then over you."

"Not if Evelyn's gone before morning and can never return."

"You'll silence her for us? For good?"

"With great pleasure. I won't let no bitch betray me again."

Dan could not believe he was standing here discussing the cold-blooded murder of a woman. He changed the subject. "How did you pull off that warehouse trick?"

"I had two notes ready to use Wednesday morning," Howard boasted. "You and Jared left so I didn't have to use but one, hers."

"What did the other note say?" Dan asked, to test the man's wits.

"That I knew who was behind the mischief and I would sell you two the information if you met me within an hour. I knew Jared would come running after I lured Maren out of the house. I had a trap set for him too, but he conveniently escaped it."

"What if Jared hadn't left and he had responded to your note? He could have done in your men; then he would have known who's involved."

"I didn't sign the note, and it wasn't in my handwriting. Ev wrote it."

"Did you destroy it?" Dan asked nervously.

"Yep. But I'll get Morgan the next time. He's in our way, Dan, and his hide is mine. We can't scare her out with him there."

"You're a fool to challenge Jared, and a bigger one to go against Eric James's orders and harm Maren. Lay low while I try to point the finger at him. Maybe I can get Maren to think Jared is romancing her to throw suspicion off of himself. I have to admit you've timed these accidents so that he'd be implicated, but I'm not sure Maren will fall for that. If you halt your pressure for now, perhaps she'll kick him out for us.

Then we can work on convincing her to sell out to Eric. That is the plan we'll follow."

Howard was angry with Dan for killing his hirelings, and he had no intention of following Dan's advice. "I'll take care of Evelyn tonight. And I'll leave them alone for a while," he added deceitfully.

On Friday afternoon, the wine delivery was made again and the manager paid the men. As Maren, Dan, and Mary were checking the cases of wine before putting it in the cellar, one of the female dealers rushed into Lady Luck. "Evelyn Sims is dead!" she cried excitedly. "She fell and broke her neck last night."

Chapter Thirteen

It was almost closing time when Jared returned
from his successful raid on the British ship in Mobile
Bay. The pirate captain of the *Sea Serpent*, René
Blanc, had not sailed last week as planned. Instead
the Water Snake had used his ship and crew to help
Captain Hawk defeat their mutual foe. It was evident
to Jared, from viewing confiscated official papers
and using his intuition, that the British were
plotting assaults on the Gulf states. Mobile and New
Orleans were vital ports, and the British must be
prevented from taking them so they could reach
America's vulnerable belly.

It was common knowledge that Andrew Jackson
had defeated the Creek Indians at Horseshoe Bend in
March and that he was steadily making his way down
the Tallapoosa and Alabama Rivers to head off a
possible invasion at Mobile, which, according to
American agents, was targeted for attack within the

next few months. Jared could not allow the British and their sympathizers to stock up on supplies and become more prepared for battle than the Americans.

As Jared was hurrying upstairs to see Maren, Dan called out to him and asked if he would wait until the employees were checked out so they could talk.

Jared knew something was wrong. He'd noticed how alert the guards were. He headed into the kitchen, and asked Mary Malone what was going on, but she said Dan should explain the trouble to him.

"Is Maren all right, Mary?" he asked worriedly, hardly able to keep himself from rushing upstairs.

"She's fine, Mister Jared. There was big trouble after you left Wednesday, but Dan wants to explain it to you."

Having finished his nightly task of collecting and counting the money, Dan joined Jared at the kitchen table. The manager carefully outlined the attack on Maren in the warehouse, and his rescue of her. Then he informed Jared of Evelyn Sims's death. Finally he described the precautions he had taken during Jared's absence. By that time both men were tired so they agreed to discuss the situation further over Sunday dinner on the following day.

About ten minutes later Jared eased himself into the bed beside his wife. "Maren," he murmured near her ear. "I'm home, love."

Aroused by his voice and touch, she happily entered his embrace. "I've been so worried about you."

"I'm safe, love," he vowed and kissed her. "And

Dan told me what happened on Wednesday. I'm sorry, love. You were lured into that trap because of me. From now on any message I send will be brought by Kip or Dan, no one else."

"I was so afraid you had been lured away, that someone was going to try to kill you. What happened? Are you hurt?"

"I'm fine, Mrs. Morgan. I've had my crew for years, and I trust every one of them. What's more, my mission was successful."

She repeated what her captors had said, and surmised, "Maybe they were trying to mislead me about Eric, or someone may be betraying him. I doubt Howard Heath or Samuel Lewis would have the courage to do that. Marc isn't smart enough to try, and Mr. Andrews is too smart to attempt it."

"Could be. We'll know when your cousin returns. But if he doesn't, we will expose his deceit, produce the real deeds, and clear up this trouble."

"Dan has had me guarded every minute, but he and I both think they'll back off for a while. Why do you suppose Evelyn Sims was killed? Dan told you about her accidental fall, didn't he?" Maren stressed the word *accidental*.

"Yes, and I doubt it was an accident. Strange, it sounds almost like your accident on the stairs. Maybe she demanded more money for spying on us, or perhaps she knew too much and whoever she worked for thought we were on to her."

"I told you she acted funny the other day when we talked. Actually, she's acted strange ever since I returned to New Orleans." Maren described her conversations with the redheaded Evelyn. "I told Dan to watch her closely, but it's too late to learn anything from her now. Mary remembered that Evelyn came to Lady Luck the day of my fall, while you and I were at Samuel Lewis's office and Dan was out getting supplies. Mary didn't think anything about it until Evelyn's death."

"What did Mary say Evelyn wanted?"

"Evelyn told her she'd left her purse under the bar. Mary was hanging out wash at the time, so she didn't see what Evelyn did inside."

"She probably loosened that step to set up your fall."

"That's what Dan thinks. He tried to hire men to follow Heath and Lewis, but both men have left town for a while. I wonder why."

"To elude my wrath and my questions," Jared replied. "Knowing that Evelyn was here on that day doesn't prove she was responsible for your fall or that she was working for Eric, or Heath. We need evidence the law will accept. Somebody is usually here day and night. Who else would have access besides me, you, Mary, and Dan?"

"As far as I know, we are the only people who have keys, but Eric gave me a set. He could have had another, or perhaps someone simply got in without a key. You are able to do that."

"Yes, but I don't do it here. Your father was a smart man; Lady Luck has locks that are hard to pick. Still, I think I'll have a locksmith come over Monday and change all of them. That way we'll know only four people have keys."

"That's a marvelous idea, Jared. I feel relieved. Now, tell me about your mission."

He smiled. "It was successful, but I'll tell you all about it tomorrow. Mary is preparing dinner for us and Dan is coming at four so we can discuss our situation at length. Right now," he murmured, getting out of bed, "I want to see for myself you're not injured." He lit the two lamps that stood on night tables on either side of the bed, and rejoined her.

"Jared, I'm fine. Dan rescued me before they . . . harmed me."

"I should have been here to protect you. I wish I had slain those bastards. They don't know how lucky they are that Dan killed them. I would have put them through hell first."

Jared's tawny eyes roamed her face, then traveled downward. His rage built when he noticed the scratches and bruises on her satiny skin. Dan had told him the condition he had found Maren in when he'd reached the warehouse, and Jared hated to think that any man would touch her intimately, cruelly, vulgarly. He wanted to beat the two men, to cut off the hands and lips that had touched his wife. Only Dan Myers's wit and courage had prevented Maren from being badly injured or slain. Jared decided he could not expose her to more perils. He would take her to Savannah and she could stay at Shady Rest Plantation with Willa Barns Morgan and the two

353

children. Willa wouldn't like that situation, but that was too bad. Right now, Maren's safety came first. When Jared recalled Willa's hands and lips on him, he realized how Maren must have felt when those two men had touched her. He decided that very soon he would tell Maren about Willa, Catharine, and Steven Morgan.

Noticing his serious expression, Maren gently teased him. "As you can see, Mr. Morgan, I was hoping you would return tonight." Upon retiring she had not donned a nightgown.

"You knew I would be starving for the sight of my beautiful wife," Jared responded.

He then kissed each scratch and bruise on her body before his soothing lips comforted her sore breasts. His caresses were gentle, for he was grateful that she was alive and uninjured, almost uninjured. He gazed at the darkened spots on her flesh, wanting to make them vanish beneath his adoring lips. Then his lips traveled over her flat stomach and kissed the discolored areas on her shapely thighs, bruised by cruel hands. As he realized how forcefully she had tried to defend herself, he ached at knowing he had not been there to help her. His mouth kept brushing against the bluish spots and his tongue kept passing over them as if he could wash away the evidence of his lack of protection.

Maren sighed and squirmed as his lips tantalized her. She had not known her inner thighs could be so sensitive, so thrilled by attention; her body was tingling and glowing. Then, suddenly, she inhaled and stiffened as she felt his hot breath teasing her cottony-soft maidenhair, and her entire body came alive with wanting. When his tongue parted her furry lower lips and made contact with her straining peak, she moaned aloud and her body writhed with delight. The longer he caressed her there, the more rapture she knew, despite the tension building within her.

Jared feasted on her, his lips creating sheer bliss, his hands stimulating her further; then his lips, hands, and manhood gave her the greatest pleasure of all. . . .

Afterward as they lay in each other's arms, she was filled with amazement as she reflected on the many ways to make love. She asked softly, "Is it also that wonderful when a woman pleasures a man?"

"Yes, my love," he murmured, kissing her shoulder and neck.

"Teach me what to do," she coaxed, wanting to share all with him.

"On another night, my inquisitive wife. It's nearly dawn."

That Sunday afternoon, Dan Myers arrived at three-thirty. While Mary and Maren completed the dinner and prepared the table, he and Jared sat in the front room and discussed the problems facing them.

"The thing which worries me most, Jared," Dan said, "is how they knew when to strike. How could they have found out you were leaving?"

Jared glanced at the man who had managed Lady Luck for years. "Surely you don't think I had anything to do with this peril?"

"Certainly not, but someone timed Maren's abduction to the minute. Who knew you would be called away Wednesday, and when it would happen?"

"Only my most trusted friend and the man who sent the message to me. Even if they couldn't be trusted, which is not the case, neither man had time to set up such a clever ruse. This was premeditated."

"I've been going over and over the plot in my head. What if the villain had two plans, one to lure you away and one to lure Maren away? When you suddenly left, he didn't have to worry about getting you out of the house to get at her. Maybe we're being watched, and maybe you eluded a second trap by leaving. You both might be in danger."

"I think you're right, Dan. That sounds logical. How else could it have worked? Some bastard was awfully lucky Wednesday."

"I was hoping it was Howard Heath or Samuel Lewis so we could entrap them and end this madness, but they're both out of town," Myers responded.

"I think I should take Maren with me when I leave," Jared declared.

But before he could say more, Dan argued, "That's reckless, Jared. What if your ship's sunk or captured? You don't want Maren at the mercy of the British. She'll be safer here with me and Ned and Harry. I won't make any more mistakes. I've learned how cunning they arc."

"Damn it, Dan, I just wish Eric James would return so I can take care of him. I don't know how much longer I can stay around here. If Heath and Lewis were behind that attack, what's to stop them from hiring more ruffians to harm Maren, or just to scare her?"

"They know we're on alert now and can't be fooled again. With three of their men dead, they should back off for a while." Dan added cautiously, "Maren and I have been giving this situation a lot of thought, Jared, and we don't think Eric James would kill her. She's like a sister to him. He might try to scare her or rough her up, but we doubt he would murder her. That means his men aren't obeying his orders. If we scare them real good, they might retreat until he returns. Once he gets back, he'll watch his moves for a while, and if this war ends soon, you'll return before he gets the courage to go after her again. If not, I'll see to her safety."

"We both know he stole her inheritance and hired these villains to torment her into selling out to him. Do you really think he wouldn't kill her if she's standing in his way? Maybe he's crazy."

Dan shook his head, playing his cards artfully. "You're letting your emotions cloud your thinking, Jared. I've been around Eric James for two years. He's sly, he's wicked, and he's greedy; but I don't think he's crazy. James Shipping is mighty important to him. I think he's decided to hold on to the firm even if he has to steal it from his cousin. But if he had wanted

357

Lady Luck as badly, he would have found a way to take it before now; it's been in his control for over a year. The more I think about it, the more I believe we're looking in the wrong direction. I think his men are disobeying him, or somebody else wants Lady Luck, wants it badly enough to do anything to get it. Whoever that is could be taking advantage of Eric's absence and your doubts. If we concentrate only on Eric James, the real villain might escape us."

Jared was intrigued. "Who, Dan? And why?"

Dan Myers shrugged. He suddenly realized he had gotten too caught up in his story and had said some things that might draw Jared's attention to him. "I'll have to think about that some more. Lady Luck's a beautiful and grand lady, and she's worth a fortune. Lots of men have offered to buy her. But don't worry about Maren if you have to leave. I'll keep my eye on her."

"Why have you changed your mind about Eric?"

"I dislike Eric James immensely, so I let that color my judgment and interfere with my reasoning. After Maren's attack, I put aside my feelings and tried to see this matter clearly. If Samuel Lewis is working with Eric as we suspect, he would have found a way to forge a partnership deed in order to fool Maren; he's a lawyer. Then when the real partner showed up, if he ever did, Eric would have gotten rid of him and taken his share. I think you're the target, not Maren. Who could get past you to harm her, or get to Lady Luck with you as her partner? Surely you realize these troubles began after your arrival. Maybe her kidnapping was intended to make you think they're after her. The more I've thought about this situation, the more I think Eric wants her to have this place, if only to keep her from questioning his other deals or trying to reclaim her father's holdings."

"I still think Eric James is behind this trouble, but I'm willing to check out the possibilities that someone else is responsible for it. We'll keep our eyes and cars open."

"I'll let you know anything I learn and I'm sure you'll do the same for me."

"I appreciate your help, Dan, especially your rescue of Maren."

Dan watched Jared leave the poker table in the front room and walk into the kitchen. Since the door was open, he could see the way Jared Morgan looked at Maren James. He turned from the enamored couple and lovingly gazed about the room he was in. This place had been his home, his work, his life, and his love until Maren had returned. What would happen if Eric James took control of it? Would the devious James keep his word?

"Ready to eat, Dan?" Mary asked from the doorway.

After dinner was consumed and the table was cleared, the men enjoyed a mellow port while the women washed the dishes and refreshed themselves. At eight o'clock, Dan asked Mary to take a walk with him. He guided her down the street and into his small apartment, where he lit only two candles so the room would be dim while he saw to the task he dreaded: deceiving this good woman into un-knowingly assisting him in his scheme. But he had to make certain that he did not fall under Jared's suspicion.

Dan sat down on the small sofa by Mary and placed an arm around her. He needed to make Mary trust him implicitly. "You know I moved out of Lady Luck because of you, not Maren," he lied.

"Why?" Mary asked in surprise.

Dan looked into her blue eyes and said, "We've been living there together for years, but I never thought you'd noticed me until lately. When I saw you watching me like I was watching you, I was afraid I would act badly if I stayed there."

"Badly? In what way, Dan?"

"Like this, Mary," he answered and fondled her breasts as he kissed her. Keeping his eyes closed to avoid seeing the woman he was duping, he said, "I've been aching to make love to you. I was afraid I'd show my feelings in front of Maren and Jared and they'd think something improper had been going on between us during our years at Lady Luck."

Mary was succumbing to Dan's good looks and his seduction. She had been many years without a man. "They couldn't say anything, Dan, because they're just as guilty."

Dan suckled at her ear lobe, sending fires of passion through her body.

"What do you mean?" he asked.

"I think they've been . . . spending the nights together," she revealed, trembling with desire and hoping Dan would continue his pursuit of her.

"Are you sure?" Dan asked as he drove her wild with caresses and kisses. After Mary related what had happened the night the squirrels had gotten into the gambling house, Dan's approaches became bolder. A half-ownership of Lady Luck was at stake, as was his home, his only love, his very life. He had to win over this woman, and it was going to be easier than he had imagined because she was igniting his passions now.

"Would you yield to me, Mary?" he asked huskily.

"Yes, Dan, yes," she replied breathlessly. She allowed him to lead her into his small bedroom, to undress her, and take her to his bed.

But as he caressed her, Dan's mind wandered. He was furious with Howard Heath for overstepping his authority. Eric had left Dan in charge, not Lewis or Heath. He considered getting rid of Heath; after all, the gambler had disposed of Evelyn Sims. Following the attack on Maren, he had berated Heath for doing such a stupid thing, and he would do the same with Lewis when the lawyer returned. He was glad that he had discovered their plot and had made himself appear a hero to Maren and the others—Eric would kill all of them if anything happened to Maren—but he regretted that it was not Jared who had been tripped on the stairs as Heath and Evelyn had planned. Still, Evelyn should have known a woman's foot from a man's, he thought. Now that Jared was having the locks changed on the following day, he couldn't chance arranging another accident inside

Lady Luck for only four people would have keys to the new locks.

And Jared was clever. It would not be easy to outwit him. He must get him relaxed, catch him off guard. Then he could take care of Maren's partner before Eric returned or Jared left. He hated to kill Jared Morgan, but he saw no other way to protect himself and to get his share of Lady Luck. Eric would never satisfy his greed, and when it came to Lady Luck, Dan was just as greedy. Perhaps after Jared's death, Maren, in her grief, would marry him. Then he could control Lady Luck without having to harm Cameron's daughter. That plan set easier on his conscience. Yes, it was better to get Lady Luck by marrying Maren and then killing Eric James.

Maren snuggled into Jared's arms. "I don't think they're back yet. I wonder what's keeping them. Do you think they're all right? I mean, our enemies wouldn't harm them to punish us, would they?"

"How do you know you didn't miss the sound of those bells while I had you distracted, woman?" Jared had mounted warning bells which could be lowered over all exterior doors at night so no one could enter without making them ring, and the bells had not sounded since Mary and Dan had left. "Maybe they went to Dan's place to be alone? You've seen how they look at each other and how much time they spend together."

"I know, and I find it incredible. They've lived

here for years, but their romance didn't start until Dan moved out. Still, I'm happy for them. They've been at Lady Luck for as long as I remember; they both love it."

Jared started to ask her a question about Mary, but Maren rolled atop him and covered his mouth with hers. As she caressed him, she commanded, "Forget about everyone but me tonight."

Jared grinned into her face, which was lit by golden candlelight. The suspicion did not quite form in his keen mind because it seemed so absurd and because his wife was blissfully tormenting him.

Lilibeth Payne arrived on Monday afternoon. She squealed with excitement and then hugged Maren tightly while Jared carried her bag to Maren's room. She would stay with Maren at least one night, possibly two. As she and Maren walked through the elegant gaming rooms and then headed upstairs, she eyed the sumptuous furnishings.

"It's wonderful, Maren, absolutely splendid and wicked. Papa may come into town this week, so I'm registered at the hotel. If he caught me here, he'd flay the hide from my beautiful back, but I can't resist spending at least a night with you. You'll help me trick him, won't you?"

"Of course I will," Maren replied, although she dreaded being separated from her husband, even for that long.

As the two young women sat on Maren's sofa, Beth

coaxed, "Tell me all about that handsome privateer across the hall. Have you hooked him yet?"

"Let's just say he doesn't see anyone else. But he'll have to leave soon, and I miss him already. Have you heard from Bart lately?"

"Nothing. I don't want to talk about him; it only makes me worry. You know me, Maren; when I worry, I'm awful to be around. Let's go shopping this afternoon."

"I can't," Maren told her; then she told Beth about the accident on the stairs and the attack at the warehouse. "Jared thinks someone is trying to hurt me, so he's ordered me to stay inside for a while."

"Whoever would want to harm my dearest friend?"

"We don't know. We think someone wants to drive me out of Lady Luck. It sounds crazy, but it's been frightening. Don't tell anyone."

"Why haven't you notified the authorites? Let them investigate."

"It isn't that simple, Beth. They can't do much. Jared and Dan are keeping an eye on me."

"But you're in danger, Maren."

"Including the two guards, four men are watching over me."

"Day and night?" Beth giggled.

"You're incorrigible, Lilibeth Payne."

"I'm not to blame for that. God and Nature made me this way."

"Whatever shall I do with . . ." Maren halted when someone knocked on her door. She went to answer it, and found Jared standing before her.

"May I speak with you privately for a moment, Maren?" he asked.

Maren turned to her petite friend and said playfully, "Make yourself comfortable, Miss Payne. I'll return shortly; business calls."

Jared led her to his room and, after closing the door, told her that Kip had brought another message from his contact at Barataria. "Most of the pirate ships of any size and speed are anchored near Grand Isle so it's the perfect time for me to try to convince the pirates to aid America. Two of the most feared or revered captains, depending on how you choose to view them, will be there." Jared chuckled. "The Water Snake and Jean Lafitte. The Water Snake is taking me to them, under his protection. If I can persuade the other captains to join our cause, we would have enough ships to wreak havoc on the Brits. We're vastly outnumbered by the Royal Navy; we need these ships, Maren. I'm offering the pirates a pardon and a chance to join the American Navy."

"Can you trust this Water Snake? I've heard terrible things about him. Suppose he intends to trick you and turn you over to the British?"

Jared laughed. "We buy our wine shipments from him, my love, and he helped me at Mobile Bay. He's got a ship I envy and a totally loyal crew. He has already agreed to join me, and he's the best man to persuade the others to unite with us, especially Lafitte. I trust him. If you're ever in trouble, ask for René Blanc. Only his most trusted friends know his real name."

"If you talk the pirates into joining you, your missions here will be over, won't they?" Maren asked reluctantly. "You'll be leaving."

He embraced her and held her close. "You forget, love, checking on Eric is one of my missions, and he hasn't returned yet."

Maren's arms encircled him as she asked, "How long will you wait for my cousin before you go in search of him?"

"I'm the absentminded one," he jested. "I'm always forgetting how quick and clever you are. You're right, Mrs. Morgan. At most I can spend only four to six weeks here."

"That means you're supposed to leave at the end of this month or during the early part of August. Why didn't you tell me you had such a schedule?"

"And make us both miserable? I didn't want you to feel rushed, Maren. I wanted you to enjoy our short time together. I'll never forsake you, woman."

"I know, Jared. But that means we have only a couple of weeks."

"Better to have a few weeks together than no time at all."

"You're right. I should be grateful for even a day with you, and I am. I love you, Jared, and I know you will do what you must to end this war soon."

They hugged and kissed, then Maren asked, "How will you find the pirates' stronghold? There are hundreds of waterways through those bayous. They're filled with snakes and alligators and quicksand and smugglers. People go into them and are never seen again."

"Fret not, little woman; Kip's going with me, and René is sending someone to take us there and bring us back. This is the notorious Captain Hawk you're looking at. Who would challenge a legend like me?"

"A fool who envies you and wants the honor of placing your sword in his sheath. You and Kip will be armed, won't you?"

"Naturally. I'd be naked without my cutlass and pistol. Remember your promise, love; tell no one about our marriage. I put the license and the deeds in the bank box where they'll be safe. The key to it is hanging on a nail just inside the hidden cabinet, to the left."

"How long will this meeting take?"

"I hope it will be resolved tonight, but I can't rush them."

"I know, but surely no war conference lasts more than two days. If you're still gone Wednesday night, I'm coming after you."

"Do you know your way through the bayous, my mischievous vixen?"

"No, but I'll find someone who does."

"You and Beth have fun, and be careful."

"I will."

He kissed her once more before he departed; then Maren rejoined Beth. The two women talked all afternoon, but Maren kept her promise to Jared and did not reveal her married state.

That night, until someone was ready to use one of the "guest rooms," Maren let Beth spy on the downstairs activities from behind the drapery on the stairway landing.

And that night the Lady Luck manager began to work on making Mary distrust Jared so she would plant seeds of doubt in Maren's mind. He did this by asking cunningly worded questions and by murmuring about how suspicious the accidents were, especially in timing. He mentioned how lucky it was for the villains that Jared had not been around to help Maren, and he cleverly pointed out what Jared had to gain if Maren was killed. When the woman asked Dan if he suspected that Jared was involved, Dan looked skeptical and replied, "They're supposed to be in love, so why would Jared Morgan try to harm her? No one should suspect a man like him of treachery and greed."

The next afternoon, Maren allowed Beth to persuade her to take a walk to get some fresh air and exercise. As they strolled across the street before Lady Luck, chatting happily, a carriage bolted down the street and nearly ran over Maren, who had lagged behind to lower her parsol. Knocked aside by the terrified horse, she landed hard and was dazed. Beth screamed, but the carriage continued headlong down the street until it vanished. Rushing to Maren's side, she then helped her friend to rise. Since Maren's ankle hurt when she put pressure on it, Beth assisted her to the sidewalk before rushing over to Lady Luck.

Within moments, Dan was lifting Maren. He

carried her home, and then he and Mary chided the young woman for leaving the house.

"It was an accident, Dan, a runaway carriage."

"Accident, my foot," Mary argued. "Something like this happens every time Jared is out of sight. You must stay home when he isn't around," she warned.

Maren glanced at the housekeeper and wondered what she was implying. "I'll be fine," she said.

"I'm so worried about you, Miss Maren. These accidents scare me."

"This was a real one. Ask Beth."

Beth's face was pale and she was shaky. "I'm not convinced it was, Maren. It looked to me like the horse was being raced wildly."

"That's silly. How could anyone know when you and I would take a walk? And who would risk being seen in daylight?" she reasoned.

"Someone lying in wait for you," Dan replied. "We can't be too cautious. Please, stay home."

"Where are Ned and Harry?" Maren asked.

"They're in the stable," Mary responded. "I asked them to feed the horses because the stableman is sick today."

"Perfect timing, just like always," Dan remarked. He knew who was responsible for this new attack, and it riled him. Howard Heath had to be dealt with quickly, before he ruined everything!

The following afternoon, Dan went to Maren's room. "Good news," he said. "Howard Heath fell off his horse and broke his neck. He's dead. He won't trouble us again, but we can't let up on our precautions, Maren; there are probably more of them.''

"Darn it, Dan! I'm tired of living like this. I don't want to be a prisoner in my own home, living every minute on alert. What can we do? What if we have a little talk with Samuel Lewis and scare him?"

"Jared would be furious if we went against his orders. Wait until he returns and then we'll discuss this new strategy with him. I'm going to check with the neighbors to see if anybody noticed anything suspicious. Ned and Harry are guarding the place. Stay put, all right?"

"If you insist," Maren reluctantly agreed. After Dan left, she paced the room on her sore ankle. The situation was vexing her. Beth had left that morning, and she needed to talk with someone. She went downstairs to see Mary.

When Maren sat down at the kitchen table, Mary joined her, then asked, "What are we going to do, Miss Maren?"

"I don't know, but we have to do something soon. These incidents are driving me crazy. I wish Jared were here."

"Do you think," Mary began hesitantly, "there's a reason why these accidents only happen when he's gone?"

"What do you mean?" Maren asked.

"I'm not certain, but I think it's mighty strange he's never around when you're in danger. Ned and Harry never see anyone watching the place, so how does this villain know when to strike?"

"You're not hinting that Jared's involved, are you?"

Mary squirmed in her chair and didn't meet Maren's gaze. "Mister Jared's been coming here for years and he seems so nice, but . . ."

"But what?" Maren probed uneasily.

"Please don't be angry with me, but I'm not sure you can trust him. How do we know he isn't the one helping Eric James? What better way to throw the suspicion off of himself than by courting you and speaking against your cousin? He's asked you to marry him. If you do, he would own all of Lady Luck if . . . you had a real accident."

"How can you say and think such things, Mary?"

"Don't you find it odd that he's never around when you're in danger? And don't you think it's impossible for a stranger to strike at the right moment every time? Maybe I'm just scared for you and thinking crazy."

"Jared was here when the step was loosened and the squirrels got inside," Maren reminded the woman.

"I know, and he has his own keys. Perhaps the other accidents took place while he was gone to keep us from looking in his direction. Where does he go? What does he do? And can he prove it?"

"My father trusted Jared, and so do I," Maren asserted worriedly.

"Mr. Cameron also trusted Eric James, and so did you."

"They're nothing alike, Mary. I wish you didn't

371

feel this way. I love Jared, and I trust him."

"I'm sorry, Miss Maren. I won't mention this again."

Maren returned to her room, depressed. She did trust Jared—her husband—and she was saddened to learn that others did not. Her joy in Lady Luck was being stolen away. Maybe she shouldn't try to hang on to a place that presented her with so many problems: treacherous employees, mistrustful help, vicious gossip, no social life, imprisoning days, dangerous accidents. . . . Someone wanted Lady Luck badly. Maybe she should sell out and leave, move to Savannah with Jared and leave this misery behind her. She would tell Jared what she was thinking when he returned.

Jared came home Thursday morning, and he became furious when he learned of the latest attack on his wife. After Maren told him how she now felt about the gambling establishment, he became thoughtful. He stalked around the room like a caged beast as he deliberated the matter, and finally he returned to the sofa to sit beside Maren.

"I don't know what to do," he confessed bitterly. "If we hang on here, I'm placing you in danger every day, whether I'm here or gone. If we sell out, we're admitting defeat and somebody will get away with this mischief." He inhaled deeply. "I can't leave you in danger and I'll have to sail soon. Would you be willing to move to Savannah and let Dan run the

372

place until we decide what to do?"

"What about your family? Would they mind?"

Jared frowned. "I guess it's about time I tell you a few things about my family. My father, Benjamin Morgan, built Shady Rest near Savannah. We raised rice and sea island cotton as our main crops. My mother, Anna, died when I was thirteen, and my father couldn't seem to get over her death. I guess that was partly why I avoided love and marriage, I didn't want to endure the anguish he'd known at Mama's death. When I was sixteen, Papa married a woman only seven years older than I was—Willa Barns, a beautiful widow who only cared about herself. But I'll tell you more about her later."

Jared shifted to relax before continuing. "My brother, Jeremy, and I worked the plantation with Papa for a while, but Willa wanted things run her way and we were quarreling all the time. So Jeremy and I decided to leave. We told Papa it was to give them privacy, but we didn't like Willa or the way she treated him. She had her hooks into him good, so it was futile to take a stand against her. She's one of the reasons I gave women a hard time; I feared they were like her. You proved they aren't," he said tenderly.

"Jeremy and I traveled together for several years, but when we took separate paths, Jeremy returned home. He stayed there for a year, but things hadn't changed so he left again. He was taken, by the British, from the *Chesapeake* in the summer of 1807 and was hanged on the *Leopard*, a British ship, for refusing to yield to impressment. That's one of the reasons I became a blockade runner and an American agent.

"My father was a good man, Maren, a special one. He was a hero in the war for independence, so he was proud of his sons' resistance of the British. For years, Papa had allowed us to sail with our exports, so we both knew the sea and ships from top to bottom. And you might say we had been introduced to adventure and worldly temptations. Papa and I met Cameron James on a business trip to New Orleans, and he and your father became good friends. That was before Willa got ahold of Papa. Jeremy and I fought in the Barbary War for President Jefferson, but I quickly lost interest in killing pirates. Since I didn't want to return home, I joined the Lewis & Clark Expedition. I was wounded in the Sioux territory and lived with the Indians while I was healing. They taught me plenty about nature and honed my skills. That's where I got the name Hawk; the chief called me Soaring Hawk. He also gave me the idea for my ship's name by saying I could slip through the early mist without leaving a trace or getting damp."

Jared chuckled as he reminisced on those exciting days. "When the expedition came back through the Sioux territory, I returned to St. Louis with it in 1806. I was twenty by then. I spent time working on a riverboat and trapping outside of town, and I fought river pirates and Indians; but that life grew tiresome. I finally headed this way, worked on the docks and did a lot of gambling. There seemed to be a flame burning in me. I had to challenge danger, to seek excitement and my fortune. I let Papa convince me that I should get my own ship and handle his exports. Lordy, I came to love the sea and that kind of experience. And as you know, my fetching wife, it was such business that brought me to New Orleans when we first met."

Jared suddenly became distressed over the facts he was about to reveal to Maren. "When I learned about Jeremy's death and war seemed imminent, I returned home for a while. Papa was real sick and he needed me. After his death, I hung around to take care of things for my stepmother and the children. My father had two by her: a girl named Catharine who's twelve, and a boy named Steven who's eight. But the war heated up pretty fast, so I went back to sea. I made a name for myself and my ship quickly, and the President asked me to become an American agent. Then I met you . . . again."

"You don't like your stepmother, do you?" Maren asked.

"Never have and never will," Jared admitted. "I understand that Papa was lonely and miserable after Mama died; he was only forty-two. But Willa made life worse for him. I know she tormented him into an early grave. She's a real bitch, Maren, but a deceptively charming one. That's why I hate to subject you to her. She's greedy, and selfish, and wicked. She had affairs while they were married, and there's no telling how she's behaving now." He looked into her eyes as he said, "So you'll understand why Jeremy and I left Papa at her mercy, I'll tell you why we really went away. Willa had a big sexual appetite, and she tried to seduce me and my brother many times. We couldn't break Papa's heart by telling him his wife was pursuing his teenage sons, but if he caught her with another man, it wasn't going to be one of us. Every time I go home, she goes after me again, even though she knows how much I detest her, and I'm sure she did the same with Jeremy on his last visit. I worry about her effect on Cathy and Steven, but there's nothing I can do about that. Can you see why I hated to reveal such wicked things about my family, and why I hate to leave you there with Willa?"

"What if she won't allow me to stay there?" Maren asked.

"It's my home, so she can't refuse my wife a place to live. You see, Papa willed the place to me just before he died. Willa Barns Morgan can live there only as long as I permit it, which I do because of Cathy and Steven. Once they're grown and gone, so is Willa, but despite how bad she is, I can't toss out my father's children."

"I understand, Jared. You're a wonderful man to take care of them."

"I don't let Willa handle anything there. I have a trusted overseer take care of the plantation for me. If we're lucky, maybe she's remarried and moved out; then we'd have it all to ourselves."

"When did you last see her?"

"I almost did before I came here. I stopped by to check on the children and the plantation, and to pick up my deed to Lady Luck. She was still there, but she was seeing a man. She was away with him when I got home, so I missed her, luckily. Cathy and Steven are good children, Maren; you'll like them. From what I understand, Willa spends little time with them, and they're being raised by a wonderful black woman." He smiled broadly and hinted, "When Willa hears I'm still alive and will be returning home soon maybe she'll trick her new lover into marrying her and be gone before our arrival. Nothing would suit me better."

"Does she know about Lady Luck?"

"Nope. Papa kept it a secret from everyone. If anything happened to me during the war, you were to be sole owner. Do you think you can endure my stepmother while I'm at sea?"

She snuggled into his arms. "I can do anything to please you. Will she be told we're married?"

"Let's decide that later. I don't want to make any rash decisions."

"Whatever you say, love."

"Aren't we being cooperative today?" he teased, then kissed her.

"I'm hoping it will pay off later," she replied seductively.

"Rest assured it will, my lusty siren."

"When will we leave for Savannah? I'll need to pack."

"If Eric isn't back by August first, we'll sail then. Don't tell anyone we're going. I don't want our foe to become desperate enough to slay us before we depart.''

Maren considered telling Jared of Mary's distrust, and probably Dan's since those two were so close, but she decided not to hurt him. "Do you think Lady Luck will be safe while we're gone?"

"The only important thing is your safety, Mrs. Morgan. If we can't settle our problems with Eric before we leave, then we'll worry about them later. I don't want anybody to know where I'm taking you. That way you'll be safe in Savannah. If possible, I don't even want anyone to learn you've left the city with me. Just before we sail, I'll circulate a story about you going upriver to visit friends. That way, if this persistent foe looks for you while I'm gone, he'll never find you."

Maren hugged Jared. "I'll be safe, so stop worrying. While you're gone, I'll give Willa lessons in manners and morals."

Jared looked serious. "Don't let her get to you, Maren. Remember that's our home, not hers."

"Our home," she echoed. "Doesn't that sound wonderful?"

"Yes, my love, it does. I can't wait for this war to end so we can get on with our life together."

Two peaceful days passed, and an enjoyable Sunday was underway when a visitor came to call: Peter Thomas. . . .

Chapter Fourteen

Thomas informed Jared Morgan that Eric James was a spy, and he added, "You'll need to sail immediately to thwart him. I'll be going with—" When Maren came to see who was at the front door, Peter was astonished to find her with his contact. He fell silent and stared at the dark-haired beauty. Then his inquisitive gaze went to Jared.

Jared chuckled heartily before he invited Peter into the kitchen, where the two men sat down at the table and Jared explained matters to the sandy-haired American agent, who was pleased to discover the truth about Maren. She was preparing hot tea and pastries, and Peter's hazel eyes lingered on her as Jared briefly discussed Maren's troubles and his missions, for he already knew James Slade was actually Eric James. Peter was intrigued as he listened to Jared's tale of Eric's curious voyage to London, after which he'd carried a gold shipment to

Jamaica. Then, Jared outlined Eric's treachery to Maren, told of his own secret partnership with her, of the progress of his missions, and of Maren's lack of involvement in Eric's traitorousness.

Despite Jared's revelations about Maren, Peter then said, "I think we should go somewhere else to talk privately, sir." His tone and expression implied that his report about Eric James was damaging.

Jared responded confidently. "There's no need, Peter; we can speak freely before her. I trust Maren with my life and honor."

As Peter glanced at Maren, he caught the look that passed between her and Jared. "I can see that you do, Captain Hawk. But perhaps you should hear what I have to say first, then you can decide what to tell Miss James and how to do it kindly."

During Peter's reply, Maren poured their tea and set pastries on the table. "I'll leave you two alone, Jared," she offered politely, for she knew her husband would tell her everything later.

But Jared wanted to prove to his wife that he trusted her implicitly, that she was a vital part of his life. Since she would be leaving with him, no villain could get to her and force her to expose crucial secrets. "I prefer her to stay, Peter, unless you object."

"I take it you two have become close, Captain Hawk, and I will do as you say. I am only concerned about how part of this news will affect Miss James. Do you still have that ruby necklace Eric gave you on the ship?" he abruptly asked Maren.

"Yes, it's at the bank in Jared's box. Why?"

"We have to get it before we sail tomorrow. Your cousin will be heading to France soon to pick up another gold shipment, and Josephine's necklace is the recognition signal. Eric's on his way here to pick it up. He had to put in at Savannah before heading to Jamaica to drop off some cargo, so I jumped ship and caught another heading this way. But he got a head start on me while I was stranded ashore, so we don't have much time. If I've calculated his schedule correctly and he hasn't confronted any trouble, he'll arrive before this week ends. I've taken many chances to spy on him, but it was worth it."

"Empress Josephine's necklace?" Maren asked, incredulous.

"The same, Miss Maren. It was specially made for her, so it will be easily recognized. When Eric hands that necklace over to Napoleon's contact in Marseilles, he'll be given gold on the assumption that it will help us fight our mutual enemy, the British. But your cousin's a sly devil. He has the Americans believing he's doing special tasks for them, the British are convinced he's using their gold to bribe people, and the French think he's taking money to America to help defeat Britain so that later we'll help put Napoleon back into power. But Eric is pocketing all the money and jewels, hiding them at his plantation in Jamaica. He wants to make certain his cache is safe until this war is over. The French gold waiting in Marseilles is to be picked up by the person who presents the empress's necklace."

"That's why Eric gave it to me, to conceal it and

protect it!''

"He used you, love, but we'll make him pay. We'll take the gold right out from under his nose by claiming it first."

"There's bad news too, especially for you, Miss Maren," Peter said. "When Eric went to Baltimore, it was to kill his brother Murray, which he did. He then sold that branch of the firm, and went to Jamaica to take everything of value to his plantation. I'm sorry to tell you that so badly."

Maren was stunned. "He killed his own brother? Are you sure?"

"I witnessed it myself, but I couldn't do anything. If I had exposed myself, I would be dead and America would not have this information."

Maren looked at Jared, and murmured, "You said he was crazy and dangerous. If he would slay Murray, he would kill me too."

"You're coming with us, Maren," Jared declared, and when Peter started to protest, he silenced him by saying, "I can't leave her here, and there's no time to take her to my home in Savannah or to find her a safe place to hide. She's my wife, Peter, but it's a secret. I didn't want anyone to know because somone might try to use her against me."

"Your wife?" Peter echoed.

Jared told Thomas of the secret wedding, and then said, "As soon as the bank opens in the morning, I'll get the necklace and put my papers in the box for safekeeping. I have evidence that Eric stole Maren's inheritance and I want to protect it. Peter, you can go to my ship to alert my crew to be ready to sail at second tide tomorrow. Tell Kip and Jacob Tarver to hurry over here and get Maren and her things." Jared turned to his wife. "You'd best pack, love. If we can get you out of here before Mary and Dan return, I can tell everyone I've sent you upriver to stay with friends. That way, no one will know you're leaving with us. I'll stay here tonight and speak with Dan before I visit the bank and join you.

They talked a while longer; then Peter left for the *Sea Mist* while Maren and Jared hurriedly packed. When Jared finished, he joined his wife. The pair embraced and kissed, and exchanged words of encouragement and caution. There wasn't enough time to make love, but they had a lifetime before them. As they discussed Peter's revelations, Maren cried softly over Murray's death and Eric's evil, and Jared comforted her.

When Kerry Osgood and Jacob Tarver arrived, Maren was compelled to leave Jared and go with them to the ship. She begged her husband to be careful and hugged him tightly, not caring about his men's watchful eyes. Jared then helped to load her belongings and his into the carriage; he didn't want to be carrying anything when he slipped out of town and traveled down the Bayou Bienvenue to Lake Borgne, then rowed out to his ship. He promised Maren and Kip he'd be aboard before noon on Monday, July twenty-fifth.

At Jared's behest Maren had disguised herself as a sailor, so no one noticed her departure, and Kip took every precaution to make certain they were not followed. It was not long before she was helped aboard Jared's ship and shown to his quarters, and she was delighted to learn that the crew had been told about their captain's marriage. She hadn't wanted them to think her wicked for sharing Jared's cabin.

Upon boarding the *Sea Mist*, she had been introduced to some of Jared's crew: Davy Douglas, the steersman; Patrick "Patty" Brennan, the cook and doctor; and Harry Epps, and Simon Carter. She had already met Jacob Tarver, ex-seaman and now Jared's cabin man. As she was shown to Jared's cabin, Maren had noted that the ship was being readied to sail.

She spent the remainder of the afternoon unpacking and settling into Jared's quarters. She was delighted to find his cabin so large and neat—there was plenty of room for her and her belongings—and she was intrigued by the papers and books on his desk. She did not examine these, however, but decided to wait for his permission to do so.

Patty prepared a delicious meal for her, and Kerry Osgood joined her for dinner. They talked for a long time because Maren explained what had taken place that day, as Jared had requested. Afterward, Kip entertained her with tales of past voyages. He was glad Jared had revealed his past to Maren, for he could now talk to her without fearing a slip. But when the hour grew late, Kip excused himself so Maren could go to bed.

After bolting the door, Maren donned a thin, cool

nightgown and then slipped into the comfortable bed. She imagined Jared lying beside her, and she smiled happily. Tomorrow they would set off on a perilous mission. She was now a part of his life, his work; and they would stalk their mutual enemy, and hopefully defeat him. She yawned and stretched, then curled up on her left side, cuddling a pillow and pretending it was her handsome husband. Surprisingly she slept very well on her first night aboard the ship. Perhaps Jared's scent lingered in the cabin and that relaxed her. Or perhaps the heady brandy Kip had enticed her to drink after dinner did that.

Peter Thomas came to Jared's cabin at midmorning, and he and Maren again spoke for a long time, going over everything she knew about Eric James and that voyage from London, and everything Peter had learned about her cousin while sailing with him. Thomas then discussed her role in the upcoming scheme, and Maren was eager to accomplish it.

As they chatted genially, noon came and went, and knowing that tide would not last much longer, Peter finally told her, "We have orders from Captain Hawk to sail at the last possible minute if he doesn't make it aboard."

Maren stared at him. "What do you mean? You can't leave without Jared? He's the captain!"

"Jared knows how vital this mission is. Kip is to act as captain if he doesn't arrive before we have to sail."

"Why wasn't I told?" Maren was worried. She envisioned a lengthy and dangerous separation from her beloved.

"He didn't want to worry you unless it was necessary, Mrs. Morgan. You're aware of the trouble back there. If Jared's being watched, he could be prevented from joining us."

"But we can't sail without him," she protested.

Peter responded softly, "We may have no choice. This mission is more important than Captain Hawk, or you, or me. We're at war, and only America matters."

"You're wrong, Peter; all of us matter. We are America."

"Then we should be willing to make any sacrifice for her."

"I'm not leaving without Jared," Maren declared firmly.

"You won't have to, love," Jared said as he entered the cabin.

Maren knocked her chair over as she jumped up to rush into his arms, causing him to chuckle. "Where have you been? What happened?"

Kip stood behind him as Jared greeted Peter, then explained, "I got the necklace and put our papers in the bank. I then told Dan and Mary that false tale about you being upriver. Dan was worried, but he agreed to take care of Lady Luck for us. I told them I was heading home for a few weeks, after which I would return and fetch you."

The three men chatted a few minutes and then

386

went topside. Alone, Maren paced the cabin. She recalled how long and boring her last voyage was, but this time she would be with Jared. Knowing the dangers they faced, she prayed they would slip through the blockade without any trouble.

As the ship moved beneath her, she inhaled deeply. This exciting journey had begun. She did not know that far away the famed Battle of Lundy's Lane was being fought at that very moment. Near the Canadian side of Niagara Falls, Jacob Jennings Brown and Winfield Scott were fighting for their lives, as she and Jared soon would be doing. . . .

They sailed out of Lake Borgne and into the Gulf of Mexico. Their route would take them between Florida and Cuba, past the Bahamas, across the Atlantic Ocean, through the Strait of Gibraltar, and into the Mediterranean Sea. They would put in at the French port of Marseilles. The voyage would take six weeks, more or less.

Maren looked through a porthole until only water was in sight. She knew Jared was busy on the deck, giving commands and watching for British ships, so she sat down to read. Hours passed, and daylight waned. She had dined alone. Jared had not even come to visit her for a few moments since they had sailed, but Patty had told her this was a dangerous area.

When she felt sleepy, Maren changed into her nightgown and climbed into the bed. She realized the ship was sailing through the night, and wondered when her husband would come to bed. She did not wonder long because Jared soon eased himself into the cabin, moving quietly as he presumed she was asleep.

"You don't have to be so sneaky, my love," she teased.

Slipping out of his clothes, he joined her. "I wish you didn't have to be here, love, but I'm glad you are. We won't be safe until we're in the Mediterranean, so I'll have to stay topside most of the time to keep from being distracted by you. I guess you realize we'll pull the same tricks Eric did to avoid being captured."

"If any captain dares to challenge Captain Hawk and the *Sea Mist* . . ."

"You flatter me, woman," he jested, then kissed her lovingly.

As his hands drifted over her receptive body, Maren let hers explore his virile frame. Then Jared drew her into his arms, and for a time he was content just to hold her. Finally his lips began to wander over her face before invading her mouth, and he cupped one of her breasts and gently fondled it. He was stimulated by the way she responded to his touch and nearness.

And Maren was stimulated by the way Jared reacted to her caresses and embraces. She loved the way their spirits soared as one, their hearts beat in rhythm, and their bodies joined in blissful pleasure. He was so easy to be with, to talk to, to trust, to share all with, to love.

Jared's caresses and kisses waxed bolder as his hunger for her increased. He hated every day and night they were apart. Even if they didn't make love, he wanted her beside him, wanted her flesh making contact with his. He wanted to see her smile, hear her laugh; wanted to share her vitality. Her magnetic pull was powerful, irresistible. He ached for this war to end so they could enjoy a bright future, and he worried over her safety on this perilous voyage. He loved her, needed her, and he could not allow her to be harmed.

Maren's fingers slid over Jared's sleek back and dipped into the shallow valley along his spine. She trailed them sensuously up and down the bumpy ridges there, then allowed them to roam freely over his hard muscles. Meanwhile she stroked his nimble legs with hers, and her lips assailed his neck, nibbling and kissing. When his mouth began to work deftly on her breasts, her hand encircled the fiery torch which was burning against her hip. Gently and stirringly, she eased her hand up and down its silky shaft.

Jared moaned and his hips writhed as his manroot grew in size and yearning. He felt it tremble with the need to burst into bloom, heard its mute plea to enter the cooling, refreshing, territory where it could be nourished and cherished. Yet, he restrained his ardor so he might savor her enticing caresses and urge her passion to blaze out of control. His fingers aroused the sensitive areas of her body, as did his mouth.

They both labored until they were breathless and feverish, then eagerly fused their bodies to lay claim to the prize which loomed before them. They kissed, caressed, and moved rhythmically until a mutual victory was attained. Joyfully, they yielded to it, freely and wildly, until their urgency passed and rapture poured over them like heavy rain. Gradually contentment claimed them, and locked together, they went to sleep.

For exercise and diversion, Maren was allowed topside twice a day: morning and evening. She enjoyed watching her husband at work in the surroundings he loved, and the crew was always busy, alert, caring, and obedient. The men rose early, took down their hammocks, bundled and stowed them, and reported for duty. They scrubbed decks, tended canvas, cleaned and greased chains and guns, mended casks, watched for enemy ships, and secured loose cargo. They were fed well and were allowed a cup of grog at the end of their shift. For relaxation, they smoked, talked, and played games. Some even did wood carvings or made decorative things from rope. This crew was happy and well trained.

By Thursday morning, the *Sea Mist* was heading across the Atlantic Ocean. Winds continued to "back her canvas," and no British ship had been sighted. As far as Maren could see, only blue water was visible. The ocean was calm, and the *Sea Mist* sailed gracefully over its surface, much like a huge water bird. The crew had taken to Maren and did not seem to mind having a woman aboard, which many sailors considered bad luck. And at sea, peace filled her. She even forgot the war for a time.

On that same morning, New Orleans was anything but peaceful after Eric James arrived. He first stopped at his office and questioned his brother, Marc. He was astounded to hear that Maren had not only moved into Lady Luck, but that she had been having numerous problems, which did not sound like those he had ordered created to entice her into selling the gambling establishment. At first he was furious to learn of Jared Morgan's partnership; then he smiled, relieved by that discovery. Marc was unaware of Maren's and Jared's departure, so he could not inform his brother of it.

Eric decided to visit Samuel Lewis before seeing Maren, and perhaps Jared. He would then find a way to meet secretly with Dan Myers to get the manager's story. After opening the safe to put some papers inside, he noticed the stack of letters. He snatched them out and studied them; the ribbon wasn't tied as it had been, and the stack was out of order. So, he mused, Maren did know the combination. She had searched his office. He berated Marc for allowing her to do that, but even he realized his brother's innocence could not be denied.

At his lawyer's office, Eric was given more disturbing news. He learned about Jared's intrusion in his affairs and Maren's near-fatal accidents. He was glad when Lewis told him Dan had gotten rid of

Howard Heath and Evelyn Sims. The lawyer
revealed everything Dan had related to him, including Dan's pretense of assisting Jared and Maren.
Eric did not like this report, and he decided he had to
do something quickly.

But the worst news came from Dan Myers. He
hurriedly entered Lewis's office, and was shocked to
find Eric James there.

Eric looked at the anxious Myers and said, "Good
to see you, Dan, but isn't this visit of yours a little
dangerous? What if you're being followed?"

"Lewis has been out of town for weeks so I couldn't
tell him what's happened. Has he told you everything?" the nervous manager asked.

"Obviously not everything or you wouldn't be so
eager to see him. Tell me what happened, all of it,"
Eric ordered.

Dan rapidly revealed his distressing news, ending
with, "Maren's gone upriver somewhere, probably to
hide. I haven't been able to get a clue as to her
location. And Jared Morgan sailed on Monday. He
left me in charge of Lady Luck until he returns, so he
doesn't suspect me."

Myers and Lewis then remained silent as Eric
walked to the window and gazed outside. "Damn,"
he muttered. "I had her partner right where I needed
him. But no matter. When Morgan returns, I'll have
him killed and Maren will be subdued. This will
work out better than I planned. I will obtain even
more than Lady Luck at his death. I'll be leaving for
France on Monday, but I'll give you strict orders how

to handle him if he returns before I do. This time, make certain my orders are obeyed perfectly. I don't want Maren injured. In fact, forget about her; I'll take care of my little cousin." Eric spoke these last words oddly.

Before leaving he made each man go over the entire story once more to make sure nothing had been omitted. He then went to the door and gestured to Horben Wolfe who stood outside.

"Let's go, Ben. I must visit the bank before it closes." Withdrawing a key from his pocket, Eric tossed it into the air, caught it easily, and laughed. "With luck, they don't know each box has two keys. If they've found anything of value, they probably locked it up there."

As the two men walked down the street toward the bank, Horben asked, "What about the necklace, Eric? What if she has it with her?"

"Maren's too smart to carry around something that expensive. If I know her, it's in the bank box. If not, we'll find her and take it."

At the bank, Eric was shocked by the contents of the metal box, but he suddenly grinned. "Let's go home," he said. "I'll go over this stuff there. I want you to gather some of the men and find Maren for me. I have a good idea where she's gone."

Eric stretched out on his bed and tossed the money from the box aside. Then he read the papers, one by one. At last the real deeds were in his hands and nobody could prove anything against him once he substituted these for the forged ones. He smiled as he went over the two wills, thrilled by what he would soon obtain. Reaching for the ribbon-bound paper, he slid off the ribbon. As he read that document, his green eyes narrowed and chilled. "Damn you, Maren James," he exclaimed, grasping the extent of her betrayal. Then he laughed. Jared's will was even more valuable when added to this marriage license.

He gulped the whiskey sitting beside his bed and savored his new victories. He had assumed Willa hadn't known about Jared's part ownership in Lady Luck or she would have told him of it when he'd visited her recently. No matter. He would soon own the plantation where she lived. She had been someone to dally with on his trips to Savannah, but he would not permit her to live on his land.

He despised people who went against him, and he always made them pay for their betrayals. He had been twenty-three when he had accidentally discovered why his father had hated him and Marc. He had returned home one day when his parents, thinking they were alone in the house, had been quarreling bitterly. Concealing himself, he had eavesdropped, and had learned of his mother's treachery and his father's crime.

Elizabeth had shouted at John, "You whored around more than I did, you bloody bastard! You've slept with every tart around, but I've only spent time with one man. You men are lucky; you don't have to worry about becoming pregnant when you enjoy your little trysts. Well, I needed love and sex just like you, my selfish husband. You wouldn't touch me, so I found a real man who loved me—and I loved him."

"You sorry bitch! You won't sleep with him again because I killed him. And if you tell anyone, I'll kill you too. I'll never let you humiliate me by leaving or exposing me. And if you try anything, I'll tell Eric and Marc who their real father is and what a whore you are. You dumb bitch, you should have stayed away from him after I forgave you and kept you around even though you were pregnant with Eric. But no, you had to start up with him again and conceive Marc, the other bastard I claimed to cover your sins, the stupid one. But if you thought I'd allow you and him a third bastard, you were dead wrong, Lizzy, just like he was. And if you dare replace him, I'll slit your whoring throat. Living with a whore for twenty-four years is more than enough for me. Behave, or you're gone, bitch."

"I should have left you for him years ago. No, I should have killed you for provoking me to turn to another man. My sins don't come near yours. He loved me, and I still love him. If you had been any kind of husband to me, none of this would have happened. I had as much right to love as you did."

"You belong to me, Lizzy, and I can do as I please with you. Check the law if you doubt my word. If you ever reveal this . . ."

John did not complete his threat, and Elizabeth replied, "You're the one who's going to expose us by treating Eric and Marc like scum, though they've been born and reared as your sons."

"I have only one son, and that's all I need or want from you. Murray is the only real James heir and he'll get everything. Your two bastards won't see a dollar of mine. Be glad I allowed you to keep them and raise them in my house to prevent a scandal. Every time I look at them I get sick to my stomach. They're just like their father, a no-good tavern owner who was drunk half the time. You would never have left me for trash like that, and if you thought I would ever touch you again after you bedded such filth, you're as stupid as Marc. Keep your mouth shut and your legs crossed, or I'll make sure your bastards lose the James name and see you all drummed out of town."

"You wouldn't dare!" Elizabeth had scoffed. "I can have you sent to jail for murder. How would you like living in a tiny cell without your money and power and slimy wenches?"

"It would be easier to prove you killed your secret lover than to prove the honorable John James did it. You have more to lose than I do, woman, so shut up and do as I tell you."

"I hate you, John, and one day you'll burn in hell for this crime."

It was this statement that had given Eric the idea of punishing his parents. Nobody would miss a whore and a killer! He had looked into the tavern owner's murder to learn who his real father was. His mother had been right. The tavern owner had been a good man, but that did not exonerate his mother. She had made him a bastard! He would destroy the two people who, in their bitterness and revenge, had destroyed him.

For months Eric had plotted their deaths, and he'd come to hate them more and more. Horben Wolfe, his best friend, had helped him carry out the lethal deed. They had rendered his parents unconscious at a hotel and had set fire to the room. John and Elizabeth James had not survived the blaze which had engulfed the hotel and two adjoining businesses before it had been controlled. After that, Eric had plotted his loathsome half-brother's death, and he had recently killed Murray. Now, he owned the James empire, or he soon would. To avoid suspicion, he would wait a year or so before ridding himself of Marc. He didn't care about Colin and Martha James. They were in London, and they were not related to him by blood, neither was Maren.

Maren had messed up his plans by marrying Jared Morgan, the famous Captain Hawk. During his voyage to Baltimore and Jamaica, Eric had decided to sell all of his American holdings and move to his plantation on that lovely island. He had intended to tell Maren they were not blood kin, and to take her as his wife. He had always craved her, but as her cousin, he had been unable to approach her. Of course, she would be a widow after Jared was killed. . . .

Little did Maren know that Eric had encouraged his friend, Daniel Redford, to marry her, so she would be out of the way. He and Daniel were a lot alike, both second in line for inheritance and both unloved by their fathers. It had not been hard to convince Daniel that Maren would be rich one day and would make him a perfect wife. Since Daniel's brother had wooed and wed Daniel's true love, Daniel had been most receptive to Eric's suggestion. Then, during one of his secret trips to London, Eric had learned of Daniel's death and he'd made new plans for Maren James. He was getting rich playing three countries against each other, but it was time to drop his pretenses before someone unmasked him. A good gambler knew when to leave the table, even if he was winning.

Now that he was within reach of Jared Morgan's wealth, Eric would soon have all he needed to live better than Britain's king . . . after he picked up that gold shipment in France. The necklace had not been in the bank box, so he would have to locate Maren to retrieve it. Horben and his men were searching for her at Payne's Point. Eric had assumed Maren was with that arrogant little blonde, Lilibeth Payne; and once Horben got her, he would take Maren with him to France, then drop her off in Jamaica and tend to his business here. Maren would be held captive until he needed Jared's widow to seize the Morgan fortune. Then he would decide whether she was worthy to marry him or not. If he didn't want her, he would hand her over to Horben.

By Sunday afternoon, Eric was certain they would not locate Maren nearby. His overseer at the dock, Andrews, had told him of the young man who had arrived last Sunday morning, looking for Jared Morgan and Lady Luck. When the sailor was described as being in his mid twenties, with sandy hair and hazel eyes, Eric recalled the man who had jumped ship in Savannah: Peter Thomas. He went aboard the *Martha J* and questioned his crew about Peter. Discovering that Peter had purchased another crewman's shore leave at Baltimore, he added up the facts, and was enraged by his conclusion.

He was positive that Jared was on his way to France, with the necklace and with Maren. He ordered his ship and crew to make ready to sail at dawn the next morning, and he offered each man a bonus if they beat the *Sea Mist* to Marseilles.

Horben Wolfe focused his ghostly eyes on his friend and asked, "What will you do if she's with him and you catch her?"

Eric's frosty green gaze met Horben's icy blue one and he replied, "I'll see if she's there by choice or if our illustrious Captain Hawk has coerced her into marrying him and betraying me. You heard what Sam and Dan said: she was against battling me, but Morgan kept pushing her. Dan said he was threatening her with the loss of Lady Luck and with jail because of that money I took. With all that pressure, it's no wonder she got scared and turned to Morgan for help and protection. Dan thinks Morgan forced her to marry him for selfish reasons, which I can understand. If she's innocent, I'll keep her. If she isn't, she's yours to do with as you choose."

Horben smiled and licked his lips as he envisioned

Maren under his control. "Damnation, I hope she's guilty."

They both laughed, then Eric said, "You're my best friend and you've stuck by me for years. I know how badly you want her. Even if she's innocent, I'll let you have her once a week, drugged of course."

Horben smiled at Eric and then clasped his hand because he knew Eric was telling the truth. "In that case, I hope she's innocent," Horben said.

"Me, too, Ben. She'll make us a perfect wife."

Friday afternoon in the mid-Atlantic, Jared and Maren were nestled together in his bed. Jared had been on deck since five o'clock yesterday, but he had finally come down to rest and sleep. Despite his exhaustion a hunger for his wife had kept him from rest. He had asked her to undress and join him for a while, and she had eagerly agreed. They had sighted a few ships, but always at too great a distance to be a threat, and since Jared knew his men were on constant alert, he felt safe in stealing a few hours with Maren.

As he removed his boots and garments, Jared asserted, "I hate to admit it, or even to think it, but I believe Dan Myers is involved with Eric or his cohorts. I keep recalling indications I didn't grasp at the time. As soon as Evelyn was exposed to him, she became a threat, and she was slain. Then Heath died mysteriously. Dan was angry about the attacks on you, so those two must have been overstepping their orders. I think he moved out of the house to throw suspicion off himself, but the incidents those two created kept pointing the finger at him. So he got rid of them."

"He was my father's friend. Why would he betray us, Jared?"

Jared lay down beside her and clasped her naked body to his. "I recall the way he looked and sounded when he talked about Lady Luck, and how nervous he was that day we searched Eric's home. Remember how relieved he seemed when we didn't find anything there?" Maren nodded and snuggled closer. "Dan loves that place. Maybe Eric offered him a share in it for his aid. The trouble started after my arrival, so maybe Dan thought we wouldn't want him there anymore and he'd be pushed out."

"But we wouldn't have done that, Jared. He's a good manager, and we need him. Doesn't he realize how much we liked him and trusted him?"

Jared sighed heavily, from fatigue and disappointment. "Perhaps he was already in too deep by then. I believe he suddenly started romancing Mary Malone to entice her to spy on us for him, just in case we doubted him."

Maren revealed the housekeeper's distrust of Jared and her warnings about him. "I didn't want to tell you because I knew she was wrong and it would hurt you. Possibly Dan planted those ideas in her mind, so he could create a breach between us."

"Yet she never swayed your faith in me. I love you, Maren Morgan," Jared vowed huskily, then covered her mouth with his.

Thoughts of Dan, and of all other matters, were quickly lost as passion seized them and carried them far away. They made love urgently, yet savored every minute of their time together. Then Maren held Jared in her arms while he slept, and she prayed for peace.

Eleven more days passed, the sea remaining calm and no hostile ships being sighted, and Maren and Jared drew closer and closer to each other and to their destination. On the twelfth day after they'd voiced their suspicions of Dan—the twenty-fourth day of their voyage—trouble came to them. A large British ship bore down on the *Sea Mist*, determined to attack.

Maren watched the enemy ship become larger and more menacing as it sailed rapidly toward their larboard side, the wind in its favor. Clouds filled the sky, and she feared a violent storm was brewing. The brisk breeze caused the canvas to whip and pop loudly, as if protesting this duel of powers. She heard the order to clap on more sail, but the British ship kept coming, closer and closer. Then, as if the elements were working in America's favor, the waves and winds rose higher. Spindrift gathered on the sails, and when struck by intermittent sun, it glittered like tiny lights. Whitecaps slapped against the ship's hull, and the smell of salt air and of impending conflict filled everyone's nostrils. The crew readied themselves for the attack, and for confronting death.

Meanwhile the British ship crowded on the sail and sped toward them, seeming to glide across the water's surface as if she were skating on an unevenly frozen pond. Jared kept his ship on course because his mission was vital and he did not have time to battle this persistent and arrogant foe. He ordered the pirate flat hoisted, indicating no quarter if overtaken, but the British ship held to her course. When she neared firing range, she sent a warning shot at the *Sea Mist*.

Jared did not reply to it. He hoped the British captain would give up his pursuit. But the *Sea Mist*'s crew swarmed over the decks and riggings, making certain their vessel was well prepared to defeat this foe. As the distance between the ships diminished, Nature became more tempestuous, and both ships were forced to reduce sail and slacken speed to achieve control. The challenge that had been given was now reluctantly accepted.

The British ship fired another round, which came closer to striking the *Sea Mist*. It was apparent that Jared's ship had been recognized, for the enemy did not wait for the *Sea Mist* to hoist a nation's flag or surrender. The British guns spit forth another volley, and within minutes the two vessels were sailing at each other head-on to test their captain's courage and skills. The British ship was larger and boasted more firepower, but Jared was the best commander and his sleek ship was easier to handle. Jared ordered his crew to open fire on their attacker and to continue firing as quickly as the guns could be reloaded.

The enemy ship did the same, and soon thunderous cannonfire and acrid smoke permeated the air. The *Sea Mist* delivered a stunning blast to the broadside of the other ship, raking her foe with expertise, and as the desperate battle continued, Jared maneuvered his ship so deftly that three staggering blasts of double shot hit the British ship. Her mizzenmast and foremast were hit, leaving only the mainmast; and much of her rigging was destroyed, while Jared's ship had received little damage.

Eventually the British guns became silent, and the ship floated aimlessly on the waves. Jared knew this was not a trick to lure him in closer; the other ship was crippled. He ordered grappling hooks be readied, intending to board her and search for papers and impressed Americans.

Though Maren covered her ears to shut out the screams of wounded men, she could smell the smoke from the fires aboard the other ship, and she wondered if they could be controlled. If not . . . Her heart pounded anxiously as she tried to imagine what Captain Hawk would do with the enemy ship and its defeated crew. She wanted to rush topside and beg him to show mercy, but she knew she must not interfere.

Time seemed to move slower than a snail. Finally, she realized the *Sea Mist* was drifting away from the other ship. She waited, eyes closed and pulse racing, to see if Jared ordered the ship blasted into the depths of the ocean, and she prayed, harder than she had ever prayed, that he would not kill helpless prisoners.

Suddenly the cabin door opened, and Maren whirled about.

"I thought you might want to see this British prisoner and speak with him," Jared said.

Chapter Fifteen

"Bart? Barton Hughes?" she asked incredulously.

"Maren James?" the man replied, equally astonished.

She and Bart rushed toward each other excitedly, and they hugged and laughed. Then Bart grasped her forearms gently and held her away from him to eye her. "You look wonderful, Maren. Lordy, it's great to be free again, thanks to Captain Hawk. What are you doing here?" As if he suddenly became aware of his unkempt state, an embarrassed expression crossed his face and he apologized before she could explain her presence. "Please excuse my sorry appearance. The British don't treat prisoners well. I hope Captain Hawk will provide me with some clean garments and will allow his barber to cut my hair and give me a shave." He ruffled his unkempt hair and rubbed his bearded face as he spoke.

Maren had studied Barton Hughes quickly because she did not want to make him undergo an impolite scrutiny. Lilibeth's fiancé had always taken great care with his appearance, and it obviously dismayed him to look so dirty and maltreated. His face and arms, pale from a lack of sunshine, were bruised and soiled. His midnight black hair was oily and shaggy; it fell into his haggard face and grazed his shoulders. He had not shaved for several weeks. He was clad in a short-sleeved sailor shirt and dark trousers which were wrinkled and dirty. His clothing hung loosely on his gaunt frame. Maren did not have to be told he had endured physical and emotional torment, his eyes revealed his suffering.

She stroked his cheek comfortingly and smiled. "Don't you worry, Bart; we'll have you fat and sassy within a week or two. What were you doing on that ship? Beth told me you were fighting near Maine."

"You've seen her?" he asked anxiously. "How is she?" His greenish blue eyes had brightened at the mention of Beth.

Maren related all she knew about Bart's love, even the jests Beth had made about going after her fiancé, and joy filled Bart's eyes as he admitted, "Lordy, I've been lonely and miserable without her. War is hellish, Maren, worse than I ever imagined. I thought it would be settled in a few months, but it's been years, terrible years."

"When was the last time you contacted Beth?"

"Right before I was captured and put to work as a slave on that British ship, around the end of May. I hope she got my letter in early June and hasn't been too worried. As soon as it's possible, will you help me get a message to her?" he asked Jared.

"We'll be heading back to America after we sail from France," Jared replied, "so it shouldn't be too long, Bart. When we reach Washington, you can either find another ship there or stay with us. I have to stop in Savannah to drop Maren off at my home; then I plan to go to New Orleans."

Bart looked from Jared to Maren. "Am I missing something here? I thought you were living in London now."

Maren didn't know how much to reveal, so she was glad when Jared's arm encircled her waist and he said, "Maren decided to marry me instead of Daniel Redford. We took our vows on July tenth, but we've kept our marriage quiet because of my mission. If you get back to New Orleans before we do, I'd appreciate it if you guard our little secret because we've had some trouble with Maren's cousin and his hirelings."

"Congratulations and best wishes, but what kind of trouble?" Bart asked.

Jared gave him a partial explanation of Eric James's takeover of Cameron James's holdings after the older man's death. "Maren and I own Lady Luck together," he added, "but he wants that too. He hired ruffians to frighten us out. When I had to sail on this mission, I couldn't leave her there because accidents kept happening to her, and several suspicious characters were killed."

"I've only met Eric James on a few occasions, but I

didn't care for him. During his visits to New Orleans, he approached me several times about some unsavory deals, and he was vexed because I refused them." Bart glanced at Maren and said, "I'm sorry about your father, Maren; he was a good man. Why are you heading for France? Isn't that kind of dangerous?"

Jared responded, "We've learned that Eric James is pretending to work for three countries, and he's taking money from each one. He's supposed to pick up a gold shipment in Marseilles, from Napoleon and his loyalists, to help us battle the Brits, but we're hoping to beat him there and claim it. As far as I know, he's a week or so behind us. That's why I didn't want to stop to fight that ship."

"I'm glad you did," Bart declared with relief.

"So are we. It must have been Fate," Maren told him.

Bart's eyes were troubled when he spoke again. "Yes, it must have been Fate, Maren, because you're heading for trouble if you sail for Washington after you leave France. Within the next two weeks, the British are plotting to attack it along with a number of major cities. They intend to shell all the leading ports, and burn the shipyards. We prisoners were kept in an area where we could hear what was going on at the officers' meetings, and they had plenty of them aboard in the last two months. I've heard plans which turned my guts inside out. I hope some American agent has uncovered those schemes and our country is preparing to thwart them, because we could never make it back in time to alert the

President, not even if we turned around this very minute. You and I must talk, Jared, but I would like to clean up first." Bart pushed his ebony hair away from his face, and he prayed he did not smell as badly as he thought he did.

Jared nodded in understanding. "I'll have my cabin man, Jacob Tarver, help you with a bath and a shave; then he can cut your hair and get you a decent meal. Kip's finding places for you and the others to bunk, and since we're about the same size, I'll locate something for you to wear. We can't get back in time to warn of the attacks, so I suggest you rest today. We can talk over dinner tomorrow. There's an American agent aboard that I'd like you to meet. You can tell him what you've learned when he and Kip join us for dinner tomorrow night. We'll reach Marseilles in about a week, so we're going to go over our strategy again. Later you can talk with Maren about Beth."

After Bart left with Jacob Tarver, Maren hugged her husband and thanked him for showing mercy to their enemies.

"So many of them were dead or wounded that I didn't see any need to sink a crippled ship," he replied. "It isn't going anywhere and it can't be repaired. All they can do is tend their injured, bury their dead, and hope for rescue. Not many of those men will heal soon enough to fight us again. But I have to get you home as quickly as I can; that could have been us. We're lucky we didn't have more than one ship after us."

"Fate, Jared Morgan, we're fated to survive and

411

be together."

"Fate's like luck, Mrs. Morgan, sometimes it needs a helping hand."

"As long as it's your talented hand doing the helping, my love." Maren's golden brown eyes danced enticingly.

Jared's blood was already fired by his recent victory. Compelling emotions surged through a man before, during, and after battle, but now, he burned with the desire Maren kindled in him. It was early afternoon and he should return to duty for there might be more British ships in this area. Still, the conflict had been won so easily he had not expended all of his energy, his tension. He knew that his crew was scrubbing up and doing repairs while the freed men were eating, cleaning up, and resting. He walked to his door and hesitated only a moment before bolting it. As he turned, Maren was already unfastening her clothing, and a seductive smile teased her lips.

He came forward and halted her movements. "You read me like a map, my apt student. Let me do it," he coaxed huskily, for he enjoyed this disrobing task which enflamed them both.

Maren relaxed as Jared lifted her dress over her head and tossed it aside. After untying her petticoat, wriggling it over her hips, and slipping it past her ankles, he knelt to remove her slippers. He stroked her silky thighs and calves as he playfully rolled her stockings down her legs. He then kissed her knees,

trailed his lips down her left leg, and nuzzled her
dainty foot against his cheek. To balance herself,
Maren rested her fingertips on his shoulders. But
when his hands traveled up her body slowly and
sensuously as he rose, hers slid down to his chest.

Jared deftly unlaced her chemise and removed it.
His smoldering gaze roaming her flawless face, now
flushed with passion and need, before it seared over
her naked shoulders and came to rest on those
enticing mounds which had risen with desire. He
fondled her breasts lightly, leisurely, lovingly, his
thumbs and forefingers trapping the two buds
between them and gently kneading them until they
grew larger and harder. Then his lips and tongue
moistened the peaks, tantalized them, made them
plead for more attention.

As Jared's mouth worked stirringly at her breasts,
his hands artfully caressed her shoulders, arms, and
back. Maren was now as sultry as a summer day, but
her fragrance was as fresh as that of early morn. Even
the cotton which grew on his plantation was not as
soft as her body, nor were the horses he reared as
sleek. She was splendid, she was temptation, she was
perfection. His strong fingers roved her satiny
texture, causing her to tingle all over. Then Jared
briefly halted his provocative behavior to remove her
remaining garment. As he cast it aside, his eyes took
in the woman he loved, from her toes to the tip of
her dark brown head. His tawny gaze fused with her
golden brown one as his hands moved around her

softly rounded hips to capture her firm buttocks. He pressed her bare groin against his clothed one and fondled her derrière, then his lips sought hers.

Maren felt the heat radiating from his manly region to her feminine one, and she was highly aroused. She wanted to titillate him to an even higher level of desire, so she pulled his shirt over his head and tossed it onto a nearby table. Then her fingernails carefully grazed his golden flesh and she spread kisses over Jared's torso as she sank to the floor. She grinned wickedly as she carefully removed his ebony boots, but comically flung his stockings away. Then, rising to her knees, she unbuckled his belt and drew it from his waist before urging his breeches down over narrow hips and muscled thighs. When he stepped out of them, she tossed them upon the table as well.

For a moment she greedily took in his magnificent physique before she bent forward and pressed kisses to his most sensitive region. As her lips covered it, she gave him a blissful pleasure much like the pleasure he had given her on several occasions since this voyage had begun. She felt him stiffen and heard his loud inhalation. When he shuddered and moaned, she knew he was both surprised and pleased. His response was gratifying and stimulating. She massaged his firm buttocks with her fingers before slipping them around to caress his moist and fiery shaft.

For a time, reality fled them. Then Jared lifted her and placed her on the bed. Their mouths fused greedily, their hands explored eagerly. With both appetites fully whetted, their bodies joined and they made love urgently and rapturously.

On the following Wednesday, the twenty-fourth of August, the British stormed Washington and burned many buildings, including the Capitol and the White House. The second stage of their three-pronged attack on the United States was also underway: invasion via Chesapeake Bay, Lake Champlain, and the Mississippi River. The British would claim that the burning of Washington was in retaliation for the American assault on York in July. Barracks had been burned there as had storehouses and eleven ships. But the Americans had not been trying to conquer Canada, only to hold the Niagara line. Now more trouble was brewing because the end of the European conflict would allow more and more British to pour into that area and into others. And in Belgium peace was being discussed, although the British were stalling the talks to gain an advantage.

The following Friday, on the eastern shore of the Gulf of Lions, the *Sea Mist* docked at the chief Mediterranean seaport of France. Marseilles was a city of many businesses: soap making, metal foundries, tile and brick works, shipyards, glass factories, and much more. They had sailed past several islands which were fortified to protect the harbor. Marseilles was the oldest city in France, rich in history and almost as large as Paris.

Maren Morgan was ready for her role in this impending drama, and exhilarating but perilous one. She had donned a white batiste gown in the Empire style. She was wearing the ruby and gold necklace which belonged to Josephine, wife of Napoleon. Her hair was gathered into an upswept style, but short curls dangled around her face and the nape of her neck.

As she stepped onto the dock, opened her parasol, and took her husband's arm, Jared admired her beauty and smiled at her. Maren returned his smile, then silently prayed for success. With luck, Eric had not uncovered their plans, had not beaten them to Marseilles.

Five men followed them, but not too closely: Harry Epps, Simon Carter, Kerry Osgood, Barton Hughes, and Peter Thomas. Jared had wanted to bring along Davy Douglas because he was quick and alert and a superb fighter, but an expert steersman was too valuable to endanger.

They made their way to the soap factory which was being used as a meeting place for loyalists and as a storage depot for supplies being gathered for Napoleon's next strike. In fluent French, Maren asked to see Antoine Gallier, and they were shown to his office. After they were seated, she introduced herself as Maren James, Eric's first cousin and his substitute. She told the Frenchman that Eric had broken a leg and could not make the journey at this time, taking that story from one of Eric's lies. She introduced

Jared as Captain Hawk and Kip as his firstmate.

As she fingered the necklace, she spoke the first line of the code, "American blood is running as red as these rubies, Monsieur Gallier. If possible, I would trade them for peace."

The Frenchman eyed Maren and Jared intensely, but did not respond correctly. "It is a pleasure to have you here, Miss James, and an honor to meet a real hero, Captain Hawk."

Maren translated for Jared and continued in the man's language, "Peace could be entrusted to no safer hands than Captain Hawk's. When I was asked to come here, I naturally chose him as my escort."

"What product do you seek, Mademoiselle James?" Antoine asked, aware she had given the beginning of the correct code, but he was being cautious because this deed was dangerous and involved high stakes.

Maren prayed that Peter Thomas's clues were the right ones. "I have heard of a special soap which is blended and sold only here, Monsieur Gallier. I believe it is called Maiden Fair. Do you have it?"

Antoine smiled and nodded. "It is crated and ready to be shipped. Have you brought men to help you transport it to your ship?"

"We have five waiting outside. Is that sufficient?" she inquired.

Antoine became serious. "Is your crew totally loyal, mademoiselle?"

"Each one was selected by Captain Hawk for this vital task."

Gallier eased into English so Jared could join the

conversation. "I will have the crates loaded onto wagons, and your men can deliver them to your ship. My drivers will go along to return the wagons. Would you care to inspect your purchase?"

Jared smiled and shook his head. "It won't be necessary. We know how important this shipment is to both sides. As we speak, the British are attacking Washington and other major ports. We need to sail immediately so we can trade the soap for supplies and deliver them."

"*Sacrebleu!*" the slender Frenchman cursed. "These British dogs dare much, Capitaine Hawk. But together we will defeat them."

"That's a promise, Monsieur Gallier." Jared lied out of necessity.

The three chatted about their wars with Britain while the loading was being done, and when Kip returned to the office and said everything was ready, Jared shook hands with Antoine Gallier and thanked him.

Maren removed the exquisite necklace and held it out to their contact. As she did so, Antoine grasped her hand and curled her fingers over it. "Keep it to wear around your beautiful throat, Mademoiselle James," he said. "I am sure its past owner would agree that a heroine as ravishing as you must be rewarded. I have also sent along a crate of my very best soap for your use."

Maren smiled radiantly and thanked him, but she kept the necklace only because she knew its sale would buy more supplies for her people.

The Americans then hurriedly returned to the ship and prepared to sail with the late tide. The gold was uncrated and concealed beneath the inner planking of the orlop deck, its weight distributed evenly to allow for the ship's smooth handling. The crates were stored elsewhere for later use.

As the moon climbed higher, the *Sea Mist* sailed through the Mediterranean toward the Strait of Gibraltar. Jared was eager to get back into the Atlantic Ocean where he could maneuver his ship better in case of trouble. He knew the additional weight she carried would slow his progress, and he could not allow the British, or any pirate or privateer, to take it from him. He had to remain on alert, ready to flee if peril approached.

Until he was certain the British had attacked Washington, he would sail in that direction. If his foes were in that area and he used a British flag, perhaps with cunning and boldness he could slip past the blockade and get the gold to land. After that, he would put Maren ashore in Savannah and then go after his foes.

The next week, on Saturday, Eric James arrived in Marseilles to make an infuriating discovery. He told the irate Gallier that the woman with Captain Hawk was not his cousin. He said she was a British spy who had stolen the necklace from Maren and had then hired Captain Hawk, who was now working for his own profit, to assist her in the clever theft. He swore to the man he could overtake them and would get back the gold.

"Make certain his treachery is exposed to your President and he is hanged," Antoine Gallier insisted.

"Do not worry, Monsieur Gallier, I will slay them myself," Eric vowed, and as soon as the tide permitted, he sailed in pursuit, assuming Jared would head first for Savannah to make certain of his wife's safety.

The *Sea Mist*'s luck was challenged on September the seventh. "She keeps coming, Jared," Kip informed his captain as he eyed the ship behind them. "She may only be heading in the same direction we are, but she's steadily closing the distance between us."

"As soon as you can make out her flag, hoist a matching one." Jared turned to Davy Douglas, his steersman, and ordered, "Give her a southward head, Davy. Let's see if our pursuer changes course too."

She did, and two hours later the ship was still gaining on them. Jared ordered, "Davy, give me a quarter turn to starboard." He shouted to his crew to "press more canvas."

"Wind be backing us, Cap'n," Harry Epps shouted as the sails were filled to capacity by nature's energy.

For a while, the *Sea Mist* increased the space between the two ships, until the one in pursuit also turned the helm to starboard and trailed them again.

"Simon, Harry, get the guns primed and the crew alert. I think she wants to tangle with us. We'll try to outrun her. If we can't, we'll turn and fight."

"She's sleek and swift, Jared," Kip remarked worriedly.

"Can you make out her firepower?" Jared inquired.

Kip stared into the eyeglass and replied, "About the same as us. Damnation," he swore suddenly. "She's pulled an old trick, Jared; there's another ship in her shadow. They're spreading now to overtake us from both sides. With this weight, we'll never . . ." Kip quieted, as there was no need to further outline their plight.

Both men frowned simultaneously. "Get the crew ready, Kip. I'll be back in a moment."

Kip knew Jared was going below to speak with his wife, and he began to pass along orders to prepare for battle.

Jared entered the cabin and approached Maren, who was repairing some of his garments. She knew from his expression that there was trouble, and she waited tensely for his explanation.

He gave it hastily because the attackers were swiftly overtaking them; then he embraced her and said, "Whatever you hear or see, stay in the cabin, love. I'll try to get us out of this."

Maren regretted that he had to be concerned for her at a time such as this, and she did not waste precious preparation time by asking questions. She tried to relax him. "Don't worry about Captain Hawk's wench. I know you'll do your best to save us. I love you."

The two ships dogged them until the next morning. But that day the sun did not appear. Dark clouds were piled above them, the winds blew with a mighty force, and turbulent waves beat against the ship's hull. As the swells rapidly grew in height and power, the ship was carried with them. Up and down and side to side she rolled, until Maren feared she was going to be sick.

The crew had taken turns catching naps, but Jared had slept little. The ship, the crew, his wife, and the cargo were his responsibilities. He could not bear the thought of those aboard falling into enemy hands, so he kept his eyes on the storm and on his persistent foes. He didn't know which menace he'd rather battle.

But the choice wasn't his. With terrible violence, the squall broke before noon. "Batten down!" The command was shouted at the last minute, for the battle with the two ships could not take place in the storm.

For the remainder of the day, all three ships were at the mercy of the elements. They were tossed to and fro like tiny toys. Jared had ridden out many storms, but this was one of the worst he'd seen. The crew worked diligently and desperately to save the ship and their lives.

When the storm finally broke, no enemy ship was

in sight. No doubt the tempest had driven the vessels in different directions. Until darkness fell, the crew continued to labor beneath lessening winds and pouring rain. Loosened cargo and equipment were secured and repaired, as were breaks in the railings. Sails were checked and mended. Broken rigging was replaced. Decks were scrubbed with freshly fallen water, and companionways were mopped. Men were checked for injuries, and those needing care were tended.

Jared, who worked with his men, was delighted to find no major damage to the masts. Patrick "Patty" Brennan shifted between cooking and doctoring, and, in rotation, the men took breaks for quick meals. Harry Epps and Simon Carter cleaned, checked, and readied the guns, and when most of the work was completed and night provided some cover, the crew took turns catching some sleep and finishing the chores. Lookouts were posted on all sides of the ship to watch for attackers, or to spot a ship adrift.

When Jared was relieved by Kip, he went below. Maren was lying on the bed, fully clothed. Her pale face and faint smile said she had weathered the turbulent storm, but not without problems. She was sipping the hot tea which Jacob Tarver had brought to the cabin.

Jared sat down carefully beside her. He eyed her from head to foot; then his gaze locked with hers. "How are you doing, love?" he asked tenderly, stroking her cheek.

"Fine now, Captain Hawk, but you have taken me on a tempestuous trip," she jested. She set the cup aside, then nestled into his arms. She always felt so loved, so protected in his strong embrace.

"When I came down earlier to change into dry clothes, you were asleep so I didn't disturb you." As he stretched out on the bed and drew her into his comforting embrace, he sighed wearily, allowing his tension to subside and his fatigue to take command of him.

Maren knew he was exhausted. It was very late, and he had been under an enormous strain for the past two days. She lay quietly in his arms, and when she realized he was asleep, she gazed into his compelling face, thankful that they were all alive and still free. She started to rise to put out the lantern, but feared awakening him. Placing her arm across his chest, she closed her eyes and went to sleep.

A few days later, in New York, Plattsburgh was viciously attacked by the British, who were resoundingly defeated in what would be called one of the greatest battles during the War of 1812. The American fleet, under Commodore Thomas MacDonough, sent the British fleeing into Canada after achieving a decisive victory over them. But British warships had left Halifax and had landed forces in Maine at Eastport, Machias, Castine, and Bangor. A large part of the Maine coast was now occupied.

On September fourteenth, with Washington in

partial ruins, the British Army laid siege on Baltimore. Defended by Fort McHenry and numerous American patriots, that city repulsed the invading force, and it was during this battle that Francis Scott Key, a prisoner on a British warship, wrote what was to become the national anthem of the United States.

During the preceding summer, most of the fighting had taken place on the Great Lakes and along the eastern seacoast. Then it was learned that the British were attempting to lure the New England states back into the empire, and some disgruntled or greedy Americans were favorable to the idea. Indeed, Massachusetts was soon to call for a convention to be held in Connecticut to vote on secession.

And that fall, American frigates were dispatched to major cities to defend them against the British strategy Barton Hughes had revealed to Jared and Maren.

The *Sea Mist* was only a few days off the eastern coast when she made contact with another American ship, an extremely fast and agile sloop of war which was stoutly built and heavily armed. As the vessels rode side by side in the tranquil water, Jared went aboard to gather news. The naval vessel had recently visited several ports, and the commodore was well informed on the progress of the war, so Jared learned what had occurred since he'd been in Washington in June.

After explaining his self-appointed mission to France, Jared decided it was best to turn half of the gold over to the naval officer. He had some of his crew recrate it and transfer it aboard the warship. That way, if anything happened to the *Sea Mist*, not all of the gold would be lost. The commodore was delighted by Jared's victory and his trust. He vowed to use the gold to obtain supplies for their country, and to do that with dispatch.

Since Jared could not get to Washington, the sloop's commander suggested he unload the remaining gold at Charleston, where several naval ships were docked. Then, after taking his wife to Savannah, Jared could rejoin the American forces as a privateer gathering supplies.

In less than a week, the *Sea Mist* had put into Charleston, had sailed, and had dropped anchor at Savannah. Although a few ships had been sighted en route, none had approached them. As quickly as possible, supplies were purchased and loaded, and the ship was readied to sail at dawn the next day.

Maren's packing was done when Jared came for her. He drew her to him and rested his cheek atop her head. "I hate to leave you, love, but we must defeat those Brits. I'll take you to Shady Rest and get you settled, but I can't spend the night with you. I must be back on the ship before midnight in case the weather changes and we're forced to sail early."

He lifted her chin and gazed into her sad eyes. "I think it's best to let everyone there know you're Mrs. Jared Morgan. That will make it easier for you to deal with Willa. You will stand up to her, won't you?"

Maren was too concerned about her husband's departure to concentrate on Willa Barns Morgan. "I'll try to keep peace until your return, but I'll remember what you told me about her. Please be careful, Jared."

"I will, love. Let's go meet a she devil," he said with a scowl.

Maren was impressed by her first view of Shady Rest Plantation, and she realized that it deserved its name. The main house, slave quarters, blacksmith shed, smokehouses, gardens, stockyards, fowl pens, stables, and barns were all shaded by moss-draped live oaks, elegant magnolias, sweeping willows, and a variety of other trees. A narrow road led straight to the main house which was spanned by porches that ran the entire length of the first and second floors. These were supported by many Grecian-style columns. The mansion was painted white with green trim and was in excellent condition. Areas were fenced off, and the grounds were enlivened by flowering bushes. Near one barn stood a huge stack of firewood and several chopping blocks, and in the distance were fruit trees and several small ponds.

After leaving the main road, they had ridden for several miles, flanked on both sides by cotton fields which stretched nearly as far as the eye could see. Clearly this sprawling plantation was self-sufficient and well managed. Even without cotton and rice exports, it could survive many years of war. Maren now understood why Willa Barns Morgan refused to leave this Georgian paradise.

In the rented carriage Jared had quietly watched his wife absorb her new surroundings. Finally she met his gaze and said, "It's magnificent, Jared. Even our place wasn't this large or well laid out. Mr. Lawton, your overseer, is a jewel; you never want to lose him."

"There he is now," Jared pointed to the muscular man approaching them on horseback. "He lives with his wife and three children on a small parcel of land west of the house." Jared halted the carriage and waited for Jim Lawton to join them. After introducing Maren as his wife, he instructed the overseer to watch over her for him, explaining that he must return to sea.

When Jim had swept off his hat and nodded at Maren, he'd revealed a steadily balding head. At forty-one, his skin was deeply tanned and wrinkled from countless days beneath the sun, but his dark gaze appeared gentle and friendly. After wishing them a happy married life, Jim quickly gave Jared a report on the plantation. Then he wished Jared safety and success at sea.

Jared asked the overseer to show Maren around the plantation on the morrow and to help her with any problems before the man bade them farewell and rode off. He then smiled at his wife and said, "You'll like Jim and he'll take good care of you. There is one thing I want to explain: our slaves are treated better than most hired workers. We feed and clothe them properly, and they're never whipped, not by Willa or Jim or any of the black bosses. And we allow them to marry and to keep their children. If you ever catch anyone breaking any of those rules, correct the situation at once, no matter who it is. My place is a happy one; that's why things go so well here.''

Maren hugged him and said, "I'm glad, Jared. I'm going to love it here. Suddenly New Orleans and Lady Luck don't seem to matter. When the war's over, let's get rid of everything there and live here.''

"That sounds good to me, love. You're home, Maren Morgan,'' he remarked, halting the carriage near the front door.

Instantly three servants left the house and joined them. Jared greeted them like old friends and made the introductions. "Robert is our butler, and he takes good care of me when I'm home. He's been with us since he was knee-high. Suzy is our housewoman and she sees that everything's kept clean. Little Suzy was born here. Her mother still helps out when she's able, but most of the time she looks after children while their parents are in the fields. And Bertha is our cook, the best in the land. I hope you've got something special cooking for tonight, Bertha, 'cause I've brought home my wife. This is Maren Morgan.''

All three servants—the petite Suzy, the stout Bertha, and the elderly Robert—were overjoyed.

"Lordy, Mister Jared, you done found yourself a beauty,'' Bertha said. "I'll git myself in that kitchen and cook up a storm for you two. A shame your papa ain't here to see this glorious day."

Jared told her, "I can only stay until midnight; then I must sail. This infernal war's still going on and there's no end in sight."

"I'll git your room ready, Mister Jared," Suzy declared, "and I'll take care of your wife whilst you're gone. Don't you worry none about her. Robert, help me git them trunks upstairs for Missy Morgan."

Jared protested gently. "They're too heavy and awkward, little Suzy. Fetch a couple of the men to carry them upstairs. I don't want you and Robert hurting your backs or falling. I need you three healthy to take care of this woman for me." He drew Maren against him and kissed her forehead, revealing his deep feeling for her.

"Where are Willa and the children?" Jared asked, knowing they should have appeared by now.

"Missy Morgan done moved them chillun into town with Bessie so they be near the school," Suzy revealed. "She bought a little house, and they lives there when school's going on. Missy Morgan says they hasta git up too early to git there from here when the weather gits bad this time of year. She says they git more resting and studying done living in town. She only let's 'em come home one time a month and on holidays. Big Bessie lives with 'em and looks out for 'em."

"When did Willa get this crazy idea?" Jared asked, annoyed.

"When school started this time," Suzy replied.

"That's too long for those young children to be away from home."

"You're right, Mister Jared," Bertha agreed. "Ever' time they comes home, they cries and begs Missy Morgan to let 'em come back, but she tells 'em it's best for 'em."

"I'll take care of that tonight before I leave. Where is Willa today?"

"She went to the Clarys yesterday. She's supposed to be home by now," Bertha answered.

"I'd like to speak with her before I leave, but I hope she doesn't return until after dinner. Let's get Maren inside and settled."

Maren and Jared had enjoyed a romantic dinner and were about to sneak upstairs for an hour alone when Willa arrived. It was after dark, so they had assumed she would not be returning that night.

Jared met his stepmother, who was only seven years older than himself, on the front porch. She was a strawberry blonde with hazel eyes, and she had not had time to collect her poise after being told Jared was home. Still, she eyed him up and down as she smiled and said, "Nice to have you home again so soon, Jared. Can you stay long?"

"I'm leaving within the hour. I was afraid I would miss you before I sailed." Before he could explain what he meant, Willa had stepped closer to him and was trailing her fingers over his chest. Jared seized her hand and pushed it away. "I wanted to introduce

431

you to my wife and to get things settled before I return to the war. She'll be living here."

"Wife?" Willa echoed. "You got married? She's here?"

"Her name is Maren James Morgan. She's the daughter of Papa's old friend Cameron James of James Shipping in New Orleans. We got married there on July tenth. Maren's parents are dead, so I brought her here to wait for me. She'll be the mistress of Shady Rest, not you. I hope you understand that and don't give her any trouble."

The situation struck Willa hard. She started to protest, but decided to handle Jared's wife after he departed. However, she was not prepared for the woman who joined them. Maren was beautiful, and she had strength. Willa realized she had a formidable rival in this stunning creature. She smiled with feigned warmth, then hugged Maren. "This is quite a surprise. I'm sure you'll be very happy here, Maren. I'll introduce you to everyone, perhaps even throw a welcoming party. We'll get along wonderfully, Jared; you don't have to worry."

"One thing that does worry me is what you've done with Cathy and Steven. They're too young to be living away from home."

Willa frowned, sighed heavily, and tossed her reddish gold hair. "You know how far it is into town, Jared. Every morning those children had to be up before dawn to get to school, and they didn't get home until dark. They were so exhausted they couldn't study, and never had time to play. They were getting scrawny and sickly covering so many miles every day, especially in stormy or cold weather, so I rented a nice house near the school and moved Bessie in with them. This way, they can sleep later every morning, they're close to the schoolhouse in bad weather, and they're home before dark. They have more time to study and to play. They're near other children, and they're healthier. Bessie cooks and cleans and protects them."

"But they must be miserable," Jared asserted.

Willa covered her vexation and slyly said, "What's a little unhappiness when their education and health are at stake? I haven't deserted them or sent them off to boarding school. I visit them every time I go into town, and they come home every few weeks. I have to do what's best for them; they are *my* children, Jared."

"I want Maren to see them and talk with them. If she agrees it's best for them to live in town during the school year, then it's fine with me. If she disagrees, I want them brought home immediately. Understand?"

Willa glared at the handsome Jared for a moment. "You have no right to interfere. I'm not your slave. We're family. If you want me to leave Shady Rest now that you're married, just say so. Don't try to embarrass me or make me cower before your new bride."

Maren excused herself from the unpleasant confrontation by saying, "I'll let you two talk for a few minutes while I freshen up." She went into the house, and as she retrieved her shawl from the sofa in the sitting room, which opened onto the porch, the tone of Jared's voice caught her attention and she halted to listen.

"I promised Papa I would take care of Cathy and Steven, and I intend to keep that vow. Remember, Maren is in charge here until I return, and don't give her any problems."

Willa inquired angrily, "Did you tell her about us? Does she know Steven isn't your father's child?"

"I told her part of it, but not about Steven. Maybe I'll tell her one day, and maybe I'll let it lie. But I won't let you hurt that boy, Willa. He's a Morgan, and I'll never let you make him a bastard."

"He looks more and more like you, Jared. He's quite handsome and bright. I wish you would spend more time with him after you come home. He needs you. Stop downing me and help me with him."

"I have to get back to the ship. Behave yourself, Willa, or . . ."

"Or what, Jared love? You'll tell little Maren all about me?"

"You're a bitch, Willa, a real bitch. Why don't you latch on to another rich man and get off my plantation?"

"Half of this plantation should be mine, or my son's!"

Jared said coldly, "Don't worry about Steven; I won't let him lose his rightful inheritance."

"Why did you marry that girl and bring her here?"

"Because I wanted to."

"And you always get everything you want, don't

you, Jared?"

To annoy Willa, he replied, "Yes, I do. Now, let's go inside."

Maren did not know what to make of the conversation. She took a seat on the sofa, sipped the cold tea, and when Jared entered the room, she rose and smiled at him. "Is it time for you to leave?"

"I'm afraid so, love, but I'll be back soon," he promised. Taking her hand, he coaxed, "Walk me to the carriage."

As they headed for the door, Jared glanced at Willa and said, "Remember, behave yourself, or you'll be sorry."

At the carriage, Maren softly chided, "You shouldn't treat her like that in front of me and others, Jared. It will only create more trouble between you two, and between her and me. I would like things to run smoothly during your absence."

"You're right, love. She just riles me because I want her gone and I can't get rid of her. And I have to think of Cathy and Steven."

"I can hardly wait to meet them."

Jared pulled her into his arms and kissed her hungrily. "Lordy, I crave you, woman."

"I'm going to miss you terribly. Please hurry home."

"Stay safe and well, Maren Morgan, or I'll make you pay dearly," he teased, then planted searing kisses over her face and throat. "I have to leave now, or I won't be able to go."

Maren watched him until he vanished from view.

Then she sighed heavily and returned to the house. Willa was nowhere in sight. Bertha told her that she had gone to her room and wouldn't be back down that night. Maren thought it odd that the woman didn't want to study her or to make her feel welcome, but she decided that perhaps Willa needed time to get accustomed to her presence, or to get over her embarrassment and irritation.

Maren went to Jared's room, put on a nightgown, and got into bed. She felt strange in this huge room with such large furniture. It was too masculine and dark, too quiet and depressing. She wanted to brighten and enliven it. None of Jared's fragrance lingered in the room, and she missed him already.

She wondered how she would get along with Willa and what the woman's conversation with her husband meant. If Benjamin Morgan was not Steven's father, but the boy was a Morgan, whose son was he? And how did Jared know the truth? She wondered why he had chosen to keep this matter a secret, but she was tired. She decided that when Jared returned, she would ask for an explanation of the implications that simmered dangerously within her.

Maren spent most of the following day in Jim Lawton's company. The overseer gave her a tour of the plantation and introduced her to the workers and to his family. She enjoyed herself and was quite relaxed.

When Jim left her at the door of the main house,

however, Maren noticed something odd; none of the servants came to greet her. She called out their names after entering, but received no response.

"Hello, little cousin." The man's voice filled her ears.

Maren whirled to find Willa standing between Eric James and Horben Wolfe. She was grinning devil-ishly

Chapter Sixteen

"Eric! What are you doing here?" Maren asked incredulously. She did not like the familiarity she perceived between her cousin and Willa, and the wicked grins on their faces made her uneasy.

"Maren, my sweet," he began playfully, "whatever are you doing here in Savannah? Why aren't you at home?"

Maren did not know how to answer because she couldn't surmise how much Eric knew. His next response partially enlightened her.

"Why did you allow Captain Hawk to trick you into betraying me? I've just come from New Orleans and France, following your traitorous wake, little cousin. What will the President have to say about you two?"

"Jared left that gold with the President's men, so he should be quite glad about that," Maren replied, hoping her voice did not quaver. She tried to remain

439

poised and clear witted, but it was difficult. She was shaking, and her palms were damp. Trying to focus attention on Eric's foul deeds, she asserted bravely, "You lied to me about my parents' deaths. Lilibeth Payne told me there was no hurricane last year."

Eric did not appear to be bothered by her words or her tone. He asked casually "Is that why you turned against me and sided with that so-called hero? If you had given me a chance, I could have explained. I'll do so right now; I thought that story would sit better with you than the truth. They were robbed, beaten, and murdered by runaway slaves from another plantation. I only wanted to spare you such gory details. Willa tells me you and Morgan are married. Is that true?"

"Yes," Maren replied tersely, keeping her eyes fixed on his.

"Why?" Eric probed, his jaw clenched and his gaze impenetrable.

"That's none of your business," Maren told him.

Annoyed, Eric nonetheless asked in a deceptively calm voice, "Speaking of business, Samuel Lewis and Dan Myers tell me Morgan's been sticking his nose into my affairs back home. Is that true?"

"Why would your hirelings lie to you?" Maren responded sarcastically.

He grinned and vowed smugly, "They wouldn't."

"Then why the foolish question?"

"I don't want an answer," he clarified. "I want an explanation."

"Do you really need one, Eric? Do you think I'm

too stupid to comprehend what you've done, and were doing?''

"No, but I was hoping you were loyal and smart."

"Loyal to the man who stole my inheritance? Surely you jest!"

"I see you found your secret partner and located those deeds for me. Thanks, little cousin." Seeing her shocked response, he chuckled and said, "Oh, did I forget to tell you? I kept the second key to the bank box.''

"You took my papers?" Maren was frantic.

"I took everything there, everything," he declared pointedly.

"How dare you trick me again!" she exclaimed, then artfully changed her tone to ask, "Why, Eric? We were so close. I can't believe you would do such horrible things, especially to me." When he approached her and stroked her flushed cheek, Maren did not flinch. She did not want to reveal her terror. If she was going to get out of this dilemma, she had to fool him.

"Ben, take Willa for a long walk. I want to speak privately with Maren. There are a few things she needs to hear about me and Morgan."

After Horben Wolfe and Willa left the house, Eric coaxed, "Sit down, Maren, you've got a few shocks coming.''

Maren knew she could not escape at that moment, so she did as Eric suggested. She sat on one end of the sofa and faced him. "Well?" she demanded. "Why did you betray me and try to destroy me?"

"Where to begin . . ." he murmured, eying her intently.

"What about with spying and treason; then the theft of my inheritance? How could you, Eric? I loved you and trusted you."

"Maren, my sweet, you're so wrong about everything. When this messy war was over, I was going to share everything with you."

"You were?" she scoffed. "After you left New Or—"

"Be quiet and listen to me. I really am working for the American government, but in a tricky way. I'm pretending to be a spy for the British, and I can prove it. As soon as it's safe, I'll take you to see the President, and he will convince you that I'm no traitor. Things aren't as they seem, Maren; I swear it. That gold I got out of London was delivered to Jamaica to be picked up by another American agent. Since I'm supposed to be working for the other side, I couldn't risk being caught passing it along. The same was true of that French shipment. You and Morgan have nearly destroyed my contacts. I'm not even sure I can carry out my missions anymore; everyone is suspicious of me now. Not that my life matters that much, but I hate to lose it without a good reason."

He moved a little closer to her. "I spoke with the President before coming here, and he's going to order Captain Hawk to stop intruding on my missions. You two have really jeopardized my position, and I'm afraid I can't allow any more interference. The war is at a critical stage, and your recklessness could lose it for us."

"Do you really expect me to believe this—"

Eric interrupted curtly, "I've reached a point at which I don't care what you think or feel! I'm hurt and disappointed, Maren. You've not only turned against me, you've been working against me and trying to get me killed. I took over James Shipping so I could use the ships to help our side. I couldn't even tell your father what I was doing. I hurt him badly, Maren; he thought I was a real British spy, and I never got the chance to tell him the truth before he died. I don't want your damned inheritance. Taking it over was only a ruse. You can have everything back the minute this war's over. But I asked you to trust me and help me. Why didn't you?"

Eric was most persuasive, but Maren remembered everything she had heard and learned. Knowing she could not dupe him by making a sudden about-face, she argued boldly, "Because I know what you say is not true. There was a *real* American spy on your ship—Peter Thomas. He came to New Orleans and told Jared Morgan all about your plans. You used me, Eric. You've been working for all three sides, but only in your own favor. And if that isn't bad enough, you've attempted to drive me out of Lady Luck and you've probably tried to have me . . . killed."

"You're wrong, Maren. Dan Myers was the one after Lady Luck. Those fools that tried to harm you were employed by him. When Lewis told me about your so-called accidents, I was furious. If Myers

443

hadn't gotten rid of his hirelings before my arrival, I surely would have. I paid Myers to watch over you, but he got greedy and was afraid you and Morgan would get rid of him. He was a friend of your father's so I thought he was trustworthy; he isn't. As for Lewis, he was the only man who knew I was secretly working for the Americans. He forged papers to help me establish an identity the British would accept, but you scared the hell out of him when you wanted me investigated. That's why he went along with Myers's ruse to scare you out of Lady Luck; he thought that would keep you from exposing me. Unfortunately, that only made me look worse to you, and it made you susceptible to Morgan's guile."

Eric edged even closer to Maren. "I would never pay anyone to hurt you. To kill you? That's absurd. Damn it, woman, I love you. I've always loved you and wanted you. I was hoping to take you with me to Jamaica after the war, to marry you. I've already bought us a home there." His green eyes and his voice were filled with passion.

Maren gaped at him. "Marry you? But we're . . ." She halted, her thoughts a maelstrom. Was her cousin crazy? she wondered. If so, how could she deal with him? How could she escape?

Eric jumped up and paced the room. "Maren, how do I tell you such humiliating news?" he asked, sounding as if he were frustrated and tormented, but totally honest.

"Tell me what, Eric?" she inquired apprehensively.

Eric turned and faced her as he admitted, "We're not kin. I'm a bastard, Maren. My real father owned a tavern in Baltimore; my mother was in love with him for years. My parents never slept together after Murray was born, so there's no doubt about my sorry lineage. My father knew all about her lengthy affair, but he kept her around for appearances. He couldn't do or say much because he'd carried on with countless women. He and my mother hated each other, tried to hurt each other whenever they could. That's why my father, or I should say John James, hated me and Marc; we weren't his sons." He rapidly fired the truth at her, then scoffed, "If John had lived, he would have exposed us one day. I'm glad he died in that fire. He was never a father to me. I'm not your cousin, Maren, no blood relation at all, and I've waited for the day when I could tell you the truth and marry you. I love you, and I would never harm you."

Maren used this stunning revelation to her advantage. She exclaimed, "Sweet heavens above! You're telling me the truth, aren't you?"

In response, Eric asked painfully, "Why did you marry him and spoil everything? I was going to take you where nobody knew us and make you my wife. Didn't you feel the attraction between us?"

Maren knew she had to think fast and take desperate steps. "Yes, but I thought we were first cousins. Why didn't you tell me sooner?"

"I was ashamed. I had to make certain you trusted me and loved me. Now it's too late. You're married to

Jared Morgan.''

Maren realized her life was in peril, as was Jared's. She quelled her nausea and went to Eric. "He forced me to marry him. He was going to jail me for the money you stole from him. He threatened to take Lady Luck and leave me without a home or money. He told me terrible things about you. I was scared and confused. Then all those accidents kept happening to me. I was helpless. What else could I do?''

Eric caught her face between his hands and stared into her misty eyes. "Do you love him, Maren?''

"Love a man who enslaved me? How could I? I've never slept with him, Eric. It's a marriage in name only. He entrapped me for some reason, but I don't know why. He said it was because I was Cameron's daughter and he wanted to protect me and help me, but I don't believe those were his motives. He took me to France so I wouldn't be in New Orleans when you arrived. He probably knew you would explain everything to me and we would get matters straightened out between us. I didn't give him the necklace, Eric; I didn't even know the truth about it. Peter Thomas revealed its significance to Jared, and he took it.''

As if Eric had heard little of what she had said, or as if his mind was only concerned with one matter, he inquired, "Would you leave him for me?''

Maren forced herself to smile and go into his arms. Glad he could not see her face, she lied, "Yes, I would. Oh, Eric, I always thought it was so wicked of me to have these feelings for one of my kin, but we aren't related. What are we going to do?"

As Eric's arms closed around her, he replied, "We'll figure something out, after the war. I'll send you to Jamaica so you can wait for me. Is that all right with you?"

When she made the mistake of looking up at him and nodding, his mouth covered hers and she was compelled to return his kiss. Afterward, his lips trailed over her face and he whispered huskily, "I love you, Maren. We'll be together soon."

Determined to carry off her desperate pretense, she cupped his face between her hands and looked into his smoldering eyes. "I love you, Eric, and I want to marry you. I'm so glad I can finally say that aloud. For years I've been tormented by my feelings for you. That's why I agreed to marry Daniel Redford, to put distance between us. I was so afraid someone would guess my secret and think me evil."

Believing another victory was within his grasp, Eric smiled. "I'll complete my mission as soon as possible and join you in Jamaica. We'll have your marriage to Jared Morgan dissolved; then we'll be married. I can't wait until we spend our first night together."

Maren hugged him and replied, "A dream come true, Eric."

"You'll have to sail at dawn. Can you be ready?"

"I'll be ready as soon as I'm packed. When can you join me?"

He cuffed her chin playfully. "Within a month, my eager vixen."

"What about Willa? Can you trust her?"

"The only two people I trust fully are you and Ben."

"How do you want me to behave when she returns, as your fiancée or as your captive? What do you want her to think and to tell Jared Morgan? If he finds us, there's no telling what he'll do to me for deserting him. Until I'm free of him, Eric, you must protect me and our secret." Maren really wanted to protect Jared from Eric, and from his evil cohorts, until she could escape this agonizing trap, but she was not sure which ruse would work best for her and Jared.

"You're right, Maren," Eric replied. "You are legally married to him, so he could give us trouble. And from what I hear, Morgan isn't one to challenge without the advantage. He would be angrier if he knows you've turned to me than he would if he thinks you were kidnapped by me. We'll let Willa believe I'm taking you to my home in Baltimore. Act as if I've ensnared you and you're frightened of me; that way, if Morgan catches up with you before I can handle him, he won't punish you for siding with me."

"We'll have to confront him eventually, but your suggestions sound wise. Is there anything between you and Willa that should concern me?" she asked, trying to appear jealous while masking a reaction to his mention of Baltimore. She knew what he had done to his brother there, and Jared would suspect that Willa was misleading him.

Eric chuckled. "Nothing, my naughty vixen. I love

only you. I once told you I was waiting for the perfect woman, but I was actually waiting until I could lay claim to her. You, Maren, are perfect for me.''

"Maybe we've known this all our lives, Eric. Maybe that's why we've always been so close. But will you change your name? What will people who know us think?" she asked, continuing her desperate deceit. Having recalled Murray's fate, she knew he was deadly.

"We'll have plenty of time to work out the details later. Right now, you must get packed. I'll take you aboard my ship after dark. Ben will go along to protect you.''

Maren concealed her shock and dismay by asking, "But who will protect you if Ben's with me? Jared will come after us the minute he learns about this. Since you're heading him toward Baltimore, you won't go near there, will you? Does Murray know about what you're doing?''

"Don't fret, little woman. Murray doesn't know anything. I'll go to New Orleans to settle our affairs there. Now, get packed so our new life can get underway.''

Maren smiled at him and turned to leave the room, but Eric gently caught her arm and pulled her into his embrace. As he kissed her hungrily, she suffered through tormenting moments, and she was relieved that he was in such a hurry because she would never allow him to make love to her. When he released her, she immediately left the room.

As Maren packed her trunks, she prayed that Jim

Lawton would return to save her. Then she prayed he would not arrive because she feared that Eric and Ben might slay the overseer. Horben Wolfe . . . she hated to leave with that intimidating man. Either Eric did not fully trust her or he actually wanted to protect her. She could not attempt to escape for doing so would expose her real feelings. She must wait until she had only one man to battle, and she hoped it wasn't going to be Horben Wolfe.

Maren wondered if any of the house servants could read. If so, she would leave Jared a note beneath the sheets so that a servant would find it while changing them. Since she had not been at Shady Rest long enough to know, she dared not take such a risk. She wondered where Willa had sent the household help and whether they would return in time to witness anything; she doubted it.

Just as she finished her task, Eric came to her room and told her all was set for her departure. "I'm ready," she declared, then smiled.

Eric and Ben loaded the carriage, and no servant was in sight. Maren was positive Willa had seen to it that they would not be observed. The servants were doubtlessly in their own cabins, dismissed for the night so this plot could be carried off without witnesses. Since it was dark and the cluster of neat cabins was a good distance from the big house, no one would be summoned to help her. If she ran off, she would only expose herself for she would be overtaken, and she did not want to endanger Jared's unarmed slaves.

Be patient and alert, Maren, she warned herself.

As Willa walked beside her to the carriage, she said, "I'm delighted Eric's taking you away, Maren; you wouldn't have liked it here. Jared would have tired of you and he would have returned to me. We share a very special bond. In fact, I only married his father to be near him. You could never satisfy him as I do."

Maren glanced at the arrogant blonde and smiled skeptically, but she thought it unwise to argue the woman's claim. Instead, she remarked sarcastically, "I'm sure you believe the same is true of Eric."

"Actually, Eric James is a better lover than Jared Morgan, but he isn't as rich and powerful."

"And, a woman like you goes after the best."

"Of course," Willa concurred after a throaty laugh.

"I suppose you'll also claim that Steven is Jared's son," Maren hinted.

A look of surprise crossed Willa's lovely face. "He told you?"

"No, I overheard you two on the porch and I figured it out."

"I wouldn't tell anyone if I were you. Jared doesn't want our son to be viewed as a bastard. Steven is to live and die as Benjamin's child."

"How considerate of you both," Maren replied.

When they reached the two men, Eric asked what they had been discussing. Willa did not reply, but Maren cleverly related their remarks. Although Willa glared at her, she smiled sweetly.

Thinking perhaps he could use this information

against Jared, Eric grinned. "Maybe that's good news. It could provide me with a nice little weapon."

"I thought so," Maren agreed, though she believed that Jeremy was Steven's father. She had recalled that Jeremy had been home the year before his death, but Jared had been out West for years. It was understandable to her that her husband loved the boy and wanted to protect him from scandal. And as the only son of Benjamin's deceased heir, Steven was entitled to a part of the Morgan inheritance. No wonder Jared despised this woman and wanted her out of their lives! Their lives . . . What would happen to them now?

Eric helped Maren into the carriage, and Ben drove it away. She looked around as they journeyed down the road, able to make out a few sights in the light of a three-quarter moon. "It is a beautiful place, isn't it?" she said genially to disarm the man.

Ben smiled and agreed. "I'm real glad you're siding with us, Maren. Eric isn't a man to cross, and you'll make him a good wife."

Maren thanked him and then pretended to settle down and enjoy the ride. She was not bound, but she realized Horben was very alert. She could see that from his tight grip on the reins, the way he sat, and his expression. She also knew he had placed a gun on the seat, on the side away from her.

Ben was tense and wary, but for reasons Maren did not know. While she had been packing, he had spoken with Eric, who planned to enjoy Willa for a few days before sailing for New Orleans. Eric had reiterated his promise to allow Ben to have Maren in Jamaica, once a week while she was under the influence of drugs he'd brought from the Orient, but Ben did not trust Maren. He intended to make certain she did not elude him. He had fantasized about his imminent nights with her, until his aching body had ordered him to halt that torment. He had to be careful how he treated her and looked at her or she might realize her plight. Once Eric had gotten to Jamaica, the fun would begin, and even if she continued her ruse, it would be enjoyable.

Maren was relieved that Ben allowed her to lock the cabin door, although she knew how easily it could be broken down if she refused to open it. She only dozed on that long night, fully clothed, and was very aware of the ship's movement as wind and tide carried her away from Savannah to a tropical island. How to escape? . . .

The early October days were still warm at sea, but the winds were brisker and the nights chillier. Naturally that would change as they sailed farther south. They had left port four days ago, on October first. Maren had remained in her cabin most of the time, and she had taken her meals only with Horben Wolfe. To pass the long hours and to ingratiate herself with her ghostly-eyed guard, she had asked him questions about himself, his family, and his travels with Eric; and Ben had cordially answered her, seemingly to enjoy himself.

When they played cards, she impressed Ben with her skills, and she often entertained him with tales of her early adventures with Eric. She even related her misfortunes in New Orleans and explained why she had doubted Eric for a time. But she wondered how long she could continue this difficult ruse, for she had noted Wolfe's desire and his distrust.

Late in the afternoon on October fourth, a ship pursued them, and Maren was thrilled. She did not care whether it was American or British. She just wanted to be taken off this vessel. But when a fierce conflict began, she doubted she would survive it.

The ship shuddered as its cannons roared and hits damaged her severely, and Maren pressed herself against the inner wall of her cabin, and clamped her hands over her ears. What if the ship was sunk? she wondered in mounting alarm.

When Ben rushed into the cabin and locked the door, Maren looked at him, her fear evident. "Who's attacking us?" she asked.

"Bloody pirates," he informed her angrily. "They won't give quarter and we can't flee them." He roughly drew her to him and declared, "But I'll be damned if they take you first."

He began to kiss her and fondle her. Maren struggled, but he forced her to the bed and flung her upon it.

"Eric will kill you for this, Ben!" she shrieked. Then her golden brown eyes filled with terror and disgust as Ben revealed Eric's promise to him.

"If I die today, I'll die as a happy and sated man," Ben said. Then he captured her hands, pinned them over her head, and straddled her.

But suddenly a gunshot rang out and Ben fell sideways off the bed. Maren immediately rose to battle her new attacker, but the man merely stared at her. She swallowed hard, her pulse raced, and she breathed rapidly. Her eyes were wide, and as he came forward, she tried to back away but the mussed covers inhibited her progress.

The pirate captain halted and studied her intently. "Come with me," he commanded, extending a hand to her.

Maren looked at his hand as if it were a death threat. "I'm Captain Hawk's wife," she declared nervously. "If you harm me, he'll kill you. These men kidnapped me, but Jared's searching for us."

"I'm sure he is," the man said with an amused grin. "Let's go, Hawk's mate; this ship is sinking."

Maren glanced at Ben's body and knew he was dead. Her gaze returned to the pirate's dark eyes. She had heard tales of what pirates did with female captives, and she feared she would have been safer with Horben!

Suddenly she noticed that Ben's gun had fallen onto the bed during her tussle with him. She lunged for it, but the man grabbed her and she struggled with him until he said, "There is no need for this, Maren Morgan. I am the Water Snake, a friend of your husband's."

Immediately she ceased thrashing. "René Blanc?"

"The same, my lovely bird. Come along. You're safe."

Maren had never fainted in her life, but she did so.

When Maren came around, she found herself in the highly decorated cabin of René. Her movements caught his attention and he rose from the table to approach her. He sat down beside her and smiled. "Feeling better?" he asked kindly. "Would some sherry put color back into your exquisite face?"

"Yes, thank you," she responded as she cleared her wits. "I don't know why I passed out like that. I've never done so before."

As he fetched the tawny liquid, he said, "Do not be embarrassed, Maren. It can be a natural reaction. What happened to you?"

Maren sketchily described her problems with Eric James and her abduction from Savannah. René nodded understandingly, then said, "I can't take you back to Savannah or to New Orleans; you would not be safe in either place. You must stay with me until we can locate your husband. We'll reach Grand Isle in a few days."

"But that's a pi—" Maren halted and flushed.

"Aye, a pirate haven, but you'll be under my protection as Captain Hawk was when he came there. Many of us have agreed to join him and the Americans. Hopefully, your government will keep its word."

"Jared says we need your help, and I'm sure it's true."

"He is a unique man, a superb seaman. He is also lucky."

Maren smiled at the compliment and thanked him for it. Her journey to Grand Isle had begun pleasantly.

During the passage she used René's bed while he slept in a hammock, and the days passed quickly and without danger. At Grand Isle she was taken ashore and transported in a boat to Barataria, where she was amazed by her surroundings. But her excitement rapidly vanished when she got a closer look at how the pirates lived.

Crude men eyed her intently, while lewd women pampered them, and stacks and stacks of stolen goods lay about. The weathered huts stood out darkly against the sandy background, as did the noisy taverns. Many of the pirates were drunk, and others were on their way to that sorry state. The women she saw were scantily attired, and they allowed any man to fondle them. Maren was embarrassed by such goings-on. Raucous singing and lively music, laughter, vulgar talk, and quarrels reached her alert ears. No wonder a man like René Blanc wanted to end his career in piracy.

She was guided to a large house which René said he owned. Two shapely Frenchwomen waited upon them there, serving them a delicious meal and preparing a refreshing bath for Maren. Then René told her to make herself at home and to remain inside the house while he went to visit his friends.

The Frenchwomen were not talkative, and they eyed Maren critically, though they had been told that she was a guest, Captain Hawk's woman. As Maren settled into her room after her bath, she wondered how long she would be compelled to remain at Barataria. If René was as powerful, feared, and respected as Jared had said, she should be safe, she thought.

In the tavern, the Water Snake passed the word that he had rescued Captain Hawk's woman, and he asked the other pirates to give that message to Hawk if they encountered him. René noticed the interest Maren had aroused, and knew he had to guard her closely.

He ordered one of his men to post a few guards around his home, and when he returned to it, he told the two serving women to be alert. He decided that the next day, as an additional precaution, he would give Maren a gun and make certain she knew how to use it. He then allowed the two women to undress him before he climbed ito bed between them.

When Maren heard telltale laughter coming from the room down the hall, she longed for Jared and prayed he would survive. She hoped he would not learn of her kidnapping before he discovered she was safe. She imagined how her husband would deal with

Eric. Then she curled up, closed her eyes, and let slumber overtake her.

By Wednesday René knew it was too hazardous to keep Maren with him. He had sent two of his men into New Orleans, and they had returned to report that Eric Jones was not there, Samuel Lewis was dead, and Dan Myers was controlling the gambling house. Based on that information, René asked Maren if she knew of a safe place where she could hide until Jared could be located.

Maren assumed that Eric would check Lady Luck and Payne's Point for her if he learned of the destruction of his ship and returned to New Orleans. But until he learned of his loss, he would not search for her. She thought about the preacher who had married her to Jared, but realizing that her presence might endanger that old couple, she decided to go to a hotel on the edge of town and hide out there. If she could, she would get a message to Mary and warn her about Dan Myers.

René gave her money for her expenses, and he escorted her to the hotel at dusk. After thanking him for his rescue and assistance, Maren roamed about her comfortable room and deliberated her problem. If anything happened to Jared, she was on her own, so she could not sit around and do nothing. She must find a way to deal with Eric and Dan.

By Friday, October the fourteenth, she had conceived no plan. But far away, the enemy force was leaving Washington. The British had failed to incite slave insurrections in and around the southern ports, but they had not been driven from Maine. Since the Indian uprisings had been halted or prevented, the British were now trying a new ploy; they were planting false stories in American papers in order to prey on fear and gullibility. Trouble abounded for America, but so did victories.

Captain Hawk and his men had succeeded in blowing up British ships which could not be taken, thereby destroying arms and supplies they could not appropriate for American use. Other British ships had been attacked and relieved of their cargoes, and many enemy cannons had been sent to the ocean floor. With each day, Captain Hawk's legend increased, and with each day he missed his wife more and more.

When René Blanc visited Maren on Saturday to make sure she was safe, she asked him to lure Dan Myers away from Lady Luck so she could sneak inside to visit Mary Malone. René argued with her, but he finally agreed to assist this daring and determined beauty who stirred his blood.

And so, wearing a heavy black veil to conceal her identity, Maren waited in a carriage while René enticed Dan to go examine a new shipment of fine wine and liquors. Maren knew she had little time to talk to Mary, and she was glad to see that the guards were not at Lady Luck that day. I have no further need for them, she angrily concluded.

When Mary answered the summons to the back door, she was astonished to see who was standing before her, for Maren lifted her veil. "I don't have much time," Maren said, "so we have to talk fast."

She immediately sat down at the table and revealed what she knew about their past troubles and those involved in them. Mary's shock over ~~her~~ revelations, of her torment. Maren knew the older woman believed her, and she also knew her revelations pained the housekeeper.

"I'm sorry to be the bearer of such terrible news, but I couldn't allow either of us to be used any longer. It's been awful, Mary, and I still don't know what to do. I have to stay in hiding because Eric's supposed to come here at any time. But I can't trust Dan, and I can't endanger any of my old friends. Just pretend nothing's wrong until Jared can help us."

"I won't have to, Miss Maren; Dan ended our . . . relationship when you left. He didn't need my help anymore. I'm sorry for giving you so much trouble and pain, but he fooled me."

"As he fooled me. It seems every man I know has been changed drastically by this war. I'll be at the hotel if you need me."

"Be careful, Miss Maren. And if there's trouble, you can trust Ned and Harry," she added.

"I'll try to keep everyone out of this. Unless I keep my presence a secret, Dan could hire new villains to harry me."

"He'll hear nothing from me, I swear."

"I know, Mary. Goodbye, and stay safe."

When Maren was entering her hotel room, she was halted by a familiar voice. She slowly turned around and looked at the man standing before her in the corridor. Then she almost fainted for the second time in her life.

"Daniel Redford, can it be you? They said you were dead."

Chapter Seventeen

Maren allowed her ex-fiancé to enter her room. "How did you get here, Daniel? You are in danger in this country."

"My life's been hell for over two years. After my ship was sunk, I was picked up by a pirate vessel and forced to work on it until I escaped. Since then, I've been hiding out around here until this infernal war ends and I can go back home. I've been keeping watch on the Lady Luck, hoping to contact you or Eric so I could get some help. I recognized you even in your widow's garb. What does it mean?" he asked, shaking her veil of midnight lace. "Why didn't you wait for me?"

Maren looked over this man with sapphire blue eyes and chestnut hair. Despite his misfortunes, he was still handsome and virile, but she realized there was much he didn't know. "Sit down, Daniel. We have a lot to discuss."

He took a seat near her and waited impatiently, but Maren wasn't sure where to begin. "Just listen to me first, and then you can talk," she said. She then told him of her trip to London, his reported death, Eric's voyage to get her, and her present plight. She ended by revealing her marriage to Jared Morgan and Eric's treachery.

Daniel overlooked everything to ask, "Isn't Jared Morgan Captain Hawk?" His blue eyes had darkened and his jaw had become taut.

"Yes, he is. I'm sorry if you're hurt and upset, but you were supposed to be dead."

"I would be if your Captain Hawk had seen me floating away from my ship before he blasted it to splinters. He's a murderer, Maren. He sank the *Merry Maiden* and countless other ships. He never gave us a chance, never even asked for surrender. We ceased fire and struck our flag, but he wasn't satisfied with defeating us."

Maren was stunned. "That doesn't sound like Jared," she protested.

"That was two years ago. Maybe he's been ordered to cease his slaughter. I know what I saw, Maren; and I have scars that prove my story. I'm lucky to be alive. Get clear of him or you'll be sorry one day."

"Maybe you've changed too, Daniel," she remarked defensively; then she disclosed what she had learned about her ex-fiancé.

Daniel lowered his head in guilt. "It's all true. I turned into a real bastard after I last saw you. I fell madly in love with the most beautiful woman alive, but my brother stole her from me and married her. I suppose a woman who can be swayed by wealth and status isn't worth having, but I wanted to show him by marrying a woman just as beautiful, one with more wealth and position and power. I know it was a rotten thing to do to you, but I was hurting too badly to care. But I've changed, Maren. I'm my old self now. If you'll call off this sham marriage, we can still be wed."

"No, Daniel, I love Jared." Since he had been honest with her about the reason for their betrothal, she told him the truth. "If we had married, it wouldn't have worked out. We were marrying for the wrong reasons. But we can still be friends, and I can help you be safe until the war ends."

"I hate to think of what the Americans would do to me if I were captured, but how can you help me, Maren? You're in trouble too."

"We'll figure something out," she promised. "I'll get you a room here and give you money for food and clothing. And I'll help you work on dropping that English accent. When Jared gets here, he'll—"

"He'll have me arrested and jailed—or hung," Daniel declared heatedly.

"He won't. He'll listen to me and he'll help you go home."

"Still the naïve innocent, Maren," he chided softly. "This is war and he's my enemy. Hear me well; he will not listen, nor will he help."

Maren could not accept his appraisal of her husband, but an idea came to her mind. She doubted

465

that Marc knew the things Eric had told her. If she revealed them to him, perhaps Marc would side with her. Since two weeks had passed and Eric had not arrived, obviously he had changed his destination or he had been killed. With Marc's help, she and Daniel could have a safe place to live—the townhouse. She would find a way to get Dan Myers out of Lady Luck and then she would take advantage of Ned Jones's and Harry Peck's loyalty.

She explained her idea to Daniel, who was wary but receptive. "If you stay out of sight most of the time, we'll be safe," she added. "I'll even hire more guards to keep Dan Myers under control. Once he sees I'm in power and on to him, he'll probably leave town. And if Eric does show up, we'll capture him. The element of surprise will be on our side."

"It's dangerous, Maren, but exciting. I'm already feeling like a new man. When do we start?" Daniel asked eagerly.

"What about Monday?" she replied, and they laughed.

On Monday night, Maren and Daniel sneaked to the townhouse. Marc was astonished to see her and surprised to meet Daniel Redford, and Maren soon sat him down and revealed Eric's treachery, including the probability that he had murdered Murray. When she told Marc that Horben Wolfe was dead, the young man almost cried with joy!

"Eric has broken many laws, Marc, and he'll be

punished. He can no longer harm you, so please help us," Maren implored.

"I'll help you," Marc replied. "I don't like Eric anymore, and I ain't gonna be scared of him. He's bad."

"We'll move in here tomorrow; then we'll all go to work together."

"Am I smart enough to help you?" Marc asked childishly.

"More than smart enough, Marc. You'll see." Maren smiled.

By nightfall on Tuesday, Maren and Daniel Redford were settling into the James townhouse. Marc was very excited about being included in her plan and he doted on Maren. When Maren finally climbed into her old bed, unbeknownst to her, Jared's ship was anchoring near Grand Isle. . . .

On Wednesday Maren and Daniel made and discarded plans while Marc observed, wide-eyed. Finally they decided to simply walk into Lady Luck and take it over on Friday morning.

On the following afternoon, someone knocked loudly and persistently at the front door. When Maren peeked out the front window near the stoop, her eyes enlarged and joy surged through her—it was Jared. But suddenly she feared for Daniel. Before answering the door, she told Marc and Daniel to hide in the carriage house until she spoke with her husband and assessed his feelings on certain matters.

When both men were gone, Maren opened the door and flung herself into Jared's arms. He eased her inside and closed the door behind them; then he kissed her.

"I just came from Barataria, and René. Did those bastards harm you?" he asked. Maren knew he was referring to Eric and Horben, and she told him everything that had happened after he'd left Savannah. When he asked why she was here, she sighed heavily and told him of her plan, excluding Daniel.

"Dang you, woman! This is too dangerous. Eric is still loose."

"I've seen Daniel," Maren disclosed softly. "He isn't dead."

Jared's expression altered. As his gaze locked with hers, he asked, "Where is the Brit? I'll take care of him."

"No, Jared, you won't. He's suffered enough. Let him be."

Jared stared at her oddly. "You're protecting one of our enemies? You could be jailed too, Maren. I forbid it. Where is he?"

"He's no longer a threat to America, or to you, Jared Morgan. You nearly killed him once. I can't allow you a second chance. He'll remain hidden until the war ends; then I'll get him home. He won't cause any trouble; I swear it. He's been my friend for years."

"Eric was your friend for years too, but look at him. No, Maren."

"You're being stubborn and mean, Jared Morgan. For just a moment forget you're Captain Hawk; be my understanding and generous husband. If you turn Daniel in, he'll be imprisoned or hanged, yet what harm can he do? He's only a man who's been through hell."

Jared scowled. "Have you forgotten what you learned about him?"

"He explained everything," Maren said rapidly. Then she told Jared what Daniel had revealed to her.

"And you believed his lies?"

"They're not lies! I know him, Jared."

"Like you knew Eric?" Jared was angry with her.

"That isn't fair. I'm not the only person Eric fooled."

"You've a blind spot, Maren. Don't be taken in again."

"Like your father was taken in by Willa Barns?" she snapped. She related what she had learned about Steven. "He is Jeremy's, isn't he?"

"For damned sure he isn't mine! I've never put a hand on that bitch."

"I know you haven't. You see, I'm not always wrong about people. Daniel did terrible things, yes, but he's paid for them. Give him a chance, Jared," she urged softly.

"Why didn't you stay put at the hotel? It's dangerous for you here."

Maren told him about Samuel Lewis's death, and she added, "I couldn't wait around for months doing nothing. I knew I would be safe if I hired plenty of guards and got rid of Dan Myers."

"I'm going to see Dan right now. By the time I return, Redford had best be gone, but we'll move into Lady Luck and carry out your plan."

"You're serious?" she asked.

"What I don't do for you, woman! You have my word."

After Jared left, she summoned Marc and Daniel and informed them of this new development. Then she gave Daniel some money and told him to try to find a safe place. "Jared says the war can't last much longer. Peace negotiations are underway. Just stay out of sight, Daniel."

Daniel hugged her and thanked her, but he was already making plans of his own as Marc took him to the warehouse, where he bedded down for the night.

Jared returned in less than an hour with stunning news: Dan Myers was badly wounded and might die. "He tried to kill himself last night. Guilt or fear of discovery, no doubt. There's no reason we can't move into Lady Luck immediately. I plan to remain here for a few days, just in case Eric shows up."

"What about the law, Jared? Can't we expose him and have the sheriff on the lookout for him?"

"I've already done that, but he could sneak past him. We're taking no more chances, Maren Morgan. Understand?"

Maren smiled and melted into his arms. As he held her tightly, she said, "I've been so worried about you, Jared."

He told her that he had been ordered to speak with the pirates again, for they had not yet accepted the government's terms and the British were going to attack New Orleans. He added, "We can certainly use their help, so I hope I'm convincing. I wish I could take you somewhere safe, but I doubt any place is safe right now. We'll make sure the Brits don't get in here."

Within the next hour, Maren and Jared entered her suite at Lady Luck. They sat down and went over everything once more; then Jared went downstairs and saw to that night's business. It was late when he returned, exhausted.

Maren was in bed, naked beneath the sheet. She smiled at her husband as he entered the room. "I thought you weren't coming back," she teased.

Jared glanced at her bare shoulders, which were revealed, and he grinned. After stripping, he joined her and they embraced and caressed each other. The desire to make love having seized them, both were highly aroused and eager to fuse their bodies.

But Jared knew the past weeks without Maren had him on a sexual precipice and he had to move cautiously. He tantalized her until she was writhing with need; then he joined their bodies and they moved rhythmically until rapture claimed them.

Later, in the golden afterglow of lovemaking, they

471

caressed each other gently and kissed tenderly. "I love you, Maren. Thank God you're safe," he said.

She shifted her head and looked into his eyes, so tender in the candlelight. "I love you, Jared Morgan, and I'm so glad you're here."

When Eric's ship had been steadily driven southward because of the blockade, he had finally decided to postpone his business in New Orleans and sail onward to Jamaica. After enjoying a brief time there with Maren and Ben, he would once more try to make it to New Orleans. . . .

On Sunday, Daniel Redford sneaked into Lady Luck and tried to kill Jared Morgan. The two men fought and quarreled for an hour, breaking some of the furniture downstairs. For his wife's benefit, Jared tried everything in every way he could to break off the conflict with Daniel. He tried reasoning, brute strength, explanations, threats, an apology, and bargaining. But Daniel was determined to slay the man who had nearly killed him and who had made his life hellish for two years. After Daniel was finally subdued, Maren realized that Jared had no choice but to turn him over to the authorities. She apologized to Jared for her mistake.

"Don't worry about it, love. I knew he would try to kill me. His pride demanded it. I would have done the same.''

That afternoon, Maren and Jared visited Dan, who, though very weak, was recovering slowly. Dan made a full confession and begged for their forgiveness. Mary Malone was with him, and he spoke of his real love for her and of his remorse over fooling her. He promised he would never come near any of them again. He explained that he had killed Evelyn Sims and Howard Heath and Samuel Lewis because they had planned to harm Maren, and he wouldn't allow that, and he swore to slay Eric if he ever saw him again. Then, suddenly realizing he would be imprisoned for his crimes, he pleaded with Jared to protect Cameron's daughter and to slay their mutual foe.

"Don't worry, Dan, I'll handle Eric, sooner or later.''

Dan wept pitifully as he murmured, "The Devil got into me and filled my head with evil desires. What I did was wrong, and I couldn't live with my guilt any longer. I tried to stop them, but it was too late. Maren wasn't supposed to be injured. It sounded so simple when Eric approached me and tempted me. I honestly thought Maren would give up without a fight, and I never imagined you were her partner. When I realized how wicked Eric was and knew he would keep coming after Maren and Lady Luck, I had to end this treachery before I was unmasked. But I couldn't find a way to defeat him. I know you two must hate me for what I've done. I'm sorry, Maren, Jared.''

"We know, Dan. Sometimes people just get caught up in their rash dreams and make mistakes," Jared replied, and Maren's heart warmed.

Using his remaining strength, Dan then revealed all he knew about Eric's treachery.

Later, at Lady Luck, Maren lay in Jared's arms. "It's nearly over," she murmured. "Only Eric is left."

"Lordy, I wish I knew where he was and what he's up to."

"Forget about him for now. Just think about us."

Jared's lips and hands worked wonders on her body, and hers did the same on his. They made love slowly and titillatingly, and when that delightful crisis seized them, they rode toward a mutual victory.

Then, as they lay in each other's arms, they talked. Jared promised to deal with Eric and Willa when time permitted and to settle their business affairs. When he told Maren that he had to leave on Wednesday morning, he added that more guards had been hired to protect her.

"I think Eric must have sailed for Jamaica. I'm going after him and the gold he took there. Maybe it will be enough to allow us to win the war."

"Don't go after him, Jared," she pleaded.

"I'll be careful, love, but this has to be done or you'll never be safe."

On Wednesday, Jared left and Maren cried. She

could not bear the thought of anything happening to him, and she knew Eric was insane, irreparably evil.

After her love's departure, Maren threw herself into the running of Lady Luck to distract herself. Business flourished, and days swept by.

Three and a half weeks passed without trouble; then one day Jared was standing at the door. The Royal Navy had many ships in the routes to Jamaica—between Florida and Cuba, and between Cuba and Central America—so he had been fighting these ships rather than sailing on to seek out Eric and the British gold. He surmised that the heavy enemy concentration on those routes would prevent Eric from getting to New Orleans, and assuming Maren was safe there, he stayed for three days, then left.

The following Sunday, November twenty-seventh, the United States soundly licked the British at Mobile Bay. Unbeknownst to Maren, Jared had been trapped in the Gulf and was fighting in that battle along with Andrew Jackson and others.

As December overtook them, though the temperature remained above fifty degrees on many days, Jared arrived by sea and Andrew Jackson by land. But due to the crucial stage of the war, Jared and Maren had little time for a proper reunion. They spent one night making love and then Jared returned to duty.

He met with Andrew Jackson and revealed what he had worked out with the pirates at Barataria and

Grand Isle. Jackson was most agreeable to pardoning those men and accepting their aid, and he met with their infamous leader, Jean Lafitte. Lafitte was very helpful in planning the defense of New Orleans and the blockage of the Mississippi River to the British, so Jackson was grateful to Jared for arranging an alliance with the pirate captain.

With Jared Morgan's assistance, Jackson set about recruiting anyone who wanted to do battle with the British: blacks, Creoles, plantation owners, freed slaves, friendly Indians, and businessmen. All went to work side by side with the soldiers, digging ramparts and building barricades. As the people of New Orleans supplied food and clothing, under the watchful eyes of Maren who was the collector and distributor, a line was formed across the Chalmette between the Mississippi and the swamp. Rotting cotton bales taken from the wharfs and plantations were used as buttresses. Jackson praised the joint efforts being made for the defense of New Orleans.

And that December saw the failure of the convention at Hartford. New England did not secede, Stuart ran the blockade with the *Constitution*, the two sides fought many minor skirmishes, and unbeknownst to their participants a peace treaty was signed in Belgium on Christmas Eve.

Jared and Maren had both been very busy, running Lady Luck and aiding in the preparations for the defense of New Orleans, but the lovers had finally planned to steal a few hours for themselves. And when Lady Luck closed on Saturday night, Maren and Jared sealed out the world beyond their door.

They spent Christmas Eve and Christmas Day together, talking, laughing, feasting, making plans, and making love. Maren gave her husband an exquisitely carved pocket watch so he would know when to quit work and hurry into her waiting arms, and Jared gave his wife a beautiful shawl which he had purchased from René Blanc.

Since Mary Malone spent the time with Dan Myers, the couple could enjoy just being together, and since their marriage was no longer a secret, they could be quite open about it.

That afternoon, Maren and Jared heated water and filled the tub in her bath closet. Then they played sensuously there, soaping and caressing each other from head to foot, until the water was chilled and passions were kindled. They laughed as they dried off each other and snuggled under the bedcovers to get warm. The house was quiet and the fire in the hearth crackled serenely.

Jared's hands and lips roamed Maren's flesh, which smelled delightful for they had bathed with the French soap Antoine Gallier had given to her. "You smell good enough to devour, my love," he murmured.

"When you return to the men and they get a whiff of you, Mr. Morgan, you'll no doubt drive them wild with lust. Make sure they don't ravish you," Maren teased.

Jared chuckled as he stroked her silky flesh. "I had forgotten about that disadvantage when I joined my wife for a bath. I'll be certain to dash a very masculine cologne all over me before I leave."

"And let the British detect your odor from miles away and be lured to your hiding place? Very careless, my love," she jested.

"I'll take my chances, woman, because that adventure was worth any risk. It isn't often a man can get clean and be inflamed at the same time. Yes, ma'am, that combination is most appealing."

Even as Jared and Maren were enjoying their tranquil Christmas at Lady Luck and making passionate love, the British struck. They sank many American gunboats and drove to within seven miles of New Orleans. Due to their proximity the city was placed under martial law and Jackson was put in full command. Stealthily and skillfully, the British had entered the area via Lake Borgne and Bayou Bienvenue—fortunately Jared's ship was elsewhere—and by Christmas Eve they had sneaked past Jackson's flank and taken control of the Villère Plantation. But luck had been with the Americans, for Major Gabriel Villère had escaped and had warned Jackson. Old Hickory had been furious, and had reacted promptly and boldly. He had attacked during the night and set up a new battle line. But the British had been given time to prepare for this new challenge.

When the alarm was sounded after dusk, Jared looked over at his sleeping wife. Hating to disturb her with such news, he gently nudged her awake. "I have to go, love," he said. "The British are attacking nearby, or they've broken through our defense line. Be alert, Maren. If you sense danger, flee inland to Payne's Point. I'll come for you when it's safe again."

Maren knew he had to leave; it hurt her to let him go. The day of reckoning was near, and she prayed the British lost the war. "I love you, Jared. Please be careful."

Maren walked him to the door and then watched him until he vanished into the chilly darkness. Tears welled in her eyes and sadness filled her. She wanted this war to be over so they could live a normal life, a safe one. Quickly, she went upstairs, dressed, and packed a small bag. She remained alert.

The Americans fought bravely and steadily, for they were determined to push the British back into the Gulf. On the twenty-eighth, Parkenham attacked. After he was repulsed, General Andrew Jackson called upon the pirates, and with their help the Americans gradually pushed back the British line.

But the battle raged on until January eighth, and Maren had not seen her husband since December twenty-fifth. She received reports from the daring

479

men who delivered medical supplies, food, and arms to the battle line, so she knew Jared was safe and well. Still, she worried about him. Due to the situation, Lady Luck's business was slack, so she had little to occupy her mind and hands. She was often tempted to go cook for the soldiers or to bandage the wounded, or even to fight. But she had promised to remain where she was.

When the major battle ended, the British had lost over two thousand men, while the Americans counted only seven dead! Due to Major Villère's warning, the defeat was decisive, and Jackson presented that brave man with Parkenham's arms.

But all did not go in Jackson's favor. A local paper, *La Courrière de La Louisane* had printed an article entreating the people not to obey Jackson, and the author, Louis Louaillier, had been arrested at Jackson's order. Judge Dominic Hall, born in England, had protested, and Jackson had then ordered that he be arrested.

On January twentieth the British admitted defeat and left New Orleans, and three days of rejoicing followed. But Maren did not join in. Jared and the other sea captains had been ordered to pursue the British ships to make certain they kept sailing homeward, and he had obeyed Jackson's request after allowing himself a brief visit with his wife, who was opposed to his facing this added peril. Despite her position, Maren knew Jared would obey Jackson, so she sent him off with a strained smile. Then she went to the wharf every day to look for his return. But as days passed, though business was better than ever at Lady Luck, Maren was lonely and worried.

Barton Hughes had been discharged, and had married Lilibeth Payne. Maren had stood beside her friend on that joyous and long-awaited occasion, and now the happy pair were living on Dart's plantation.

But Marc James had lost his courage. Unable to stand up to his brother, he had fled into the wilderness. Maren feared for his life, and she doubted that she would ever see her pitiful cousin again.

During this time Dan Myers's wound had healed and he returned to work at Lady Luck. He was romancing Mary Malone again, and things seemed to be right between them now. Maren had forgiven the man, but she hoped he would remain loyal this time.

In Savannah, Jared Morgan had received distressing news. Willa had been slain by a strapping male slave she had been savagely beating. The black had escaped, and Jared had decided not to send the law after him. He did bring Cathy and Steven home from town, however, and Bessie was placed in charge of them. After he made certain the children would be all right, Jared sailed for New Orleans to retrieve his wife.

He had been away from Maren for a long time and he did not doubt that she was becoming frantic. But the retreating British ships had sailed toward Nassau, and when he was just about to stop tailing them and return to New Orleans, several had turned northward to attack the eastern coastline or to attempt to join up with the British fleet. Jared and the other captains had been compelled to pursue these ships and to defeat them. That done, Jared had realized he was near Savannah, so he had decided to make a brief stop there to deal with Willa before fetching Maren home.

On February thirteenth news of the peace treaty reached New Orleans, and on the sixteenth, Congress ratified it and the War of 1812 was officially ended. All British prisoners were pardoned and released; they were placed aboard a Spanish merchant ship to work their way home, Daniel Redford among them. Still Jared did not return, and Maren did not know what to think. She had last seen him on January nineteenth of 1815; it was now February eighteenth.

As she turned to leave the wharf, for it was growing late, her heart was heavy. She felt that something terrible had happened because Jared would not willingly stay away now that peace was assured. She wondered if he was searching for her cousin, if her cousin had found him, had harmed him. Her spirits lagged as she returned to Lady Luck.

It was a busy night and a noisy one. People were

celebrating America's victory and the end of the war. Maren tried to join in the fun, but she could not. Finally she went upstairs and lay across her bed.

Around two in the morning, a hand was clamped over her mouth and she was shaken into full consciousness. The night candle revealed the rage-twisted face of her assailant: Eric James.

He glared at Maren and whispered, "It's your day of reckoning, you traitorous bitch."

Chapter Eighteen

Eric bound and gagged Maren, threatening her as he did so. She tried to resist him, failed; and panic surged through her as she was rendered helpless. She had to keep a clear head to foil such a hostile foe, but Eric had given her no chance to dupe him.

"After all I told you and how I trusted you, I come here to find you living with that bastard again," he muttered as he worked. "I'll find out later how you got away from Ben. No doubt he's dead, damn you. Lewis is gone, Marc's vanished, and Dan's turned against me. But I'll kill you all," he ranted.

"Did you think Sam and Dan were my only loyal men? Fool," he berated her. "Did you forget about Andrews? Of course you did. And I sprung Daniel, so he's on my side now. Don't expect him to help you."

Maren knew Daniel Redford had been pardoned Wednesday and placed on a Spanish ship. She had watched her ex-fiancé sail, so she did not know why

Eric had mentioned him.

"All because of that damned Captain Hawk and Lady Luck! You could have had the world with me, Maren. But you betrayed me, so you'll have to pay. Morgan is dead and this place will be burned to the ground before we sail. When I finish with you, you'll be as good as dead. But not by my hand," he said, and laughed wildly.

"My little false cousin, I'm selling you into slavery. You'll be an asset to some foreign brothel. Every time you're pierced, you'll curse the day you betrayed the only man who truly loved you. You'll know endless days and nights of torment, and you'll reflect on your wickedness."

As Eric carried her downstairs wrapped securely in the quilt from her bed, Maren noticed Dan Myers's battered body near the front door. It was obvious that the manager had put up a terrible struggle. Maren reflected on the ironic reality that he was now fully vindicated, but she could not tell whether Dan was alive or dead. Mary was nowhere in sight, and Maren wondered frantically whether she was alive.

Eric halted long enough for her to watch his men toss whale oil here and there. Then he ordered, "Give me ten minutes head start; then set the place ablaze. Be aboard on time or we'll sail without you."

Maren was carried to Eric's ship and taken to his cabin. He then forced her to stand at the porthole and watch smoke roll heavenward as flames brightened the dark sky. Tears gathered in Maren's eyes, but she contained them. Everything that had belonged to her parents was at Lady Luck. A sentimental and a monetary fortune was going up in vengeful flames, and two of her friends were probably dead. Maren gazed sadly at the blaze illuminating the night.

When a knock told him they were ready to sail, Eric pulled her over to the bed, and laughing devilishly, he declared, "I'll return later, my false little cousin." He then left quickly and bolted the door from the outside.

Maren lay on her side, trying to think. Since Eric had installed a bolt on the outside of the door, she could not sneak topside and jump overboard. Her world was coming apart, and it seemed there was nothing she could do to prevent catastrophe, at least not yet. She did not believe Jared was dead, but she could not imagine where he was. No doubt, Eric had discovered how long Jared had been gone, so he had lied about him as he had lied about Daniel Redford. She did fear she had seen her love for the last time, however, for locating her might not be possible if Eric carried out his horrible threat.

Maren warned herself that she mustn't lose hope, mustn't surrender to terror. Until she was dead, she was not defeated. She closed her eyes tightly as she felt the ship move. God, help me, she prayed.

Then she wriggled and squirmed until she forced her bound hands past her buttocks, beneath her legs, and over her secured feet. Removing her gag, she worked at the knotted ropes until her teeth and gums were sore. At last she freed her wrists. She then untied her ankles. But the door was locked. She considered using a chair to break out the large porthole, intending to jump overboard and swim ashore, but when she looked out, she realized they had sailed too far for her to attempt such a feat. She decided she had no choice but to endure this torment until she had a better chance to escape.

Barefoot and clad only in a flannel nightgown, she cuddled into the heavy quilt in which Eric had brought her to his ship. The February night was cold, and the coals on the sturdy brazier had gone out. She did not see more wood, so she endured the ever-increasing chill, thinking it one of Eric's torments.

For some inexplicable reason, he did not return to his quarters that night. Having had plenty of time to poke about the cabin, Maren knew she was not aboard the *Martha J*. How, she wondered, could Jared pursue an unknown ship? And if there had been no witnesses to Eric's evil deeds, what were the chances that her husband would realize what had happened? Did she even want her love to come after her? she asked herself. Jared would be reluctant to attack this ship and endanger her, and so he might endanger his life, his crew, and his ship by trying to rescue her. She would rather confront Eric's treachery than be responsible for the destruction of the man she loved. She tossed and plotted, and

occasionally dozed, until morning was well underway, as was the ship on which she was held captive.

A few hours later, she heard the bolt being released.
A cautious man slid a wooden tray into the room
and quickly bolted the door again. Maren gazed at
the unappetizing meal and then rolled onto her side
and snuggled into the warm confines of the bedcovers. She wondered when Eric would appear and
what he would do.

At midafternoon, the animal-like feeding procedure was repeated. Once more she refused to eat the
unappealing fare. Instead, she boldly searched Eric's
closet for his smallest shirt and trousers and donned
them, along with two pairs of fuzzy socks. It was not
unbearably cold during the day, but she knew the
temperature would drop swiftly at night. She paced
the cabin in an attempt to keep her wits sharp and her
muscles warm and agile, so she might seize an
opportunity to escape. However, she did not intend
to be reckless. She knew she would be permitted only
one chance. After her attempt failed, Eric would
make certain no more were presented, and he would
be extremely hostile.

At dusk, the second tray was recovered, but a new
one was not left. After that, Maren was brought
neither food or water, nor any fuel for the brazier. She
longed to bathe, but her water supply was miniscule
and she feared an intrusion. She used Eric's brush on
her hair to relax herself a little. Then she wrapped
herself in the covers and reclined on the bed. The

later it got, the cooler it got. It seemed she was being ignored, and Maren could not figure out Eric's intent.

He came to visit Maren the next morning, and he grinned wickedly when he saw that she had managed to free herself and had found something to wear. He had assumed her intelligence and her courage would not fail her. "Hungry and cold, my fetching bitch?" he inquired hatefully.

Having plotted her strategy during his absence, Maren glared at him and then turned away. "Don't even speak to me, you hateful traitor!" she said haughtily, though she was waiting for her torment to begin.

Eric James rushed to her and yanked her around so she faced him. Then he slapped her, and she struggled with him. Freeing herself from his grip, Maren backed away and cursed him, "You vile bastard, you're lower than I imagined! You'll pay for this and your many crimes."

"How so, bitch? Your husband is dead. I caught up with him in Savannah and had my men slit his throat. You're a widow, Maren, and you deserve to be after your final betrayal."

"My betrayal?" she scoffed. "Eric James, you—"

"What happened to Ben?" he asked, his green eyes cold.

Furious, Maren shouted, "Peter Thomas said you

490

killed Murray just to get his inheritance. You were only duping me until you could kill me and take mine too, weren't you? And to think I actually believed your pretty words! How dare you tell that beast Horben Wolfe he could have me once a week, even after we were wed! He told me all about your filthy little scheme when he tried to rape me on the way to Jamaica! That's when he was shot by that pirate, while he was tearing my clothes off! But what do you care? You were behind it all."

"What the hell are you talking about?" Eric demanded angrily.

Having decided how to handle this man, she revealed how the *Martha J* had been attacked by pirates and she had been taken to Barataria. She described in detail the destruction of his ship and the killing of Horben Wolfe, elaborating on what the man had disclosed while trying to ravish her. She told Eric her pirate captor had been the raider who had supplied Lady Luck with wine and liquor, so he had rescued her and had freed her for a price. She mentioned that, after she'd returned to New Orleans, Daniel Redford had contacted her and had offered to help her retake the gambling house from Dan Myers. But she said that Jared Morgan had arrived before they could act. He had arrested Daniel and had forced her to move into Lady Luck with him. Then she had remained at home while Captain Hawk had gone off to battle. He had not returned. Maren claimed she had been unable to do anything except obey Jared in

491

order to avoid exposure and punishment.

She scolded Eric harshly. "You have no right or reason to mistreat me, Eric James! What was I supposed to do, tell Morgan the truth? When we talked in Savannah, you told me to pretend I was your captive if I was caught escaping Morgan! You said to act as if I were terrified of you so he wouldn't harm me for taking off with you. I did what you suggested, but look where it's gotten me! Damn you, Eric!"

"Who killed Samuel Lewis and shot Dan Myers?" he questioned.

"I don't know about Mr. Lewis; that happened before I reached New Orleans. As for Dan, he tried to kill himself, probably because of guilt. He told Jared in front of me that you paid him to harass me."

"What was Dan doing at Lady Luck? Surely Morgan was on to him."

"He told us everything he knew, Eric, and asked for our forgiveness. Jared believed him and put him back to work when he was well. Damn it, I don't know who or what to believe anymore. You and Morgan both give me different stories! Dan said you never wanted me harmed, just frightened out of Lady Luck. Is that true?" she queried, guilefully softening her gaze and tone.

"I told you, my fiery vixen, that you were going to get everything back by marrying me. Now everything is spoiled."

"And you blame me?" she asked in a dejected voice.

492

"If you had trusted me and been loyal, things would be fine."

"If you had truly loved me and trusted me, I wouldn't have intruded, wouldn't have doubted you. But what was I supposed to think and to feel when people were terrorizing me? Your people, Eric James!"

"I told you I didn't give those orders! But that doesn't matter now. It's too late to change my plans. I've been exposed and lots of people will be after me. After I take care of you, I'll have to disappear."

"You hate me that much?" she asked, staring sadly at him.

"You must be punished."

"For your crimes and failures? That isn't fair, Eric."

"Life hasn't been fair to me either." He sneered.

"But I'm not the one to blame! I'm caught in the middle of a private war between you and Morgan. Why hurt me?"

"If you think I'll let Morgan have—" He halted and glared at her.

"You said he was dead," she reminded him, unwisely.

"He will be if he comes after us. I'll blast him out of the water. I swear he'll never see you again, Mrs. Morgan. And if he settles down somewhere and drops his guard, I'll track him and slay him."

"Let it go, Eric, or you'll be killed. Find a safe place and begin a new life, with or without me," she urged,

493

wanting to protect her love.

"What do you care if I'm killed!" he stormed.

"We were so close for years, Eric, and I loved you. Stop this madness before it's too late."

"I told you, bitch; it is too late—for all of us."

Before Maren could argue further, Eric left the cabin and locked it.

Two long and agonizing days passed without another visit from Eric. Food and water were placed inside the door twice a day, and now Maren consumed them to keep up her strength. They had sailed farther south, and the weather had warmed. She knew, even if she could get the door open, she would not jump overboard in the middle of the ocean. So she waited tensely, and she prayed constantly.

At dawn on February twenty-fourth, Maren heard shouts and boots scraping the deck. She hurried to the porthole, gazed out and saw a ship on the horizon. Her heart pounded wildly, for its sails were the color of the sky and its hull was painted to match the sea. Eric entered the cabin, laughing wickedly. Maren frantically eyed him as he casually stripped to the skin before her and changed into clean clothes. As he brushed his freshly clipped hair, she could see that he had shaved recently. His curious behavior intrigued and dismayed her.

He glanced at her and said, "You might want to witness this battle, Maren. Your husband's ship is gaining on us, and I'm going to kill him today."

"Jared . . ." she murmured fearfully. She knew it was futile to beg or bargain for her love's life.

"I thought so," Eric concluded aloud. "But what a superb little liar you are. I'll let you watch me send him below before you meet your own fate."

Maren watched from the large porthole as the *Sea Mist* closed the distance between the two ships, then slowed its pace and rode the waves just out of cannon range. The two vessels continued their crafty cat-and-mouse game for over an hour, and Maren feared her heart would explode from tension before the first shot was fired. She could not guess either man's strategy, so she kept her eyes on the ship trailing them.

Eric's vessel abruptly slowed and made a half-turn, placing her broadside to Jared's stern, and suddenly it shuddered as several cannons were fired simultaneously at Jared's ship. Maren screamed, and panic flooded her. She was relieved to see that her husband's vessel was not hit; nonetheless she was breathing so rapidly that she became dizzy. She felt hot, then cold, then hot again. Moisture glistened on her face and dampened her flesh. Her entire body was trembling.

Eric's ship blasted away again, and made a hit on Jared's vessel at railing level on the port side. Maren gripped the porthole frame so tightly that her knuckles blanched. Then, nothing happened for a while.

Jared's ship had ceased its forward progress and its

sails were now lowered, as were those on Eric's vessel. Yet, Jared did not fire, no doubt because his wife was aboard and could be injured. Knowing he was at a grave disadvantage, Maren was alarmed, and she prayed he would abandon the attack and sail away.

As the opposing ships waited each other out, the sun grew hotter. Maren was not served any food or water, and no one came to check on her. But finally Eric's vessel began to move once more, and so did Jared's.

Not much later, Eric came to Maren's cabin. "He must want you badly, and alive," he teased. "Let's see how badly. We'll sail down his throat. Come with me. I want to make certain you're in full view."

Maren fought him wildly, not wanting to aid him in his attack on her beloved, but Eric called two of his men and had them bind her snugly. They hauled her topside and secured her hands to the rail on the starboard side.

Eric then commanded his steersman to turn the ship and head for the *Sea Mist* so that the starboard side faced her, and he ordered the cannons to be loaded with shot. "When we're in range, fire at my signal, not before!" he shouted.

Maren heard grumblings to her right and left, for Eric's crew dreaded to challenge Captain Hawk. She noted that the closer they got to Jared's ship, the greater was their apprehension. She shouted, "If you obey Eric James, Captain Hawk will sink you! My husband will kill me before allowing Eric to keep me! Throw me overboard and get out of here!''

Eric ran to her side and slapped her several times. ''Shut up, bitch! My men won't mutiny.'' He looked at his disgruntled crew and shouted, ''She's our only hope of survival! Even if we gave up our beautiful shield, he'd come after us and sink us!''

Upon hearing that Maren was Captain Hawk's wife, and knowing the man's reputation, some crewmen protested aloud, saying Captain Hawk could be trusted to keep his word not to attack if they released their captive. Others said they could never escape the Hawk's wrath if she was harmed or slain.

Eric vowed, ''For every man who remains loyal to me, there'll be a reward when we reach Jamaica: twenty gold pieces each and an hour with Morgan's bitch to enjoy her as you wish.''

''You wouldn't dare!'' Maren shrieked.

But Eric coolly replied, ''I damned sure would.''

''Jared Morgan will hunt down any man who harms me and—''

Eric's forearm cut off her air and words, and he smiled evilly. ''Shut up, Maren, or I'll give Morgan a demonstration of my crew's lust. Give him an eyeglassful of my men raping you right here on this deck while he sits out there, helpless as a newborn pup.''

''You're mad, Eric. My God, you're mad,'' she murmured.

While Eric was distracted, Jared guided his ship into position and fired twice, once to the bow and once to the stern. The blasts shook Eric's vessel and ripped away decking and equipment. The crew of the damaged ship scrambled for cover, worried because Captain Hawk was so close and was obviously unafraid to open fire even though his wife was their hostage.

"She's right, Cap'n! Morgan won't let us get away with her! Let's make a deal with him before we're sunk!" a frightened sailor shouted, and others agreed.

"Never!" Eric bellowed. "I'll slit her throat while he watches!"

"Then we won't have any protection against him!" a muscular crewman argued.

"I know how to send him fleeing," Eric asserted, his eyes darting about. His mental disturbance was becoming more evident in the face of defeat. He no longer had Ben to help him, to protect and advise him.

Eric ordered two men to unleash a cannon, roll it backward, and secure Maren before the opening of its barrel. The ships were now within shouting distance of each other, so Eric grasped a torch and held it on high, ready to light the fuse on the deadly big gun. He then yelled to Jared, "Get out of my sights, Morgan, or I'll send her over to you in pieces!" Turning to his crew, he bellowed, "Load every cannon and fire at my command! We won't sink alone!"

Maren could see her husband, Kerry Osgood, and many of the *Sea Mist*'s crew along her rail. Never had she viewed such hatred and fury on her love's face, nor such determination. Quickly scanning the faces around him, she saw expressions that matched his, and her heart was warmed.

"Jared, please!" she called out. "I love you! Save your ship and crew! Forget about me and destroy him!"

One of Jared's crewmen shouted, "We don't sail without Captain Hawk's wife!"

"You'll have her in shreds, and your ship, too!" Eric screamed.

Then Jared spoke for the first time, his voice confident. "Put Maren in a longboat and sail away, and I won't pursue you! I won't even approach the boat until you're out of gun range! If you don't open fire, we won't! If you do fire, prepare to meet your Maker, you spawn of the Devil! I'll see my wife dead, here and now, before I'll let you take her where you can torture her and slay her!"

Jared could hear the murmurings of Eric's crew as they urged their captain to accept Jared's offer. He knew Eric's guns could rip his vessel apart at this range, but he prayed his bluff would work.

As Eric lowered the torch toward the fuse of the cannon before which Maren had been placed, Jared's heart seemed to stop beating. But Eric's first mate grabbed his wrist and prevented him from carrying out his mad intention. As the two men began to scuffle, others surged forward to help subdue their captain, but Eric got free and drew his cutlass, waved it wildly at his men.

Then a desperate struggle ensued, one in which the odds were against Eric James. His men were resolved to end his mad leadership and to save their lives. Yet Eric was filled with strength born of madness and rage, cunning born of years of deceit. Suddenly death meant nothing to him. He attacked his own men with a vengeance, and fought skillfully to get at the helpless Maren, screaming that she was going to die with him and be his forever.

Maren's heart was racing as frantically as was Jared's, yet they could do nothing except watch this struggle take place. They both prayed fervently that Eric's men would be victorious and would accept Jared's terms. Time seemed to stand still as the fateful battle continued. Maren's gaze locked with Jared's and she hoped they would be together again.

Within minutes, Eric was slain by his crew, and his body was tossed overboard. Then the first mate shouted to Jared, "If you still want to trade your wife for our freedom, swear you'll honor your word!"

Jared sighed with relief as he nodded. Then he declared loudly, "You have the promise of Captain Hawk. Put her in the boat and leave peacefully."

Maren was cut free, and the longboat was lowered. On trembly legs she was guided to the rail and told to climb down the rope ladder into the boat. She was so weak from prolonged stress and from relief that her hands slipped twice. Both times she used her legs, tightly wrapped around the rope, to slow herself until she regained her grip. At last, her feet touched the boat and she dropped into it. As she looked up at her husband and waved to let him know she was all right, she hoped their ordeal was over. Let all go well, she thought, as the ropes securing the longboat were cut and she was set adrift, still tense and doubtful.

The sails of Eric's ship were raised, and the first mate took command. The vessel moved away slowly until her canvas was filled with wind.

Jared made no suspicious moves, for the other ship's guns were still trained on his vessel, and Maren was between the two ships. Fearing that Eric's crew could not be trusted to leave peacefully, he watched closely for any sign of treachery. Thankfully, none came. When a good distance had been put between the ships, Jared and Kip went after Maren. She fought the urge to weep, as her husband spread kisses over her hair and face, and when he cupped her jaw to raise it so he might look into her golden brown eyes, his tawny gaze revealed his love.

Jared smiled. "Still have me chasing you, wench," he teased.

Maren returned his smile as she hugged him tightly. "I was so afraid for you and the others. You shouldn't have taken such a terrible risk."

"Allow that motley crew to steal my favorite treasure? No way."

"You're an excellent judge of character, Mr. Morgan, or the lack of it. You knew they would be terrified of Captain Hawk, didn't you?"

"Well," he murmured as they rowed toward his ship, "I was hoping they would accept my bluff. If they hadn't, I would have sailed off."

"You would have what?" she asked, astonished.

"I would have sailed just far enough to trail them without being noticed. Remember, I can become invisible like the mist when I need to. I would have followed you until they anchored somewhere; then I would have sneaked aboard, ripped out Eric's black heart, and rescued you."

"How did you locate us in that strange ship?" she inquired.

"I reached New Orleans shortly after you sailed. In fact, our ships passed at a distance in the Gulf. When I got to Lady Luck and learned what had happened, I knew only one ship had sailed, and which direction she had taken," he explained.

"He burned Lady Luck, Jared. There was nothing I could do."

"No, love, he didn't."

"But I saw the flames from the ship."

"You saw the stable burning. Dan recovered and prevented them from setting the house aflame. Some of it smells of whale oil, but that can be cleansed away or concealed with paint. Dan and Mary are fine," he declared, sensing the question she was about to ask.

"You are a wonder, Captain Hawk, and I love you."

"I'm glad you appreciate me, woman, and I love you."

They had reached the ship, so conversation ceased while they climbed aboard amidst cheers. Maren thanked everyone for rescuing her, and Jared's crew greeted her enthusiastically. As they did so, Jared ordered a second round of grog, the best aboard, for his crew that night. When one man asked about the fate of the other ship, Jared said he would let it go and would head homeward for a long-awaited shore leave. He put his arm around Maren's waist and guided her to his cabin. The only flames burning that night were in their hearts and bodies. Their fortune couldn't have been better or brighter.

Chapter Nineteen

April tenth of 1815 was a beautiful day at Shady Rest Plantation in Savannah, Georgia, and everything seemed to be working out for all concerned. Napoleon Bonaparte had been defeated at Waterloo on February twenty-sixth, two days after Jared's daring rescue of Maren. America and Great Britain had made peace. The shipping firm in New Orleans had been recovered and sold, and Marc James was working for the new owner. The townhouse and the Jamaican plantation, also recovered, had been sold as well, but Maren and Jared had not attempted to take her family's main home from the couple who had purchased it in good faith. And Maren was still in possession of Empress Josephine's necklace, but it lay forgotten in Jared's safe. Later she would decide its fate.

Dan Myers and Mary Malone had married in the previous month, and were now the proud owners of

Lady Luck. While Lilibeth Payne Hughes was expecting a baby before Christmas, and Barton couldn't be happier. Daniel Redford was back in England, and his bitterness had diminished. Peter Thomas was still in the employment of the President, but René Blanc now lived like a proper gentleman. He owned a plantation near Baton Rouge. Kerry Osgood was now captain of the *Sea Mist*, and Cathy and Steven Morgan had adjusted after their mother's death. They were living with Maren and Jared.

With much to be happy for, Maren smiled at her husband when he revealed a further delight: a visit to London to see her grandparents, Colin and Martha James. She raced to his side and hugged him tightly. "I love you, Jared Morgan, alias Captain Hawk."

Jared's hands teased up her bare arms to cup her face. As he gazed into it, he smiled contentedly. "I'm a damned lucky man, Maren Morgan."

Their bodies and lips met, and they kissed tranquilly. Then as their hands began to wander, passions were kindled and clothes were discarded. What did they care if it was only a little past noon and there were things to be done?

As they cuddled on the big bed and exchanged caresses and endearments, Jared stroked Maren's gradually rounding stomach and grinned. "I can hardly wait to see this little rogue—or vixen. You've made me happier than I ever imagined possible. The day Kip enticed me to attack your ship was the turning point in my life. Lordy, I love you and need you, my beautiful treasure."

"Then plunder your treasure gently and greedily, my love, for I need you fiercely today," Maren coaxed seductively.

Jared chuckled and Maren laughed as they came together. Blissfully, they spent hours sating their fiery passions. Isn't that what life is really about . . . love and rapture?

Author's Note

I hope you have a good time reading this story; I enjoyed writing it. I love it when a story flows as easily and swiftly as Jared's and Maren's lovestory did.

I also hope you'll be watching for my next release, a rip-roaring romantic western. You'll be surprised by the adventures and delighted by the passions which Randee Hollis and Marsh Tanner share as they travel through the Wild West, loving and helping each other as they seek to unmask and defeat a vicious killer.

Thanks for your support and GOOD READING. . . .

For a *Janelle Taylor Newsletter* and bookmark, please send a self-addressed, stamped envelope to Janelle Taylor Enterprises, P.O. Box 11646, Augusta, Georgia, 30907-8646.

BESTSELLING HISTORICAL ROMANCES
From Zebra Books and Sylvie F. Sommerfield

MOONLIT MAGIC (1941, $3.95)

How dare that slick railroad negotiator, Trace Cord, bathe in innocent Jenny Graham's river and sneak around her property? Jenny could barely contain her rage . . . then her gaze swept over Trace's magnificent physique, and the beauty's seething fury became burning desire. And once he carried her into the refreshing cascade and stroked her satiny skin, all she wanted was to be spellbound by ecstasy — forever captured by MOONLIT MAGIC.

ELUSIVE SWAN (2061, $3.95)

Amethyst-eyed Arianne had fled the shackles of an arranged marriage for the freedom of boisterous St. Augustine — only to be trapped by her own traitorous desires. Just a glance from the handsome stranger she had met in a dockside tavern made her tremble with excitement. But the young woman was running from one man . . . she dared not submit to another. Her only choice was to once again take flight, as far and as fleet as an ELUSIVE SWAN.

CATALINA'S CARESS (2202, $3.95)

Catalina Carrington was determined to buy her riverboat back from the handsome gambler who had beaten her brother at cards. But when dashing Marc Copeland named his price — three days as his mistress — she swore she'd never meet his terms, even as she imagined the rapture just one night in his arms would bring! Marc had vengeance in his mind when he planned Catalina's seduction, but soon his desire for the golden-eyed witch made him forget his lust for revenge against her family . . . tonight he would reap the rewards at hand and glory in the passionate delights of CATALINA'S CARESS.

ZEBRA HAS THE SUPERSTARS
OF PASSIONATE ROMANCE!

CRIMSON OBSESSION (2272, $3.95)
by Deana James

Cassandra MacDaermond was determined to make the handsome gambling hall owner Edward Sandron pay for the fortune he had stolen from her father. But she never counted on being struck speechless by his seductive gaze. And soon Cassandra was sneaking into Sandron's room, more intent on sharing his rapture than causing his ruin!

TEXAS CAPTIVE (2251, $3.95)
by Wanda Owen

Ever since two outlaws had killed her ma, Talleha had been suspicious of all men. But one glimpse of virile Victor Maurier standing by the lake in the Texas Blacklands and the half-Indian princess was helpless before the sensual tide that swept her in its wake!

TEXAS STAR (2088, $3.95)
by Deana James

Star Garner was a wanted woman—and Chris Gillard was determined to collect the generous bounty being offered for her capture. But when the beautiful outlaw made love to him as if her life depended on it, Gillard's firm resolve melted away, replaced with a raging obsession for his fiery TEXAS STAR.

MOONLIT SPLENDOR (2008, $3.95)
by Wanda Owen

When the handsome stranger emerged from the shadows and pulled Charmaine Lamoureux into his strong embrace, she sighed with pleasure at his seductive caresses. Tomorrow she would be wed against her will—so tonight she would take whatever exhilarating happiness she could!

TEXAS TEMPEST (1906, $3.95)
by Deana James

Sensuous Eugenia Leahy had an iron will that intimidated even the most powerful of men. But after rescuing her from a bad fall, the virile stranger MacPherson resolved to take the steel-hearted beauty whether she consented or not!

Available wherever paperbacks are sold, or order direct from the Publisher. Send cover price plus 50¢ per copy for mailing and handling to Zebra Books, Dept. 2250, 475 Park Avenue South, New York, N.Y. 10016. Residents of New York, New Jersey and Pennsylvania must include sales tax. DO NOT SEND CASH.